D0464043

JFIC
Vaderhill
7/23

ALWAYS
THE
ALMOST

ALWAYS THE ALMOST

A NOVEL

EDWARD UNDERHILL

WEDNESDAY BOOKS
NEW YORK

First published in the United States by Wednesday Books, an imprint of
St. Martin's Publishing Group

www.wednesdaybooks.com

Designed by Nicola Ferguson
Case stamp by Erik Rose

Library of Congress Cataloging-in-Publication Data

Names: Underhill, Edward, author.
Title: Always the almost : a novel / Edward Underhill.
Description: First edition. | New York : Wednesday Books, 2023.
    Audience: Ages 12–18.
Identifiers: LCCN 2022043684 | ISBN 9781250835208 (hardcover)
    ISBN 9781250835215 (ebook)
Subjects: CYAC: Dating—Fiction. | Piano—Fiction. | Transgender
    people—Fiction. | Competition—Fiction. | LCGFT: Novels.
Classification: LCC PZ7.1.U483 Al 2023 | DDC [Fic]—dc23
LC record available at https://lccn.loc.gov/2022043684

Our books may be purchased in bulk for promotional, educational,
or business use. Please contact your local bookseller or the Macmillan
Corporate and Premium Sales Department at 1-800-221-7945, extension 5442,
or by email at MacmillanSpecialMarkets@macmillan.com.

First Edition: 2023

10 9 8 7 6 5 4 3 2 1

To every trans and queer reader—
you are always, always enough

Before you read this book, I want you to know two things:

First, this book is full of joy. Queer joy. Trans joy. (And some snark.)

Second, this book also has moments of heaviness, hurtful language, and the ripple effects of that language.

I'm a trans person, and while Miles is not me and his story is not mine, some of his experiences are drawn from my own. And, as is often true for queer folks, they are not all joyful experiences.

If you'd like a list of content warnings, you can find that on my website.

As for content promises: I promise this book has a happy ending.

ALWAYS THE ALMOST

CHAPTER ONE

In the empty, half-lit auditorium, the strength of my whole body surges through my shoulders, down my skinny arms and bony wrists, through my hands, my fingertips, into the piano keys, until I'm nothing but a kinetic force making the massive instrument in front of me shudder. The sound bounces up to the rafters and back to the farthest row of seats; I can hear violins like they're playing around me on the empty stage, the grit of rosin against their strings as they take off on a soaring melody.

And each chord I play spells out *I. AM. REAL.*

The piano is an extension of my body—this weird body that is neither here nor there, everything and nothing all at once. I pound out each chord, just me and the piano, because here, my button-down shirt, plaid sleeves rolled to my elbows, stops being a cheap costume I found at Goodwill. Just like Pinocchio, I turn into a real boy.

Here, I can push aside the number of times this week that Mr. Gracie called me *Melissa* instead of *Miles* (seven). I can drown out Ms. Harding saying "Hey, girls" to me and Paige and Rachel and then fumbling for the next ten seconds trying to fix it. I can even turn off that vague buzz that's always in the back of my head: *You'll have to go to the bathroom sooner or later . . .*

I can ignore everything that says *ALMOST* and just *be*. As long as I'm playing the piano in this empty room by myself.

And not thinking about the new piano teacher I'm supposed to meet next week.

Or the Tri-State Piano Competition coming up in four and a half months.

Or Cameron Hart's smug, leering face every time he wins that competition—which he has every year for the *past three years,* while I've ended up second. Every single time.

But most of all, I can ignore any thought of Shane McIntyre, ex-boyfriend extraordinaire, because seriously, *fuck that guy.*

CHAPTER TWO

Upton, Wisconsin, on New Year's Eve is *cold*. The kind of cold that makes my ears ache and my nose hurt and makes me deeply regret volunteering to pick up the pizza. Sure, it's on my way to Rachel's house, and yeah, Paige picked up the pizza last time, but the wind spiraling off the lake is freezing my whole face. And that's just on the walk from the parking lot to the lime green door of Sal's.

I pull open the door and get hit with a blast of warm air and classic rock. My glasses fog up like I just opened the dishwasher, but it doesn't really matter. I could probably find my way through Sal's with a blindfold on. Just follow the smell of melting cheese.

Sal's is deader than I thought it would be—usually I can't even hear the classic rock. Maybe everybody else decided to pay extra for delivery rather than go out in this winter vortex.

When I'm pretty sure I'm at the counter, I say, "Hi, I'm picking up?"

The blurry guy behind the counter waves at me and points to the blob pressed against his ear that's slowly resolving itself into a phone.

"Oh. Sorry." I step back. Pull out my own phone to stare at so I don't look awkward.

"Mel?"

I look up. And there, standing next to me at the counter, holding a pizza box and totally visible now that my glasses have cleared, is Shane McIntyre.

Chestnut-hair-and-chiseled-jaw Shane McIntyre.

Looks-broad-and-strong-even-in-a-puffy-coat Shane McIntyre.

Star-running-back-who-broke-up-with-me-two-weeks-ago Shane McIntyre.

I have got to stop walking into buildings with fogged-up glasses.

"Um." I somehow manage to find my voice. "Actually, my name is—"

"Miles." Shane's shoulders hunch up under his orange-and-black down coat—the same coat he was wearing the last time we were this close. "Right. Sorry."

I don't want to think about the last time we were this close, sitting on a bench in Palmer Park, staring at flat gray Lake Michigan, while he told me he *didn't want to hurt my feelings* and was *trying to get it,* but we should break up. Because, yeah, when I cut my hair short (six months ago), he thought it was cute. And it was totally fine if I didn't like girl clothes anymore (three months ago). But now I was *Miles.* (Four weeks ago.)

And Shane McIntyre is Pretty Sure He's Not Gay. In that can't-look-you-in-the-eye, don't-you-see-how-awkward-this-would-be-for-football kind of way.

"It's okay." I shrug like it's no big deal, because I don't want it to be a big deal. "Picking up pizza?"

He looks down at the pizza box in his hands. *Obviously* he's picking up pizza. What's wrong with me?

But it's Shane, so he just says, "Yeah. I'm going over to DeShawn's with some of the guys from the team. You?"

"Going over to Rachel's." I try to grin. "A little less romantic than last year, huh?"

Shane's forehead wrinkles and he looks away. *Way to go, Miles. Foot right in mouth.* Because now we're both thinking about last New Year's Eve, when we'd been dating for two weeks. We sat wrapped up in blankets on Shane's front porch, watching the fireworks livestream from Milwaukee on his laptop. It was sort of silly—we could have just watched inside—but it felt special, in that moment. Sitting outside like we were watching the fireworks for real. Using the freezing temperature as an excuse to get closer to each other.

Shane recovers first. "Yeah, I guess."

I clear my throat, stuff my hands in my pockets, and look at the guy behind the counter. But he's still on the phone, with what is apparently the world's longest pizza order.

"Well." Shane's shoulders hunch even higher. "Guess I better go."

"Yeah." I attempt another grin, but it feels like a grimace. "Have fun with the guys."

"Thanks." He turns away without looking at me.

Behind the counter, Pizza Guy finally hangs up the phone. "Jacobson?" He points to me. "Picking up?"

"Yeah." But I'm looking after Shane, already pushing back out the door. I fumble with my wallet. "Just the large cheese—"

"Here you go." Pizza Guy slides a box across the counter.

I pull out a twenty. "Thanks. Keep the change." I grab the pizza box, dodge past the people by the window, and lean my shoulder into the door. The wind hits me like a hundred icicles. "Shane! Wait!"

He's halfway across the quiet street, but he pauses. Wanders back to the curb.

"Sorry, I just . . ." *Come on, Miles. You've been wanting to say this for two weeks. Now's your chance.* "I'm the same person, Shane. I'm not any different."

It sounds hollow, even to me. I thought it was true the first time I said it (to Rachel), and it still felt sort of true the second time (to my parents), but now it's starting to feel like a line I got off the internet.

Which I did. Late-night anxious Googling: *how to tell people you're trans.*

Shane lets his breath out. It puffs in a cloud in front of him. "I know you keep saying that, but you *are* different. You're a guy now."

"Yeah, but that doesn't make me a different person."

"Look, I gotta go." He retreats a step, holding up the pizza box like an excuse.

"Shane—"

"Happy New Year." He meets my eyes, briefly, and then he turns and walks away, crossing the street toward the white Ford pickup with the bashed-in bumper that he's been driving to school all semester. The dent in the bumper kind of cradles you when you lean against it—which I discovered while waiting for Shane after a football game. When I pointed it out to him, I thought he might laugh at me, but he just grinned and promised never to get the dent fixed.

Part of me wants to run across the street after him now. Point to that dent and come up with something cool to say about it, so we could laugh and have—I don't know—a *moment*.

But he's already climbing into his truck. The engine roars to life. And there goes Shane McIntyre, ex-boyfriend extraordinaire, rumbling down the street and leaving me and my large cheese pizza freezing on the sidewalk.

The thing is, I don't believe Shane—that we're done just because I'm a guy now. You don't date someone for a whole year, tell them you love them, and then ditch them the second they, well, change. Who cares what the change is.

I still love Shane. That's something that *hasn't* changed. Not after I cut my hair, not after I changed my clothes, not after I changed my name and my pronouns. Not even after I crashed out those chords on the piano in the auditorium because *fuck that guy.*

You like who you like. I just need to help Shane figure that out. Remind him why he liked me in the first place. Prove to him I'm still the same person, and he can like the new exterior. It doesn't have to be more complicated than that.

When I try to explain this to Rachel and Paige, they look at me like I've just grown a second head.

We're sitting in Rachel's room. The pizza is almost gone and the TV downstairs gently vibrates the carpeted floor underneath us. Rachel's parents are watching the ball drop live from New York City.

"It's *way* more complicated than that," says Rachel.

"No, it's not. Look at you guys."

Rachel and Paige look at each other. They're the only two people who haven't messed up my name or pronouns once. When I came out to them, I got a squeal and a hug from Rachel, and a fist-bump and *Hell yeah* from Paige. Honestly, I think they both saw it coming. Rachel was just a little disappointed I didn't also seem to be interested in girls. She wanted to set me up with someone— even though we seem to be the only three queerdos in all of Grant East High.

Well, us plus Shane. I hope.

"It's different," Paige says to me. Paige has been friends with us since middle school and has had the same chin-length black hair the entire time. It definitely should not be cool, especially with the barrettes she wears, but somehow she pulls it off. Maybe it's the Doc Martens boots she's constantly wearing, or her oversized but perfectly draped punk rock T-shirts.

"Only because we started dating *after* we came out," Rachel says quickly.

Rachel told me she liked girls when we were ten. She wore a suit to her bat mitzvah and only got vaguely frustrated looks from the rabbi. Her dark hair is long and frizzy, but you still know immediately that she's queer. It's probably the plaid shirts and the boots. The large rainbow pin on her backpack definitely helps.

"It's just"—Paige reaches across Rachel for another piece of room temperature pizza—"we both knew who we were. Are. You know—before we got together."

"Gay," I say.

"*Super* gay," says Rachel. She leans over and kisses Paige on the cheek. "Look, I know you just saw him, but you should forget about Shane. If he wants to break up, he doesn't deserve you. He's just a straight and narrow-minded jock. Fuck that guy."

"Yeah," I say, but mostly because I want to drop it. I thought Rachel and Paige would get it—that they'd agree that love should transcend stuff like short hair and clothes and pronouns. It should see who you really are. Or at least take your word for it.

I shouldn't have called Rachel after the breakup, when I was angry. I shouldn't have said *fuck that guy,* because now she won't let it go. The truth is, Rachel never really liked Shane. Paige wasn't that into him either, but Paige is ambivalent about most people. Rachel, though, really couldn't see past the football. At first she thought it was fun that I was dating him—her best friend with such a *hunk.* But the longer it went on, the less into him she was. She didn't think there was any *there* there.

"He's a jock," she would say. "I know I'm stereotyping, but he plays *football.*"

And then she'd look at me like maybe, this time, I'd have a different reaction.

"You *are* stereotyping," I'd say. "He's more than that."

And he was. He is. He loves true crime podcasts. He's weirdly obsessed with submarines. He asked me out for the first time after I played a Mozart concerto with our truly shitty high school orchestra, which means he's the kind of guy who goes to a truly shitty high school orchestra concert.

But I don't want to get into it tonight, so I lean back against

Rachel's bed and let it go. Lick pizza grease off my fingers while Rachel nuzzles her face against Paige's shoulder and Paige rolls her eyes, grinning. I'm happy for them. Really. I can see how happy they make each other. I mean, Paige doesn't grin like that for just anybody.

But it's weird when your two best friends start dating. They're suddenly in their own club. I didn't used to mind because I had membership in that club with Shane; we were all on equal footing. Without Shane, I'm out, demoted to Awkward Third Wheel. I know they're not trying to exclude me. Paige and I still share a secret look when Rachel finds a new cause to have Feelings about. And I still tell Rachel some things before I tell Paige, because Rachel has been my friend forever and that's how it works. But they take up space in a different way. More of our space belongs to them.

We go to bed shortly before midnight. It's already long past midnight in New York and Rachel's parents are asleep. We make up a mound of blankets on the floor of Rachel's bedroom because Rachel says it's too unequal for one person to get her bed.

Rachel and Paige are breathing quietly within five minutes, all that pizza we ate catching up with them. But I'm awake when we hit the New Year. Staring at my phone.

11:59.

12:00.

January first. I need a New Year's resolution.

I roll over onto my back. Above me, the mobile of tarot cards hanging from Rachel's ceiling spins slowly in the dry breeze of the house's central heating. (Rachel might have been raised Jewish, but she identifies firmly as "atheist pagan.")

I know exactly what my resolutions are. They're sitting there, right on top of my brain, like they've been waiting for the right moment.

One: Beat Cameron Hart at the Tri-State Piano Competition.

Two: Win back Shane McIntyre.

Because *fuck that guy,* and also, I really miss him.

Two resolutions. That seems like a good number. Not too complicated. I have four months for one, and, well, however long it takes for the other.

How hard can that be?

CHAPTER THREE

My dad used to play piano in a jazz band in college, and still keeps his dinky old upright piano in his home office. When I was little, I'd climb up on the piano bench and bang on the keys. Dad would flip the lights on and off like lightning, and I'd bang around on the low end of the piano like thunder. Dad dubbed this game *Thunderstorm*. Not incredibly imaginative, but he always manned the light switch enthusiastically.

When I turned five, my parents decided if I was going to bang on the piano anyway, I might as well learn how to do it properly.

That dinky upright is buried under tax law books and stacks of papers now, and I have my own piano—a baby grand stuffed into a corner of the living room. But lately, I've been practicing at school as much as I can. The piano in the auditorium is a full-size grand and actually pretty nice. Plus, the music director says if the school sees it get used more often, they'll take better care of it. All good reasons, but really I practice there because I can be alone, as long as the theater kids aren't using it for whatever musical they're putting on.

My piano teacher for the past eleven years has been Mrs. Kim, who also happens to be Paige's mom. We weren't friends when I started taking lessons with Mrs. Kim, though, and until middle school, Paige totally ignored me. She said later it was because I was one of her mom's students. Paige acts like she has no desire to play any musical instrument—apparently something she and Mrs. Kim

used to fight about all the time. Mrs. Kim wanted Paige to play violin, or piano, or flute, or *something*, and Paige stubbornly refused
to play anything except air guitar. (And only when listening to
punk bands.)

Once we got to middle school, Paige started hanging out with
Rachel, and that meant hanging out with me, and by that time,
Mrs. Kim was giving up anyway. She decided Paige was too old to
start learning an instrument and let it go.

I kind of wonder, though, if Paige really doesn't want to play
music, or if it's just too much pressure when your mom is the
go-to piano teacher in town and your older sister got a full violin
scholarship to UW-Madison.

I always liked Mrs. Kim as a piano teacher. But at my lesson
right before this past Thanksgiving, she said to me, "I think it's
time you move on."

"Great. I'm actually getting really sick of this Chopin Étude—"

"No, no." Mrs. Kim frowned at me. "The Chopin you keep
working on. You need to move to a new teacher."

I stared at her. "I'll stop complaining about the Chopin."

Mrs. Kim smiled. "Mel," she said (the name and pronoun
changes weren't coming for another week), "I taught you everything I can. If you want to keep getting better, you need to find a
new teacher, who can *push*! Push you further."

Crap. I knew what was coming. Besides Mrs. Kim, there are
only two piano teachers in the whole of southeastern Wisconsin who teach advanced students. Like, the kind of students who
compete in the Tri-State Piano Competition and actually have a
chance of winning.

The one with the best reputation, who's so fancy he teaches in
Chicago half the time, is Pierre Fontaine. He's French. He has a
website with an incredibly dramatic black-and-white headshot.
He wears a lot of turtleneck sweaters.

He also teaches Cameron Hart.

"I want you to have the best," Mrs. Kim said. She scribbled on a sticky note. "So I already called. You just call and make a lesson time to start after Christmas."

"Mrs. Kim, I really don't want to study with—"

"Stefania Smith," she said, handing me the sticky note. "Best you can have."

My mouth actually fell open in surprise.

So now, here I am, on January third, freezing my ass off in front of Stefania Smith's adorable blue craftsman house, because I haven't yet worked up the courage to ring the doorbell.

The idea of studying with Pierre Fontaine and still having to listen to Cameron play the coveted final spot in every damn studio recital was enough to make me want to vomit. But the idea of studying with Stefania Smith isn't much better. Sure, she's so close that I can walk from my house. And yeah, she actually soloed with the Milwaukee Symphony Orchestra last year.

I tried to talk Mrs. Kim out of it. But she just smiled and waved me off. "I'm done teaching you after Christmas. You call Stefania or you teach yourself!"

I wasn't going to win this argument, especially after Mrs. Kim called my parents and told them Stefania would happily take me on as a student. I listened to Dad gush through two whole dinners about how he was listening-to-her-old-recordings-and-have-you-*heard*-her-play-Rachmaninov. It was the most he'd talked to me in weeks. I had to call Stefania to schedule a lesson after that.

I legitimately cannot feel my toes anymore, so I ring the bell. Mostly out of self-preservation.

BARKBARKBARKBARKBARK—

Crash.

Something that sounds big enough to be a freaking *bear* scrabbles around inside the house and then comes pounding closer, closer, *closer.* The porch underneath me shakes.

"OLGA!"

Skidding. Sliding. The barking stops. For a blissful second, there's dead silence.

And then the door opens.

The first thing I see is the huge shaggy dog standing in the doorway like it answered the door itself. It looks like the love child of a wolf and Bigfoot.

"Olga!" A woman appears behind the dog and begins pushing at its butt. "Are you Miles?" She's not being very effective. "Come in, come in, Olga won't bite."

Is she sure about that? "I'm here for a piano lesson. With Stefania Smith?"

"Yes, yes, I'm Stefania. Olga, *move*!" With a herculean effort, she heaves the giant Bigfootwolf out of the way and beckons to me. "Come in."

I step over the threshold. Stefania shuts the door. And we stare at each other.

She's not at all what I expected. I've heard plenty about her— born in Russia, trained in St. Petersburg and then at Juilliard, winner of several major competitions in Europe before she married a doctor whose name is literally John Smith and somehow ended up in Wisconsin.

The Stefania I've heard about is terrifying. Last year at the Tri-State Competition, Andrew Morris told me she scared off five different students in a month (including him) and at least one other had a nervous breakdown and quit piano altogether.

The Stefania in front of me is a tiny, birdlike woman with large blue eyes in a pale, pointed face that looks too young for her frizzy mane of wild gray hair. There's a glittering butterfly comb stuck in there, but there's so much hair going every which way around it that I wonder if it got lost and she forgot about it. Big silver butterflies dangle from her ears, but the rest of her isn't glamorous at all. She's wearing jeans and a sweatshirt with a penguin on it.

"You didn't wear gloves, Miles," she says.

I look at my bare hands like a fool.

"It's winter. Wear gloves so we don't have to spend twenty minutes warming up." Stefania turns and clomps away—she's wearing high-heeled clogs. "Piano's this way!"

I follow her through a dining room with crown molding that would make Mom drool, and through a kitchen with impeccable white tile and oiled butcher block counters that smells overwhelmingly of *coffee*. She opens a pocket door into a room behind the kitchen and waves me through.

It's a small room. The only things in it are a floral-printed armchair, an old, faded Persian rug, and, on top of the rug, a beautiful, scuffed-black, six-foot Steinway grand piano.

My mouth drops open.

This is the nicest piano I've ever seen outside of the Tri-State Competition.

"Sit!" Stefania waves her hand at the piano bench and settles down in the floral armchair, picking up a blue coffee mug from the windowsill.

I shrug out of my coat, rub my hands on my pants, and sit down on the piano bench. My right foot goes out to find the pedal.

"Scales," Stefania says. "B-flat major. Go."

So I go. The keys under my fingers aren't thin, slick plastic like my piano back home, or the one at school. These keys are ivory, thick and textured. They sink without extra force and they spring back up with no stickiness. The whole instrument seems to be alive, vibrating with excitement, even though I'm just playing scales.

Up and down my hands go, while Stefania watches me. Scale after scale. Key after key. I wait for her to say something, but she's silent, except for barking out which scale to play next.

When we've gone through all twelve major scales, she holds up her hand. "That's enough. Now, Mrs. Kim tells me you're playing Tchaikovsky for the competition."

"Tchaikovsky's Piano Concerto Number One, yeah. The first movement."

Stefania looks at me like this is obvious. "Play it."

"Now?"

Another look.

So I play it.

Chord, chord, chord. My hands move up the keyboard. The sound fills the little room, big and round.

I take off on the melody. *Expressive!* I hear Mrs. Kim in my head. *More, more expressive!*

And now the first virtuosic passage. Notes flash by in cascading waves . . .

"Stop," Stefania says.

Her voice cuts through like an axe. My fingers stumble. I hit wrong notes. Stop with all the grace of wiping out on roller skates.

Stefania regards me from behind her coffee mug. "Do you like this piece?"

"Yeah."

(Although when Cameron Hart found out I was playing Tchaikovsky, last summer at the Midwestern Piano Arts Fundraiser, he sighed. "I'm over Tchaikovsky," he said. "Just, like, so *overdone,* you know? I'm playing Rachmaninov. Way more subtle.")

"Why do you like it?" Stefania asks.

Why? What kind of question is that?

My palms sweat. "It's pretty. I like the melody. Um."

"Play it again," says Stefania. "And think about that."

I wipe my hands on my jeans. Maybe she *is* terrifying.

Deep breath.

Chord, chord, chord.

I try to be more expressive. Sway my body with the melody. Sing the notes in my head.

"Stop!"

I jump. Yank my hands away from the keys.

Stefania sets her mug down on the windowsill with a grumpy *thunk*. "Get up." She waves her hands at me. I slide off the piano bench and press up awkwardly against the wall.

Stefania sits down, and without taking a moment to breathe or think or prepare at all, she plays.

Her hands bounce off each chord like the keys are springboards. She throws her entire being at the piano, and she looks tiny but the sound coming out is huge.

Huge. Beautiful. *Incredible.*

It's not just about the piano. This piano is amazing, but all pianos are just keys and soundboards and felt hammers that hit strings. It's Stefania. When she plays, the piano sounds *different.* I thought it was alive when I played it, but now it's singing. It's an extension of Stefania—it's her huge and percussive and beautiful voice, and it's completely fearless.

She races her way through that first virtuosic passage and stops where I stopped. She turns to me. "You hear the difference?"

I nod.

"Good." Stefania stands up and goes back to her chair. "Show me."

I sit down. *Play fearlessly and perfectly without even thinking about it.* That's all I have to do.

Chord, chord, chord.

"Stop!"

Am I getting worse?

"Miles," says Stefania.

"Yeah?"

"Are you scared of me?"

I blink at her. Actually blink. "Um. What?"

She just raises her eyebrows.

I am completely certain that if I lie, she'll know. "Yeah. I am. Kind of."

"Why?"

"Uh, I just . . . heard stuff. I mean, I'm sure it's not true—"

"What *stuff*?"

Might as well just throw it all out there. "Like you used to teach Andrew Morris and he said you're a bitch."

Stefania stares at me. My hands are sweating again.

She throws her head back and laughs, so loud and uproarious that I jump and Olga the Bigfootwolf comes thundering into the room barking.

Stefania stops laughing. "Olga, hush!" The dog stops barking and looks between us, wagging a long bushy tail. It thumps against the piano hard enough to make the strings vibrate.

"Andrew Morris," Stefania says calmly, "is a pretentious ass of a kid who fancies himself a genius and doesn't want to work on his stiff pinky fingers, so he left to find a teacher who wouldn't make him work. Are you willing to work, Miles Jacobson?"

"Yes. Ma'am."

"Good. Never call me *ma'am* again." Stefania gives Olga's butt a mighty shove and the dog ambles back out of the room. "You have tension in your shoulders that's getting in your way. Your pedaling is sloppy, especially in the melody. Your left hand is behind your right. But most of all, you play safe. You play like this piece doesn't belong to you. You play like you don't know who you are."

Oh.

That's so much worse than stiff pinky fingers. Worse than sloppy pedaling. Worse than her screaming or laughing at me.

Worse than anything I had imagined.

"I know who I am." It comes out defensive. She's known me for all of twenty minutes.

"So tell me," says Stefania. "Who are you?"

"I'm Miles."

"Who is Miles?"

Miles is me. I am Miles. I'm the same as I was when I was Melissa, but Miles is also everything Melissa was not.

I'm not telling her that.

"Why is Miles playing this concerto?" Stefania asks.

"Mrs. Kim thought it would be good for the competition—"

"No." Stefania gulps coffee. "Not a good enough reason."

"Because I want to beat this guy Cameron Hart—"

"I know who Cameron Hart is. Not a good enough reason."

"Then I don't know." This is ridiculous. Maybe I can still beg Mrs. Kim to take me back. I'm not above groveling. At least she doesn't play mind games.

"Okay," says Stefania.

"What?"

"Not knowing is fine, as long as you admit it." She stands up. "Come with me."

I follow her out of the piano room and into the kitchen. She picks up a pot of coffee and pours herself more. "You want some?"

I nod, because I don't know what else to do. She pours coffee into a red mug and hands it to me. I sip at it. It tastes as bitter as I feel.

Stefania lifts the lid of a record player sitting on the edge of the kitchen counter, as though that's a perfectly sane place for a record player. "Wait here." She disappears through the dining room into some other unseen place. I hear her rummaging around. When she reappears, she's holding a record. She sets it carefully on the turntable and drops the needle.

Static. Crackles. And then a harsh stab of brass—the opening fanfare of the concerto I've listened to countless times, imagined in my head countless times, played countless times.

Stefania turns to me. "Did you know Tchaikovsky was gay?"

I choke on my mouthful of coffee. Cough and hack while Stefania watches, as blank as a marble statue.

Finally, I manage to say, "Seriously?"

Her mouth twitches. "Seriously. I'm not surprised Mrs. Kim didn't tell you."

Hang on. "Her daughter Paige is gay. She's totally fine with me—" I stop, because all I did when I called Stefania was introduce myself as Miles. What did Mrs. Kim tell her?

But Stefania just leans over and turns the volume down slightly on the record player. "Colorful things like queerness tend to be left out of classical music history."

"So . . ." (No going back now.) "You know I'm trans. And stuff."

Stefania actually smiles. "And stuff."

"Why are you telling me about Tchaikovsky?"

"This music doesn't exist in a vacuum. We practice these pieces and try to play them perfectly to win competitions, to get into schools, to play with orchestras, but that's not why anybody wrote music, or why we really play music." She arches her eyebrow. The smile vanishes. "If that's why *you* play music, we have a problem."

Well. It's not why I *started* playing music.

"If you want to play this music in front of other people, and have it really *mean* something, then it has to mean something to you," Stefania says. "You can't play it safe. Mrs. Kim taught you decent technique—except for the sloppy pedaling—but you're staying in your comfort zone. You play like someone who has only ever been told what to play and how to play it. You play like this music doesn't belong to *you*."

Through the crackles on the record, the orchestra surges around the pianist. The melody climbs, reaching higher and higher.

"I figured since you and Tchaikovsky are both a bit *queer,* it might help you find your way into this concerto. Figure out why you want to play it. Figure out what this music means to you, outside of competitions and teachers and schools."

"Oh."

We listen to the record, drinking coffee.

Finally, I say, "Who's playing?"

"Van Cliburn," says Stefania. She gives me a pointed look. "Also gay."

When I get home, I go straight to my room. Open my laptop. Open Google.

I don't know why it didn't occur to me to do this before.

But then again, why would it? Composers are names on concerto pages. Names that come before numbers. Tchaikovsky's First. Rachmaninov's Second. You're supposed to care about the notes on the page and whether you're playing them right.

But scrolling through the results on Google . . . Stefania isn't pulling my leg. Peter Ilyich Tchaikovsky was gay. In nineteenth-century Russia. That can't have been fun.

And Camille Saint-Saëns was gay in nineteenth-century France, writing symphonies and concertos and *Carnival of the Animals.*

And Samuel Barber and Aaron Copland were gay in twentieth-century America. Although not, as far as I can tell, together.

And Wendy Carlos, who recorded a whole bunch of Bach pieces on synthesizers, is still alive and a trans woman.

I lie on my bed with my eyes closed, listening to Barber's *Adagio for Strings,* and Copland's *Appalachian Spring,* and Carlos's *Switched-On Bach.*

Who else was out there? Who else *is* out there?

Why didn't Mrs. Kim tell me?

I listen until Mom knocks on my door and tells me I'd better go to bed. Tomorrow's a school day.

CHAPTER FOUR

When I wake up, I'm not thinking about music. Or gay composers. I'm thinking about Shane McIntyre.

Today I see Shane for the first time since Sal's on New Year's Eve. That second New Year's resolution starts now.

I don't have to spend time picking out an outfit because I planned what to wear three days ago, right down to the underwear (gray with purple stars because yes, my butt could use a little magic today).

I put on the underwear and my newest binder, smushing my chest around until it doesn't pinch. Then I pull on a T-shirt. Jeans. My favorite flannel button-down shirt. Striped socks. Boots. Cheap wristwatch I picked up at the mall. It's too clunky for piano playing, but it makes me feel more like a guy.

Sideways check. I turn and look in the mirror. Chest flat. I face the mirror. Hips not *too* wide. I suppose I can thank the Universe's great sense of irony that it made me a scrawny person with pathetic boobs. Not big enough to make me a Real Girl and too big to make me a Real Boy. Hilarious.

I'm ready. So ready that I can almost ignore the look Dad gives me when I go downstairs.

"Ready for school?" he says.

Translation: *I see by what you're wearing that you haven't changed your mind and turned back into the daughter I'm not-so-secretly hoping is still in there.*

"Yeah," I say.

Dad nods and goes back to his iPad. Dad is a total feminist who wishes he'd pursued a career as a novelist instead of listening to *his* dad and becoming a tax attorney. Having a feminist as a dad should be great. It *was* great—until I came out as a boy, which he took to mean that he had personally failed at passing on his feminist agenda. Because the only reason a girl would want to be a boy is if she doesn't think she can get what she wants in the world as a girl.

Not that Dad said any of this to me. He just kept leaving Betty Friedan's autobiography on my nightstand. When Mom caught me putting the book back on the shelf (for the third time), she tried to explain, quietly telling me *your dad was just so excited to have a girl,* all the while looking like she was getting a root canal. I guess she must have said something to Dad, though, because the book hasn't turned up again.

And now Dad and I don't talk about much of anything. He just smiles awkwardly and looks wistful, and I pretend I don't notice.

"Chop, chop, Miles!" Mom marches into the kitchen, wearing one of her fifty gray business suits and carrying her briefcase. "I've got a showing at nine and I need time to pick up more cinnamon candles before Brian cleans out Walmart."

Mom is a real estate agent and absolutely convinced that her co-worker, Brian Kingsley, who overuses both hair gel and whitening strips, is stealing her selling methods and her favorite scented candles. He's basically her Cameron Hart. Mom works all the time, which I'd get if the work was repping sellers who wanted to dump their house and get out of Upton as fast as possible. But half her clients are buyers. She says the lake is a big draw.

It doesn't even have a proper beach.

"I haven't had breakfast yet," I say.

"So grab something to go. I'm driving you today and we need to go!"

Dad gives me a sympathetic look over his glasses. Mom's

constant job stress is something we've been dealing with for years. It used to be a bonding thing, until I made everything awkward.

I give him something like a grin, grab a granola bar and my coat and my bag, and head outside.

"Seat warmer?" Mom asks as I climb into the passenger seat.

In my mind, the stars on my underwear catch fire and burst into supernovas. "No, thanks."

Last summer, Mom said that if she was going to take her career to the next level, she needed to drive something more respectable. People expected to see a nice car in the driveway when they showed up to tour a house. So now she drives a sleek black BMW, while Dad still drives his ancient Subaru. I think he's had it since law school.

The BMW is nice and all, but I still think it's weird when it warms my butt. And weirder still when my mother asks if my butt is cold.

We pull out into the street and Mom glances at me. "You look nice, Miles."

"Thanks, Mom." Unlike Dad, Mom's been just fine having a son. She got used to the idea so fast it made me wonder if she secretly always wanted a boy. Morning compliments like this have become pretty standard. I know I don't really look *that* nice and she's just trying to prove she's on board, but I don't mind.

We turn onto a busier street. "Ready for the new semester?" Mom asks.

"It's not gonna be much different."

"Oh, come on. New piano teacher? No boyfriend?"

Uh-oh. "Yeah, that's true."

She puts on her sunglasses. "I think it's good to start fresh again sometimes. You know, I was watching this TED Talk the other day with a life coach who said to be really successful, you need to reinvent yourself every five to ten years. That was about careers, of course, but I think it applies personally, too."

Smile and nod. "Mm-hmm."

"Could be good for you—not having a boyfriend. You can refocus on piano. Make more time for yourself."

(Hilarious coming from a woman who makes no time for herself, ever.)

"You've had a lot going on. Maybe taking a break from, you know, boys and stuff will feel nice. Nothing else to distract you."

There it is.

It's not that Mom has a problem with Shane. She liked him just fine when I was a girl. Her enthusiasm wore off when I came out. She was *really* supportive when we broke up.

Don't poke the bear. Don't poke the bear.

I poke the bear. "You know, Shane might just need time to adjust. Like you said about Dad."

Her lips tighten. It's not fair of me to throw Dad in her face, but I'm getting sick of her going above and beyond to support one part of me—and only one part.

"I just think you hang out with girls a lot," she says. "You spend so much time with Paige and Rachel—"

"Friends, Mom. I don't want to date them."

"I know, but maybe with another girl, if you give it some time—"

"I'm gay."

Her breath huffs out. "What does that even mean, really, in this situation?"

It means the same thing it meant the last five times we had this conversation.

It means you still don't believe me.

"It means—"

Her phone rings, loud and jangling, over the car speakers. She holds up a finger to me and presses a button on her steering wheel. "Tanya Jacobson speaking."

Well, that's that. She dives into a conversation about bathroom paint and kitchen built-ins with an anxious house seller, and I know that's going to take the rest of the drive.

I lean my head against the window, watching the bare trees flash by.

Mom likes having a son. She just wishes he liked girls.

Mom is still on the phone when we pull up to the flat concrete brick that is Grant East High School. I've heard Mom describe "picturesque, charming Upton Main Street" to clients more times than I can count, but the high school has to be one of the ugliest things ever built. It squats at the end of Main Street, the abrupt end to a row of cute red brick buildings. If it had a sound effect, it'd be a sad trombone. *Wah-waah.*

Since she's still on the phone, Mom blows me a kiss through the car window as I slam the door. Rachel and Paige are waiting by the empty bike racks. There's only an inch of snow on the ground, which, honestly, probably wouldn't deter the hardcore bikers, but it's supposed to sleet later, which means the roads will be solid ice by this evening.

"Was she on the phone the whole drive?" says Paige, as Mom pulls away.

"No. She just got a call at the end."

Paige and Rachel exchange glances. I feel defensive. Mrs. Kim doesn't do anything besides teach piano and play at her church, and Rachel's mom stays home.

"She's good at her job," I say. "Her Yelp reviews are amazing."

"It's freezing," says Rachel. "Come on."

The funny thing about going *just kidding, actually a boy* halfway through high school is that basically everybody finds out, whether or not you tell them, because they all pass you, look at you, stalk you online, or know someone who does one of those things. At the same time, most of them have other things they care about way more than how flat your chest is today.

I know this, but somehow I can't stop hunching my shoulders anyway.

We file into homeroom and choose the three chairs in the third row that we've been sitting in for months. Shane shares homeroom with us—or he's supposed to, but looking around, I don't see him.

Morning announcements crackle over the loudspeakers: student body elections, community volunteer day, active shooter drills next week . . .

I kick the back of Tyler Johnson's chair in front of me. He turns around, glaring. "*What?*"

"Where's Shane?"

Tyler glares harder. "Extra conditioning practice. Because the team *sucks.*" He turns away. Tyler was the second-string QB until he tore something in his knee last semester. Now he's hobbling around in a knee brace and the football team *sucks.*

Tyler definitely has too many of his own problems to care what pronouns I use.

Rachel gives me her signature Judgy Look, probably because I asked about Shane. I smile blandly and ignore her. Lean back in my chair. Cross my ankles in front of me. That's how comfortable I am.

If Shane isn't in homeroom, then I won't see him until American History this afternoon. Fine. I've got plenty of time for this New Year's resolution. No rush.

Rachel gives me a judgier look. I realize I'm chewing my thumbnail. I glower back at her because I'm not in the mood for her to police my nail biting. She looks away.

And that's when I notice the guy staring at me. He's sitting several desks past Rachel, and he's chewing his thumbnail, too. We lock eyes and both drop our hands back to our desks. His lips twitch. He looks down at his hands, tapping his fingers.

I have no idea who he is. I don't know *everybody* in school, but I recognize most of them. Despite being named Grant *East* High School, this is, in fact, the only high school in town. And "town" is not that big. And I *definitely* know everybody in my homeroom, and he was not here before break.

His hair is black and wavy. His skin is brown. There's a tiny silver hoop in his ear and a silver ring on one finger. His shoulders are hunched up like he's trying to hide in his black hoodie.

I realize I'm the one staring now and look back down at my desk. Check the time on my watch.

So many hours before American History.

A week after the Coming Out, Rachel and Paige declared themselves the Bathroom Brigade: defenders of my right to use my restroom of choice. Which is why, when Rachel finds me in the cafeteria for lunch, she asks, completely seriously, "Do you have to pee?"

There's absolutely no stopping Rachel when she's found A Cause, which is why I didn't argue with the Bathroom Brigade's formation. And honestly, it's kind of nice to know they have my back. But right now, I'm busy scouring the cafeteria for Shane. "No, Rachel, I do not have to pee."

"Are you sure?"

"Oh my god, I'm not five. Yes, I'm sure."

Rachel shrugs, and we go stand in the lunch line—or the chaotic mob that counts as a lunch line. Paige joins us a minute later. Julian Wozniak groans at us like Paige is cutting into some orderly process instead of a swarm. She shoots him a withering look.

I barely pay attention to what ends up on my tray because I'm still looking around for Shane.

Seriously, how does someone that tall turn invisible?

"Miles!"

I whip around. Realize I've reached the register. Rachel and Paige are waiting for me, and everyone behind me looks annoyed.

"Sorry." I fumble for my wallet, waving at Rachel and Paige. "Go find a table. I'll be right there."

They leave and I pay for my lunch. It doesn't take that long, but I want a minute alone to look for Shane without Rachel's Judgy Look.

There. Finally. He's all the way across the cafeteria from me, good-naturedly punching DeShawn Wallis's shoulder. DeShawn says something. Shane laughs.

I can't hear his laugh over all the noise bouncing around in this big space, but I remember what it sounds like. Friendly. Open. Surprisingly big and unashamed. I really miss that laugh.

I can't talk to him now—not in front of the whole football team. It seemed like a good idea, slowly forming in the back of my mind before lunch: just walk up to the football table and be like, "Hey," and he would say, "Hey," and then it would be just like last semester. Easy.

That seems like a terrible idea now. It's so loud here. Maybe he wouldn't hear my "Hey" and would say "What?" and then it would be awkward. Or maybe the rest of the team would stare at me. Shane is always nice, but he was nicest when we were alone.

I need to get out of here before he sees me. I turn, balancing my tray in one hand while I stuff my wallet back in my bag with the other—

Whump.

Bump right into someone. Half my soup sloshes out of the bowl. "Sorry!"

It's Staring Guy from homeroom, as frozen as I am, no tray, just holding a brown paper bag. His eyes are really dark. His lashes are really long.

"Hi," he says.

"Hi." I see Rachel and Paige behind him, sitting at a table and waving at me. "Sorry, I gotta go." I dodge around him without looking back. I'm focusing on Shane today, and I don't have time to explain my whole identity to some rando, no matter how long his eyelashes are.

Besides, I know by now that there's no short introduction for me.

I'm practically buzzing when I finally get to American History. My focus is so bad it's like someone keeps flipping the channel on one of those old TVs that had bursts of static in between. Thought—*static*—thought—*static*. Going by a mile a minute.

Rachel and Paige have AP Spanish this period, so I find a seat by myself, not too far forward, not too far back, off to one side. I basically ran here, determined to beat Shane, so I could be cool and casual when he walked in—like, *oh, hey there, I just happened to save this seat for you,* and . . . it's Shane. He's friendly and polite. He'll take the seat.

Of course, now I'm the first person in the room. Mrs. Reed beams at me. She must think I'm *really* excited for history.

More people trickle in, and then, *yes,* there's Shane, and he's by himself. Letter jacket slung over his shoulder. Sleeves rolled to his elbows. Chestnut hair falling messy in all the right ways.

He weaves through the desks and I call out, "Hey!"

He pauses, looks up and around, and sees me. No smile. No wave. He jerks his chin, barely—the universal guy sign for "What's up." It's the chin-jerk you give people you only recognize, not people you care about.

And then he turns away and chooses a desk in the back, on the opposite side of the room.

I've gone through this scene a dozen times in my head. I knew every possible direction this encounter could go.

MILES: Hey.

SHANE: [hesitating, turning hopefully] Miles?

MILES: [slowly removing glasses] I've been saving this seat—
  for you.
SHANE: [shedding a single, manly tear] I love you.
MILES: [tossing hair, which looks as floppily dashing as
  Shane's] I know.

Okay, so maybe I got carried away in my late-night fantasies,
and yes, I stole the last bit from Star Wars, but I still thought
things through. I played this moment out in every setting and
every genre I could think of. I even had an answer ready if Shane
said, "I mistook thee for a fair maid, sir, but now I see, by my troth,
thou art a most handsome lad."

(We're reading *Twelfth Night* for English.)

But I hadn't played out *this*. Shane digging through his bag,
noodling on his phone, not looking at me. Not even *avoiding*
looking at me. More like he just doesn't care if I'm here or not.

The channels in my brain stop flipping. The whole TV turns off.

"Can I sit here?"

I tear my eyes away from Shane and look up.

It's Staring Guy. Again. Pointing at the desk next to me. He's
the last person standing in the classroom and of course there's
no one next to me, because I'm weird and I'm staring at my ex-
boyfriend the football star like a total creep.

"Yeah. Sure." I hunch my shoulders. The last thing I need right
now is Staring Guy trying to figure out if I have boobs.

He sits down next to me and pulls a notebook out of his bag. I
have no choice but to stare ahead as class starts. Why did I get here
before Shane? I should have waited outside the room until I saw
him walk in, and then I could have sat down next to him.

Right, Miles. Because that *wouldn't have been creepy.*

Too late to change anything now. All I can do is dart little
glances over my shoulder at Shane, but each time I do, he's looking
elsewhere. Out the window. At the board. Down at his notes.

Fifty minutes crawl by.

The bell rings. Here's the fifty-first minute, and I shove my books in my bag and get up as fast as I can. Too fast. I trip over the leg of my chair.

Staring Guy grabs my elbow. "You okay?"

"Yeah. Fine." Except I'm not, because I wasn't fast enough and Shane is already leaving. Damn tall people cruising effortlessly through crowds. By the time I get out to the hall in all my five-foot-five glory, Shane is receding into the distance.

I find Rachel and Paige at my locker.

"Bathroom?" says Paige, jerking a thumb over her shoulder.

"Yeah. But I'm just gonna go to the single stall upstairs."

Rachel takes a deep breath of righteousness. "You have the right to use the bathroom of the gender you identify with, and we are here to guard that bathroom and protect your rights because separate is *not* equal—"

"It's fine, Rache, I'd rather just go upstairs. See you guys in trig."

I turn and push my way through the stairwell door. I'm not about to tell them the real reason I want the single-stall bathroom: I'm going to cry.

CHAPTER FIVE

After the crowded hallways, the dark, vast auditorium feels like outer space. It's empty and silent and might as well be a million miles away from everything outside.

Outside is getting quieter—everyone's going home, except for the teachers. They'll be here awhile yet. I learned that after I kept bumping into them on my way out after practicing.

This morning, I wasn't sure if I would stay at school and practice, but after the last bell, I needed to regroup and think. The empty school auditorium is the best place for that, especially now. The spring musical won't even hold auditions for three more weeks, so I can be in here as long as I want.

The auditorium is never completely dark. Dim yellow lights on the ceiling are always on—a few over the stage, more scattered throughout the audience. Just enough light to read music by. I've never bothered looking for the lightboard to see if I can brighten the place up. The dimness helps me focus. It turns the auditorium into a space outside of reality, where there's nothing but me and the piano.

I walk down the center aisle, shuffling through the books in my bag for my music. Four steps up to the stage. Seven steps to the piano on the left. Uncovered, because I'm here so much. I push up the fallboard to reveal the keys and open the lid—just a little, on the short stick, so it's not too loud. Spread out my music, sit down on the bench, stretch fingers.

Begin.

Chord, chord, chord.

Crash, crash, crash.

But I can't hear the orchestra in my head. Can't follow the music in front of me. All I hear is Stefania: *You play like you don't know who you are.*

I yank my hands away from the keys and rub them on my jeans. Sweaty palms again.

"That was amazing."

JUMP—so far I almost fall off the piano bench. I barely save myself by catching the heel of my hand against the bench corner. *Ouch.*

"Sorry!" A few rows from the stage, in the shadowy seats, someone straightens up. Wavy hair. Brown skin. Black hoodie and a wink of silver . . .

Staring Guy. *Again.* In the auditorium this time—my auditorium. The only place I can be alone besides the second floor single-stall bathroom.

I flex my wrist. It hurts. "How long have you been there?"

He looks embarrassed. "Uh, I was here before you came in, actually."

Great. So I walked right past this guy without seeing him. Go, me.

Then again, I was looking in my bag for my music. He could have said something.

"There usually isn't anyone here." I mean it as a hint for him to leave, but he misses it. Or he chooses to ignore it.

All he says is, "Do you come here a lot?"

"Yeah. I practice here. If I have a free period, or after school."

"That's cool." He chews his lip. Then he jerks, like something prodded him in the back, and slips out of his row and down the center aisle. "I'm Eric, by the way." He holds out his hand, which means I have to get up . . .

We meet halfway down (up?) the stairs to the stage and shake hands. I worry mine is sweaty. His is warm and dry.

"I'm Miles."

"Nice to meet you." He lets go of my hand. "What pronouns do you use?"

I freeze. My stomach clenches.

Nobody has ever asked me this before. When I came out to Rachel and Paige and my parents, it was more like an identity announcement. I just told them my pronouns. My parents called the school. I re-explained to teachers, more than once. But nobody has ever looked at me—just looked—and thought this was a question they should ask.

I wish people could look at me and just *know* the right pronouns to use. But in the meantime . . .

"He, him, his." My voice works, somehow, but it goes up at the end. Like a question. Like a girl.

Eric ignores this, too. "Cool. Same."

I frown at him. Sure, he's got an earring, but he's taller than me, and his wrists are thicker, and he definitely shaves. He looks like a cis dude. But cis dudes don't say their pronouns. Even Rachel only started saying hers after I came out—and only on social media.

Say something, Miles. "What were—are—you doing in here?"

"Oh." He turns and looks back to the row he was sitting in, like there's something to see there. "Well, it was open, and I needed somewhere to do some work. Plus, I really like the lighting."

"Oh, yeah. It's . . . moody."

We both look up at the dim yellow bulbs overhead.

He shrugs. "Yeah, but it's cool."

So he was being serious? I mean, that's what I think, too, but I'm weird.

"Do you mind if I keep working here?" he asks. "I mean, if you're going to keep practicing. I'm quiet, I promise." He grins. He has a dimple in one cheek.

I do mind. Practicing alone is when I can fuck up. When I can swear. When I can try something wild and see if it works. The whole point of practicing here is I know nobody's listening—not even my parents.

But I can't say no without being a giant asshole. He was here first. "Sure. If you don't mind listening to me butcher Tchaikovsky."

Eric only shrugs. "I'm butchering everything I'm working on today, so we can be comrades in butchering."

I grin. I can't help it. "What are you working on?"

He gives me a dubious look but sidles back into his row. "I guess it's fair, since I eavesdropped on you." He comes back holding a notebook.

I'm expecting homework. The essay on the Gettysburg Address we're supposed to write by next Tuesday, or the slew of trigonometry problems I'm really not looking forward to.

But the notebook page in front of me isn't lined or patterned in tiny graph squares. It's thick, rough, and covered in cartoons. Fat stripey cats in pencil chase each other across the top of the page. A little round boy in black marker rides a puffy lion in highlighter green. More pencil drawings of two dogs sword fighting, a tall skinny girl playing trombone, a bear reading a magazine. And in blue pen near the bottom, what looks like a laughing waffle.

"You draw," I say. (Captain Obvious.) "This is really good."

Eric doesn't look happy. "It's kind of silly."

(A laughing waffle? You don't say.)

"I meant to do some character design work for this, um, comic-graphic-novel thing I'm working on. But I wasn't getting anywhere. So I doodled." He closes the notebook.

The idea of practicing angst-ridden Tchaikovsky while Eric the Staring Guy draws laughing breakfast food is absurd—and kind of appealing. It takes the pressure off.

"You can stay," I say. "I'll probably only be here an hour or so anyway, until my mom picks me up."

"Cool." He grins. Dimple again. "I'll just, um, sit back where I was. Unless that's too close."

"No, it's fine. I mean, I obviously didn't see you before."

He laughs. Not as big or free as Shane. More self-conscious. Shy. "Yeah, I'm super stealthy." He heads back to his seat and I climb the stairs back onto the stage.

If Shane were here, I would pick the hardest passage and race off on it, and afterward, he would say, "Damn, you are such a maestro." He asked me what the lady version of "maestro" was when we first started dating, but I just laughed and said there wasn't one. I'm sure that's a lie, but I liked being called "maestro."

Add that to the list of Things That Make a Lot More Sense in Hindsight.

I sit down at the piano and look out into the audience. Eric's dark head is bent over his notebook. His feet are up on the chair in front of him. The soles of his green Chuck Taylors poke over the top.

I think of the laughing waffle, and start from the beginning. *Chord, chord, chord.*

I don't have to show off for Eric. I don't know him. And he's doodling cartoon food.

I don't know how much time has passed when Eric stands up. I see him wave from the corner of my eye. I don't stop playing, but I nod at him. Grin. The universal guy sign. He walks up the aisle out of the auditorium.

I make it through the end of the phrase, and I stop. The sound dies away. The auditorium is empty and quiet again, like I wanted.

Except now it's filling up with Stefania and Shane and *you don't know who you are.*

On the piano bench next to me, my phone vibrates. I pick it up, expecting a text from Mom.

ericmdraws wants to follow you on Instagram

I haven't posted on Instagram in ages. Most of the time, I honestly forget I have one.

I open my phone. The last picture I posted is me and Rachel and Paige at the Upton summer boat festival. An awkward selfie in front of the lake. Paige in sunglasses. Rachel holding a root beer float. All of us, even Paige, with big, goofy grins. My hair is short but I'm still wearing earrings. And mascara, which I can tell because I'm not wearing my glasses in this picture, either. I was still wearing contacts sometimes.

I locked my Instagram halfway through my first shopping trip in the boys' section. At this point, after the Coming Out, everybody knows. Everybody at school. Anybody who sees me regularly in town. They must at least know that *something* is up.

But that's different. Coming out in this curated album of my life, online, is something else. What do I even do? Erase all the old pictures of me—of Melissa? Leave them and just start posting new ones and hope nobody comments? I don't even like looking at old pictures of me. In every single one, I look like a big, uncomfortable fake.

The most recent post on ericmdraws's page is that laughing waffle. Posted ten minutes ago. I scroll back through his feed. It's all drawings. Cartoon after cartoon. Silly sketches in pen or pencil of fat stripey cats and food with faces.

But there's one character who keeps popping up shaded and colored and polished. Always with a ponytail and a hat. Sometimes it's a baseball hat, and the character wears shorts and sandals and a shirt with a fat, stripey cat on it. Sometimes it's a hat like Robin Hood, and the character has a tunic and a sword.

But it's always the same face. Same body. Same polished look— like it already belongs in a graphic novel. Maybe this is what Eric was talking about. The character he's designing. The graphic novel he's planning.

The posts don't say.

I scroll back up. In his profile picture, Eric is balancing a pencil on his nose. He looks ridiculous.

```
Eric Mendez
I draw things. A lot of them are cats.
Location: Seattle, WA
```

So he must have just moved here from Seattle. That's why I haven't seen him before.

I go through his feed again. I'm still scrolling when Mom texts that she's outside.

CHAPTER SIX

Cameron Hart is simultaneously the biggest tool on the planet and the shining star of the Midwestern piano world. He's sixteen, just like me, and we once played the same Mozart piano concerto at the Tri-State Piano Competition's Junior Level—but that's where the similarities end.

Cameron Hart is what old books would call *blond and fair*. He's also six feet tall and built like a ballet dancer. Lanky. Graceful. He looks like the love child of an Abercrombie model and an anime dream boy. When he plays the piano, his blond hair flops across his forehead while his long fingers dance across the keys like each one is freaking Fred Astaire. He might as well shoot sparkles out of his eyes. The judges eat it all up.

It doesn't matter what he plays: Mozart, Beethoven, Chopin. Cameron wins the Tri-State Piano Competition every damn year. You'd think the judges would be bored by now, but no—they seem to enjoy it. More accolades for the all-American, apple-pie-and-freedom-fries piano genius!

I hate Cameron.

I hate the way he manages to mention he studies in *Chicago* with *Pierre Fontaine* every time I see him. Like I've forgotten since the last time he mentioned it.

I hate the way he finds the most noticeable spot in any warm-up room or hallway to do his breathing exercises, finger stretches, shoulder rolls. Like he's some Olympic athlete.

I hate the way he talks about all the conservatories and music schools he's going to apply to for college. Like he'll have his choice because he'll get into all of them with a full scholarship.

But most of all, I hate what happens right after he beats me. It's always the same: rakish grin, gentlemanly handshake. "Man, you made me work for it this year. Keeping me on my toes, Jacobson."

Like I'm nothing but a short, forgettable footnote in the Legendary Chronicles of Cameron Hart's Success.

The only comfort I can take is this: Cameron has never come close to winning the National Competition.

Every year, the winner of the Tri-State Piano Competition's Senior Level automatically gets an audition spot at the bigger National Young Artists' Piano Arts Competition, which is open to high school–age pianists from anywhere in the country. Most people apply for a spot in the National Competition the good old-fashioned way, by sending in an audition tape. I don't know how many people apply—probably hundreds—but only the top thirty are picked to fly to New York City (all expenses paid) and play in the final rounds at Carnegie Hall.

The top three pianists get cash prizes. But if you win, if you come in first at National, your first year of college is paid for, no matter where you go. As long as you major in music, you're covered.

Plus, it looks really good on a college application. Even a win at Tri-State would look good. A win at National would really make a music school sit up and pay attention.

Cameron's been to New York twice, performed at National twice, but he's never even made it to the top ten.

I'd love to go to New York. I'd love to play at Carnegie Hall. And I'd really love to win. A whole first year of covered tuition would make me feel a lot less guilty about pursuing piano in college. Mom and Dad would support it (I think) but sometimes I wonder if Mom's constant work stress is because she's thinking about paying for college.

But National is a far-off pipe dream at this point. First, I have to beat Cameron at the Tri-State Competition. And not just Cameron. Any pianist from Wisconsin, Illinois, or Indiana can enter, provided they can play a concerto and are in middle school (for the Junior Level) or high school (Senior Level). First step is a preliminary round in your state. Then the top ten from each state (five juniors, five seniors) move on to the finals. The location of the finals changes every year. An attempt to make it fair, I guess. This year, it's in Milwaukee, Wisconsin.

I would *love* to beat Cameron in our home state.

The preliminary round is in two months—the second week-end in March. I've never worried about it much before. I've made it to the finals every year so far. The prelims are just a chance to see everybody play and figure out who your main competition is.

Or so I keep telling myself. Because right now, I feel terrified.

The rest of the week went by in a frustrated blur. Each morning, I picked out clothes I felt confident in, and by lunch, I felt awkward and fake, sweaty under my binder, and none of the clothes fit right anymore. Each day, I planned out casual, cool things to say to Shane and never got the chance because he stayed twenty feet away from me at all times.

Even practicing in the empty auditorium didn't help. No matter how much I tried to play each note with Meaning, they all sounded as fake as I felt.

So now it's Saturday afternoon, and I'm terrified, worried, and grumpy. I've been working on this concerto since July. I thought I was ready. I thought I could really compete with Cameron this time. Sure, he's playing Rachmaninov, but both concertos are virtuosic classics that famous pianists perform with famous orchestras all the time. We should be on equal footing.

Except, according to Stefania, I'm not ready at all, and I can't figure out what to do about it.

I lean over and thunk my head on the piano keys of my baby grand. Dissonant noise.

"Okay in there?" Dad calls from the kitchen.

"Peachy," I yell back.

It's only the second conversation we've had today. The first was both of us saying "Morning" this morning.

I wish Mom wasn't at open houses all day. Before the Coming Out, we butted heads all the time, and Dad was always patching things up. But after the Coming Out, the pressure on both of us evaporated. I don't know why. Maybe I just don't have to compare myself to Mom anymore. Except now it's Dad I can't talk to.

Ugh.

I get up from the piano, stomp upstairs, open my laptop, and fall over on my bed, listening to Van Cliburn's recording of Tchaikovsky. It was cool of Stefania to pull out an old record, but I found the same recording online in about ten seconds.

I study the network of tiny shadows in the popcorn ceiling. Another architectural feature of our house that Mom says is *so outdated* and *just despised these days* but makes no move to fix. I don't mind it that much. My main disappointment is that I can't put posters up there. I tried once. The poster fell down in a shower of white dust. I was vacuuming my bed for days.

But Mom did change other things in my room. I didn't ask, but she did, and I said sure. So the pink floral lamp on my dresser is gone, swapped for the plain white one from Mom's nightstand. My peach-colored curtains moved to the laundry room, and I've got the plaid green ones. We took down my ribbon-trimmed corkboard and put up a plainer one. It has school notes pinned to it now, instead of pictures of me and Shane.

I feel better and weird about it all at the same time. The floral lamp was pretty. I kind of liked the ribbons on the corkboard. Now I'm *participating in binary gender roles dictated by a patriarchal society that enforces oppressive, narrowly defined identity boxes,* as Rachel would say.

But at least I can be in my room without feeling like it's questioning my identity.

I pull out my phone, while tinny strings wail over my laptop speakers. I still haven't responded to Eric's follow request on Instagram. I just look at it every day and don't do anything. We didn't talk in person the rest of the week either. He grinned at me in homeroom. I nodded to him in history. And I spent the rest of the time with Paige and Rachel, looking at Shane, thinking about Shane, trying and failing to talk to Shane.

> ericmdraws wants to follow you on Instagram

Here goes nothing.
I tap *Accept*. And then I start a new message.

> Hey—I was thinking of going to school tomorrow to practice in the auditorium. Totally no pressure, wondered if you wanted to join?

I send it. Drop my phone on the bed. Breathe. Listen to Van Cliburn's static-laced notes flashing by.
Buzz.
I grab my phone. It's a message from Eric.

> Hey! Sure, I'm down. Study hall?

Five seconds later:

> Get it? Study hall? Because the auditorium is a hall

Three seconds after that:

> Have u heard that one 500 times already

Who is this guy who makes puns about concert halls?
But I grin and type:

> I see you make dad jokes. Is 10am too early?

> Nope. Do u drink coffee

I think of Stefania.

> Not sure. Maybe.

> Then maybe I'll bring some. See u at 10.

> See u at 10.

I turn my phone facedown on the bed. My stomach feels light.

The phone buzzes again. Message from Eric.

It's a drawing. A laughing waffle playing a tiny piano.

I send him a thumbs-up emoji.

On Sunday morning, I pull up to school in Dad's ancient Subaru at 9:51 A.M. I guess I should have listened to Dad when he reminded me it doesn't take twenty minutes to drive to school. But it snowed last night. And not all the roads are plowed. And this is the first winter I've had my license.

Several other cars are already parked in the lot. I recognize Mrs. Reed's old blue Corolla and Janitor Bob's salt-stained Jeep. Somebody's always here, no matter what day it is.

At the end of a row is a dark green Subaru that looks a lot like my dad's. Washington State plates. A peeling National Parks sticker in the window. A rainbow sticker on the bumper.

I lock Dad's car and head into school. The front door is open, but as usual for weekends, only about half the lights are on inside.

I unwrap my scarf, pull off my gloves, and head for the auditorium.

Eric is sitting on the floor outside the auditorium doors, still in his coat, a dark plaid scarf, and a knitted hat with a shockingly orange reindeer on it. And glasses—clear, round, plastic glasses.

"You're here early," I say.

"I overestimated the coffee line." He picks up two paper cups from the floor next to him, straightens up, and hands me one. "In that I thought there would be one."

"You actually brought coffee." The paper cup has a happy purple bee printed on it. "And you went to Hive?"

"Is that bad?"

"There's a Starbucks, like, two blocks from here."

Eric laughs—self-conscious again. "I'm from Seattle. We take coffee really seriously."

"I thought Starbucks started in Seattle."

Eric's grin vanishes. "We don't talk about that."

I stare at him. He stares back.

Then he grins. "Joking. I didn't know how you like your coffee, and I got worried you might be lactose intolerant or something, so I just put oat milk in. It's really good though. Here's some sugar." He pulls a few white packets out of his coat pocket and drops them in my hand.

"Thanks." I'm not lactose intolerant but I also don't know how I like my coffee, and I'm not about to tell him that.

"So what's your excuse?" says Eric.

"For what?"

"Being early."

"Wasn't sure how many roads would be plowed." I stuff the sugar packets into my pocket and open the auditorium door.

"Uh, Miles, it says . . ." Eric points to the threatening sign next to the door: NO FOOD OR DRINK IN THE AUDITORIUM.

"It's fine. Janitor Bob knows me. Come on."

"Janitor Bob?" In the empty auditorium, his voice echoes.

"Yeah. We've got three janitors: Bob, Dave, and José. Bob works the weekends. He looks like a scraggly old Jesus."

"And you know them all?"

Shrug. Sheepish grin. "I told you I practice here a lot."

We dump our coats over a few seats near the front. I pull out my music while Eric pulls out a notebook and pencil.

"More food?" I ask.

He looks blank.

"Drawing." My face turns hot. I point to his notebook. "I mean, are you drawing more—"

"Oh. No." Eric twirls his pencil. "Still trying to do character design. Attempt number one hundred and fifty-three starts now."

I can't tell if he's being serious or not, but he doesn't look too bothered either way. Just shrugs off his coat and settles down in a seat, reindeer hat still on his head. He takes a swig of coffee. Opens his notebook.

So I go up on stage to the piano. Fallboard. Lid. Sit down. Stretch. Begin.

Chord, chord, chord.

Maybe it's the coffee (not as bad as I was prepared for), or Eric with his Chuck Taylors up on the seat in front of him, but I feel more alive, crashing up and down the piano in the boomy auditorium, than I have for days. I don't know who I am or why I like this piece any more than I did the last time I thought about it, but today I don't care. I like playing this music. I like hearing the chords bounce back to me off the ceiling and the walls.

I like not being alone.

When I stop for another sip of coffee, Eric calls out, "So what are you playing over and over, anyway?"

"Tchaikovsky. Piano Concerto."

"That's cool. Do you just study one piece at a time?"

"No, but I'm playing this piece for a big competition coming up, so I'm . . . focusing on it."

"Cool." He goes back to drawing.

I go back to playing.

The next time I stop, I say, "When did you move from Seattle?"

"End of December." When he looks up, his glasses catch the dim lights. "Worst. Christmas. Ever. But the snow was nice."

"It doesn't snow in Seattle?"

"Not often."

"Why'd you move? And if you tell me the lake is a draw, I'll punch you."

Eric laughs, less self-conscious this time. "My mom got a tenure-track position at UW-Milwaukee. Not many options in art history, so we moved."

"If she's at UWM, why are you in Upton?"

"Because Dad's teaching at a high school near Chicago. Upton, I have learned"—he twirls his pencil in the air—"is conveniently halfway between the two places. Plus the lake is a huge draw."

I roll my eyes, start to play again, and then stop. "You didn't buy your house from Tanya Jacobson, did you?"

"No, we're renting. Why?"

"She's my mom. Real estate agent."

"Oh." He grins. "Well, if we buy a house in the future, I'll have my mom call your mom."

I grimace at him and go back to Tchaikovsky.

But now we have a routine. When I stop to stretch my fingers, or drink coffee, or get up and walk around, one of us asks a question.

MILES: What's Seattle like?

ERIC: Rainy but green. Coffee's more expensive.

[More Tchaikovsky]

MILES: What do you think of Upton?

ERIC: Is it always this cold?

MILES: No. In the summer it's disgustingly humid and we have loads of mosquitos.

[Yet more Tchaikovsky]

ERIC: When did you start playing piano?

MILES: Age five.

ERIC: Do you like it?

The coffee is gone when he asks me this. I'm standing behind the piano, head hanging back, staring at the ceiling. My back hurts. *Posture!* I can practically hear Mrs. Kim shouting at me.

I look at Eric. Or where I think he is. Staring into the dim ceiling lights was not a great idea—now I can't see a thing. "What do you mean?"

"Do you like playing piano?"

"Yeah. I mean. It's what I've always done."

"Mm."

"What?"

I can see him now, glasses catching the light again. "Nothing. I just mean, like, I get that it's complicated."

I bristle. "What's complicated?"

"You and piano. I love drawing and I've always done it, but sometimes I don't *like* it. You know?"

No.

"Like sometimes . . ." The Chuck Taylors come down and he leans forward, elbows on the back of the seat in front of him. "I get stuck. Like now, I guess. I draw, and everything is wrong, and it feels terrible. But I know—because that's how it always is—that I'll just keep trying stuff, and eventually I'll figure it out, and then I'll like it again. But in the meantime, it sucks."

Clear as mud. "How can you love something and not like it at the same time?"

Eric shrugs and leans back, pushing the sleeves of his black hoodie up to his elbows. "I don't know. But that's what it feels like. I mean, I never quit drawing, even when I don't like it."

Oh.

Do I feel like that about piano? I have no idea. I've never thought about it before. But I suddenly realize that's exactly how I feel about Shane. *Fuck that guy* and also I really miss him. I don't like him and I love him. "Yeah. I guess I get it."

Eric goes back to drawing. From my spot on the stage, I can just barely hear the *scratch-scratch* of his pencil on paper.

I sit back down on the piano bench.

How do I know if I love piano?

Well, I never wanted to quit, even when I fought with my parents about practicing. That was years ago—I wanted to play outside, they said I had to practice, we shouted at each other. But whenever they pulled out the big guns—the *if-you-don't-want-to-practice-maybe-you-should-quit* guns—I always caved. That must mean something.

And I want to win the Tri-State Competition. But is that about loving piano or beating Cameron?

Maybe Stefania's on to something.

I rub my hands on my jeans. Sweaty palms. "Hey, Eric?"

He looks up. "Yeah?"

"I'm getting kind of hungry. Do you want to go for a slice of pizza or something?"

"There's pizza here?" The Chuck Taylors come down again and he pops up like a jack-in-the-box.

"We're in Wisconsin, not under a rock." I stand up. I feel better as soon as I walk away from the piano. "Haven't you noticed half the school disappear during lunch break?"

"There's *walkable* pizza here?" We pull on our coats. Wrap up our scarves. "Well *dang,* that's real city stuff."

"Har-har." But I'm grinning. "Sal's also has pretty good deep-fried cheese curds if you want to go really Wisconsin."

"Deep fried . . ." Eric pulls on his gloves. "You do that to *cheese?*"

"Cheese *curds,* and in Minnesota they deep-fry Twinkies."

Eric blinks, shaking his head. "I understand your words but not your meaning, sir."

My stomach goes all light again. He called me *sir.* Like it was easy. Like it was nothing.

I lead the way out of the auditorium because my face feels hot. Janitor Bob looks up from his floor buffer as we head for the front door, and gives us his usual two-finger peace sign. We return it.

I'm pretty sure Janitor Bob's a hippie.

Outside, the sidewalks are still not plowed, but there's probably no point now. The snow has been packed down by tromping feet. On the curb, it's turned gritty with sand. Upton gave up salt years ago. Rachel, who spent half of one winter outside with a sign that read *Salt Is For Oceans Not Roads,* claimed a victory, but the official reason was that everybody was tired of salt ruining their shoes.

I look down at Eric's Chuck Taylors, which are turning darker green around the edges where they're getting damp. Based on what I've seen so far, these shoes and the orange reindeer hat seem to be the only pops of color he owns. "Don't you have real boots?"

"No." He sounds sheepish. "You can laugh. I didn't take winter seriously."

"You're legit gonna get frostbite by February." Right on cue, a blast of arctic wind hits our faces. I burrow deeper into my scarf. "Go look in the clearance section at Upton Sporting Goods. It's late enough that they'll have something now."

"Late enough? It's only January."

"Yeah, and everybody smarter than you already bought their boots. This way."

We walk down Main Street, which, despite the cold, is still as busy as it usually is, especially now that it's noon and everything is open. People brunch behind the arched window of Izzie's Café, music pounds out through the seams of Upton CrossFit, the door of Starbucks swings open and *coffee* and *talking* waft out. A little kid is even riding the coin-operated rocking horse outside of Gilbert's, the little supermarket that's somehow still in business, despite the giant Festival Foods a mile away.

Eric looks at the kid like he thinks her choices are very questionable.

"And here we are." I push through the lime green door of Sal's and we both stop.

"Well, it *smells* great," says Eric.

I grin, because I'm finally not the only one with fogged glasses. "Yeah, welcome to winter." I have to raise my voice because unlike New Year's Eve, Sal's is crowded. Everybody over thirty is brunching at Izzie's; everybody under thirty is getting pizza at Sal's. I definitely can't hear the classic rock now. "What do you want?"

"What's good?"

"Everything." I sidle past a couple guys from school to get closer to the counter. Eric follows me. "The sausage and pepperoni is amazing if you're into that sort of thing." Talking over my shoulder. "Rachel gets the veggie slices sometimes and says they're good. The only thing I wouldn't get is the Sconnie Hawaiian, because putting ham and pineapple together just sounds—"

Whump.

It's a soft bump, at least. The advantage of everybody wearing winter coats. I turn to see who I bumped into . . .

It's Shane. Right here, between me and the counter.

Again? *Seriously?* Is this going to happen every time I walk into Sal's? I can't even blame my glasses this time. They're clear now.

"Miles," Shane says.

"Hi. Shane." I have to crane my neck to see his face but I'm too packed in to move farther away. "You're here. Again."

He blinks at me. "Yeah. Me and DeShawn come most Sundays."

He jerks his thumb. I can just barely see DeShawn's tight braids at the cash register.

"That's cool. That you're hanging out with DeShawn so much." *Stop. What are you doing?* "This is Eric, by the way." I grab his sleeve and pull him forward. "Eric, Shane."

"Hi," Eric says.

And then, *thank god,* DeShawn shouts, "Shane! Come on, man, let's go!"

"I gotta go," says Shane. And he goes. Turns around, magically parts the sea of people with his tallness, and joins DeShawn at the register. Leans forward. Orders. I can't hear what he says, but I have a good guess. Shane is a sausage-and-pepperoni kind of guy.

"Um, Miles?"

"Yeah." I turn back to Eric, who's right smack up against me thanks to all these people.

"You okay?" he asks.

"Yeah, I'm good." I avoid his eyes and shrug it off. "Let's get pizza."

We were basically in line already, but I pretend we weren't and find us a spot behind a group of girls I also recognize from school.

Clearly I can't come to Sal's on Sundays anymore. Or maybe ever again, since apparently Shane is *always here.* But I can't leave now. That would make it super obvious I'm *not* okay, and anyway, I promised Eric pizza.

Which he's obviously excited about, since he doesn't talk about anything else until after we've gotten our slices (he goes for mushroom and olive—apparently not a sausage and pepperoni kind of guy). I'm ready to get takeout boxes and just head back to the school, but a couple stools open up in a corner by the window and Eric swoops in and grabs them.

Shane and DeShawn don't stay. They take their slices in boxes and leave. I watch them walk by outside the window, wondering when they started coming to Sal's "most Sundays," wondering where they're going now . . .

"So." Eric sets down napkins and water in plastic cups. "Who's Shane?"

I try to sound casual. "Oh, he plays football. Running back. At our school."

Eric is watching me from the corner of his eyes. His reindeer hat has slid back on his head and a wavy lock of black hair is poking out. "Okay."

I know he's waiting for more. I might as well get it over with. "He's also my ex." Pick up pizza slice. Take bite. Burn mouth.

Eric has a strange look on his face. "You guys dated?"

"Yeah, for, like, a year." Sip water to cool mouth. "He broke up with me right before Christmas."

"Oh." Eric finally stops looking at me, and picks up his pizza. "So was that his new boyfriend?"

I very nearly do a spit take. Manage not to, but the water goes up my nose. "DeShawn? No, they're not gay."

"But I thought you said—Oh." Eric looks at me again. That strange expression is still there, but now it looks more . . . sad. "I'm sorry, man."

"It's fine. I mean . . ." And then I realize I don't have to explain. Eric knows Shane and I started dating when I was a girl. He knows we broke up when I was a boy. And he called me *man* to make me feel better.

I don't know how he got all of that so quickly, but he got it. That was the short introduction I've never had.

"Thanks," I say.

"Oh wow," Eric says with his mouth full. "This pizza is great."

"Told you."

"I thought Wisconsin was just bratwurst and beer. Because of all the Germans."

"Who told you that?"

"Wikipedia."

I roll my eyes. "I promise there's a whole brat fest in the summer. Feel better?"

"Much." He grins at me, and I can't help grinning back.

Maybe this pizza trip isn't a total bust after all.

CHAPTER SEVEN

Mortification at bumping into Shane does not last. Partly because neither Shane nor Eric tells the entire school, like my Sunday-at-midnight brain was convinced they would.

Shane goes back to pretending I don't exist.

Eric pretends that Shane doesn't exist.

"I should talk to Shane," I say, watching him from our table across the lunchroom.

"Nope," says Rachel, firmly.

"At least tell him I wasn't, like, stalking him."

"Nope," says Paige, bored.

My phone vibrates in my pocket. It's an Instagram message from ericmdraws.

Study hall after school?

"What are you smiling about?" Rachel sounds suspicious.

I look at her, perfectly expressionless. "I'm not smiling."

And that's how the week goes. I watch Shane. Shane ignores me. I eat lunch with Rachel and Paige. And I spend my afternoons practicing in the auditorium, while Eric draws. Time goes faster with the *scratch-scratch* of his pencil filling the silence every time I pause, reminding me I'm not alone and kicking my butt to keep going. It's nice.

Less nice is trying to figure out *who I am* and *why the hell I care about Tchaikovsky.* When I head back to Stefania's house on Thursday after school, I feel as clueless as last week.

I can already see the headlines: *Useless Piano Student Can't Answer Simple Question, Is Fed to Dog by Teacher.*

I ring the bell and Olga immediately launches into another barkfest. This time, when Stefania opens the door, her frizzy gray hair is pinned on top of her head with at least five butterfly combs. She shoves Olga's butt out of the way. "Any answers to those questions yet?"

I could try to come up with something on the spot, I guess, but I have a feeling Stefania has an excellent bullshit detector. I brace myself. "No."

She just shrugs and beckons me inside.

I spend the whole lesson waiting for the other shoe to drop, but she doesn't say anything existential at all. It's just scales and arpeggios and Tchaikovsky broken down into tiny, technical pieces. *Left hand behind. Watch that pedaling. What kind of wrist position is that?* She paces up and down the tiny room with her coffee mug like a drill sergeant. *No. Again. Better. Again.* I have to do everything five times in a row *right* before she'll let me move on. I'm beginning to see why Andrew hates her.

When the lesson is over, Stefania walks me to the door. "I'll see you next week," she says. "Keep thinking." And she shuts the door.

I have another Instagram message from Eric when I get home:

> How'd it go?

I'd told him about Stefania in the auditorium the day before. Nothing about the Questions. Just that Stefania was intense. Really intense.

> Better than expected. She didn't rip
> my head off.

> Can I have ur phone number so I don't
> have to keep using Instagram

I give it to him.

The next week is pretty much the same, except that Eric texts me now. About auditorium "Study Hall." About the boots he found at Upton Sporting Goods. (My feet are so warm what is this black magic.) About a giant mound of snow he saw in a parking lot. (U didn't tell me there were glaciers here.)

And I spend way too long thinking up responses. In the car with Mom. (Oh did you miss the cauldrons in the back of the store?) Procrastinating on homework. (I probably should've told you about our resident mammoth too, his name is Steve.)

When Stefania opens the door the next Thursday, this time with her hair in a very high ponytail and wearing an enormous cable-knit sweater, all she says is, "Well?"

I like piano. I keep playing it. I don't quit.

But none of those are the Answer. "I don't know," I mumble.

She still doesn't give me grief about it. Just stalks the room with her coffee mug again, breaking Tchaikovsky into yet more technical pieces. No emotion, or phrases, or *meaning*. Just notes on a page, and all she cares about is how cleanly and accurately I play them. She goes after my pedaling so hard that I fully expect my foot to fall off walking home.

"What's the matter with you?" Mom asks, as I shuffle into the kitchen, limping.

"Does that yoga you do have stuff to work out your ankles?"

"Your ankles?"

"For piano."

She looks at me like I've grown another head and makes a beeline for her office.

* * *

On the first day of February, Rachel, Paige, Eric, and I are sitting around our lunch table, brainstorming more accurate names for the cafeteria's tuna casserole (lead contender: *The Guts of a Thousand Enemies*) when we notice Sophie Hubbard handing out pink invitation flyers for Valentine's Night.

"I really thought she might not do it this year," says Paige, idly leaning her chair back on its hind legs.

"This is something she does every year?" Eric asks. He's been sitting with us during lunch for a few days now, after I bumped into him on the way to the cafeteria, and then we bumped into Rachel and Paige, and we all ended up at the same table. Paige doesn't seem to mind him, which is definitely worth something. I can tell Rachel is still sizing him up, but she hasn't said anything to me about him yet.

"Sophie Hubbard started dating Ben Yang in, like, seventh grade," I say to Eric, pushing my tuna casserole away. I can't stop seeing guts now. "She was a huge believer in romance, until Ben broke up with her last summer."

"I think he finally figured out she's never gonna grow boobs," says Paige.

Rachel shoots her a look. "Don't objectify."

Paige shrugs. "I wasn't. I'm just reporting."

"She had this Valentine's Night party at her house every year," I say. "Well, every year that she was dating Ben. Invite required. Desserts and hot chocolate and a lot of cheesy music."

"Given that her heart is broken," says Paige, "I thought maybe she'd skip the party this year."

"So do you guys go?" Eric asks. "To the party?"

Paige's chair legs hit the floor again and she grins. "We're not cool enough to score invites. Except for Miles. He went last year." I kick her under the table and she glares at me. "What? You did."

Now Eric is looking at me with raised eyebrows. "I went with Shane," I mumble. "We just got invited because we were a couple."

"False," says Paige. "You got invited because *Shane* is a jock." She rolls her eyes at Eric. "It's all Valentine's and romance-themed, so if you're in a couple, Sophie's more likely to invite you even if you're not that cool, because *she's* romance-themed. Or romance-obsessed. That's what Cody Barnett said last year, anyway."

"We're in a couple!" says Rachel. She leans over and bumps her shoulder against Paige. "Maybe we could go this year. See what it's like."

Paige raises an eyebrow. "Seriously? I thought Valentine's Day was a bullshit holiday set up to support the patriarchal industrial complex."

Rachel turns pink. "Yeah, but we're dating now," she mumbles. "It's just a party."

"Well," Paige says, with another shrug, "Miles is single, so he'd be left out."

Eric looks at me. "We could pretend to date, if you want to go."

I'm thinking about Shane when he says this. Remembering going with Shane last year. He put whipped cream on my hot chocolate and drew a heart in it with a plastic spoon. We were both totally embarrassed about it and it was also kind of wonderful.

It takes a few seconds for Eric's words to hit me.

My mind goes blank. I open my mouth with no idea what to say, but Rachel beats me. "That would be so cool!" She leans across the table and grabs my hands. "Miles! We could all go! We'd get a Valentine's Day party *and* we'd get to upset its heteronormative expectations!"

Paige looks at me. Our secret *Rachel's-found-a-cause* look. "I mean, we could always just crash," she offers.

Except that last year, Sophie actually took people's invitations at the door and checked them off her list. And if she's single this year, and thus not eager to start dancing with Ben Yang, we might not be able to sneak in late either.

Anyway, why not go with Eric? We're friends. He offered. And,

I don't know, maybe I should feel weird about it, but it actually sounds . . . kind of fun.

Also, Rachel is giving me puppy dog eyes.

"Sure," I say. "We can pretend to date."

Rachel immediately pops up from her seat, waving her hand in the air. "Sophie! Over here!"

Paige raises her eyebrows at me.

"What?" I say. "You guys might have fun."

"Nah, dude, I was just thinking that was mighty big of you." Paige grins. "No offense, but Rachel wouldn't shut up last year about how you were going with Shane and life was deeply unfair."

Rachel has dashed over to Sophie. The two of them are in the middle of an animated discussion, with way too much smiling. Rachel points to Paige, who waves, and then points to me and Eric.

Sophie gives us a doubtful look.

Eric and I lean toward each other. He puts his arm around me. I smile and give Sophie a thumbs-up, my heart beating faster. (Why is my heart beating faster?)

Sophie mouths something that looks a lot like *whatever*, writes on her clipboard, and hands Rachel two flyers.

Rachel practically skips back to the table, the flannel shirt tied around her waist flying behind her like a gay mini-cape. She slaps the flyers down on the table. "We're in. Here, queer, and ready to couple it up."

"So she's really doing it," says Paige, "even while single?"

"No, I guess she has a new boyfriend." Rachel shrugs. "Some guy from a different school. I escaped before she could start gushing. I mean, it put her in a good enough mood to invite us. Look!" She waves the flyer in Paige's face and squeals.

Paige stands up. "Yeah, I'm going to the bathroom before the whole cafeteria starts staring at you."

"Wait, I'll go with you." Rachel shoves a flyer toward me and stuffs the other one in her bag. "Miles—?"

I quickly shake my head because I really don't need the Bathroom Brigade making an appearance in front of Eric.

"Okay, see you guys later," Rachel says, and dashes after Paige.

Eric leans forward and picks up the flyer from the table. "'The Sweetest Night of the Year,'" he reads. "Wow, that promises a lot."

I'm looking across the cafeteria to the football table.

"'Dress to match your sweetheart. Cutest couple outfit wins a prize!'" Eric is still reading. "I realize I haven't known Rachel and Paige for that long, but I'm confused why they aren't vomiting at this."

"Because deep down Rachel is a total teddy bear who wants everything the Straights have," I say, "and Paige doesn't actually mind this stuff. She just rolls her eyes at everything."

I've found Shane. There's a pink flyer on the football table in front of him. *Who did Sophie hand it to? Is it for the whole table? Did Sophie invite the whole football table least year?*

"We don't really have to go," Eric says. "Or, I mean, we can go but, like, not together. If you just want to go and hang out with Rachel and Paige."

What if Shane is going with someone? What if he's dating and I don't even know?

"No." I tear my eyes away from Shane. "Let's go. We can pretend we're dating to get past Sophie at the door, and then . . . whatever. It'll be fun."

"Okay." Eric pushes his chair back and stands up.

"Um, wait a minute." I scramble up, too. "Just wondering . . ."

Eric slings his backpack over his shoulder and looks at me, eyebrows raised. He hasn't worn his glasses again since that one ill-fated pizza excursion, but I sort of wish he would. He looked good in them.

"You're, like, pretending to be gay." (Thank god for loud cafeterias. I don't think anybody but Eric can hear me.) "I mean, that's . . . that's what you just did, right?"

Eric gives me a strange look. I don't know what it means, but it's the same look he gave me on that pizza Sunday, when I told him about Shane.

"I mean, I . . ." His look makes me nervous, and maybe I should turn back, but I can't. I have to know. "You've got a rainbow bumper sticker on your car."

"Yeah."

"Well, I wasn't sure if it was yours or not."

"Miles," he says calmly, "are you asking if I'm gay?"

I consider my options. "No." Change my mind. "Yes?"

Eric grins—there's that dimple in his cheek again. "I'm not really gay."

"Oh. That's cool." So why is my stomach sinking? What do I care? We're *faking* to make Rachel and Paige happy, and if that also means I can spy on Shane and see if he shows up with a date, well, I'm fine with that. "I know Rachel can be a lot, but we don't hate straight people or anything, really—"

"I'm not straight." His grin turns self-conscious. "I'm just—I like people. Just . . . people. And I gotta grab a book before English. I guess we'll coordinate outfits later?"

My mouth is open. I can't figure out how to shut it.

"Okay, see you." He spins on his heel and waves over his shoulder. "I'll text you."

My phone buzzes in my pocket. I pull it out, half expecting Eric to have somehow texted me already.

But it's Rachel.

> Eric totally wants to date youuuuuu . . .

> Haha we're just friends, he was just being nice.

> Whatever, he gets my approval. Also, he's queer.

I pick up my bag. There's no way I'm telling Rachel I have, in fact, just confirmed this. The last thing I need is her trying to set us up. I'm focused on *Shane*. I care about *Shane*.

I really wish my heartbeat would slow down.

> you've seen the bumper sticker
> on his car, right

Ignore it, Miles. Just ignore it.

Paige gives me a ride home and (thank god) does not bring up Valentine's Night or who may or may not be queer the entire drive. We talk about the clear need for more lesbian punk bands instead.

My driveway is empty, and when I flip on the lights in the kitchen, there's a note on the counter in Mom's handwriting. Dad is out at a training on tax law changes and Mom is house shopping with buyers. There's a frozen pizza in the freezer. Broccoli in the fridge. Yada yada.

I dump my coat and bag on the table. Stick the frozen pizza in the oven. Set the timer. (Ignore the broccoli.)

And then I go up to my room and stare at myself in the mirror.

I'm going to Valentine's Night. As a boy. With my two lesbian best friends and a guy who has an earring and just told me he likes *people*. It's about as far from last year's Valentine's Night as you can get.

I roll my shoulders until my back is straight. What would it be like if I could always stand like this, and be perfectly flat? No hunching, no slouching, no picking shirts based on how well they hide my boobs.

What would I do, if I could just *be*? Like Rachel and Paige and Eric. Without so much trying and posturing and waiting, con-stantly, for someone to call me the wrong name, the wrong pronoun. Without the clock constantly counting down to the next time I feel like a weirdo.

I unbutton my flannel shirt. Shrug out of it. Put on the black button-down shirt I found at Goodwill a month ago, when I was there with Rachel and Paige. It's a little too long in the sleeves, so I roll them up.

Then I turn and dig around in my closet. Where's that box? Oh, here we go. I pull out my new dress shoes. They're just from Target, but Mom sprang for them right after I came out, and they look pretty nice, for Target.

I sit down, put on the shoes, and then reach under my bed for my old jewelry box. I haven't looked at this stuff in months. I totally forgot about half of it. But for years, earrings and necklaces were the easiest presents for anybody to give me. *Oh, you need nice things for your concerts.* I never even got around to wearing some of these things, but I don't feel like I can get rid of them. Not yet. People *gave* me this stuff.

I fish out a pair of plain silver stud earrings and carefully stick them in my ears—my holes haven't closed up at least.

I grab my laptop and head back downstairs.

In the living room, I turn on the study lamp on the piano. Find the loose cord I want from Dad's stereo system by the TV. Plug in my laptop. Crank the volume and sit down at the piano, closing my eyes.

A harsh brass fanfare vibrates the big stereo speakers. Stabs of full orchestra rumble the floor under me.

And I lift my hands and play my opening chords along with Van Cliburn.

Fifty string players surge into the big beautiful melody around us. And when we reach the melody, I'm an echo of Van Cliburn, or he's an echo of me. We chase each other through the maze of virtuosic passages. Octaves tumble. Arpeggios rise.

And here, now, in my earrings and my black shirt and my dress shoes, I am not trying to be. I just *am*. Trans. Queer. He, him, his. The labels I've chosen, and no labels at all.

Just a person.

Van Cliburn and I play through all twenty minutes and fifty-six seconds of the first movement. And then I hear the oven timer beeping in the kitchen. I turn off the stereo system and run to rescue the pizza.

By the time Mom gets home, I'm back in my flannel shirt, in my socks, the earrings put away, with most of the pizza eaten, doing homework at the table.

"Sorry to leave you alone all evening," she says, dropping her briefcase on a chair and picking up the last slice of pizza.

"It's okay." I grin, because I didn't feel alone at all. "I didn't mind."

When Stefania opens the door Thursday afternoon, I say, "I am a gay trans boy who plays the piano because it's the only time I don't have to explain myself in order to feel whole."

Stefania pushes Olga's wagging butt out of the doorway. "Well," she says, straightening up and blowing her frizzy hair out of her eyes, "that I can work with."

CHAPTER EIGHT

If I thought Stefania was intense before, it's nothing compared to now. She talks so fast I can barely keep up. She occasionally shouts in Russian. She leans over my shoulder and pounds out the melody with me on the piano's tinkly high notes. She gestures wildly while she paces the tiny room, yelling instructions.

The lesson goes fifteen minutes over, but when I ask if I owe her more money, she just waves me away.

Saturday is clear, cold, and windy, and Rachel, Paige, Eric, and I hit the Goodwill to look for coordinating outfits. Or anything we can claim coordinates without making us want to barf.

We're not the only people who have deemed Goodwill a decent place to look. The store is an overview of current high school couples, holding hands and wandering through the aisles.

"I can't believe Steven Gerber is still with Holly Hanks," Paige mutters, as we stand just inside the door, looking around. "He so clearly wants to be dating Robbie Novak."

"Oh my god, *fedoras,*" says Rachel, and yanks Paige toward a wall of hats on hooks.

Which leaves me with Eric, who's standing with his hands in the pockets of his black jeans and his dark plaid scarf loose around his neck. He's wearing his glasses again. And his orange reindeer hat. Maybe it's his weekend look.

"We don't have to do that much," I say. "For the outfits. We could get, like, matching pins or something."

Eric tears his eyes away from Rachel, who is putting one hat after another on Paige's head, and grins at me. "Are you kidding? We're going all out. There are prizes on the line."

"The prize is a bag of chocolate kisses. Sophie and Ben won it last year."

"The host of the party won the costume contest?"

"It's 'best couple outfit.' But yeah."

He raises an eyebrow. "That seems fishy."

Long-suffering sigh. "It was a scandal."

"Guys!" Rachel shouts.

Eric and I look at her, along with half the couples in the store. She's holding up two enormous rainbow tie-dyed shirts. Behind her, Paige is biting back a grin.

"Is Rachel suggesting those for us?" Eric asks.

"Yep. We better get looking before she picks out more stuff."

The best thing about Goodwill is that none of the people who work here give you looks. Nobody cares what section you're shopping in or what you pick out. Of course, there's also no guarantee I'll like any of the clothes they have at any given time. But that's true of most shopping I've done.

"So," Eric says as we start into the aisles, "what kind of theme are we going for here?"

"Definitely not hideous-rainbow-tie-dye."

He shoots me a grin. "Fair enough. Anything else we should avoid?"

I lift the sleeve of a camo jacket. Post–hunting season, a good quarter of Goodwill turns into various shades of camouflage. Jackets, pants, hats. We got it all. "Um, I don't know. Maybe no drag."

"Well, I had a ball gown picked out, but okay." Eric grins at me and points. "I think drag is covered already anyway."

I follow his gaze. Rachel and Paige, wearing matching fedoras, are now trying on pinstriped suit jackets.

"Yeah, they're into that stuff." I look away and riffle through a few more coats on the rack. "Rachel might show up with a glitter goatee, so prepare yourself."

"What are you into?" he asks.

"Passing."

It comes out harsher than I mean it to. I look at Eric, but he's inspecting a sequined bomber jacket. "You know you're a guy regardless of what you wear, right?" He looks up, sees me staring at him, and shrugs a shoulder. "I just mean—you feel like a guy, you're a guy."

Is he serious? "Yeah, that doesn't do a whole lot of good if everyone else thinks you're a girl."

"You're right. Sorry." He looks back down at the bomber jacket. "I just meant that I see you as a guy. And I still would, you know, if you were in drag. Or whatever. You're a guy."

He's serious. I think of my earrings and dress shoes and that night banging out Tchaikovsky with Van Cliburn, and my face turns hot. "Thanks."

"You don't need to thank me. It's not hard."

Well, that's a lie. It *is* hard. For some people. Just not, apparently, for Eric.

How is it not hard for Eric?

"Anyway." Eric shrugs one shoulder. "Drag isn't really my thing, either."

"There's a whole section of ugly Christmas sweater castoffs over there," I say, jerking my thumb.

"Oh, god, *yes*," says Eric.

We spend the next hour trying on the ugliest sweaters we can find, with occasional interruptions from Rachel and Paige in fedoras and suit jackets, twirling for us and asking our opinions. Eric takes this quite seriously—frowning, squinting, tilting his head and adjusting his glasses.

He looks so good in glasses.

Because "fair is fair," Rachel and Paige demand to see our top sweater options, so Eric dons a green monstrosity covered in cats wearing Santa hats. He waves Rachel and Paige out of his way, puts his hand on his hip, and runway walks up and down the aisle.

Rachel and Paige cheer. People are turning to look at us, but Eric doesn't seem to notice. He bows with a flourish.

"You're up, Miles," says Rachel. "Show us what you got."

"Yeah, I'll just stand here."

"Do the *walk*," says Paige.

Are they joking? I'm wearing a sweater that says *#elfie* on the front. People are staring at us.

Eric cups his hands around his mouth. "Do the walk!"

"Fine!" I know Rachel's ability to make a scene. The only way out is through. So I put my hand on my hip, like Eric, and walk—saunter—down the aisle.

Rachel, Paige, and Eric applaud enthusiastically. And I'm grinning by the time I reach them. I can't help it.

Rachel and Paige eventually settle on vaguely similar pinstriped suit jackets and matching black fedoras, and wander off to keep browsing while Eric and I narrow down our ugly sweater options.

"I think it's Hideous Plaid or Animals in Santa Hats." I look down at the gold monstrosity I'm currently wearing, featuring an iguana dressed as Santa Claus. "Although I might draw the line with this one. Why does this even exist?"

"Nothing says Christmas like iguanas." Eric wriggles into another sweater. "Okay, here's Hideous Plaid. What do you think?"

I look him up and down. "Queer lumberjack?"

He grins. "I'll take it."

"Hey, Miles!" Paige waves at me. "Do you need new concert clothes?"

"Why?"

She points at Rachel, who's holding up a black suit jacket on a hanger.

"Oh." I pull the iguana sweater over my head. Eric takes it and I dodge happy couples until I reach Paige and Rachel.

"It's a boy's suit," Paige says. "But I thought it might be your size."

I slide the jacket off the hanger. Rachel helps me into it. I turn to face the narrow mirror on the wall.

It fits.

Like, *really* fits.

I raise my arms to piano height and the shoulders move with me. Twist back and forth and the body moves with me, too.

I look at Paige and Rachel. "Are there pants?"

Rachel holds them up.

"I guess I'll try them on?"

"Yeah." Rachel hands them to me. "Go for it."

I head for the dressing rooms. There's an open one, so I don't have to wait, which means no shoppers can judge me either.

I lock the door. Double-check it. Triple-check it. One of my new nightmares is someone walking in on me pantsless.

With the suit jacket still on, I unlace my boots, slip out of my jeans, and slip on the dress pants. Zip. Button. Turn and face the mirror.

I'm wearing the wrong shirt for this—my favorite flannel button-down—and my socks have orange polka dots on them, but still. The pants fit. The jacket fits. It all fits. And I look a lot closer to how I felt, banging out Tchaikovsky in the dark while my frozen pizza cooked.

Closer to *me.*

I unlock the door and open it a crack. Wave a hand frantically at Rachel, who is now looking at boots. She sees me, grabs Paige, waves at Eric, and all three of them come over.

"So?" Rachel says when they reach me.

I open the dressing room door all the way.

"*Damn,*" says Paige.

"Oh my god," says Rachel.

Eric doesn't say anything.

"Can you play in it?" Rachel asks seriously. "Have you tried the Piano Sit?"

I sit down on the bench in the dressing room, lift my hands, and stick my right foot out to where an imaginary pedal would be. "Yeah. It's good."

"You look rockin'," says Paige, with an approving nod. She elbows Eric. "Don't you think?"

"Yeah." He clears his throat. "Yeah, definitely."

"How much is it?" Rachel asks.

I check the tags. "Forty dollars. Altogether."

"You're getting it."

"Well, but does it . . ." I stand up and look in the mirror again. "Does it make my . . . or, I mean . . ." I wave a hand vaguely at my hips. At my chest.

Rachel knows the questions I want to ask. She shakes her head. "It looks great."

"Okay." Of course, do I *have* forty dollars? That's the next question.

Rachel is already fishing in her wallet. "I've got an extra ten. What do you have?"

"Rache, you don't need to—"

"You can pay me back later. Paige?"

"Shit, I don't have much cash. I can give you five?"

"I've got a ten," Eric says.

They're all fishing in their wallets now, and my face is so hot it might as well be on fire. "You really don't have to do that."

Rachel just waves her hand at me. "Come on, get changed. I want hot chocolate."

I close the door and pull out my own wallet. I don't have enough cash. I could use my emergency credit card, but this isn't really an emergency, and Mom is running an open house, which means she probably won't pick up her phone.

I've got only one option.

I press myself into the corner of the dressing room and dial.

Dad answers his phone the way he always does—like he's vaguely confused by someone calling it. "Uh, hello?"

"Hi, Dad. It's me. I'm, um, at Goodwill with Rachel and Paige and Eric."

"Who's Eric?"

"A friend. Look, I found a suit. A really good suit. It fits me. For piano." Silence. "It's forty dollars and I don't have enough cash. I was wondering if I could use my credit card? I can pay you and Mom back." More silence. "Dad?"

"Yeah. I'm here." A pause. "Sure, honey. Buddy. You should have something for piano."

"Okay. Thanks, Dad."

"Yep. Sure. Yep." He hangs up.

I change back into my jeans and shoes. Open the door.

"We've got twenty-five bucks." Rachel holds out the cash to me.

"It's okay. My dad said I can use a card."

Rachel's eyebrows shoot up. "Oh. He was okay?"

I shrug. Carefully casual. "Okay enough."

She and Paige look at each other. Eric looks at both of them, but I can't deal with explaining for him right now.

Rachel shrugs. "Okay, well, that's cool." She hands Paige and Eric back their cash, and then turns to me with an enormous grin. "You got a suit! Miles, you got a fantastic *suit!*"

"Hell yeah," Paige says.

I smile and glance at Eric. He's smiling, too.

With Rachel and Paige's help, Eric and I officially nix the iguana in favor of matching red plaid sweaters, and then we all head for the cash register. I chew my lip while the girl behind the counter folds up my suit and puts it in a bag.

As we push out into the gusty winter wind, holding our bags, Eric elbows me gently. "You'll need a tie now."

"Crap, I didn't think of that."

"You should go hideous-rainbow-tie-dye. Make a statement."

"Oh, shut up." But I'm laughing.

Hive has started having hot chocolate for a dollar on Saturdays, in an effort to attract students from the community college on the outskirts of town. Instead, they get swarms of teenagers who have nowhere else to hang out when it's freezing and the lake is less of a draw. It's already crowded when Rachel pushes the door open, letting out a rush of warm, sweet air.

"I see a table!" Paige shouts. She grabs my shopping bag, and Rachel shouts that they want two hot chocolates, and then they head for the last free table, leaving me and Eric in line, waiting for our glasses to unfog.

"So this place does have lines," Eric says.

"Yeah. You were too early last time. Most of these people weren't awake yet."

He grins. Dimple. "Or maybe, unlike me, they aren't addicted to caffeine."

I'm staring into his dark eyes, and it hits me that he's spent hours in the auditorium with me at this point. He's at our lunch table every day. He was with me when I found this suit. And that means there's something very obvious that I should have asked earlier . . .

"Eric?"

"Yeah?"

"Do you want to come see me play in the prelim rounds of the competition?"

He blinks at me. His eyelashes are so long. "Definitely." He smiles. "People can just come watch?"

"Yeah. It's kind of like a concert. Except for the judges. Rachel and Paige always come. And my parents."

"That would be awesome. I'd . . . I'd love to see you play. Thanks."

Why does my face feel warm? "Well, I mean, you're my friend, and my other friends are coming, so . . ." I shrug and look away, staring at the menu on the wall behind the counter. *Be cool, Miles, what's wrong with you?* "Anyway, you deserve it, since I've been torturing you with that piece for, like, a month."

He laughs—that self-conscious, shy laugh. "You haven't been torturing me, but it'd be cool to hear the whole thing. You know—at one time."

My stomach turns light. I grin. "Okay. Well, cool." And then we're up, and it's time to order.

We carry four hot chocolates to the table where Paige and Rachel are waiting for us. We tap the paper cups together like they're champagne glasses, and listen to Rachel talk about a plant-based food campaign she wants to start in the high school cafeteria.

But I keep stealing glances at Eric. He's coming to see me play. And I have a suit.

A little shiver runs through me.

Now I really have something to work toward.

CHAPTER NINE

Mom, it turns out, is thrilled that I found a suit at Goodwill. She waves away my offers to pay for it myself and insists I put it on so she can see it. So I do—with a nicer buttondown shirt and my dress shoes, because I might as well try to sell the look.

Mom's work is spread out all over the table, but she hops up immediately when I come down to the kitchen. She walks around me in a circle, wearing an expression I've seen dozens of times when she's inspecting a house. Pursed lips. Frown. Folded arms and tapping fingertips.

Finally, she says, "It really fits you. I wonder if we might get the jacket tailored a little at some point. Maybe the pants hemmed? But it's not bad as is. Arthur!"

"What?"

"Come here for a minute."

Dad wanders into the kitchen, his glasses pulled down to the tip of his nose and a folder of somebody's taxes in his hands. He stops as soon as he sees me.

"What do you think?" Mom asks.

Dad meets my eyes and then looks away. "About what?"

"You wear suits every day! You think this needs tailoring?"

I decide not to point out that Dad does *not* wear suits every day. Dad wears suits two months of the year when he's actually meeting a lot of clients at his office. And he clearly does it grudgingly.

Dad meets my eyes again. Manages a small smile. "Looks fine." He turns and leaves the kitchen.

Mom sighs. "Unhelpful as usual." She dusts off my shoulder, like there's actually dust there. "Well, you'll need a nicer shirt than that, obviously. And a tie. But we'll find those things." She smiles at me. "You look good, sweetheart."

Nice of her to say, but I'm pretty sure I look terrible. My throat's closing up, my mouth is trembling, my whole face is hot, and my eyes are swimming.

I'll pretend it's because of what Mom said. Not what Dad couldn't say.

My next lesson with Stefania lasts an hour and a half.

"Good," she says. "Your pedaling is better."

My chest inflates. Smile starts.

"But your phrasing makes no sense here, here, and here. Again!"

Pop goes the balloon.

But she still doesn't ask for extra money, even though the lesson went fifty percent longer. She just sends me off with, "Getting better. Now figure out what this concerto is saying. We haven't got all the time in the world! Next time you show up here, you tell me what it's about."

And she shuts the door before I can argue.

I totter home and collapse face first on the couch.

Dad pauses the episode of the cooking show he's watching from his armchair and looks over at me. "Tough day tickling the ivories?"

I give him the finger.

That gets a chuckle, and he goes back to his show.

Eric offers to drive all of us to Valentine's Night, but Rachel and Paige decide to go on a date to Juku Ramen beforehand, so Eric shows up at my house on Saturday night alone.

I'm in the middle of stuffing my head through my hideous red plaid sweater when the doorbell rings, which means Mom gets to it first. She calls up the stairs, "Miles, are you going to a really late Christmas party?"

On with the sweater, back on with my glasses, quick curl scrunch, and then I rush downstairs. There's Eric, standing in the entryway in an unbuttoned black pea coat, red plaid sweater, glasses, and neatly combed hair, saying to my mother, "It's an annual thing. Miles said he went last year."

He's holding a single red rose. Mom turns and looks at me. *Crap.*

I'd told Mom and Dad I was going out with friends. I did not say it was to the Valentine's Night party at Sophie's house, and I *definitely* did not say I was getting picked up by a guy Mom has never seen before who would be bringing me a rose.

"Mom"—I grab my coat from the closet—"this is my *friend.* Eric." On with the coat. "Eric, this is my mom, Tanya Jacobson. I guess you guys have met."

Eric gives Mom a smile. (Will she resist the dimple?) "Miles says you're the best real estate agent in town."

(She will not.) "Does he really?" Mom shoots me a pleased look. "Is your family looking for a home?"

"Not right now, but I'll give my parents your name."

Mom practically beams. "That's lovely of you. You guys have fun." She closes the door behind us.

As we walk to Eric's old Subaru parked at the curb, I say, "A rose?"

He hands it to me. "I'm selling the romance fraud."

"Right." But I can't think of anything smart to say. I've gotten stuck staring at the little hoop in his ear. It's gold tonight. "Thanks."

Eric opens the passenger door with a bow, like the car is a limo.

It's definitely not. The seats are leather but they're faded, cracked, and peeling, and the floor mats are caked with mud and sand. The tray between the seats is filled with colored pencils and crumpled bits of paper. The whole car smells musty, despite the mini pine tree dangling from the mirror that says *Fresh*.

Eric starts the car, and the seat under me shakes. The dashboard lights up. The radio starts to play: Indie guitars and slightly out-of-tune piano filter through the speakers. The station on the display reads WUPT, which everybody in town calls *Whupped*. It comes out of the community college and is the only radio station around worth listening to.

"I like this song," I say, and immediately realize that was a really cheesy thing to say.

But Eric just says, "Yeah, me, too." We pull into the street. "So, how do we get to Sophie's house?"

I put her address into my phone, and from then on, I just give him directions, which makes it easier to ignore the fact that I'm suddenly nervous, that I have no idea what to do with this delicate rose on its short stem except twirl it slowly around and around in my fingers.

The street lamps leave pools of yellow light on the road as we rumble down Main Street. There's not much snow on the ground—just sad, dirty mounds left by snowplows—but the pavement is still gritty under the tires. Next week is supposed to be warmer, which might melt the rest of the snow. Tonight, though, it's bitingly cold. I can see my breath, even in the car.

Sophie's house is in the Lake View Estates subdivision of Upton, which is small, but (as Mom says) "exclusive"—which apparently means it has a name, a sign, and people who tell you what mailbox you're allowed to buy. The name sort of overpromises, since only a few of the large beige houses actually have a view of the lake. Mostly the subdivision is just giant lawns and confusingly winding roads with names like *Turnberry Trail* and *Starbridge Lane*.

Eric turns the car past the WELCOME TO LAKE VIEW sign and says, "I guess we won't have trouble finding it."

I was ready to squint and try to remember what distinguishes Sophie's beige house from every other beige house here, but he's right. There's a line of taillights going up the street in front of us to a house on the corner with heart-shaped balloons tied to its mailbox. In the glow of the yard lights, I see people hustling up the wide driveway toward the front door.

Eric manages to find a parking spot on the street, several houses down from the heart-shaped balloons, and turns off the car. "Did Sophie invite the whole school?"

I'm watching the steady stream of couples hurrying past us. Boy-girl, boy-girl. Coats and scarves and some brave souls wearing dresses and tights. "I doubt it. Last year it was maybe a hundred people."

He stares at me. "How the hell does Sophie know a hundred people?"

"Supposedly she keeps a spreadsheet of who's dating." I grin as his eyebrows shoot higher. "I'm not kidding."

Our phones buzz in perfect unison. We pull them out.

"Rachel's waiting out front," I say, even though we're both reading the same text.

"Well, here we go then." Eric kicks open his door. I do the same.

Boots on the sidewalk. Deep breath. Was I this nervous last year? With Shane? What did I wear? What did Shane wear? Did he bring me a flower? I can't even remember.

"You okay, Miles?"

Eric is watching me across the salt-stained hood of the car. When I look at him, he smiles.

My stomach flips. "Yeah. I'm fine. Just . . . nothing."

We cross the street, joining the line of people hurrying up the sidewalk, and Eric grasps my hand and squeezes it.

My stomach flips again. But before I can decide if I should

squeeze back or tug free, look at him or not, he lets go. And now he's waving to Rachel and Paige, who are standing at the end of Sophie's driveway.

"Hurry up, I'm freezing!" Rachel shouts, hopping up and down.

"She was worried you weren't gonna show," says Paige, when we reach them. Her fedora is cocked at a jaunty angle and she's wearing very dark lipstick. She looks like she belongs in a really gay cabaret.

"I was not," says Rachel, who is (thankfully) not wearing a glitter goatee. "Let's go."

Last year, Sophie stood just inside her enormous front door, checking everyone's names off her master spreadsheet. But this year, Sophie is nowhere to be seen, and we're greeted by Katie Nelson, a freshman I recognize because Dad does her family's taxes every year, which means we get invited to their summer barbecues.

Katie's blond hair is carefully straightened and her makeup looks carefully applied, but she looks ready to barf.

"Sophie has outsourced," Paige mutters, squinting at Katie. "The rumors of a new boyfriend must be true."

Rachel frowns. "That wasn't a rumor. *I* told you that."

Katie holds her hand out for our invites. "Names?" She looks up and sees me. "Oh, hey, Miles."

"Hey, Katie. Are you okay?"

"Yeah!" She turns around and scrolls frantically on the laptop balanced on the farmhouse-chic entryway table. "I just maybe should have charged more than my usual babysitting rate for this."

"Sophie's *paying* you?"

"Yeah. She wanted to spend the whole evening with her boyfriend."

"Vindicated," whispers Paige.

Rachel rolls her eyes.

"Drinks and snacks are in the kitchen, upstairs is off limits, and you can leave your coats down the hall," says Katie, picking up a rubber stamp. She plants little black hearts on the backs of our hands. "Thanks for coming."

I shove Eric, who shoves Paige, who shoves Rachel, and we press into Sophie's house.

"But she didn't get our names," says Rachel.

"Miles distracted her with his good looks," says Paige.

"But that's not fair to everyone else!"

"You just wanted to tell someone we're a couple." Paige pats her shoulder. "People know, babe."

Sophie's house is what Mom would call an *entertainer's dream*: open floor plan, high ceilings, all bathed in the warm glow of the red-and-white twinkle lights strung up overhead. The matching dark leather couches have been pushed up against the walls to make plenty of space for a dance floor, although not many people are dancing yet. The pop songs echoing over the speakers on the living room bookshelf are decidedly cheesy. Not WUPT.

Paige steers us down a hallway lined with perfectly posed family photos. "Let's ditch our coats."

We leave our coats piled over the back of an armchair in a small room with a TV and a treadmill, and then head back into the crowd. Most of the couples around us have opted for easy color coordination for their matching getups: blue shirt, blue dress, red shirt, red dress. Some have matching flowers pinned to their collars. And, like last year, a few people have gone all out. Greg Greer and Haley Lopez have reprised their Mickey and Minnie Mouse costumes. Preston Cox and Amber Griffin might be going for a Ken and Barbie look—but then again, they look like that most of the time.

Rachel immediately tugs Paige onto the living room dance floor. I have to hand it to them. The suit jackets and fedoras work. They manage to look confident and queer and fabulous, all at once.

I'm a tiny bit jealous.

"Do you want to dance?" Eric asks.

I fumble the rose in my fingers and accidentally pull off a leaf. Put my hand behind my back. Drop the leaf and hope nobody notices. "Um . . ."

Eric is watching me, hands in his pockets, eyebrows raised above his glasses. Just a hint of a smile, barely any dimple at all.

I'm nervous all over again. It must be because I'm about to be really *out*. Here as a guy, with another guy, even if we're committing romance fraud.

That has to be it.

I look again at Rachel and Paige. What the hell.

"Sure," I say. "Let's dance."

Eric grins and holds out his hand.

I stick the rose in my back pocket (it pokes up a little awkwardly over my sweater, but at least it doesn't have thorns). Then I grab his hand and we sidle through people to Rachel and Paige. Rachel bounces up and down with excitement when we reach her. She takes my free hand, and Paige (with only one eye-roll) takes Eric's free hand, and the four of us dance in a circle. Four queerdos on a freezing night in Upton, surrounded by straight couples, some of whom are definitely giving us weird looks. But Paige makes a point of not caring as a general principle, and Eric doesn't seem to be paying attention to anyone around him, and Rachel looks so ecstatically happy, her long curly hair bouncing around her shoulders . . .

. . . that I don't really care either. They're my buffer. More people are joining the dancing, but all I see is Rachel as I twirl her and she twirls me. All I see are Paige and Eric dancing back to back, and Paige shouting at Eric that he dances like a girl, and Eric taking it as a great compliment.

We dance through song after song, until the inevitable happens: a slow, romantic, cheeseball song. Rachel groans. Paige announces she needs something to drink, and we all head for the kitchen.

Sophie's house is full of people now—swaying in the living room, pressed up against the walls with their snacks, and still more coming in. Paige has to use elbows to get us to the kitchen counter, where there are stacks of paper cups, aerosol containers of whipped cream, and a giant bowl of ginger snap cookies. Two hot beverage dispensers covered with glittery heart stickers display cards handwritten in red marker that say *Spiced Cider* and *Hot Chocolate*.

"What are you going for?" Eric says in my ear, while Rachel squirts whipped cream on her hot chocolate.

"I'm thinking cider."

"Me, too." And before I can figure out how to get between two very cuddly couples, Eric has dodged around them and carefully filled two paper cups with cider.

"Thanks." I take the one he holds out to me. The rising steam fogs my glasses.

"I had an opening." He grins. "Cheers."

We tap our paper cups together.

Rachel and Paige have moved over to a corner of the kitchen, sharing their hot chocolate and a paper bowl of cookies, talking to each other. I can't hear what they're saying. I can't tell if they want us to join them.

"So, I figured out some character stuff," Eric says—fast. Like it tumbled out.

"Oh. You mean your art stuff? Or . . . your graphic novel?"

He holds out his phone. On it is a quick snap of a notebook page, and I recognize the character that I've seen several times on his Instagram. Ponytail, hoodie, jeans, baseball hat, all sketched in gray pencil. But there's something different in the design. Is it the face? The eyes? The slope of the shoulders? I can't quite put my finger on it.

"I decided to make them nonbinary," Eric says.

"Who?"

"This character." He points to the phone.

I stare at the drawing on the screen. I guess I shouldn't be surprised. Eric's from Seattle—of course he knows what *nonbinary* means. It's not like Upton, where Rachel discovered a Tumblr thread about nonbinary identities in middle school and then blew me and Paige away with her queer knowledge.

Eric must see the surprise on my face, because his shoulders hunch up. "I know, but I was trying to figure out their gender and I just couldn't. I tried all these variations, and I finally realized it was pointless. They're both. Or neither. I'm not sure."

"No, I didn't mean . . . I just meant, that's cool! I haven't read a graphic novel with a nonbinary character before." I also haven't read any graphic novels, but he doesn't need to know that.

He grins. Self-conscious. Shy. Like when I first met him. "Sometimes it's how I feel. Both, or neither. Like at this sort of thing." He twirls a finger, vaguely, at the room around us.

I look back into the living room at all the swaying couples. Boy-girl, boy-girl. He's always taller. She's resting her head on his shoulder.

"Like you don't know where you fit in?" I say.

"More like I do, it's just not in either of the available slots."

Boy, do I know that Feel.

Or maybe I don't. I *do* fit in a slot—sort of. I want to. It's just not the slot people see when they look at me. "I could use different pronouns for you, if you want."

He smiles at me. Nothing self-conscious or shy now. "That's okay. Most of the time I feel like a guy. Sometimes . . . I just don't. Or maybe I *do,* but it's not how guys are supposed to be. I don't know. I'll tell you if I change my mind, though."

"Okay." We watch the dance floor, sipping cider. Then I say, "So this character is that part of you?"

"I guess so. And probably a little bit of my friend Sam."

He doesn't explain more. So I don't ask who Sam is. "What's your character's name?"

"Cielo," he says. "It's Spanish for sky."

I form the word, soundlessly, to myself. *Cielo.* "I picked my name because I thought it would be easy for everyone to remember, since it starts with the same letter as my old name. Miles. Melissa." Shrug. "Not very inventive, I guess."

"I like your name," Eric says. "It's distance." He catches me frowning at him. "I mean, literal miles. Like, plenty of distance for you to go. Paths to take you can't see yet. It matches you. You can go as far as you want." He blinks and rubs the back of his neck. "Maybe that sounds weird."

"No." I don't know if I understand what he means. But I like what he's saying.

The song changes—fast tempo, booming bass. A cheer goes up around us. Rachel appears at my shoulder. "Come on, let's go!"

I gulp the last of my cider. Rachel is already pulling Paige and Eric into the crowd.

"Be right there!" I shout. "Just gonna ditch this sweater!"

Eric gives me a thumbs-up as Rachel drags him away.

I head for the hallway, pulling my hot, itchy sweater over my head. The pile of coats on the armchair has turned into a mountain, and it takes me ages to unearth my coat. When I do, I stuff the sweater into my coat sleeve so I won't lose it. I straighten my glasses and walk back into the hall, trying to smooth my buttondown shirt . . .

And find myself face-to-face with Cameron Hart.

ameron Hart, obnoxiously tall and effortlessly slouchy, all at the same time.

Cameron Hart, blond hair as shiny and floppy as a Hallmark Channel Christmas prince's.

Cameron Hart, crisp white collar poking up above his subtle maroon sweater, because Cameron Hart does not do silly couples' outfits.

Wait a minute.

Cameron Hart is *in a couple*?

Cameron Hart *knows Sophie*?

I watch, stuck in some terrible nightmare, as Sophie comes up beside him, and (god, no) slips her hand into his, because *Cameron Hart is Sophie Hubbard's new boyfriend.*

"Hi, Miles," she says to me, and then goes back to gazing adoringly at Cameron.

Cameron is gazing at me. "Hi, Miles."

Is his face permanently stuck in a smirk?

"Hey, Cameron." My hands are sweaty. Cameron hasn't seen me since—well, the Midwestern Piano Arts Fundraiser when he dissed Tchaikovsky. Two weeks before the Coming Out. What has Sophie told him? What has anybody told him?

"I sort of wondered if I'd see you," he says, looking like he could care less. "Sophie was just showing me around. You know, I never even knew where Upton *was* until today?"

I find that unlikely. Cameron lives twenty minutes north on the freeway, which means he drives right past Upton every time he goes to Chicago for a lesson with Pierre. But I'm not going to get into that. Paste on a smile instead. "So, how'd you two meet?"

Sophie is still beaming up at Cameron. "He was playing at the nursing home in Kenosha. I volunteer there on the weekends." (Of course she does.) "It took me two weeks, but I finally said hello. He's just so brilliant at piano, I was totally intimidated."

Kill me now. "That's great."

"I like to use it as a venue to practice performing ahead of the competition," Cameron says, with a shrug.

"Oh, so does Pierre come with you and play the orchestra parts on another piano?" I ask.

Cameron's ears turn red. "No, he's too busy for something like that."

"So you play just the solo part. By yourself."

Cameron glares at me.

Sophie says, "Everyone just feels so lucky to have him there."

"I heard you're studying with Stefania Smith," Cameron says, as if Sophie doesn't exist. "How's that going?"

"Great." There's no point asking how he knows this. The only thing Pierre Fontaine cares about more than everyone else knowing about *him* is him knowing everything about everyone else. I wouldn't be surprised if he's the one who told Cameron my new name and pronouns. "She's a pretty incredible pianist."

"Well," Cameron says, "you're brave for studying with somebody none of the judges like."

What's that supposed to mean? "I'm learning a lot from Stefania. That's the point."

His smirk returns. "Hey, whatever works for you. I need a challenge this year." He puts an arm around Sophie and gives her a squeeze. "Good for you for trying new things."

He turns, arm still draped around Sophie's shoulders, and the two of them walk back down the hall and disappear into the crowd.

My fists are curled so tightly my fingers hurt. I'm sweaty and hot and feeling exactly the same as I always feel after I see Cameron: like one big *almost*.

Almost good enough.

Almost smart enough.

Almost *everything*—but not quite anything. Some things don't change with gender.

Cold water. I need cold water on my face. And a private place to scream.

There's a door in the hallway with a handwritten card on it that says *Bathroom*. I try the door, but it's locked.

Wait. There's another bathroom in the basement. I remember because the toilet up here got clogged last year and Sophie had to send everyone down to the one in the basement. The lines were epic.

I turn around. Back down the hall, into the kitchen. My memory is right—here's the door to the basement, and the stairs down to the nicely carpeted and completely deserted room. Guess nobody's discovered the Ping-Pong table down here yet.

But just as I reach out a hand for the bathroom doorknob, the door opens . . .

. . . and there's Shane.

Frozen in the doorway, hand still on the knob, staring at me. Wearing the same black shirt and red tie that he wore last year when we were here together—*now* I remember, seeing it. He dressed to match a black and red concert dress that I had. We were ridiculously overdressed compared to everyone else but we didn't care. It was fun.

"Miles," Shane says.

What do I say? *What do I say?* Oh, hi, it's me, apparently running into you every time we leave school?

"Sorry," is what comes out. "I was just . . . I came down here to . . ." My hand seems to be flailing in the direction of the bathroom.

Shane quickly steps out of the way. "Yeah, sure. Go ahead. I didn't mean to—"

"I just wanted to hide." It slips out before I can catch myself.

Shane frowns. "Why?"

No going back now. "Cameron Hart is here."

Now Shane's eyebrows shoot up. "Seriously? Is he playing another benefit concert he can brag about or something?"

Shane met Cameron twice—at the preliminary and final rounds for the Tri-State Competition last year—and hated him.

I grin. A little. Even though the idea of Cameron playing a benefit concert anywhere in Upton makes no sense. "Apparently he's Sophie Hubbard's new boyfriend."

Shane gives me a look that's exactly what I'm feeling. "Wow. That's . . . just . . . *Why?*"

I laugh. It kind of bursts out of me—painful—but I feel better. "I have no idea."

"How long you think that'll last?"

"Beats me. I didn't know Cameron could pay attention to anything except himself."

Shane shakes his head. "I feel bad for Sophie."

"Yeah." I don't. If she can't recognize Cameron is a total jerk, that's on her.

"You okay?"

I look up, meet Shane's eyes, and both of us look away. "Yeah. It just . . ."

"Threw you for a loop?"

I glance up again. This time, when he looks at me, he doesn't look away. "Yeah," I say. "Threw me for a loop."

He smiles, barely.

"What are you doing here?" I ask. I have to.

"I came with DeShawn."

For a second, Eric's *is DeShawn Shane's new boyfriend* question goes through my mind.

"DeShawn just started dating this cheerleader and she wanted to go, so I tagged along," Shane says, and the thought evaporates. "Honestly, I didn't really think Sophie would let me in without one of her fancy flyers. But that girl at the door didn't seem to care."

"So you don't have a date?" I just can't seem to stop.

"Not this time."

I nod. Rub my arm. I'm cold now.

"You?" he asks.

"I came with Rachel and Paige. And this guy, Eric." I try to grin. "It's a funny story, actually. Rachel really wanted to go, so Eric and I pretended to be a couple so Sophie would invite us . . ."

But it doesn't seem funny, the way Shane is looking at me, so I stop.

"Well." Shane clears his throat. "I guess I should get back up there." He points, vaguely, to the stairs.

"Yeah. Yeah, of course." I step sideways, out of his way.

But he pauses when he reaches me, and his hand comes up and he squeezes my shoulder. "Don't let Cameron get to you. He's got nothing on you. Seriously."

And then his hand leaves my shoulder. I turn around, but he's already creaking up the basement stairs, and I can't think of anything to say to stop him. Every cool, casual, remotely appealing thing I've planned for a moment like this has flown out of my head.

He ducks through the door at the top of the stairs, and he's gone.

I go into the bathroom. Turn on the tap and run my hands under the freezing water. Well, Miles, you got your answer. Shane showed up, and he's not dating anyone. You even had a *moment,* and all you talked about was Cameron.

I lift my hands and touch them to my face. *No.* That wasn't the moment to say anything more because I came here with my *friends.* With *Eric.* And yeah, it's romance fraud, but . . .

I suddenly remember the rose that Eric gave me and pat my wet hands to my back pockets. The rose is gone. It must have fallen out. It's probably been trampled by now.

Great.

I leave the bathroom and jog back up the stairs. The party is really going now. Everybody in the kitchen is shouting at each other. The music is pounding. The living room dance floor is packed.

I stand on my toes to survey the crowd. There's DeShawn dancing with the cheerleader—Rhoda Something. There's Shane in a corner of the kitchen, holding a cup and talking to another guy from the football team whose name I can't remember. But Shane is looking across the room. I follow his gaze, and there are Sophie and Cameron, in the opposite corner of the living room, next to the massive arched window ringed with twinkle lights. Sophie watching the dancers. Cameron talking, of course. Presumably to her. Probably about himself.

And in the middle of all the dancing are Rachel and Paige, still in their fedoras and blazers. Rachel's arms over her head, hair bouncing on her shoulders. Paige more contained, like she always is, but I can tell she's smiling.

And here, coming toward me, weaving through the crowd, is Eric. His sweater sleeves are pushed to his elbows. His hair is rumpled, messy, with a few bits sticking straight up.

"Hey," he says. "What's up? You've been gone for ages."

Really? It all happened too fast for me. "Sorry. I got sidetracked." I hesitate, torn between wanting to tell him everything and wanting to forget it ever happened.

Of course, how can I forget if we're all at the same freaking party? Wherever I go, Cameron will probably be leering from the sidelines.

"Um, listen." I really wish I didn't have to raise my voice for this. "I think I'm gonna bail. You can stay, if you want. I can probably walk home. Or call my mom for a ride or something."

Eric watches me. "You okay?"

"Yeah." I try to sound like I could care less. "Just ran into someone."

He nods slowly. "Okay. Well, we can totally bail, if you want. Or . . ." He looks over his shoulder at the dance floor. He's so close that the sleeve of his sweater brushes my arm—and I'm suddenly warm again. "We could stay and dance another song or two, and me and Rachel and Paige can distract you and also fend off any *someones* that you might run into." He looks back at me, smiling.

It's funny, I could swear that red sweater was hideous on the rack at Goodwill, but it doesn't look hideous on him.

And I could swear that this night was spiraling downhill a minute ago, and now it's suddenly standing perfectly still. There's just Eric in front of me, and everything else fades into a blur of muted colors and white noise.

"Yeah," I say. "That sounds good."

He holds out his hand, and I grasp it, and he pulls me back into the crowd. We dodge around swaying bodies and duck under raised arms until we find Rachel and Paige. Rachel gives me a two-hand high-five, and she looks so happy that I can't help but smile back at her.

From here, in the middle of the living room dance floor, I can't see Shane or Cameron. Only Rachel and Paige in front of me. And Eric next to me. I don't know if he's staying close to me, or if I'm staying close to him, but his sweater sleeve against my arm is like an anchor, keeping my thoughts from floating away.

Here, with Eric, I can dance however I want to, because he's dancing however he wants to, and doesn't seem to care what anyone else thinks.

And I feel . . .

Oh.

Eric stops dancing. "What's the matter?"

He's stopped because I've stopped, and I'm staring at him with my mouth open. "I have to call Stefania."

He looks confused, but he nods. "Okay. Want me to come?"

"No, it'll just take a minute."

I turn. Push my way through the crowd toward the front door. Katie is slumped in a chair, resting her head on the entryway table. Not that it matters—there's no line anymore.

Through the front door, out onto Sophie's beige brick porch. Cold air hits me like a crashing wave. My breath clouds in front of my face. I pull out my phone and dial Stefania's number.

It rings. Once. Twice. Three times. "Hello?"

"Stefania, it's Miles."

Silence. Then, "What did you figure out?"

"It's about joy." The cold air burns my throat. "Tchaikovsky. The concerto. The brass and the orchestra are all this doom and gloom from the outside world that keeps trying to barge in. But the piano—I'm pushing it all away. The piano keeps being joyful, in spite of everything. It's about joy."

"So Miles the trans boy will show he is whole by playing a joyful concerto."

Swallow. Nervously. "Yeah."

Silence again. The balloons on Sophie's mailbox bob gently. God, it's cold out here.

"Works for me," Stefania says. "You?"

"Yeah."

"Good. See you Thursday." She hangs up.

I lower my phone, holding it against my chest. Sophie's neighborhood is a collection of yard lights, all up and down the street—little networks of fireflies in the dark. Overhead, through patchy clouds, I can see the stars.

The door behind me opens, and the music and voices are suddenly louder. Eric comes up beside me, holding out my sweater and coat. "Ready to bail?"

It's funny what a difference a few inches makes. I don't have to look up so far to meet Eric's eyes—not the way I do with Shane, or Cameron—and he never seems to look down on me.

I wriggle back into my sweater. "Yeah. I think so."

"Did you get ahold of Stefania?"

"Yeah." Pull on my coat. "Sorry about that, and about disappearing before. I ran into this guy who keeps beating me in the competition, and it sort of threw me, and he's kind of a jerk, and if you can believe it, now he's dating *Sophie*—"

Eric leans forward and kisses me.

Full on.

On the mouth.

My thoughts skid to a stop. I forget to close my eyes, or even take my hands out of my pockets. And before I can remember to do any of those things, he's pulled away.

We stare at each other, so close that I could count his long eyelashes, if I wanted to.

"Sorry," he mumbles. "I should have asked. I know this was a pretend date, with romance fraud and everything, but I really like you. That's why I got you a rose. I kind of wanted this to be a real date."

It takes a colossal effort to find my voice. "So, when you said you like people . . ."

He smiles, tentatively. "You're a person."

My stomach flips, just like it has several times this evening. And now I get why.

Proverbial ton of bricks.

"You can ask," I say. "If you want."

"Ask what?"

"You said you should have asked, so—"

"Oh. Right." He clears his throat. "Miles Jacobson, may I kiss you?"

I'm grinning now, too. "Sure."

He leans forward again, and this time I close my eyes, and I take my hands out of my pockets and grasp his jacket. He kisses me, and I very much kiss him back.

We pull away at the same time.

"So," Eric says, "are you ready to bail?"

"Yeah. We should tell Rachel and Paige, though."

"I did. I mean, I said I thought you probably wanted to go."

"I see. You blamed it all on me, so I'll get all their wrath on Monday."

He laughs. "I think they'll be fine without us."

I look back at Sophie's house. Through the arched living room windows, everybody is still dancing. Out here, the music is a dull *thump-thump-thump*. Nobody is looking at us.

"Yeah," I say. "Let's bail."

We turn, and halfway down the driveway, Eric reaches down and takes my hand. This time, he doesn't let go, and neither do I.

CHAPTER ELEVEN

Rachel says *I told you so* as soon as I tell her and Paige, which is right before homeroom on Monday morning. I started about a hundred texts to Rachel over the weekend, but I didn't send any of them, because what if Eric woke up Sunday morning, or from a nap Sunday afternoon, or halfway through Sunday night, realized he'd made a grave error, and changed his mind?

That didn't happen. All his texts to me were nice texts. He called me Sunday afternoon just to talk.

"It was *painfully* obvious," Rachel says. "Did you see the way he looked at you in your suit?"

"What? When?"

"At Goodwill!"

"Dude," Paige says, "what are you gonna tell your mom?"

Good question. I've been trying not to think about it. *So, Mom, remember the guy I swore was just a friend? PSYCH.*

"I don't know yet," I say.

Rachel doesn't seem concerned. "Our numbers have doubled!" she crows. "This school now has *twice* the queer couples!"

"Rache, I was still queer before Eric kissed me. And so was Eric."

Rachel turns pink. "Yeah, I know. I didn't mean to, like, prioritize traditional coupledom. Single identity is valid, too."

"She's still riding that Valentine's Night high," Paige says with a yawn.

About half the school seems to be riding that Valentine's Night high. There are four passionate hallway make-outs and three equally passionate hallway breakups before noon, none of them involving the same couples.

Which means that even though Eric smiled at me when he dashed into homeroom along with the last bell, I still feel relieved when he sits down next to me at lunch and just says, "Hi."

"Hi," I say. My stomach flutters.

"Are they okay?" Eric asks.

I look across the table. Rachel and Paige are staring at us so intensely I can practically see their eyeballs burning. "They're fine. They just, you know, *know*. And have feelings."

"Oh." Eric raises his eyebrows. "Are they expecting me to kiss you now?"

"Please don't."

Paige leans across the table and fixes Eric with a glare. "Just so we're clear, my dad is a landscaper, which means if you hurt Miles, I have access to a lot of shovels and plenty of gardens to bury the evidence."

"Okay," Eric says mildly.

"*Guys.*" Rachel can't contain herself anymore. "We can *double date.* Paige and I know *all* the good queer-friendly spots in Upton."

Paige rolls her eyes. "Babe, they're not queer-friendly. Literally none of those establishments have figured out we're a couple."

I glance at Eric, who's watching Rachel and Paige argue about which Upton restaurants and coffee shops might know they're a couple. I definitely do not want to go on a double date with Rachel and Paige—that would be A Lot. But there's still something that feels so *easy,* all of us sitting here thinking about it. Joking about it. Rachel and Paige arguing about where we would go on said date.

Maybe it's because I'm not the Awkward Third Wheel anymore.

I'm back in the club. We're all on equal footing again. And Rachel's not judging me, like she did when I was with Shane.

Eric catches my eye and grins. I grin back.

And that's when I see Shane, over Eric's shoulder. Right in the middle of the cafeteria. Holding his tray, heading for the football table with DeShawn.

He turns his head, like he knows I'm watching him. Our eyes meet.

And he smiles at me.

Smiles.

I turn away, quickly, before Rachel or Paige or Eric can figure out where I'm looking. Not that I needed to worry. They're still busy discussing Upton food establishments.

I can't help it. I sneak another look over my shoulder. Shane is gone.

Eric and I spend every afternoon together now, in the auditorium after school. It's only for an hour, before the theater crowd barges in to start rehearsals for *Guys and Dolls,* and it always flies by. Of course, that's partly because there's a lot of kissing. Which is nice. *Really* nice. I mean, of course I spent a lot of time kissing Shane, but this is different because *I'm a boy kissing a boy.* And that boy is Eric, and it's magical and normal all at the same time . . .

"We need ground rules," I say on Wednesday.

I'm sitting on Eric's knees in the front row of chairs, one arm looped around his shoulders. His notebook is on the floor next to us, and it's been ignored for at least ten minutes.

He raises an eyebrow. "Ground rules?"

"Kissing breaks are nice, but they need to be breaks." I look at him seriously. "Not the main activity with practicing and drawing breaks."

He grins. "You're the one who sat on my lap, Miles."

I stand up. "Fine, point taken. I'm just saying I still have to practice. I have to prove to Stefania that I know who I am and I can play this music like it belongs to me *tomorrow*."

"I know."

"The preliminary rounds are in less than a month."

"I know that, too." Eric pushes himself up so the chair folds up underneath him. He perches on the upturned seat. "This guy Cameron must be a real piece of work if you'd rather practice piano than hang out with me."

I told Eric about Cameron during the drive home after Valentine's Night, when he asked if I wanted to tell him who I'd run into. I'm not sure he expected a ten-minute rant.

I know he's joking, but I can't help it. "This isn't just about Cameron. I want to do well this year for *me*. It's important. Piano is important."

His grin vanishes. "You're right. I'm sorry. I get it—really."

And he does. He gets it in a way Shane never did. Yeah, Shane loves football and he cares about practices and games. He wants an athletic scholarship to college. But somehow he still never understood why I had to choose piano over him sometimes. He'd smile and let it go, but really, I think he just didn't want to argue.

Great. Now I'm thinking about Shane's smile, and I'm right back to wondering what that look in the cafeteria meant.

What's wrong with me? Shane *never got it*. So why do I keep thinking about him? Even here with Eric, Shane Thoughts keep elbowing in, and I start wondering if maybe he'd get it now. If now that he's smiling at me again, and talking to me again, maybe he could just . . . get everything?

Eric reaches out. Pokes my arm. "You okay?"

"Yeah!" Blink. Turn for the stage and the piano. "Back to work."

* * *

On Thursday, I stand on the sidewalk for a long time, staring at Stefania's door. It's lighter in the sky behind Stefania's house today than it was last Thursday. The days are getting longer.

Okay, Miles. Stefania won't laugh at you.

Probably.

I climb the stairs. Ring the doorbell. Olga goes ballistic, like always, and a second later, so does Stefania, shouting at Olga to quit barking. When she opens the door this time, her frizzy hair is up in an extremely messy bun and she's wearing a long flannel garment that might be a bathrobe masquerading as a shirt.

"Hello, Miles-who-is-going-to-play-a-joyful-concerto," she says, heaving Olga out of the way. "Come in."

Is she making fun of me? But she looks totally serious as we walk through the house to the piano room. Doesn't even pause to refill her coffee mug. Just sits down in her floral armchair and says, "Play."

I take off my coat and gloves. Not quite warm enough to go without them yet. "What scales?"

"No scales. Tchaikovsky. Show me."

Oh, god.

Well, here goes nothing.

I close my eyes. Think of that night, me and Van Cliburn, in my living room. Think of dancing with Eric and Rachel and Paige at Sophie's party. Think of *joy.*

The fanfare booms through my head. Doom. Gloom. Tragedy.

I lift my hands. Open my eyes.

Crash, crash, crash.

Joy surges through my body, from the pit of my stomach through my arms to my fingertips. I throw myself at the piano so hard that my glasses bounce on my nose. The pedal is not just a pedal—it's a drum that I stomp on in the rhythm that courses through me.

I play through the soaring melody and the cascading arpeggios.

Through the booming octaves and the playful notes that chase each other up the keys. Through the return of those brilliant, joyful chords.

I wait for Stefania to stop me, but she doesn't. So I keep going. Here the music is sweet and rolling. Here it's angsty; I'm speeding up, speeding up, praying my fingers don't slip. Now into a moment of darkness, and I let out all my frustration and pummel the keys like they're Cameron's smug face. But just before the darkness goes too far—before the whole thing turns to tragedy—the sweetness returns. The music breathes, and I breathe with it.

I keep playing all the way to the triumphant finish of the first movement—an end that refuses to be beaten down—and lean into the last note as though I can make it louder that way, sustaining it with the orchestra in my head, even as the sound of the piano fades away.

Twenty minutes after I started, I pull my hands from the keys. All I can hear is my own breathing, shallow and fast.

I look at Stefania. She's watching me over her coffee mug.

What if she hates it?

She sets her mug down on the windowsill.

She hates it. I'm in trouble now . . .

Stefania stands up and clomps over to the piano. She leans over my shoulder, one delicate hand hovering over the keys. "When you're playing the melody, let your hand roll. If you reach *with* the melody, your pinky finger will make that extension more easily. Let the music help you with your technique, so the technique becomes the phrasing. Try, with me."

We play the right-hand melody together, in octaves. I copy her movements.

"Better," she says. "Whole arm, down to the fingertips. That's it. Good." She turns a page in the music. "I don't understand this phrase. I think it needs to lead more—all the way to *here*. Don't give up before you get there. Make us *want* that high note. Again."

It's not just about pedaling now. It's not just *your left hand is behind your right.* It's about the flow of each note to the next, each gesture to the next, each phrase to the next. It's about where the music rises and falls, where it tumbles forward and where it holds back. It's about the choices I make to build a story—where the music is coming from and where it's going.

Which means that she understood. She got it. This piece belongs to me.

Or at least, I showed her it could.

The lesson only lasts an hour this time. But as I'm packing up my music and putting on my coat, Stefania says, "We need to start rehearsing for the competition."

I stare at her blankly. "We?"

"Someone has to play the piano reduction of the orchestra part for you. You can't just sit up there and play the solo piano part by yourself with no accompaniment."

"I know, but I just thought . . . You're going to do that? Play the accompaniment?"

"Who else would?"

Well, I don't know. Mrs. Kim always played for me, but I thought Stefania might consider herself above that. Pierre Fontaine only plays for Cameron; the rest of his students fend for themselves, even if they compete. One of them actually hired Mrs. Kim to be her accompanist last year.

"Thanks," I say. "I just didn't want to assume. I mean—"

Stefania waves a hand at me. "I have the score already. I'll look at it this week. Next week, we should practice together. Mrs. Kim said the two of you used the high school's pianos?"

When did she talk to Mrs. Kim? "Uh, yeah. I practice at the high school sometimes, and they have a second piano. It's just an upright—"

"Fine, fine." Stefania clomps out of the piano room. "We'll use your regular Thursday lesson time. Will that work?"

I follow her, trying to picture Stefania Smith playing a terrible school upright. "Yeah, the musical doesn't rehearse on Thursday or Friday, so—"

"Good." Olga trots after us, giant tongue lolling out of her mouth. "You have a suit?"

"Yeah."

"Has it been tailored?"

"No. It's just from Goodwill—"

"I don't care where it's from." Stefania stops in the living room. "I'll call my tailor and make you an appointment. You should get your clothes squared away now so you can practice in them. Shoes, too."

Practice in them? "That's really nice of you, but, um, how much would . . . ? I mean, I don't know what alteration costs—"

"My tailor owes me a favor," Stefania says. "Do you have shoes?"

"Yeah."

"Start practicing in them now." She gives me an almost gentle smile. "The point, Miles, is to feel as comfortable as you can when you walk onstage. You'll have plenty of other distractions without worrying about your shoes."

"I've done this competition before."

"As your actual trans self?"

Oh. She's got me there.

Stefania absently strokes Olga's head. "Maybe Mrs. Kim already told you this, but a six-foot-tall guy like Cameron Hart will always look more impressive playing the piano than me, or Mrs. Kim, or you . . . at least as you used to be. In a perfect world, that wouldn't matter, but in reality, it does. The piano is not a *feminine* instrument—it's not a flute or a harp or even a violin. It's big. It's percussive and commanding.

"Now you'll be competing in a suit with a different identity. And maybe—*eventually*—that will help you, as unfair as it is." She gives me a pointed look. "But even though the classical music world isn't nearly as sexist as it used to be, we both know that, despite a proliferation of gay tenors, it's *straight*."

I feel a little sick. Mumble, "I didn't know Tchaikovsky was gay."

"Exactly. And why would you? Nobody discusses it. Not that it needs to be front-and-center all the time. Who you date isn't on display when you perform. But who you *are* . . . that's visible. That's why I wanted you to know who you are when you play piano, and that this piece belongs to you—before you have to go out and play it in front of a lot of people who have seen you as someone very different in the past."

Now I definitely feel sick. "So the suit—"

"—will be perfectly tailored and then practiced in so it feels as much a part of you as anything else when you walk out onstage." Stefania smiles. "Don't worry. I practice in all my gowns ahead of time." She nudges Olga out of the way and opens the front door. "Out you go."

The afternoon light is fading now, the sun slipping behind the trees. Which means the temperature is plummeting. So much for springtime.

I pull off a glove so I can dial Eric's number.

Eric picks up on the first ring. "Hey, Miles."

Glove back on. I start walking. "Eric, I need a tie."

"Did you just get out of your lesson?"

"Yeah." I hunch up my shoulders to bury my ears in the collar of my jacket. "And apparently I need to practice in my suit, so I need a tie."

"Oh. Well, the good news is, the world has no shortage of ties. Actually . . ." I hear a door open and close, and then a horrible grating sound.

I jerk the phone away from my ear. "What the hell is that?"

"My janky closet door. I'm going back into the closet for you, Miles."

"What?"

"I think I've got some ties that would probably work for you, if you want to borrow one. I'm just looking in my closet."

My heart leaps. "Really? That would be great."

"Yeah. Just wait, though—once everybody really *gets* your identity, you'll start getting a tie for every birthday *and* Christmas. It's the easiest gift to buy, so everybody does it. I've got way too many ties and the last time I wore one was, like, a year ago at least."

My vague panic is already melting away. "Thanks, Eric."

"Hey, somebody should use these ties. What's best for a concert? Plain black?"

"Yeah. Plain black is good." What has Cameron worn in the past? I can't remember. Ugh, do I need to look up pictures of *Cameron*?

"Maybe you could come over on Saturday," Eric says. "You could bring your suit and try these on? I'd say I could bring them to you, but my parents both need to go into work, so I'm babysitting my little sister."

"I didn't know you had a sister."

"Yeah. Nina. So does Saturday work?"

"I'll check, but probably."

We talk for a few more minutes—about random things—and then Eric has to go help with dinner, so I spend the rest of my walk home with thoughts swirling around so fast I feel dizzy.

I'm entering a competition where *everyone* will find out I'm trans. And yeah, I basically knew this, but now it's really hitting me. I have to write a new name on an application and hope they believe me, even if it's not my legal name. I have to perform in front of a bunch of people who saw me perform last year, and hope they believe me, too.

And on top of that, I'm getting my suit tailored and I'm going over to Eric's house to try on ties.

Eric invited me over. That's a whole new level. Shane and I dated for at least a month before he came over to my house.

And now I'm thinking about Shane again. Perfect hair and letter jacket. Smiling in the cafeteria.

Shit.

CHAPTER TWELVE

Mom is strangely silent when she drives me over to Eric's on Saturday afternoon, on her way to an open house. NPR buzzes quietly in the background over the car speakers. She doesn't even ask if my butt is cold.

Eric's address is on "the wrong side of the tracks" in Upton. Not that there's much difference, honestly, but there are actual freight train tracks and his house is on the other side of them, and farther away from the lake. The houses here are smaller and older, and some have peeling paint. One yard has a swing set—a plain, basic metal one instead of the top-of-the-line wood monstrosities you see on my street that look like they belong on a playground.

Mom stops the car in front of a house with white wooden siding, a pointed roof, and a rusty, leaning mailbox.

I reach for the passenger door handle, but Mom says, "Miles . . ."

She's gripping the steering wheel with both hands. Sitting forward in her seat. Looking anxious.

"Mom, Paige used to live, like, two blocks from here, remember? It's fine."

She frowns at me. "Good grief, Miles, I'm not worried about the neighborhood. I'm glad you have a new friend. And he's . . . helping you with your suit."

She stares at me. I stare back. It's there, between us. The Big, Unanswered Question.

She breaks first. "Are you dating Eric?"

Here we go. Tread carefully, Miles. "Yeah. I think I am."

"You *think* you are?"

"Well, I wasn't when he picked me up for Sophie's party. We were just friends—really." (Does Rachel's mom ask this many questions? Does Mrs. Kim?) "And then when we were leaving, he kissed me, and it was really nice. He *gets* me, Mom. He asked my pronouns before I could even tell him. And he's an artist, so I feel like he understands my piano stuff. Rachel and Paige love him."

I might be reaching with this last endorsement, but I can't help throwing it in.

She says, stiffly, "He seemed nice."

"He's really nice."

"And he understands you." She looks searchingly at me. "Your identity and your . . . gender."

"Yeah. He does."

She nods, but she looks about as comfortable as if she were sitting on a tarantula. "Home by dinnertime, remember."

That's my cue. Time to escape while I can. "Thanks, Mom." I grab my suit, zipped into one of Mom's garment bags. "Good luck with the open house."

I feel like I owe her something nice, and she manages a smile. I slam the car door behind me. Watch the BMW pull away from the curb and rumble away down the street.

"Hey, Miles!"

It's Eric, padding down the front steps of the house in thick socks. He's wearing that red plaid sweater from Valentine's Night and his glasses.

I meet him at the bottom of the steps, and he leans down and kisses me, quickly.

"Nice sweater." I poke his arm. I'm a little jealous how good he looks in it. Mine just makes me look like Christmas Waldo.

He grins. "You know, it's actually pretty comfortable. Not bad for five bucks." We go back up the steps and into the house.

"Here, I can hold that." He takes the garment bag while I shrug out of my coat and slip out of my shoes. Add the coat to what I assume must be a coat rack, though I can't actually see the rack—just a mountain of coats.

Eric leads me into a living room with a lot of wood paneling, and green carpet that makes the whole thing look sort of like a forest, with sun streaming in through the big picture window. It's outdated, but it's cozy, with a saggy sofa and saggy armchairs and paintings of flowers on the walls.

"Welcome to our grand abode," Eric says, carefully draping my suit over one of the armchairs. "It's granny chic. My mom is still here, actually. Want to say hi?"

"Is she as intense as my mom?"

Eric looks puzzled. "Your mom isn't intense."

Ha, what a joke that is. "Sure, okay."

He takes my hand and we go through a dining room with delicate floral wallpaper and a mustard yellow fifties-style dinette and into the kitchen. Like the living room, it's dated, with beige tile floor, off-white tile countertops, and plain wood cabinets. But it's cozy, too. The yellow polka-dot curtains above the sink match the dinette, and there's a bright red toaster on the counter with googly eyes pasted to it.

Sitting at a small wooden island in the middle of it all is a woman with long, curly black hair and light brown skin, carefully cutting a sandwich into triangles for the little girl sitting across from her, who has her head bent over the stuffed toy she's holding.

"Mami," says Eric, "this is Miles. Miles, this is my mom, Gabriela."

The woman looks up and smiles. She has a dimple, just like Eric. Behind her lavender-purple glasses, her eyes crinkle.

"Miles, hi!" She leaves the sandwich, shuffles across the kitchen (she's wearing fluffy slippers), and wraps me in a hug. "It's so nice to finally meet you!"

I return the hug—gingerly, because I don't need Eric's mom noticing my boobs.

"Eric's been telling me about your piano playing." She lets me go. "I used to sing—a long time ago. I'm thrilled to meet another musician! I hope I can hear you play sometime. Come in, come in!" She goes back to the kitchen island. "I'm just getting Nina's sandwich ready and then I'm afraid I've got to go to work. Grading to do and an extra lecture to teach. I'm sure Eric told you."

"Um . . ." My brain tries to catch up in the face of her big, warm smile. "Yeah, he did."

"Good. Well, I'm happy to have you here. I hope we can chat more another time, maybe when Dan's around, too."

"My dad," Eric whispers to me.

"Okay, sweetheart." Gabriela pushes the sandwich toward the little girl, who must be Nina. "Here's your lunch."

Nina looks up for the first time. She has glasses, too—little plastic pink ones that make her wide-set dark eyes look enormous—and a round face. Her black hair is done up in pigtails.

She sees me and smiles wide and loose. "Hi, Eric's friend." Then she goes back to her stuffed toy—which looks like a stripey cat—and her sandwich.

Gabriela is pulling on a pair of boots. "Eric, there's pizza and taquitos in the freezer. I can answer my phone except between four and five—"

"I know, Mami, I got it."

She kisses him quickly on the cheek. "Have fun, boys!"

And she shuffles out of the kitchen. Thumps of boots and the swish of a coat, and then I hear the front door close behind her.

She called us *boys*.

"So . . ." Eric leans his elbows on the kitchen island. "Nina has Down syndrome, so I usually try not to be too far away, but she doesn't need constant supervision or anything."

"Sure. Of course. I mean, I'm the one crashing your babysitting afternoon."

He grins and leans across the kitchen island. "Hey, Neens, how about we take the sandwich upstairs and eat it in the tent?"

She looks up with a big smile. "Tent lunch?"

"Tent lunch."

"Okay." She grabs his hand and slides off her stool. She's short enough to be five, but I have a feeling she's actually older than that. "This way!" she says, and back through the dining room and living room we go. I grab my suit off the saggy armchair.

Nina leads the way up a flight of carpeted stairs to the tent, which turns out to be a bed sheet draped over two metal folding chairs on the second floor landing. Under the bed sheet is a kid-sized beanbag chair. Nestled in the beanbag chair is a very fluffy black cat.

"Mr. Pudge, that's my chair," Nina says.

Mr. Pudge shows no signs of budging.

Nina crawls into the tent and sits next to the beanbag chair, petting Mr. Pudge, who emits a low, gravelly rumble. "He's purring now," Nina says to Eric, "and it's my turn for the chair."

"Okay, then let's move him." Eric kneels down and awkwardly crawls into the tent. "Come here, Mr. Pudge."

The cat lets out an indignant and very loud meow, but he doesn't put up a fight as Eric hauls him out. Nina quickly takes Mr. Pudge's place. Eric hands her the plate of sandwich.

"Okay, so you're going to eat your sandwich here and I'm gonna go hang out in my room with Miles," Eric says.

"Okay."

"Where will I be?"

"Hanging out in your room with Miles."

"Yep." Eric opens the drawer of a side table next to the tent and pulls out an iPad and a pair of small headphones. "You want *Finding Dory* or *Frozen*?"

Nina thinks about this long and hard, her forehead scrunched up. Finally she says, "I would like a different princess."

"How about *Moana*?"

Nina shakes her head. "*Cinderella*."

"We don't have that on the iPad, Neens. How about we watch *Cinderella* later on the TV?"

She looks disappointed, but she nods. "Okay. Then I would like *Dory,* please."

She carefully puts the headphones on, waiting patiently while Eric cues up the movie. He hands her the iPad and she balances it on her knees with her plate of sandwich. Mr. Pudge jumps up into the beanbag chair next to her. It's a tight fit, but she doesn't seem to mind.

Eric jerks his head and we go down the creaky hallway lined with framed prints from art museums. It's easy to tell which door is his before he even opens it—it's the one with a drawing of a fat stripey cat.

I don't really know what I expected Eric's room to look like. A desk littered with paintbrushes? Floor-to-ceiling stacks of comic books? An actual easel?

There are no paintbrushes and no easel, but there are drawings. Everywhere. Fat stripey cats chasing each other across the wall over his bed. Laughing waffles on either side of the single window. A pencil sketch of Nina over his desk.

There *is* a stack of comic books—a very short stack—on top of the stool that's acting as a nightstand.

I point to the nearest stripey cat. "Is that Mr. Pudge?"

"No." Eric nudges the door closed behind us. "I sort of base the cats on our last cat—Mrs. Fiddlesticks. She died a few years ago."

"Oh." Foot right in mouth. "I'm sorry."

"It's okay. She was really old." Eric goes over to his sliding closet doors. "You might want to cover your ears."

I don't cover my ears, which turns out to be a mistake. The full glory of the closet doors shrieking open sets my teeth on edge. "That's lovely."

"Isn't it?" Eric grabs a shoebox down from a shelf. "Here are the ties." He upends the box on his bed, pushes up his sleeves, and begins detangling the mess. "Okay, so we've got argyle ... polka-dot ... plaid ... How about a Charlie Brown tie? Oh, or here we go. Santa hats."

"We got Christmas sweaters for Valentine's Night and you didn't *also* bust out a Santa hats tie?"

He grins, self-consciously. "Well, we wouldn't have matched. Oh, this is what I was looking for." He holds up a plain black tie. "What do you think?"

I don't know what it's made of, but it looks soft and just a little bit shiny, like silk. I feel suddenly nervous. "Yeah. That looks good."

"Want to try it on?" He's gathering up the rest of the ties and flinging them back into the box. "Since you brought your suit, you could just try it all on together and make sure you like how it looks."

I look down at the garment bag in my hands. I brought the suit to try it on, obviously, but now that I'm here ...

I'm starting to realize *trying it on* means changing clothes in Eric's house.

Oh, come on, Miles, it's not like anybody will be watching. Stop being a weirdo.

"The bathroom is just down the hall," Eric says. "Right across from Nina's tent."

Well, I can't say *no* now. "Okay. Uh. I'll be right back."

Just last night I braved a solo shopping trip to the mall in search of a plain white dress shirt to go with my suit. I managed to slip away without a lot of explanation because Mom was on the phone with a client, and Dad doesn't ask that many questions. Shopping alone at the mall is brutal, but I eventually found a decent white shirt in the boys' section. I haven't shown it to anybody yet.

Breathe, Miles.

The bathroom is small, covered in teal tile, teal bath mats, and a shower curtain with an enormous portrait of Frida Kahlo on it. I change in the corner, out of Frida's view. Pants on. Shirt on. Jacket on.

Mirror check. Pretty flat.

I bundle my regular clothes back into the garment bag and stuff it into the bathroom corner. I should have brought my dress shoes. I feel silly walking out of the bathroom in purple socks.

Nina looks up from her iPad. "Look sharp!" She gives me a thumbs-up.

It's so earnest I actually feel better. "Thanks, Nina."

She goes back to her movie, and I go back down the hall. When I open Eric's bedroom door, his eyebrows jump.

My heart stops. "What?"

"Nothing!" He shakes his head. "You look . . ."

Oh, no. I look wide. Busty. Like a girl.

"Amazing," he says.

My ears feel hot. "It's not tailored yet. Stefania's going to set me up with her guy, apparently."

"Looks pretty good to me." Eric hands me the black tie.

I take it and stand there, looking at him.

He looks at me. "Miles, do you know how to tie a tie?"

My face is on fire. "I haven't worn that many ties, okay, and Rachel always tied them for me. They all belonged to her anyway." I glower. "Don't laugh!"

He's laughing. "I'm sorry, I'm sorry. Okay, let's assume your lesbian friends won't always be there to bail you out." He takes the tie from me. "I'll show you. Turn up your shirt collar."

I quickly button my top button. Turn the collar up. He gently grasps my shoulders and steers me over to face the mirror next to the closet. "Okay, so . . ." He drapes the tie around my neck. "First, make sure the fat end is longer than the skinny end . . ."

I'm listening to his instructions. I swear I am. But I'm also stealing looks at him in the mirror—standing behind me and tying an invisible tie, while I mimic his motions with the real one. "Around in back, up and through again . . ."

How does his hair look so good when it's messy? Mine turns into frizzy chaos if I don't use cream and scrunch it just right.

"Then you pull it down . . ."

But now I'm distracted. I missed the final step. The tie looks like a bird's nest.

Eric laughs again. "Here." He reaches around my shoulders and undoes the mistake. "So, you go like this . . ." His sweater sleeves brush against my shoulders as he loops one end of the tie around the other. His hands are graceful, tucking the end of the tie through the knot. Not in a pretentious way. Not even in a flamboyant way. Just . . . ordinary. An ordinary kind of grace.

"Then you tuck it through here, and now you're all set!"

He steps away from me. Leaving me staring at . . .

Me. My reflection. Obviously. But I look good. From the waist up. The socks are a little silly, but from the waist up I look like a guy.

Like *me.* Like a new me. But also like the me I've always been.

"What do you think?" Eric asks.

"I think it works."

"It's yours."

"Really?"

He shrugs. "I guess it's possible I'll need an extremely dressy tie at some point in the future, and then my parents will wonder where mine went, but you can keep it for the concerts."

"I'll give it back after the competition." I fumble with the knot. "How do I get it off?"

Another grin. "Turn around."

I turn to face him, and he gently loosens the knot and undoes the tie.

We're close again. And now he's holding the ends of the tie, still draped around my neck.

"Miles Jacobson," he says quietly, "may I kiss you?"

"Yeah." I barely manage a whisper. "Definitely."

It's just as wonderful as Valentine's Night and every afternoon in the auditorium since. I wrap my arms around his neck. He wraps his arms around my back, under my suit jacket.

And his fingers find the edge of my binder.

No.

Pull away. Fast. Messy. Fumbling step backward, breaking out of his grasp.

"Sorry!" He holds up his hands, eyes wide. "Are you okay? Did I do something?"

"No." (Don't apologize.) "No, I just . . ." (Don't look at me. Don't try to guess. Don't notice my chest.) "I'm gonna go change."

I escape into the hallway. Walk as fast as I dare past Nina, into the bathroom.

I close the door behind me and sink to the floor.

What was I thinking? Or really, why *wasn't* I thinking? I can flatten them out and slouch and pretend they aren't there, but surprise! I've got boobs! Sitting there like two grenades on my chest, waiting for the worst possible moment to blow up any illusion that I'm a real boy.

And Eric wasn't even under my shirt.

I got to second base with Shane, more than once, but *ha,* what does that even mean now? There's nothing sexy about a binder. It's a sports bra on steroids. Always walking the line between hiding my boobs and letting me actually *breathe.* It's stifling, sweaty, and uncomfortable, and it's not even summer yet.

But taking it off is worse. Then I can't even convince *myself* I'm a boy.

Get off the floor, Miles. This is just sad.

I stand up and change clothes like it's a race, because the last thing I need is to look at myself right now. I fold up the suit pants and jacket and shirt and carefully slip them back into the garment bag, along with the tie. Tug on the binder to straighten it out. Tug on my jeans to straighten out my briefs underneath them. Yet

another reminder that I don't fit into clothes the way manufac-
turers expect. At least I don't feel like I'm missing anything down
there. I could honestly care less.

Does Eric care?

Has he thought about it?

Oh, god. No. Don't go there. Eric likes you. He said so.

I pick up the garment bag and give the bathroom mirror the
finger. I don't know who it's for. My reflection? My binder?

Me?

Eric is sitting on his bed when I open his bedroom door again,
but he pops up as soon as he sees me. "Hey."

"Hey."

"Are you okay?"

His shoulders are hunched up just like mine. Like we're both
trying to hide.

What do I say to that? Do I say *I don't know*? "I think I just
needed to slow down."

He nods, looking at me. Anxious. "Sure."

"Thanks for the tie."

"If you want to stay for a bit, I have an idea for a very low-key
activity."

I sort of figured he'd want to get rid of me ASAP. But he sounds
genuine. "Okay?"

He heads back down the hallway and I follow him. "Hey,
Neens, how about some *Cinderella*?"

Nina pulls off her headphones. "Yes!"

Eric takes her iPad and pauses her movie. He glances at me. "Is
that okay?"

"Yeah." I try to smile. "Sounds great."

Nina claps her hands and jumps up from her beanbag chair so
quickly that Mr. Pudge lets out a surprised grunt.

I leave the suit hanging on the coat rack downstairs and we all
settle onto the saggy sofa in the living room, with Nina on one side

of Eric and me on the other. Halfway through Cinderella singing to soap bubbles, Mr. Pudge saunters into the room. He ponders us for a moment with his big green eyes, and then hops up and squeezes himself between Eric and Nina, purring noisily.

The knot in my stomach slowly unwinds. I move my hand closer to Eric's. He turns his hand over, open, and I twine my fingers through his.

Eric gives me a ride home after the movie. His parents aren't back yet, so Nina rides along in the back seat, telling me about her school and her teacher and the goldfish in her classroom.

When we pull up to my house, though, she stops talking and sits back, humming vaguely to herself. Almost like she knows Eric and I need a moment.

Shrewd.

I reach for the door handle. "Thanks for the ride."

"Sure." He chews his lip. "Sure you're okay?"

"Yeah." I grin, to convince him. "Can I text you later?"

He nods. "You can text me anytime."

I lean around my seat. "Thanks for the movie, Nina."

She smiles. "You're welcome."

I get out of the car with my suit. Watch as they pull away from the curb.

And then I call Rachel. She answers before I even get to my front door.

"What's up, Miles?"

"Rache," I say, "I have a boob problem."

CHAPTER THIRTEEN

Boobs are never a problem," Rachel says seriously. "That's the patriarchy talking."

"I know, but I'm talking about *me* here, not you."

"Oh. Right." Rachel's tone gets even more serious, if that's possible. "What boob problems are you having?"

"Hang on." I ditch my shoes and my coat by the door, say the requisite *hello* to Dad, and run upstairs to my room. "I *have* them."

"Yeah, Miles, we know this."

I close my door. "So, what am I supposed to do if I'm making out with a guy and then, like, I *have boobs*?"

Rachel is silent. For so long that I start to get nervous. "Rache?"

"Is this about Eric?" she says. "Because he *likes* you."

"Yeah, I know." I sit down on my bed. "I mean, I know that's what he said."

"It's what he *means*. He knows you're trans."

"Yeah."

"And he said he likes *people*."

"I know."

"So, why would he care?"

"Well, I don't look like I have boobs when I have clothes on. I'm flat. But that's not . . . how my body is."

"Are you getting *naked* with him?"

"Rachel! I don't have a guy's body!"

"You *do* have a guy's body." I've never heard her sound this serious. Not even when she talks about climate change. "It's a guy's body that happens to have boobs. If you don't want boobs, you don't have to have them forever. But you're a guy. What's under your binder or in your pants doesn't change that."

I feel ashamed that she has to tell me that. Even more ashamed that it helps. "I should've thought of this."

"What do you mean?"

(I mean I didn't believe Shane—that it would be different, now that I'm a guy. I mean I didn't think about logistics. I was all *love* and *romance* and not *boobs* and *binders*. But that's me. Always late to the party. Always *almost* getting it.)

My voice comes out a murmur. "I just mean it's complicated."

"Dude," Rachel says, "it's *always* complicated. It's complicated for everybody, and then when you're queer, it's, like, ten times *more* complicated."

"Yeah. I guess."

"Miles, Eric asked your pronouns. He said he likes you. He's a big old queerdo. You just gotta talk to him about this stuff. He's not gonna think you're weird, I promise."

"Yeah."

For a while, we're quiet, and then Rachel says, "For the record, I don't care if you have boobs, either."

"I'm not dating you, Rache."

"I'm just saying."

"Yeah, I know. Thanks."

After I've had dinner, and practiced, and done my homework, and after I've taken off my binder and climbed into bed, I pull out my phone and text Eric.

> Sorry I freaked out on you.

Eric texts back immediately.

> No apology necessary. Ever.

> I wear a binder and forgot to think about that and when you touched it I sort of flipped out.

> I'm sorry! You can totally tell me if u want me to avoid it

How would he avoid it? I can't even avoid it.

> I don't know? It just surprised me.

> I have boobs.

> It's weird.

My heart is going to hammer straight out of my chest. My infuriating, boob-burdened chest.

> not really weird? I mean, if u don't like it that's fair, but I don't really care?

> I don't want to have them forever.

> ok

> but I have them now

My phone buzzes. Eric is calling me.
Crap. I didn't want to actually *talk*.

"Hi."

"I should have said it earlier," he says, "but you call the shots. Like, we can just avoid your whole chest area if you want to. Or pretend you don't have anything there. Or whatever. I'm not expecting to get your shirt off or something."

I thought my face was on fire before, but now it feels like a freaking volcano. "I know, I know we weren't even going there, but—"

"No, I get it. But I just wanted to tell you . . . I don't think there are rules. Do you think there are rules?"

"No? I guess not."

"Okay. So we can just talk about it. Figure it out as we go."

"Yeah. As we go."

"I like you."

"I like you, too."

"Okay, then."

I hesitate. Take a breath. "Eric?"

"Yeah?"

My heart has stopped hammering. It's gone quiet. I wonder if it's beating at all. "Do you see me as a guy?"

"Miles," he says, "I see you as everything you tell me you are or want to be."

Compared to talking to Eric about boobs, getting my suit tailored isn't that big a deal. It's only a little bit awkward—and that's just because Mom, Rachel, and Stefania all insist on coming. Mom says she has to be there to pay for it (refusing to believe that Stefania's calling in a favor). Rachel says she has to be there to make sure everyone's respecting me. And Stefania says she has to be there because she's the only one who speaks Russian.

Stefania's tailor turns out to be an old Russian lady with frizzy short hair that can only be described as *beige,* penciled-on eyebrows, and no lips. She doesn't smile at anyone, not even Stefania, not even when she says, with a thick Russian accent, "Stefa, I am so happy to see you." She kisses Stefania on both cheeks and then turns to me. "You have the suit?"

I hold it up, still in Mom's garment bag.

Mom takes that as her cue. "We found it at Goodwill and I think it's fairly decent quality, but it ought to be tailored to fit better and allow for the right amount of movement while playing piano."

Stefania and Stefania's tailor both turn and stare at Mom.

Then they begin a fast conversation in Russian. Stefania holds out a hand for the suit and I give it to her. They take it out of the bag, look it over, keep talking. Stefania mimes piano motions. The old Russian lady nods.

Finally, they both turn to me. "Yula needs you to try it on now," Stefania says.

Yula points to a tiny dressing room behind a curtain. "In there," she says.

Rachel accompanies me the five feet to the dressing room, like something might happen on the way. "You okay?" she whispers.

"I'm fine, Rachel."

"I'll stand guard."

I'm not going to dignify that with a response. I change behind the curtain—pants, white shirt, jacket. When I come back out, Yula points to a short, wide stool. Up on the stool I go. Rachel, Mom, and Stefania vie for the best position to see my reflection in the long mirror in front of me. Stefania wins, and Mom and Rachel crowd behind her.

Yula takes her time looking me up and down. "Pretend to play piano," she says.

I lift my arms to piano keyboard height. Wiggle my fingers.

She plunges in. Pulls pins out of her pockets, her sleeves, and (I swear) thin air. Pins here. Pins there. Back seam. Arm seams. Cuffs. "Let me see the pants." Tugs on the legs of my pants. "Too long." More pins. "Now jacket off."

Off comes the jacket. Mom beats Rachel and grabs it from me.

Yula studies my white shirt. Frowns but nods. "Is good. I fix the back." Even more pins. "Now jacket on again."

Mom helps me into it.

"Come over to chair. Sit."

I toddle over. I feel like a walking pincushion. Lowering myself into a chair has never felt so dangerous.

"Feel good?" Yula asks.

I stick my right foot out to an imaginary pedal. Lift my hands to an imaginary keyboard.

Even with all the pins, it does feel good. Like it hugs me without being tight. There's nothing extra in the way.

"Yeah. Feels good."

"Good. Leave pins in and go change. Then bring me the suit."

I toddle back to the dressing room. It takes me much longer to change this time, carefully slipping out of each piece of the suit, trying not to disturb any of the pins. By the time I emerge, back in my regular clothes, Mom is arguing with Yula about payment.

"Please," she says. "We can pay you. I insist."

Yula is waving her hand. "No! I owe Stefa favor."

Mom gives Stefania an exasperated look. "Really, I insist."

Mom is a good head taller than Stefania, but Stefania doesn't look the least bit intimidated. "I've already arranged it with Yula. We'll take care of this, and then you'll have more money to spend when Miles needs a proper tux."

Mom blinks. "A proper what?"

"I have a crush on your piano teacher," Rachel whispers to me.

"Come back next week," Yula says. "Saturday." She shoos us out the door. "Bye-bye. Dasvidaniya."

Mom is so flustered she heads straight for the car. I say goodbye to Rachel and wait until she drives away before I turn to Stefania.

"What favor does Yula owe you?" I ask. "You didn't, like, kill someone for her, did you?"

Stefania rolls her eyes. "I played the cocktail hour at her son's wedding for free." She pulls her keys out of her purse. "After Pierre Fontaine canceled at the last minute."

"*What?*"

Stefania raises an eyebrow. "You think we all make enough money teaching a few pig-headed Cameron Harts? Pierre doesn't just solo with orchestras, whatever his website says. When I told Yula you were trying to beat Pierre's star student, she was on board."

Wow. I don't know what to say to any of that.

"See you for rehearsal on Thursday," Stefania says, and clomps toward her car.

The idea of Stefania walking into my school for a rehearsal is mildly terrifying. It's too easy to imagine her clomping into the auditorium, taking one look at the sad upright piano she's supposed to play, swearing in Russian, and clomping right back out again. And then I'd be stuck.

I can't do anything about the sad upright, so instead, I practice. Even more. If I sound *good* when Stefania shows up, that might distract her from the terrible piano, right?

So I spend every free period and every afternoon after school in the auditorium, practicing right up until Mr. Goodman the music director kicks me out for *Guys and Dolls* warm-ups. I even skip lunch on Tuesday. Wednesday night, I practice at home until Mom stomps down the stairs and tells me I have to stop because *she* needs to sleep even if I don't.

On Thursday, Eric sets down his brown paper lunch bag at our table and says, "So, do we think Miles learned anything today?"

Paige snorts. "Nope."

I blink. Realize I'm staring straight through Eric's nose to the Great Beyond. "What?"

"Yeah," he says, "you've been doing nothing except thinking about piano."

"Have you met his piano teacher yet?" Rachel asks eagerly.

"I've heard she's terrifying."

"She's *hot*."

I groan. "Rachel. *No*."

"What? She *is*. I found a picture on Google from that time Stefania played with the Milwaukee Symphony and showed it to Paige, and she totally agrees with me. Right?" She elbows Paige, who's been staring at something or someone across the cafeteria.

Paige looks at her, and then at me. "What are we talking about?"

Rachel glowers at her.

"Today's the day, right?" Eric says. "Stefania Smith descends on Grant East?"

I push my plate of sad pizza away. "Ugh."

"Paige and I could come for moral support," Rachel says. She looks at Paige, who has gone back to staring across the cafeteria. "*What* is so interesting?"

Paige jumps. "Nothing."

"I don't need moral support." And I really don't need Rachel making googly eyes at Stefania while Stefania is yelling at me. Or at the upright piano. "I'll be fine."

So while everyone else pushes for the exit after the last bell, I push for the auditorium. I've only got fifteen minutes before Stefania shows up, and my hands are cold.

Eric is standing by the auditorium doors.

"What are you doing here? I told Rachel not to come."

"Yeah. You told *Rachel*." He grins. "Don't worry, I'm just saying good luck and then I'm leaving, I promise."

"Sorry. Stefania's not . . . She's just kind of intense."

"Right. I definitely don't know anyone else like that."

I frown. "What's that supposed to mean?"

But he just smiles innocently. "Nothing. I also wanted to give you this." He pulls a folded piece of paper out of his coat pocket and hands it to me.

I unfold it. It's a drawing, but not one of Eric's. A blobby figure with a round head and a smiling face, extra black circles around the eyes, and wearing what I'm about fifty percent sure is supposed to be a suit.

And signed in big blocky letters at the bottom: NINA.

"She said you looked sharp," says Eric, "and wanted you to have something to remind you of that."

"She drew this?"

"Yep. She approves. I feel lucky."

I can't help but smile. "Lucky?"

"Let's just say she didn't approve of my ex, and she was right."

I look up. "You have an ex?"

"Yeah." He shrugs.

(Of course he has an ex. Why wouldn't he?)

"It wasn't really a good idea," he says. "I was just, um, really excited that somebody liked me. She wasn't very nice, but I ignored that for a long time."

She? "Oh." My stomach turns to an anxiety ball.

He looks at me sideways. "You okay?"

"Yeah. Yeah, totally fine. I just didn't—"

"Miles!"

Oh, *no.*

But oh, yes, because here's Stefania, clomping through the thinning crowds of students, all her gray hair piled on top of her head, beaded butterflies swinging from her ears, and a long wool coat billowing behind her. People are turning to look at her. Turning to look at *us.*

There's no escape now.

Stefania clomps up to us, pulling off her leather gloves. "Hello," she says to Eric.

"Hi." He smiles politely, and holds out his hand. Stefania shakes it, glancing at me with a raised eyebrow.

"Stefania, this is Eric. Eric, Stefania." What does that eyebrow mean? "I was just going to warm up, I didn't know you'd be—"

"On time is late," Stefania says. "We'd better go, don't you think?"

"Yeah," Eric and I say at the same time. He tries to get past me. I try to get past him.

"Oh, no, let's all go." Stefania pulls open the auditorium door. "I hear there's a piano to move."

So all of us end up on the auditorium stage, heaving the sad upright piano out from its usual backstage corner. I expect Stefania to stand back and yell instructions to me and Eric, but she ditches her coat over a row of chairs and throws her shoulder into it with us. The piano rolls and squeaks across the floor (thank god for wheels) until it's finally more or less across from the grand piano, and (*squeak-squeak*) slanted slightly so Stefania and I will be able to see each other.

Stefania bangs out a few chords on the upright. "Not bad."

"Okay, see you guys later," Eric says.

"No, no!" Stefania waves at him. "Stay! Give us your opinion."

I try to shake my head at him, but Stefania notices, so I have to pretend I've gotten dust in my eye. Pull off my glasses. Rub my eye with my sleeve.

"Well." Eric glances between us. "If I wouldn't be in the way . . ."

"Nonsense!" Stefania sits down at the upright piano. "We don't mind at all. Miles, you're not fooling anyone. Sit down."

Eric shrugs at me and jumps off the stage, taking up residence in his usual row. Shoes up. Notebook out.

I sit down at the grand piano. My hands are sweating.

"Let's warm up," Stefania says. "B-flat major. Follow me, please."

We play through several scales together. My fingers loosen and grow warmer, but my stomach is still a knot of anxiety.

"Good, good." Stefania spreads her music across her piano. "Let's give it a try. Ready?"

No, but when has that ever stopped her?

She launches into the opening fanfare—big, percussive, not-quite-in-tune octaves on the piano instead of a clear, cold brass fanfare, but in my head I hear the full orchestra. Horns. Strings.

Deep breath. Lift my hands. And crash in on my chords of joy.

It's rough going—Stefania following me while I try to follow Stefania. Wrong notes. Chords that should line up and don't, like uneven heartbeats. *Ba-dump, ba-dump, ba-dump.* Phrasing gets forgotten and pedaling gets sloppy and Stefania playing at the same time is just *distracting* . . .

But still, when we muddle all the way through the first movement, Eric lets out a loud whoop and applauds.

Face on fire. I wave my hand at him. *Stop.*

But Stefania looks pleased. "We need him at every rehearsal." She turns to Eric, and, in complete seriousness, says, "What did you think?"

"I think Miles is gonna kill it."

How does nothing intimidate him?

"I think so, too." Stefania turns back to me. "But first, you have to stop following me. I'm following you. You get nervous and your pedaling turns to mush. Where's the joy? I'm not going to give that to you. You have to channel that joy by yourself. You're playing with the enthusiasm of a bump on a log."

Sigh. Here we go.

CHAPTER FOURTEEN

It's just me and Mom when we pick up my suit from Yula on Saturday. I've brought my dress shoes with me, but I left the tie at home because I'm not sure I can tie it by myself yet, and it would be super embarrassing if I ended up with a mess around my neck in front of Yula.

Yula hands me the suit in a much nicer plastic bag and waves me behind the curtain again. "Change. Make sure it fits."

My hands shake as I pull on the pants, the shirt, the jacket. Does it fit? Is it any different? It must be different because Yula altered it, but I can't tell. I can't remember what it used to feel like.

I lace up my dress shoes and push back the curtain. Mom and Yula stare at me.

"What?" I'm starting to sweat. "Does it fit?"

Mom gives me a slightly misty smile. "You look great, honey."

I step onto Yula's stool once more and turn to face myself in the mirror.

It *is* different. I thought the suit fit before, but now it *really* fits. Now it looks like it was made for me. And I look ... I look like I belong in it. I don't know what deal with the devil this old Russian lady made, but staring back at me is the pianist that I always was. I thought I'd seen the real me before, staring at myself in this suit, in Eric's mirror. But I was wrong. *This* is the real me. This is Miles the pianist.

"Well?" Yula says.

"It's great." Cough. Hack. This giant lump in my throat is getting in the way of my voice. "It's perfect. Thanks so much."

Yula regards my reflection with a frown. Then she nods. "Looks good. Change back." She waves me toward the changing room.

When I reemerge in my regular clothes, Mom is making one last attempt to pay Yula, but Yula has folded her arms and is stubbornly ignoring the credit card Mom is waving at her. Mom gives up, thanks her profusely, and ushers me out the door.

"Thanks!" I call over my shoulder.

Yula gives me a very small smile. "Tell Stefa we are even," she grunts. "And kill Pierre Fontaine's student."

"I will." I'm not sure she means metaphorically.

She slams the door.

It's tempting to change into the suit as soon as I get home and rush to the piano to try it out, but I resist. I just can't handle Dad wandering in, seeing me in my suit, and getting one of his wistful looks again. I want my first time playing piano in my suit to feel—I don't know—*special*.

So I take the suit with me to school on Monday, and after the last bell, Eric hangs out with me in the bathroom while I change. When I come out of the stall, he stares.

I grin. Tentatively. "It's good, right?"

"It's *awesome*." He holds out his hand. "Tie, please?"

I feel a little ridiculous, walking through my high school in a suit, but Eric just talks casually about his latest graphic novel ideas (a time-traveling closet portal and a sidekick cat named Walnut), and when we get to the auditorium, he settles in to draw like nothing's different.

I sit down at the piano and start warming up, and . . . The suit feels different. Heavier than any dress I ever played in. A little stiff. My elbows can't bend as easily. The tie hits the keys if I lean too far forward.

But I don't stop playing. And the longer I play, launching into Tchaikovsky, and stubbornly practicing like it's any other day in the auditorium, the better the suit feels. I learn how to move my body so the tie doesn't get in my way. My arms figure out how to move around in their stiffer sleeves. I'm okay. By the time we leave, dodging the theater kids coming in, I'm getting used to it.

I'm getting used to my rehearsals with Stefania, too. They're intense, but we're making progress. Fewer *ba-dump, ba-dump* chords. Fewer wrong notes. I'm getting more confident about leading, playing the way I want to play, trusting that she's there supporting me. The whole thing is just *tighter*.

And every time I look out into the audience, there's Eric, giving me a thumbs-up. And after every rehearsal or practice session, he drives me home, and kisses me outside my house.

I haven't thought about Shane McIntyre in over a week. Barely looked at him in the hallways. If I didn't have a giant competition coming up, life might feel close to perfect.

Eric even starts driving me to school early in the morning to practice, before anybody else is up. The sun is just a pink blob on the horizon when he rolls up with a thermos of coffee in his hand and the heat blasting in his Subaru. We're at the school by six thirty.

"You really don't have to do this," I tell him (again), as we blunder sleepily into the auditorium halfway through the week before the preliminary round.

But (again) he just shrugs. He's been wearing his glasses all week, and his eyes look puffy behind them. "I think if Stefania found out I wasn't fully supporting your piano practicing, she'd kill me."

"She wouldn't . . . I'm not going to *tell* her."

He grins. "I'm kidding. I've got coffee. I'm good. I like hearing piano in the morning."

What's he talking about? *I* don't even like hearing this much piano in the morning.

The Friday before the prelims, Eric has to take care of Nina after school, so Stefania and I are alone in the auditorium for a last dress rehearsal. Me in my suit and dress shoes and tie. Stefania in a long, silver velour dress and her clogs. We go through the piece once—start to finish—and then Stefania stands up.

"Good," she says. "That's enough."

"What? Really?"

She just raises her eyebrows at me.

"Um." I was expecting her to tear into five hundred things I need to do better, like she has every rehearsal before this. "I just mean . . . shouldn't we go through it again? There's no musical rehearsal."

"No." Stefania stands up and clomps across the stage. "Let's go, Miles!"

She drives me home, and the whole drive, I keep going over that last run-through in my head, thinking of more and more mistakes. A missed note. An unclear phrase. Blurry pedaling. *Why* haven't I gotten better at pedaling?

I'm chewing my thumbnail when we pull up in front of my house.

"Now," Stefania says, "what are your plans for tonight?"

My brain is still stuck on an uneven arpeggio. "Tonight? Uh, practice, I guess."

"No." Stefania glares at me. "No practicing."

"What? The competition is *tomorrow*."

"And I suppose you think cramming for an exam the night before is also a good idea? Take a break, Miles. Sleep on it."

"But—"

"No."

"Stefania—"

"*Don't. Practice.*" She sticks a finger in my face. "All it's going to do is make you tired. You can't play joy if you're tired."

I open my mouth, but I don't have a comeback. She has a point. So I get out of the car.

"See you tomorrow," she says, and pulls away.

I open my front door, ditch my boots and my coat—and there's my piano, sitting in the living room. Waiting.

Ugh. This is never going to work.

I pull out my phone and text Eric.

> Can I come over?

And he texts back: Yes.

I run upstairs to drop my suit and dress shoes in my room. Then back downstairs, where Mom is sitting at the kitchen table, with her laptop and folders of house listings.

"Can I go over to Eric's?"

She jerks out of her real estate reverie. "The competition is to-morrow."

"I know, but Stefania told me not to practice any more . And I feel like if I'm here, I'll end up practicing."

"Oh." Mom's forehead wrinkles. I can see her trying to work out the logic of this. "Well, if Stefania thinks so. Dad's still at work, and I've got things to do here . . ."

"I was hoping I could borrow your car." It's a big ask. Really big. I never drive the BMW.

She hesitates, but she nods. "Keys are in my purse."

"Thanks, Mom." I dash down the hallway. Fish the keys out of her purse while stumbling into my boots and coat.

The BMW is sitting in the garage. It unlocks with a chirpy little *beep-beep*. I start the car, and the dashboard lights up. It's like a spaceship compared to Dad's car—fancy digital displays and pleasant dinging sounds. My breath clouds in front of my face while I squeak around in the leather driver's seat, groping for the levers to adjust it and for the ignition button and the gas pedal, like somehow it might be in a different place in a car this fancy.

It takes me twice as long to get to Eric's as it should. I can't bear to drive even close to the speed limit. I'm utterly convinced that if I reach thirty-five miles per hour, I will lose control, spin out, and wrap Mom's Symbol of Success around a lamppost.

When I finally park in front of Eric's house, I beep the car locked over and over, and then tug on the door handle because *what if it's still not locked.*

"Did you *walk?*" Eric says when he opens the door.

"No. I took my mom's car."

"Hello, Piano Miles!" Nina shouts from somewhere upstairs.

"Hi, Nina!" I shout back.

Eric leads me up the stairs. "So, you're here."

"Yeah. Stefania says I can't practice any more."

"Oh." He gives me a concerned look. "Not easy, huh?"

Nina emerges from her tent on the landing and barrels toward me. "Piano Miles!" She wraps me in a hug so tight that I cough, and then dashes back under her tent. "Miles plays piano!"

I take a gasping breath. "Hi, Nina. How are you?"

"Good." She sits down cross-legged in a circle of stuffed animals, and Mr. Pudge.

"Um . . ." Eric jerks his head, and we go down the hallway to his bedroom. He closes the door behind us. "Nina really wants to come to your concert. Would that be okay? She's good with things like this—she's been to plays and movies and she loves music."

"Oh. Yeah, sure. Of course."

He looks relieved. "Awesome. She'll be happy about that, she's been asking me all day."

All the mistakes I was thinking about earlier come rushing back, and I have an overwhelming urge to run back to the car.

Maybe I could go to the school auditorium. Janitor Dave works Friday nights. He'd probably let me in, and he definitely wouldn't ask any questions if I practiced some more . . .

Eric must see something on my face, because he says, "What's up?"

Sigh. "I know it's the prelim round, and it shouldn't really worry me, because I've always gotten through before, but this time feels different. More important. I'm really nervous."

"It's your last chance," he says.

"Yeah."

"And you're different than last time."

"Yeah."

He chews his lip. And then he goes to his desk, opens a drawer, and takes out a small piece of paper. "I know Nina already gave you a good-luck drawing, but I thought you might like this."

I take it. It's the laughing waffle playing the tiny piano. The cartoon he drew the first Sunday morning we hung out in the auditorium together, when he brought me coffee.

"For what it's worth," he says, "it's small enough to fit inside a jacket pocket."

It's so perfect that for a second, I can't think of anything to say. "I love it. Thank you."

"So what would be a good distraction? We've got movies. Board games. A couple video games, if you're into that."

I carefully fold the waffle drawing in half and tuck it into my shirt pocket. "Actually, I'd really like to kiss you."

"Oh." The corner of his mouth twitches. "As a distraction?"

"As a distraction." I reach up and carefully take off his glasses. Fold them. Set them on his desk. And then I take mine off, too.

He leans down—not nearly as far as Shane had to—and kisses me. I wrap my arms around his neck. He wraps his arms around me. I shiver.

He pulls away. "Sorry."

"No, it's okay."

"You sure?"

"Yeah." His face is just a blur without my glasses. "I'm sure."

His arms wrap around me again, pulling me close. His hand rises up my back—outside my shirt, but I feel his fingertips cross the edge of my binder.

This time I don't flinch.

Beepbeepbeepbeepbeep.

I reach over and turn off the alarm. It's seven thirty, but I've already been awake for half an hour, lying in bed, staring at the ceiling. Carefully (very carefully) thinking about nothing.

Okay, Miles. Here we go.

I sit up, throw off the blankets, and head for the shower.

I put on my dress shirt and suit pants right out of the shower. It's a bit early, but what's the point of putting on other clothes and changing in an hour? I spend time running curl cream through my hair and scrunching. More time cleaning my glasses. But all that still takes half as long as I thought it would, because I don't have a makeup routine anymore.

It does take me five minutes to get the tie right. Even after Eric's teaching and several YouTube videos.

Back in my bedroom, I lace up my dress shoes and pull on my suit jacket, just to check everything one last time. I tuck Eric's laughing waffle drawing into the inside pocket of the jacket. Sideways mirror check. Flat.

Mom is already cooking scrambled eggs when I get downstairs. "Just got some new bananas!" she says, waving a hand over her shoulder to point them out.

Scrambled eggs and a banana—what I eat before any concert, no matter what time of day it is. Eggs because Mom believes in

PROTEIN, and a banana because Mrs. Kim once told me they help with nerves. I have no idea if it's actually true, but I can't stop doing it now.

I pull two bananas off the bunch. One for now, one to take with me.

"How are you doing?" Mom is trying really hard to sound casual.

"Fine. Usual." The banana tastes like nothing.

"You look great," Mom says.

Dad comes downstairs a few minutes later, says his usual *Morning* to me, and goes about making coffee in silence. But when he sits down at the table, he looks at me and says, "Feeling good?"

"Feeling okay." Bald-faced lie.

He smiles—not wistfully, for once. "You'll be great." And he picks up his iPad.

Twenty minutes later, we all get in Dad's car. Mom on the phone with a client. Dad punching the radio to play NPR even though Mom's on the phone. And me in the back with a banana in my coat pocket.

We swing by Rachel's house first, where Rachel and Paige pile into the backseat with me. "Is Eric coming?" Rachel asks, while Paige frowns at Mom, who's gesturing wildly as she talks to her client.

"Yeah, I think so. He's bringing his sister."

"He has a sister?"

"Yeah. Nina."

Rachel pulls a banana out of her coat pocket. "I brought you this."

"I already have one."

"Now you have two."

Paige shakes her head. "There are so many jokes I could make."

It's a forty-minute drive to the Wisconsin Cultural Arts Center in the suburbs of Milwaukee. The final rounds of the competition will be in downtown Milwaukee, in the big, beautiful hall that the Milwaukee Symphony plays in. But the prelim rounds are in the Arts Center, which still isn't bad, as far as concert venues go. It's modern and tasteful, with rows of stadium seats in blue velvet and a pale wood stage. It's not nearly as big as the Symphony's hall, but big enough that you don't feel like the audience is breathing on you when you play. And big enough that you can't see the judges through the glare of the stage lights—unless you look really hard. I don't plan to look too hard.

Dad drops me, Rachel, Paige, and Mom off at the curb in front and goes to find a parking space.

Inside, the lobby is buzzing. Piano music filters over speakers in the ceiling—Mozart sonatas, probably recorded by Pierre Fontaine, because he's always pushing his CDs at the competition reps. Anxious parents and grandparents mill around, twisting programs in their hands. Other old people are calmly taking in the big open space with its tall, narrow windows letting in thin bands of warm morning sun. You can always spot the retirees who just come for a free concert—they're the only ones smiling.

I see Cassandra O'Brian eyeing me from the corner where she's huddling under a giant parka. She gives me the same cold, appraising look every year, like we're total strangers who haven't been playing the same competitions and fundraisers since we were twelve. Cassandra has never made it to the finals.

Over the whole lobby is a big purple banner that reads *Tri-State Piano Competition Preliminaries,* and under it is a card table staffed by the same cheerful old ladies who are there every year. I saw one of them roll her eyes at Pierre Fontaine last year and she's been my favorite old lady ever since.

I go up to her, leaving Mom and Paige and Rachel hovering near the wall. "Um. Hi."

The Eye-Roller looks up. Her nametag says Patrice. That's right—she's Patrice Keller, and she used to teach piano at UW-Milwaukee.

Her eyebrows jump. She looks me up and down. The eyebrows go even higher.

Here we go.

I mentally go over the introduction for my new self that I prepared last night, while trying and failing to go to sleep. Another second and I'll go for it . . .

But—"Hi!" she says, bursting into a smile. "I didn't recognize you, sweetheart. How're you doing?"

"Good." Except for my knees mysteriously turning to water. "I'm just checking in." Deep breath. "Miles Jacobson."

Patrice looks at me for a long moment, and then pages through the notebook on the table in front of her. "Ah yes, here you are." She picks up a Sharpie, scribbles something, and then peels off a sticker and hands it to me. "You're in group three. The time printed there is when you report backstage. You can use the warm-up room ten minutes before that. It's hard to know if we'll get behind or not. But you know this." She smiles. "Nice to see you, hon. Good luck."

I head back to Rachel and Paige and Mom, glancing down at the pre-printed sticker she gave me. *Group 3, 11:35 A.M.* Below that is my name, *Jacobson.* But where my first name should be, there's a big black scribble, and above it, written carefully in Sharpie, *Miles.*

My heart beats faster. "Rachel." Elbow her, voice low. "Have you seen a program yet? Is my name—?"

"Correct?" Rachel waves the program in her hand. "Yep."

My knees turn to water again. "Oh. Good. Thanks." There were two spaces for name on the application form, weren't there? *Name* and then *Name for Concert Program.* I put *Miles* in both spots. I guess they didn't believe me.

Thank god for Patrice.

"When's your time?" Mom asks.

"Eleven thirty-five."

Mom looks at her watch. "Two hours."

"Do you want to go warm up?" Rachel asks me.

"No. I can't use the warm-up room until ten minutes before my printed time."

The big glass door opens and Dad comes in, and just behind him—Andrew Morris. Or, as Stefania continues to refer to him, *the pretentious ass who wouldn't work on his stiff pinky fingers.* Andrew is my age but he looks like he grew another six inches since I last saw him. His suit pants are a little short.

Dad pulls off his coat as he reaches us. "All checked in? All good?"

I don't feel like telling anybody about the name stuff, so I just nod. And then Mom spots Cassandra O'Brian's parents, who she's friendly with—they seem nice enough, even though Cassandra always looks like she's plotting my murder—and drags Dad off to talk to them.

Just in time, because here comes Andrew, time sticker in his hand. "What up, Miles."

So he knows my new name. I wonder how fast that made its way around the piano gossip circle. If it means I won't have to explain myself fifty times today, I'll take it.

"Hey, Andrew."

"When's your time?" Cutting right to the chase, like he always does.

"Eleven thirty-five."

He grimaces. "Man, I'm ten thirty. I always end up going before you. They won't remember me."

He's got a point. You always want to be early in the first group, or late in the last group. Make an early impression or a late one. Nobody wants to be in the blurry mess of the middle where it all runs together and everybody's kind of falling asleep.

I'm middle in the last group, but I'd rather not tell him that.

I wonder what group Cameron is in.

"You're good, Andrew," I say. (Comes out a little stiff, but I do mean it.) "They'll remember you."

"So how's Stefania working out?"

News really does travel fast. I'm not sure I like the way he's looking at me—like he's waiting for some juicy bit of gossip to jump on. I'm sorely tempted to ask him how his stiff pinky fingers are working out, but Andrew's never been a pretentious ass to *me*. Just kind of . . . aggressively desperate. Like he thinks he'll have *made it* once he can find a high horse to get on.

"She's great," I say. "I really like her."

He looks surprised. Quickly tries to hide it. "Oh, cool. So what are you playing?"

It's in the program, but whatever. "Tchaikovsky Number One. You?"

He turns a little pale. "Beethoven Emperor Concerto."

"Nice." He's in trouble, and judging by his face, he knows it. If I'm playing Tchaikovsky and Cameron is playing Rachmaninov, he's going to have a hard time matching us with Beethoven.

The big glass door opens again, and all of us turn to look. It's Eric—glasses fogged, rumpled dark hair poking out from under his reindeer hat—ushering Nina in front of him. She's bundled up in a puffy pink coat, hood pulled close around her face. I wave at them, and Nina waves back, and starts pulling Eric toward us.

"Who's that?" says Andrew.

I'm not sure I like this look either. Something on his face—and the glower that Paige is giving him—makes me suddenly very aware that aside from Paige (and Jenny Chang, who's currently checking in), Eric and Nina are the only people of color in the room.

"That's my boyfriend," I say. Stonily.

Andrew looks confused. Paige looks like she wants to punch him. And Rachel raises her arms and shouts, "Eric!"

Nina lets go of Eric and gives me another surprisingly tight hug. "Hi, Piano Miles."

"Hi, Nina."

Eric dodges around her and kisses my cheek. "Hey."

Andrew is staring at us. So my relationship status, at least, hasn't made the piano gossip rounds.

"Hey." I ignore Andrew. "You came."

"Yeah. I said I would." Eric looks around. "When does it start?"

"In, like, twenty minutes, but I'm not on for a couple hours."

"Wow." He blinks. "That's so much piano music."

"Yeah," Andrew says stiffly. "A lot of us are competing."

Eric gives him a friendly grin, but before he can say anything, Jenny Chang comes barreling over looking just as excited as Nina. "Hi!" she shrieks, throwing her arms around me. "How are you? I missed you! You abandoned the Girl Club!"

Jenny lives up in Oshkosh, and I only ever see her at the Tri-State Competition. She's always made it to the finals with me, and last year she got third place. Way back when we were still in the Junior Level, she decided we were a Girl Club with Andrea Wang and Trilby Malone, because we were the only girls in the finals that year. (It was a messed-up year.) But we sort of bonded, in a weird way, and the name stuck. Andrea and Trilby have made it to finals with us every year since.

"So you got my message." I'd sent Jenny an email when I came out. She was the only person from my piano world that I told, besides Mrs. Kim. She'd never replied to my email.

"Yes, I'm sorry, I was *so* busy visiting colleges." She brushes a perfectly curled lock of black hair away from her eyes. "Did I tell you my mom wants me to go a year early? And then I lost track of it . . ." Now she's shaking out the skirt of her emerald-green dress, trying to get rid of a crease. "I'm happy for you! That's great. Except now you can't be in the Girl Club anymore. Maybe we'll let you be an honorary member anyway. Hi, Andrew."

Andrew gives Jenny a disdainful look. He thinks Jenny talks too much. "Hi."

"What are you playing?" Jenny asks me.

"Tchaikovsky."

"Oh, that's great. I'm playing Chopin." She's completely ignoring Andrew now. "Did you hear Cameron's playing Rachmaninov? What a tool, am I right? Like, who does he think he is—Lang Lang? Okay, I'd better go warm up. Miles, you coming?"

"Yeah." I turn to Rachel, but she just waves at me. "No worries, I got it," she says.

"Where do we sit?" Eric asks.

"I have answers to *all* your questions," Rachel says, pulling him away from me. "Now we have to go find Arthur and Tanya for tickets."

"See you later," I say to Eric.

He and Nina give me a simultaneous thumbs-up.

My phone reads 9:30 on the dot when we go through the door from the lobby into the hallway that leads to the warm-up rooms and backstage. The hallway is already full of competitors. A lot of them I've seen before, but some of them I haven't. Either they were in the Junior Level last year and this is their first year at the Senior Level, or they're totally new and never entered the competition before. I'm guessing the latter for Mr. Bug-Eyes over there, who looks green enough to barf. Around him, people are sitting on the floor biting their nails, or leaning against the wall staring at their phones, or aimlessly pacing back and forth. Andrew splits off from us and joins the pacing crowd. Jenny and I lean against the wall. Andrew is right that Jenny can talk a lot, but now she's suddenly quiet.

9:45 A.M.: Jenny hands me a program. We glance over the names. The pieces. The order everyone is playing in.

Cameron is playing right after me. *How is he playing right after me?*

At least he's not last. Some poor sucker has to play Mendelssohn after him. There's no way that performance won't bomb.

10:00 A.M.: The competition officially starts. I imagine Darcy Dawson starting in on her Mozart, even though I can't actually hear anything from the hallway. I don't recognize her name from last year, and she doesn't stand a chance with that Mozart.

10:30 A.M.: Andrew heads for the doors to the warm-up room at the end of the hall, looking vaguely sick. Jenny turns her program into a paper airplane.

10:45 A.M.: Jenny hands me the paper airplane and follows Andrew.

10:50 A.M.: In walks Cameron Hart, followed by the tall, willowy figure of Pierre Fontaine.

The superstar is here. The entire hallway of nervous pianists turns to look. The competition newbies stare with their mouths open. Cameron and Pierre, of course, don't look at anybody. They just part the pianist-sea and take up residence against the wall near the door to the warm-up room. Pierre frowns at several nearby newbies until they slink away.

I wish Jenny were here to roll her eyes with me. She's the only other person who doesn't buy Cameron's bullshit. Even Andrew looks at him like he's a god.

10:53 A.M.: The door opens again, and in clomps Stefania.

Everyone turns. Even Cameron and Pierre are staring, but Stefania doesn't seem to notice. She sweeps down the hall in her long, silver velour dress, her gray hair twirled up on her head, long beaded butterflies swinging from her ears, twinkling under the fluorescent lights. She's still wearing her usual high-heeled clogs, but even they look like a Statement.

She stops in front of me. She's wearing makeup—dark eyeshadow and red lipstick. It's stunning.

I realize my mouth is open. I close it.

"What are you doing here?" Stefania says.

"Um," I whisper. (Doesn't she realize everybody can hear us?) "Waiting for my warm-up time."

"Waiting."

"Yeah."

"Waiting."

I stare blankly at her.

"We don't wait," Stefania says. "We have things to do." She loops her arm through mine and yanks me off, steering us down the hall. Cameron and Pierre get closer and closer—*oh god they're going to say something*—and the volunteer guarding the door to the warm-up room stands up from her chair like she's ready for a fight.

But Stefania turns us around the corner, leaving Cameron and Pierre and everybody else behind.

All that's down here are the restrooms. Is she taking me to the *restroom*?

No. She opens another door in the wall and pushes me inside.

The room is tiny. Filled with brooms, buckets, folding tables and chairs leaning against the wall. Mysterious box labeled THEATER PROPS teetering dangerously on top.

We're in a closet. *Why are we in a closet?*

But Stefania just sighs contentedly. "Now we can get ready in peace."

"Wh— Huh?"

"I'm going to show you what I do before every performance." She rolls back her shoulders and closes her eyes. "Deep breath in."

My brain hasn't caught up.

"Miles. Deep breath *in*."

"Your eyes are closed! How can you see—"

"Miles."

Okay, okay. I close my eyes. Breathe in.

"And deep breath *out*."

Breathe out.

"In. And out. Bring your shoulders up. And let them down."

My knees slowly firm up.

"Up again. And down."

My stomach unknots.

"Miles, what on earth do you have in your pocket?"

I open my eyes. Stefania is looking accusingly at my jacket pocket. "Oh. It's a banana. For nerves."

Stefania rolls her eyes. "So you, like everyone else, have been brainwashed into assuming nerves are a purely negative thing." She holds out her hand. "Give me the banana."

I hand it to her.

"You get nervous because you *care*. Your kryptonite can also be your superpower, you know." She sets the banana on top of an overturned bucket. Great. No way I'm going to eat it now. Who knows what's been around that bucket?

"For now," Stefania says, "you're going to play Tchaikovsky."

Has she lost it? "There's no piano."

She looks at me like *I've* lost it. "You don't say. In your *head*, Miles. You're going to go through it in your head. Imagine yourself playing it. Every note. Every gesture. Feel it in your fingers. Sing it in your head."

"What's that going to do?"

Stefania taps her forehead. "You think music is all in your fingers? Your brain tells them what to do. Use your brain."

I consider making a grab for the banana and a break for the exit. Stefania's tiny. I could probably take her.

And then I remember every other year I've been here—standing in the hallway, eating a banana with shaky hands, while Cameron Hart preens and everybody else watches him preen.

"Okay. Fine." I roll my shoulders back. Wiggle my fingers. Close my eyes. Deep breath.

Chord, chord, chord.

At first, I can still hear my breathing.

At first, I think I'm just remembering Van Cliburn's performance. Dredging up some distant echo of that recording.

But then, I get to the little expressive pause I always take, at the top of a phrase, before tumbling back down again. And here's the moment my pinky finger always does a funny little bend when I hit this low octave. And now I'm singing my way through the melody, and even though my fingers aren't moving, I can feel it all happening in my gut, in my throat, in the twinges running up and down my arms.

I'm only halfway through the first movement when Stefania touches my arm. I open my eyes.

She's got a tiny smile on her face. "Time to warm up on a real piano." And just like that, she turns, opens the door, and out we go.

Out of the closet. It's so bad I almost groan.

Back down the hallway, up to the volunteer standing in front of the door. I can feel Cameron watching me, but I don't look at him.

"Miles Jacobson," I say, and the volunteer looks down at the list in her hands. (Please let her have the right name.) She nods and opens the door for us.

The warm-up room is small, with two tall upright pianos facing each other, sitting on green carpet. The walls are carpeted, too. It's maybe my least favorite room on the planet—the whole thing feels dead, the notes swallowed up as soon as you play them. I know that's the point—since the concert hall is right upstairs—but it still creeps me out.

We've only got ten minutes, which isn't nearly enough time to get through the whole first movement.

Stefania pulls out her music. "Where'd you get up to?"

Oh. Now I get it. "Um . . ." I lean over her shoulder. "Here. Right where that kind of sweet theme comes back."

She goes to one of the pianos and spreads out her music. "Okay, let's start from there and keep going."

So I sit down at the other piano. *Don't think. Just do.*

I dive back in where I'd left off in my head.

And the funny thing is, my hands react like I've been playing for real all along. Sure, my fingers might be a little stiff, but they loosen up quickly, and my brain is ready for them when they do. *Here* is this phrase, and *there* is that one, and they tumble out as easy and natural as if I'm already ten minutes into playing, instead of just finding my footing.

Damn, Stefania is smart.

We're only a few phrases from the end when the door on the other side of the room opens. A man in a black shirt sticks his head through. "Miles Jacobson? Time to go."

CHAPTER FIFTEEN

It's always dusty in concert halls. That's the first thing you see when you walk onstage. It's invisible from the audience, but all around you onstage—hanging suspended in the air under the lights, coating the floor in a silver film. It's sort of disturbing when you think about it. It's like concert halls *want* you to think they're stuffy and musty and full of old people listening to music written by dead people.

There's always a moment, too, when you first walk out, where you get three, maybe four steps in before the audience sees you and starts clapping. In that moment, it's totally silent.

My shoes are much quieter this time. I'm not wearing heels. Those three steps have a hollower sound. I don't have to think about balance, either. I feel the floor, from my heels to my toes, flat (and dusty) underneath me.

Three steps and then the applause starts. Stefania clomps behind me, and we take our places at the two six-foot grand pianos that face each other on the stage—Stefania at the piano with its lid only open a few inches, me at the piano with its lid open all the way. An easy volume boost for the soloist.

Smile. Bow together, for long enough to whisper *Dodge the flying tomatoes.* That's how Mrs. Kim taught me to bow.

We sit down. I feel for the pedal as the applause fades.

The judges are sitting a few rows back in the audience—five straight-faced people with pads of paper who don't look remotely excited about any of this.

I don't think they sat that close last year. I thought I'd have an easier time avoiding looking at them. At least my glasses kind of help. The keyboard in front of me is all that's in focus.

I look up. Meet Stefania's eyes across the row of felt dampers and the long expanse of steel piano strings hovering over the soundboard.

I am Miles.

I am trans.

I am gay.

This music belongs to me.

I nod.

She plays the opening fanfare, octaves piercing the silence, ringing to the last row and back. Doom and gloom and then . . .

Chord, chord, chord.

I play the joy.

I throw myself at the keys, hands springing back. Across from me, Stefania's whole body sways as she plays the strings' melody in great sweeping octaves.

And then I take the melody from her. Working my way up and up the keyboard, and then down and down, octaves pounding into a fury. My pinky slips. I hit a wrong note.

Keep going. Keep going.

The first really virtuosic passage. Me all by myself, while Stefania waits. My fingers are going so fast. *They're going to run away from me. I'm going to lose control . . .*

I don't. I get through it, plunging back into the chords while Stefania crashes back in with the orchestra part.

Now a chance to catch my breath. Stefania plays the orchestral interlude. I stretch my fingers. Roll my shoulders.

And back in.

Dashing octaves.

Cascading runs.

Soaring melodies.

My fingers slip again, in the easiest, slowest passage—*I got too relaxed*—and in the middle of spiraling arpeggios, I panic *(what comes next, what comes next)*, but my fingers remember, even if my brain doesn't.

I'm okay.

I'm okay.

Here's the big cadenza. Just me, alone, for several minutes. I let myself fill up the space. Let the pauses mean as much as the phrases. Listen to the decay of each note.

Now, lilting, into the sweet and gentle theme as Stefania joins me. Slowly gathering steam. Gathering speed. Brighter. Bigger.

Into the final minute. Arpeggio after arpeggio. Hurtling down one last run of octaves.

Joy, joy, joy.

Chord after chord to the last long note. I lean into the piano, fingers shaking with effort, and then *lift*. Hands come up. Breath rushes out.

Applause. I catch Stefania's eyes. She smiles. We both stand, one hand on the piano, turning to face the audience. Bow.

The judges are busy scribbling, bent over their pads of paper. *Don't watch them.* I turn and walk off the stage, Stefania behind me. A volunteer behind the stage door opens it, and then we're out. Preliminary round over.

My knees turn to jelly. I lean against the wall.

Stefania stops with me.

"Okay." I nod. Swallow. "I think that was okay."

Stefania's lips twitch. "It *was* okay. You just performed as yourself. That's a victory."

Hollow footsteps echo behind us. We turn around, and here come Cameron and Pierre, practically in lockstep. Pierre is wearing a black turtleneck under his suit jacket.

Stefania rolls her eyes so hard I can almost hear her eyeballs creak.

"Hey, Miles," Cameron says, like he could care less.

"Hey, Cameron."

"Stefania," Pierre says stiffly.

Stefania's eyes narrow. "I'm sorry . . . what's your name again?"

Cameron turns pink. Pierre's thin upper lip gets even thinner. "Amusing," he says in his lilting accent, and continues to the stage door. Cameron hurries to catch up.

The door opens. They walk out. Applause.

I look at Stefania. "You know that was Pierre Fontaine, right?"

She snorts. "Of course I do. I just enjoy bruising his ego." She folds her arms, studying the stage door. "Are you able to listen?"

"You think I should." It's not a question. I already know the answer.

"I think if you can, it would be good to hear him play before the final round."

To know what you're up against. She doesn't say that part, but it must be what she's thinking. It's what I'm thinking.

Well, this might be a total lie, but—"Sure, I can listen."

Cameron is already playing the opening of Rachmaninov's Second Piano Concerto. Slow, moody chords ring out like chimes. Stefania and I step closer to the stage door, peering through its small square window. From here, I can only see Cameron's back, but that's plenty. He rolls to the music like a boat on the sea. His long-fingered hands lift gracefully from the piano, as if he's showing off how easily he can play those giant, spread-eagle chords. I can just imagine his forehead puckering in theatrical anguish, his hair falling perfectly across his forehead.

He sinks into the rolling arpeggios, and Pierre enters with the orchestra part—the melody as firm as his eyes, which are all I can see of him from here.

They already sound amazing. Cameron's right—Rachmaninov *is* more subtle. It's dark and edgy, all simmering angst and effortless cool. Maybe that's good. Maybe that's what the judges want.

I chew my thumbnail, squinting through the window, trying to find the judges' faces in the audience. But I can't. The window is too small and they're too far away.

Fuck, why is Cameron so good?

It would be one thing if he was a trash fire and it was obviously unfair when the judges picked him. But he's good. The overly graceful hands and the swoopy hair annoy the hell out of me, but I get it. He knows how to sell it. He's convincing. And he's tackling one of the hardest piano concertos ever written, and hitting all the right notes.

What made me think Tchaikovsky could compete with this?

What made me think *I* could compete with this?

By the time Cameron finally crashes to the end and the last chord fades, I've bitten half my nails off. I didn't even see the last competitor come up—but now he's here, looking as sick as I feel. How's he supposed to follow *that*?

The audience doesn't just applaud. They roar. They explode.

"Miles!" Stefania is slapping my arm. "Wake up!"

I jerk. Blink. Look at her.

"Still with me?"

"Yeah." My throat feels raw. "I'm fine, that was just—"

"A lot of flash and no panache," Stefania says firmly. "We'll discuss at our next lesson."

I can't even form words. What does she mean?

"Cameron is good, Miles, but he has his shortcomings." She gives me an appraising look. "I imagine you just can't hear them."

Now she's being ridiculous. "Cameron is *great*, Stefania. I'm never going to beat him!"

The backstage door opens. We both jump out of the way, along with the guy playing last, as Cameron and Pierre breeze through. Pierre walks straight past us, but Cameron pauses and turns his dazzling smile on me.

Down on me.

"Good to be back in the game, isn't it?" He heaves a contented sigh. "Like, I thought maybe I could play Rachmaninov and it turns out *yeah,* I can play Rachmaninov." He brushes his hair out of his eyes with those long fingers. "Anyway, see you next time, Jacobson."

And he turns and follows Pierre.

The last competitor goes out onstage, his accompanist appearing from the shadows and running after him just in time.

I realize Stefania is frowning at me. "What?"

"You're going to give yourself tendonitis if you keep balling your fists like that," she says.

I look down. My fists are clenched so tight that my knuckles are white. *Relax, Miles.* I stretch my fingers. There are fingernail dents in my palms. "I'm fine. Cameron's just annoying."

"Hm." Stefania squints at me, and then she turns on her heel. "We'll discuss Thursday. Go out and meet your fans. Now. No dawdling."

And she clomps away.

I can't bear to go out to the lobby until the competition is actually over, so I lurk by the bathrooms backstage until I hear distant applause. Mendelssohn finished.

I go down the hall. Push open the door to the lobby, blinking in the brighter light, and Rachel plows into me with enough force to send us both back into the hallway.

"Full-frontal hug!" she yells.

"You have *got* to stop calling it that." Paige opens the door and pulls us back out into the lobby. "Seriously, though, you were on fire." She grins at me. "Fucking *owned* that piano."

"Thanks, guys." I manage to slither out of Rachel's grasp.

"Great job, sweetheart!" Here's Mom, nudging Rachel and Paige out of the way and wrapping me in a hug.

"Thanks—"

And here's Dad, but all he manages is a smile and a pat on my shoulder.

And there, holding Nina's hand and sidling through the crowds of parents and grandparents and ecstatic (or occasionally tearful) competitors, is Eric. Nina lets go of his hand as soon as she sees me and races over, hitting me with almost as much force as Rachel.

"A-plus!" she says. She holds up her hands, stubby fingers outstretched. "I give you a score of perfect ten!"

"Thanks, Nina. I'm glad you liked it."

"Are there cookies?" she asks.

"Yup." I point to the reception tables and she marches off. Girl with a mission.

"Only two!" Eric calls after her.

She ignores him.

"We got it," Paige says, and drags Rachel after Nina.

Mom and Dad have drifted away, talking to other parents, which means it's just me and Eric now.

"You were amazing," he says.

"It was a little rough. But I got through it."

"I just watched my boyfriend play a super complicated piano piece in a smashing suit. To me, it was amazing."

A smile creeps onto my face. "Thanks for coming."

"Are you kidding? I wouldn't have missed it for the world. Plus, I'm now a super awesome big brother because Nina was completely *transfixed,* let me tell you . . ."

I grasp his hands, pull him forward, and kiss him, closing my eyes, oblivious to the piped piano music and the hum of excited conversation all around me. It's not a long kiss—I mean, we're in the middle of a packed lobby—and when I open my eyes and pull back, I see . . .

"Shane." Drop Eric's hands. "Hi, Shane."

Shane is standing a few feet away, shoulders hunched up under his letter jacket, hands in his pockets, looking uncomfortable. But he manages a smile. "Hey, Miles."

Eric follows my gaze and also sees Shane. "Oh. Hey." He holds out his hand. "Eric. We met a while ago."

Shane steps forward and shakes Eric's hand. "Right. Nice to see you."

"Shane . . ." (Do I shake his hand? Hug him? Is he expecting a hug?) "What are you doing here?"

He stuffs his hands back in his pockets. No hug, then. We just stare awkwardly at each other. "I just, uh, wanted to come hear you play. You were great."

What do I say? *What do I say?*

"Yeah, he was amazing, right?" Eric smiles at me and reaches down to take my hand.

I move my hand away. Fold my arms and manage a smile at Shane. "Thanks. And thanks for coming."

Eric quickly tucks his hand in his back pocket. Almost fast enough to look natural.

Shane smiles. "Yeah. I mean, of course." (Did he really just smile?) "Anyway." He retreats. "I better go. Let me know when you find out."

"I will. Thanks again."

Shane gives Eric the chin-jerk and turns and walks away. He gets swallowed by the crowd immediately, but it's Shane—he stands a head above most people, so I can watch him all the way to the door.

"It was nice of him to come hear you play." Eric's voice is soft. Neutral.

I feel terrible. "Yeah. It was." *It was my ex-boyfriend, Eric. I felt awkward.* I smile and hold out my hand. "Cookies now?"

That strange expression crosses his face. The same one from that day at Sal's, when he first met Shane. But he takes my hand. "Sure. When do you get the results?"

"Oh, probably an hour." We turn for the reception table. "Everybody inhales sugar to make themselves feel better and then they post the results after the reception."

"Yikes."

"Yeah. Last year Chelsea Pencyszki had a pretty dramatic fight with her piano teacher in front of everyone after she didn't make the top five. It was brutal."

"Is she here this year?"

"No. That was her last shot before college. I think she went to Penn State."

"Wow." Eric looks around. "Speaking of piano teachers, where's Stefania?"

"I think she left. It seemed like she was leaving." She certainly blasted down the hall fast enough. She was out the door and into the lobby before I could even decide whether to follow her.

"Oh." Eric is idly watching Nina point to the cookies she wants, while Paige puts them on a plate for her. "Miles, do you actually—"

"Stefania leave you alone already?" Cameron Hart comes up next to us, paper plate of brownies in one hand and a plastic cup of soda in the other.

I grasp Eric's hand tighter. "Cameron, don't you have any actual friends to talk to?"

He shrugs. Takes a sip of soda. "They've seen me perform so many times it's boring for them. They're waiting for the finals."

"Yeah, plus they'd really have to turn up their hearing aids for that hall."

Cameron glowers. "You know, playing at nursing homes actually looks really good on college applications."

He probably has a point there. Crap. "I don't see Pierre around, either."

Now he leers. "He's saying hello to the judges."

Eric calmly raises his eyebrows. "Dude, that kind of sounds like competition tampering, doesn't it?"

Cameron turns his pale eyes to Eric. "He's old friends with several of them. It's just social." He looks back down at me. "See, when the judges don't hate your guts, you actually have a reason to stick around and be friendly."

"What's that supposed to mean?"

"Ask Stefania." Cameron turns on his heel and wanders away, sipping his soda.

Eric glances at me. "What's he talking about?"

I have a nasty feeling I somehow walked into a trap. "Beats me." It has to be a trap. Cameron's just fucking with me. Why would the judges hate Stefania?

"Oh my god." Rachel appears at my elbow, shoving a plateful of brownies at me. "Miles, you have to try these. They're so good."

I let her pull me into the reception with Paige and Nina and Eric and my parents. I sip apple juice while my parents talk to other parents. I nibble on a brownie but I can't finish it. Eric and Rachel and Paige are joking with each other. Nina is drawing on a copy of the program with a colored pencil she got from Eric. That poor Mendelssohn kid is standing in a corner looking like a nervous wreck.

What happened to my banana? Did I leave it in that closet? Did Stefania throw it away?

Why did Stefania leave? Why didn't she wait with me for the results?

Maybe I'm not going to make it. Maybe she actually thinks I performed terribly, and she doesn't want to be embarrassed when the results are posted. Maybe I'm so bad that I crashed and burned and I can't even *tell*.

She didn't tell me I did a good job. She said I did *okay*.

I'm biting my nails, still holding my plate of nibbled brownie when Rachel shakes my shoulder. "Miles. Miles!"

"What?"

She's pointing. Everybody is swarming to the corkboard just outside the entrance to the auditorium. They've posted the results. I see Andrew craning his neck. Cassandra standing on her toes. Cameron trying to look cool and collected . . .

I join the swarm, inching closer to the corkboard. Why is everyone so tall? I can't see anything.

Jenny appears in front of me. "Miles! We're going to the finals, baby!"

"We are? Did you—"

"Final five!" She grabs my elbow, pushing through the crowd, and suddenly there's the list, alphabetical, printed in big block letters:

Jenny Chang
Cameron Hart
Miles Jacobson
Andrew Morris
Cassandra O'Brian

I'm going to the final round with Cameron Hart. Again.

Jenny and I duck and weave our way out of the crush, past several people crying, some more looking stricken, and a few just looking pissed. Jenny hugs me quickly and then runs for the door, where her mom is waiting.

"You made it?" Rachel asks.

I nod. Rachel and Paige hug me and Eric hugs all of us. Nina demands a high five. Mom hands me my winter coat.

Cameron walks past, Pierre at his side. "See you at the finals, Jacobson." And then he's gone, out the front door.

There goes another prime chance to give him the finger.

"Okay, now we celebrate," says Rachel. "Hive, hot chocolate on me."

I pull out my phone as we walk outside. I feel a twinge of guilt, but Shane wanted to know the results. I owe him. He came to see me play.

So I text:

> I'm in the final round.

Shane texts back right away:

> Tell Cameron he better watch his back.

CHAPTER SIXTEEN

The preliminary round is held on the same day in Wisconsin, Illinois, and Indiana, so by the evening, Jenny is texting me about the results:

> Gunnar Edmonson again ugh can u believe

And:

> YES ANDREA AND TRILBY girls club REUNITED
> (plus you Miles)

And a few minutes later:

> Miles who is this wench

She sends me a screenshot from the Tri-State Competition website—a list of the finalists from each state. She's circled a name: Lily Shimada, finalist from Finchport, Illinois.

I start searching—internet, social media—but Jenny beats me and texts me a link to Instagram.

Lily Shimada's account is private, but her profile picture shows a girl with long black hair holding a yellow puppy that's licking her face. Her bio says *Pianist & Puppy luvr.* Location: *Illinois.*

I can't decide if it's cute or if I want to barf, but it must be her.

> I think she's new this year.

> Dude I don't even think she was in the Junior Levels before.

> Maybe she just moved to Illinois.

> Or she had a life, unlike us, and this is her first Tri-State lol

I'm a ball of anxiety when I walk up Stefania's front steps for my first lesson after the prelims. Cameron's comments about the judges hating her have been bumping around in my brain since Saturday, and I still don't have any idea how to ask her about it. I mean, what am I supposed to say? *So, Stefania, I've heard even more people hate you.* That wouldn't go well.

Besides, we're going to talk about Cameron's performance. What I'm up against. That's terrifying enough.

Stefania's back in her penguin sweatshirt when she answers the door. She waves me inside and we walk back to the piano room, Olga excitedly bouncing off my legs with enough force that I crash into the wall several times.

"So." Stefania sits down in her chair. I sit down on the piano bench. And she stares at me.

Am I supposed to say something? "What?"

"What did you think of Cameron's Rachmaninov?"

What did I *think?* I think I'm totally fucked, Stefania. Don't make me say it. "Um . . . it was good."

Her eyes narrow.

"Like . . . subtle. He . . . uh . . . sells it."

Stefania sighs loudly. "Yes, he does, like a used car salesman. Like I said—all flash and no panache. He's technically very, very good, Miles. Probably better than you."

Well. That's just great.

"But he *performs*. He doesn't give a rat's ass what the piece he's playing is about and it shows. The emotion is about as deep as a puddle. He's just learned to cover it up the same way Pierre has—playing the hardest, most complicated concertos and putting on such a theatrical show that it's almost convincing. Cameron hides behind fast, fancy notes and a bunch of hair flipping and if you aren't paying that much attention, it sounds impressive. But I'd like to see him sound impressive playing Mozart."

"Yeah, but nobody can sound impressive playing Mozart. You can't win Tri-State with Mozart."

Stefania frowns at me. "It is much harder to play a brilliant Mozart than you think, Miles. Just because it wouldn't win a competition doesn't mean it's easy."

I can see there's no point arguing that one. "Okay, so Cameron is technically perfect. How am I supposed to compete with that?"

Stefania frowns harder. "He's *not* technically perfect. He's technically very, very good. But *you* have something to say. You already told me. You'll keep practicing and your technique will get better—that's what happens when you practice. But having something *real* to say—that isn't something anybody else can just *teach* you, because it has to come from you yourself. So before the finals, we'll work on your technique so you have the flash where you need it. It's the combination of technique and emotion that makes a great musician."

"So . . ." I fidget, rubbing my thumb over the corner of the piano bench. "I can compete? I mean, I *could* compete with Cameron?"

Stefania rolls her eyes. "Yes, Miles, I just told you that. Let's not waste time. B-flat major scale. Go."

And now she's leaning back in her chair. That's it. Talking over. I turn to the piano and start a B-flat major scale. What else am I supposed to do? Stefania told me I have a chance. I'm not totally fucked.

I can't ask her anything about the judges now.

When the snow finally melts in March I discover that Eric bikes, because he starts meeting me and Paige and Rachel at the bike racks before school, gliding up on a rusty red three-speed that looks even older than his car.

Paige shoots it a disdainful look. "Since when do you bike?"

Eric takes off his helmet. "Since always."

"So why haven't we seen it before?"

Now he looks confused. "Because it was winter and I don't have a death wish?"

"Most people here do," I tell him.

Paige shrugs. "I'd rather get ten more minutes of sleep and drive."

"Biking is better for the environment," Eric says, at the same time Rachel says, "Biking is more eco-friendly!" and they grin at each other.

I glance at my phone to check how much time we have before the first bell—and open up my text messages to look again at Shane's last text, just like I do practically every time I look at my phone now.

> Tell Cameron he better watch his back.

"Earth to Miles." Paige elbows me. "What are you staring at?"

"Nothing." I stuff my phone in my pocket. Eric has locked his bike up and they're all waiting for me. "Sorry, just spacing. Let's go."

Eric and I don't just see each other in school and the auditorium anymore. Whenever I'm not with Stefania, or practicing at home, or actually in class, I'm with Eric. Getting pizza at Sal's after a Saturday morning practice session at the auditorium. Taking a walk by the lake where crocuses are poking up purple and white through the thawing ground.

It's all perfect—except that whenever I'm alone, I keep looking at that text message and thinking about Shane. Wondering if he'll text me again. Sneaking looks over my shoulder at school, wondering if he'll smile at me again.

I don't *need* him to. I'm just . . . thinking about the what-ifs. And yeah, I get a warm little rush of familiarity every time Shane's dented pickup rumbles past me in the school parking lot, but that's just a leftover habit. It doesn't mean anything.

Because everything with Eric is *perfect*. Too new to be familiar, but so what? The pizza trips and the lake walks are nice. And the best times are when his parents are at work, and we spend the evening making tacos with Nina, while Mr. Pudge perches on a stool at the kitchen island and makes an occasional swipe for the cheese with his huge fluffy paw.

And after dinner, while Nina curls up on the couch with a movie, we go up to Eric's room.

He takes off my glasses and I take off his.

He kisses me, and I kiss him.

And his eyelashes brush against my face.

And his hand slides up my back, underneath my shirt now . . .

I pull back, but this time, I say, "I want to take my shirt off."

It slips out quickly, and he blinks. "Um. Okay?"

I second-guess immediately, even though I've been thinking about this for the last week. "I don't have to."

"No, I didn't mean . . . I would be into that, I just don't have expectations. I don't want you to think I have expectations—"

"I know." I know he's giving me a way out, if I want one. But I don't want one. I step back. Pull my sweater over my head, and then my binder, too. Drop it all on the floor.

Leaving, well, *me*.

Eric looks. He obviously looks. And then he pulls his T-shirt over his head.

My heart beats faster. "What are you doing?"

"Keeping things equal." He emerges from his shirt and tosses it at his bed.

I look, because he did. Keeping things equal. And I realize that in all my thinking about taking my shirt off, I never thought about *after*. It was too scary. What Eric would do. What he would say.

Now I'm staring at his chest (it's a very nice chest) and trying to figure out what to say.

He says, "You can tell me if I should pretend they aren't there."

I look up at his face. "Pretend my boobs aren't there?"

He considers. "Avoid a certain part of my boyfriend's body that makes him uncomfortable?"

It's a few seconds before I can manage a whisper. "I'm still your boyfriend?"

"I see you as everything you tell me you are or want to be." He smiles, a little shy, a little self-conscious. "You're my boyfriend who currently has, um . . ."

He's looking again.

"Boobs," I say.

"I was going to say *breasts,* but whatever. I really don't care." He hesitates, and then says, in a rush, "I think you're hot."

I'm certainly not cold anymore. "What if I get rid of the boobs? I mean, eventually?"

He shrugs. "I'll still think you're hot."

How can he sound so sure? How can he look at me, shirtless, and still see a boy, when I can't even always see that myself?

I don't understand at all, but I believe him.

"Kiss me?" I ask.

He smiles, and he's not shy anymore. "Yeah."

* * *

April first arrives with an epic thunderstorm. Dad drives me to school on his way to work, windshield wipers squeaking back and forth, rain pounding on the roof of the car, lightning flashing and thunder booming.

It fills up the awkward silence nicely.

Rachel, Paige, and Eric are huddled just inside the school entrance, all wearing drenched raincoats, waiting for me.

"You didn't bike today, did you?" I ask Eric.

"God, no." He sticks out a foot. "Look at this, I had to pull my winter boots out again. You didn't tell me Wisconsin also has biblical rains, Miles."

"Oh, just wait until the tornado warnings in June," Paige says, deadpan, heading for her locker.

Eric looks alarmed. "She's kidding, right?" He jogs after Paige. "Hey, you're kidding, right?"

It's still pouring after school, so Eric drives me to Stefania's. And since it's still pouring when we get there, he offers to stick around for the hour so he can drive me home. Stefania's eyebrows go up when she answers the door and sees both of us, but she lets us in and directs Eric to the living room. Olga is overjoyed to have another visitor. She bounces up and down like a puppy until the whole house shakes.

With Eric sitting on the couch (under a pile of dog because Olga thinks she fits in his lap), I *still* can't ask Stefania whether the Tri-State judges hate her. I've been trying—ever since that first week when I failed miserably—but there's never a good moment. Whenever I'm not playing the piano, Stefania's talking, and she's so *focused*, trying to make me better, that I just can't figure out how to interrupt her.

If I can't actually ask Stefania about it, there's only one other option. So, back home, after I've changed into dry clothes and had dinner, I head upstairs to my room, sit cross-legged on my bed, and open my laptop.

The Tri-State Competition website has its own online forum, restricted to past and present competitors, and it's about as useless as any other online forum. Half of it is people asking serious questions that nobody answers, and the rest of it is people asking inane questions that fifty other people answer before the whole thing devolves into trash-talking Mozart.

I've only gone on the forum twice before. The first time was in middle school, before my very first Tri-State Competition at the Junior Level, because I was so anxious that I wanted to know everything I possibly could about the experience beforehand. Hot or cold auditorium, where the judges sit, whether anyone has ever gotten a wedgie during a performance (my thirteen-year-old brain was *really* worried about that).

The second time was before my first competition at the Senior Level, when I decided that I wanted to know what everyone was saying about Cameron Hart. I regretted that search within the first ten seconds.

The closer the competition gets, the more ridiculous the forum gets. Too many anxious pianists taking breaks from practicing. But given Stefania's reputation, I have a feeling there's gossip about her somewhere on it.

I log in with my email and try five times to remember my password before I give up and reset it. Five minutes later, I'm finally typing Stefania's name into the search bar.

Five results. Huh. Honestly thought there would be more.

I click on the first one.

OK so does anyone know why Stephania Smith quit piano because look at this video she was AWWWWWWESOME.

I click the link. The video is grainy—the dappled browns of the string instruments and blacks of the suits and dresses all sort of fading to gray. A small woman in red walks out onto the stage. Her frizzy hair is jet black, piled on top of her head, but even pixelated I recognize her: it's Stefania.

She bows to tinny applause, takes her seat, and the orchestra plunges into a Brahms concerto. Stefania throws herself at the piano the same way she does now. The audio quality is terrible, but she's still amazing. There's no doubting that.

I leave the video playing in the background and go back to the forum. Scroll through the replies:

Probably got knocked up and quit to have babies.

Ugh. Moving on.

She was never that special. You should look up Pierre Fontaine, he's actually good.

Twenty bucks says that's Cameron.

I heard she had an affair with her mentor or something and it derailed her career

---

Well, this isn't helpful. I hit the back button and scroll through the other posts.

How tall is Stefania Smith? Nope.

How old is Stefania Smith? Nope.

Stefania Smith is a TERRIBLE teacher and NOBODY should study with her!!! Hi, Andrew. Nice to see you here.

The last post is also the newest. Posted last night. I click on it.

Does anybody know what's up with "Miles" Jacobson? Studying with Stefania Smith now? Looks like a boy?

My heart thuds. I scroll down to the replies.

> Didn't "he" used to be a "she"?
> Once a she, always a she.
> I thought his name was Melissa???
> Ugh, take your stupid suit off "Miles", you're just an ugly girl.

My heart is beating so loud I can hear it in my ears. Drumming its way through the bad-quality Brahms still filtering through my laptop speakers. My fingers don't even seem like my fingers as they reach out and scroll back up to the top of the post, and then, slowly, back down so I can read all the replies again.

> Once a she, always a she.

I can't blink.

> Ugh, take your stupid suit off "Miles"

Can't breathe.

> You're just an ugly girl

My fingers are shaking now. I can't scroll smoothly. The words jump up and down on the screen.

Stop looking. Close your laptop.

But I can't.

Don't don't don't don't don't—

But I type my name into the forum search bar.

More posts.

> Is Miles Jacobson the same as Melissa Jacobson?
> Lol I guess we don't have to use our real names for the

competition now, I'm gonna be Spaghetti Meatball for all performances . . .

I type my old name into the search bar. Even more posts.

Uhhhh what happened to Melissa Jacobson?
Is Melissa Jacobson gay now or???

None of these posts have responses. Yet.

Log out.

LOG. OUT.

I log out. Manage to hit pause on the video of Stefania. Reach for my phone and open up my contacts. I can't call Rachel—she'll get righteous—and I don't talk to Paige about shit like this. I hesitate, staring at the name that's suddenly come into focus. He knows the competition. He's met the people there. *Tell Cameron he better watch his back.* That has to be worth something, right?

I press Call.

"Miles?"

"Hi." My voice sounds thick. I clear my throat. "Sorry to call you." But now my voice is shaky and that's no better. "This thing happened and I just—"

"Hang on a sec." Muffled noises on the other end. A door closing? And then clearer, soft, and so familiar it hurts, Shane's voice. "You okay? What's up?"

Don't cry. "You remember how the Tri-State Competition has that online forum?"

"Yeah."

"I was just on it to look something up, and . . . I ended up finding a post about me. Well, *posts.*"

"Was Cameron whining about how good you are?" He's trying to be light. Funny.

My vision swims. "No, everything's anonymous, so I wouldn't

be able to tell anyway. They don't display names. Competition privacy, or something. But someone started a post about me, saying 'didn't he used to be a she,' and all of that and . . ." My voice breaks. *Don't cry.* "Anyway, the last reply on the post said 'Take your stupid suit off, you're just an ugly girl.'"

Silence. Except for my shuddering breath.

What am I doing? "I'm sorry I called you. I just knew if I called Rachel, she'd launch into some tirade about queer rights and I just . . . *can't* with that right now . . ."

And you know me, I want to say. *You've been there, at this competition, with me. You watched me perform this year, in my suit, even though we broke up . . .*

Finally, Shane says, "Fuck. That's really terrible." He sounds just like he did in Sophie's basement at the Valentine's Night party. Uncomfortable—so uncomfortable—but like he means every word. "They're just . . . I mean, whoever wrote that is an asshole. A troll and an asshole."

"I know." *How do I breathe?* "I know it shouldn't matter, but . . . It must have been somebody *at* the preliminary round. Somebody who saw me, in my suit and everything. And that feels different."

"Why? They're still an asshole."

"But they *saw* me. They thought that when they saw me. And I probably saw them."

"And they're bitter they didn't make it to the next round so they posted something disgusting because they didn't have anything better to do. So what? It doesn't matter."

"It does to me."

Shane is quiet for a moment. Then he says, "Yeah, I know. Sorry. I can't even imagine how much it sucks to read that."

"It's okay." It's not, and we both know it, but what else am I going to say?

"Is there a way to report that post or something?" he says.

"Like, what, as hate speech?"

"As anything."

"I don't know." And I don't want to go back and look.

"I could check, if you want. Like, see if I can report it . . ."

It's such a kind thing to say that I want to curl up in a ball and hide. "That's okay. You need a password to log in anyway. It's . . . it's fine."

"Okay." After another minute, Shane says, "Maybe you could tell Jenny. That's the girl you're friends with, right? Is she going to the finals?"

"Jenny Chang? Yeah."

"So tell her. So you have someone on your team at the competition."

"Yeah." (I guess he's right.) "Maybe." (I know he's right.)

"Miles, uh . . . I'm sorry, I gotta go. DeShawn's over, and—"

"Oh. God, I'm sorry."

"No, I didn't mean . . . It's fine that you called. Really."

"Okay." Breathe. In and out. "Thanks for talking."

"Sure." A pause. "I'm sorry."

"Thanks." The call ends and I lower my phone. Spin it around on the bed in front of me.

What did I just do?

Because now it hits me so hard that my insides twist. *I should have called Eric.*

Eric knows me. Eric cares about me. And yeah, Eric doesn't know the competition that well, but I could have explained it to him. It wouldn't have been that hard to explain it to him. He *gets* my piano stuff. He could *get* the competition.

If there was ever a Call Your Boyfriend moment, that was it.

But instead I called Shane—the guy I keep thinking about, the guy whose text I keep staring at, the guy who broke up with me because I'm a dude now and he's *not into dudes.*

What is *wrong* with me?

I curl up on my bed and stuff my head under a pillow. But I don't feel angry enough to scream. I don't feel angry at all. I just feel . . .

Sad.

Ugly.

Fake.

A sad, ugly, fake loser.

It's too stuffy under the pillow. I pull my head out. Stare at my popcorn ceiling, listening to the rain drum on the roof.

I pick up my phone and text Jenny.

> Hey, when you get a chance, could you look up my name on the Tri-State forum? Some asshole said something kind of shitty. I don't need you to do anything. I just wanted to tell you.

And then, with my stomach in knots, I do what I should have done in the first place. I call Eric.

He picks up right away. "Hey! How are you?"

He's excited that I called him.

I feel worse.

I tell him what happened. My voice is steady. My eyes are dry. My heart beats faster when I remember the words on the screen, but my hands don't shake.

I don't tell him I called Shane. How would I explain that, anyway?

Eric listens, and he's as gentle and understanding as I knew he would be. Asks if I can report it. Asks if I'm okay. Asks if there's anything he can do.

I don't know.

I'm fine.

That's okay.

"What are you going to tell Rachel and Paige?" he asks.

Nothing? Is that an option? "I don't know. I guess I have to figure something out."

"You don't *have* to."

"Yeah, but . . . they're my friends." Sigh. Rub my eyes. "I want to stop thinking about this. I bet the asshole that wrote that shit has stopped thinking about me."

"Yeah. That's how it always works."

"You speak from great experience?" I mean it to be sarcastic. Funny. But it comes out mean and bitter. "Sorry," I mumble.

Eric is silent for a few seconds. Then he says, quietly, "Remember the ex I told you about?"

(She. Her. A girl. Of course I remember that.) "I remember the ex you *mentioned*."

"Right. Yeah." He goes quiet again—for so long that I start to wonder if he's still there. I'm about to ask when he says, "I shouldn't have dated her. I mean, I should have known better. Or I feel like I should have. She wasn't very nice to my friend Sam, even before we started dating—she never made any effort on Sam's pronouns. Sam is nonbinary, but she said 'they' isn't a singular pronoun."

Oh. So that's how he knows what *nonbinary* means. "That's ridiculous," I say. "People are always saying 'they' when they don't know somebody's gender."

"Yeah, and language changes all the time. I know. I should've been a better friend to Sam, too, but I never stood up for them. I was so distracted by somebody liking me. Plus, my mom was having a rough time finding a job and Nina was having a super rough time in school, so it was just . . . nice to have someone act like I was special. Jocelyn—that's my ex—she was also an artist, so I felt like she *got* me."

"But?" (Because I can tell there's a *but*. He sounds too sad for there not to be.)

"But after a couple months she asked if I could be more straight."

What? "More *straight*?"

"Yeah. She wasn't homophobic or anything. Or, I mean, she said she wasn't—she had *gay friends,* you know . . . But I was her boyfriend and that was different." He sighs. "I guess her friends were poking fun at her because her boyfriend was gay and 'hadn't figured it out yet.'"

"Eric"—I can't stop myself—"no offense, but you don't seem *that* gay."

He laughs. "No offense, but neither do you."

"Oh." (Really? I haven't thought about it.)

"I probably seem less gay now," he says slowly. "I used to dress a little different. I wore rainbow socks, if you can believe it."

"You wore *color*?"

"I know." This time the sarcasm worked—I can hear his smile. He's silent for a moment, and then he says, "I wonder a little bit if Jocelyn wanted me to be straighter because *she* got called a 'dyke' sometimes, which is just . . . so backward and I kind of can't believe people still do that. I mean, who knows, maybe she just started dating me to prove a point. And now this has become a long-winded story—"

"It's okay." I don't want him to stop talking. He's never talked this way before—he's never talked about *Seattle*—and I want to know, want to listen, want to feel less alone.

"The point is, this band came to Seattle that I wanted to see, and Jocelyn and I were going to go, but then she didn't show up. She'd blown me off before—like, whenever we were supposed to hang out with my friends—but she'd never done it when it was just the two of us. I was pretty upset, but she apologized the next day and said she'd gotten food poisoning. Only Sam found out she'd been out with her friends instead. Sam and I got into this huge fight about it when they told me, because I didn't believe them at first." He sighs. "I confronted Jocelyn about it eventually, and she admitted it, like it wasn't even a big deal. And that was finally it. I said I wanted to break up. But I guess she didn't want to be broken up with, because when I got to school the next day, I found out she'd told everyone that she'd broken up with *me,* because she'd caught me dressing up in her mom's clothes."

He stops. I know I'm supposed to say something now, but what do you say to that? *That sucks* doesn't even begin to cover it, even if it's true.

"Eric, I'm . . . sorry."

"It's okay." (It isn't.) "I mean, the thing is . . . even if I *was* dressing up in clothes that people think are supposed to be for women . . . who cares? Clothes are cool. Drag is fun. People should wear whatever. But Jocelyn said it because she knew people would think it was funny, or weird, or gross. And . . . well, I just wanted to tell you because . . . I get it. I promise I spent way more time thinking about how Jocelyn could do that or why she did it than she ever spent doing it. Or probably even planning to do it."

"If I ever meet your ex, I'll dig into my teen girl past and bitch-slap her for you."

He snorts. "Oh, believe me, I have, like, five hundred comebacks if I ever see her again. Really good one-liners, too."

Bitterness creeps back into me. "People suck."

"I don't know. I felt like everybody sucked for a long time after that happened, but now . . ." I can almost hear him shrug. "I guess ignorant people say mean shit sometimes. Honestly, I think it hurts the most when there's some small part of you that wonders if they're right."

Take off your stupid suit.

You're just an ugly girl.

I know what he means.

"Do you want me to tell Rachel and Paige?" he asks. "About the forum post?"

I rub a finger over my bitten thumbnail. "No, it's okay. I'll tell them. Just not until tomorrow."

"You sure?"

(No.) "Yeah. But thanks. For asking."

We fall back into silence. But it's a nice silence this time. A silence where I know he's listening, but I don't have to speak. I didn't know silence could feel this close, or this safe.

Finally, I say, "I guess I should go to bed."

"Okay. Talk tomorrow?"

"Talk tomorrow."

I put my phone and my laptop back on my desk. Take a shower, breathing deep. Put on my pajamas, convincing myself my heart is slowing down.

When I go back to my bedroom, I have a text from Jenny:

> Found an admin email for the forum so
> i'm reporting these losers. Bet it's the
> same a-holes who posted that i should
> go back to china last year.

CHAPTER SEVENTEEN

The rain has cleared off into a gloomy gray sky in the morning, but everything still smells like wet dirt, and I have to leap over puddles in the parking lot potholes. Rachel and Paige are waiting by the bike racks like usual, but they aren't looking at me. They haven't even noticed me.

They're arguing. With each other. They must be—I can't hear what they're saying, but they don't look happy and Rachel is waving her arms around.

"Hey!" I shout. Because nobody needs the embarrassment of me walking right into their fight.

"Hey!" Rachel waves and smiles, but it looks pinched.

"No Eric yet?" I ask.

"Nope." Paige has pulled out her phone, but she's clearly not doing anything with it, except avoiding looking at Rachel.

"Speaking of Eric," Rachel says, "he texted us last night and said you were gonna tell us something and we weren't allowed to have an opinion unless you wanted one."

Oh, thank god.

"Just to be clear," Paige says, looking up, "we are actually two separate people who would have *opinions*. Plural."

Rachel shoots her a glare.

I ignore it and plunge in. Tell them about the forum posting. Quick. Simple. No frills. I leave out the part where I called Shane, and the details of my conversation with Eric. I do say I texted Jenny, just to head off Rachel's inevitable tirade.

But when I'm done, all Rachel says is, "I'm really sorry," and she looks like she means it.

"That sucks," Paige says. She glances at Rachel. "You're really going to hold it in?"

"This isn't about *us,* Paige."

Paige looks annoyed. "Yeah. Obviously."

Rachel glowers, and Paige goes back to her phone, and I'm about three seconds away from throwing caution to the wind and asking what the hell is going on, when Rachel says, "Oh, there's Eric!"

He glides through the parking lot on his bike, tires spitting water up behind him. No jacket today—just his black hoodie. He has more faith in spring than I do.

"Hey, guys." He pulls up to the bike rack.

"Miles told us," Rachel says promptly. She shoots Paige a look. "And we *didn't* have *opinions.*"

Paige rolls her eyes.

"Okay." Eric locks up his bike and pulls off his helmet. "Hey, it's finally warmer, huh?"

"Yeah," Paige says, and turns for the school.

Rachel lets her breath out with a huff and storms after her.

Eric looks at me with raised eyebrows. "What's up with them?"

"I think they're arguing."

"About what?"

"No idea."

He shakes his head and takes my hand. "You okay today?"

"Yeah. I'm okay." And I am, more or less, except that I feel guilty all over again when we go into homeroom and there's Shane, sitting in a chair near the back. He doesn't look at me.

Whatever's up with Rachel and Paige, it goes on all morning. They sit on either side of me and Eric in homeroom, instead of next to each other. When we go to lunch, Rachel asks me if I have to pee, but Paige heads straight for the food line. Eric shoots me a puzzled glance and goes after her.

That's it. "Rache, what's going on with you two?"

She avoids my eyes. "Nothing."

"Rachel."

"Fine!" It bursts out of her and she looks around anxiously, like she thinks someone might be paying attention. (Nobody is.) "We're having a minor disagreement."

"About what?"

Rachel looks at the food line. Looks back at me. Looks desperate. "We were going to . . . I mean, we tried to . . . We were, *you know.*"

"I really don't, Rachel."

"We were *doing it,*" she whispers, looking ready to cry, "and it didn't work, and we stopped, and now everything is terrible."

I don't know what I was expecting, but it wasn't this. My brain screeches to a halt. "You were . . . You had *sex?*"

It comes out louder than I mean it to, and Rachel grabs my arm and pulls me into a corner. "No! We started to, but it didn't work."

We're standing way too close to the trash bins. It reeks over here. I lower my voice. "What do you mean, *it didn't work?* How does it not work?"

"I don't know." Rachel furiously wipes her eyes. "I was so excited, and I was looking forward to it, but then Paige wasn't into it. Everything I did made her annoyed, and suddenly she's telling me she never gets to be herself, whatever that means, and now I feel terrible at everything. Do you need to pee?"

"What? Rache, what happened? I mean, is that why you're fighting?"

"We're not fighting! I'm going to pee." She wipes her eyes again and pushes her way back into the crowded cafeteria and out into the hallway.

Crap. I also have to pee, but I can't follow her now. I don't know what to say, which means I'll say the wrong thing, and anyway, I have to follow Eric and Paige. Because as much as I really don't want to think about my two best friends *doing it* when I'm trying to eat lunch, I can't just leave Eric in the middle of their argument.

So I grab a tray and head for the cafeteria line.

Shane and I never got past second base. I guess I figured we'd go farther at some point—I wasn't intentionally avoiding it, there just didn't seem to be any rush. Plus, I didn't want to think about condoms. Or birth control pills. *Especially* birth control pills. Talk about a marker of being female. Dealing with a period every month is bad enough.

Rachel asked me plenty of times if Shane and I were *doing it.* Even though she didn't like Shane, and he was *so straight,* she asked me about my love life constantly. But I never wanted to ask about her and Paige because . . . *weird.*

I guess I sort of assumed they'd done it ages ago. Why wouldn't you, if you didn't have to deal with birth control?

Eric is showing Paige his most recent sketches when I set down my tray at the table. I don't interrupt them. He doesn't look freaked out, so Paige must not have said anything.

Rachel shows up ten minutes later. Sets her tray down next to me without looking at anybody.

Paige acts like she doesn't exist.

It's the most uncomfortable meal I've ever sat through. And that includes Thanksgiving with my racist grandpa. Rachel stabs her wilted, sad-looking salad with increasing violence, while Paige ignores her and talks to Eric. I can't think of anything to say to anybody. Not that it would help. When Eric tries to start a whole-table conversation about webcomics with queer characters, he gets stony silence from Rachel, and Paige just looks at her phone.

"Did you find anything out?" Eric whispers to me as we bus our trays.

"Um." Rachel and Paige are already leaving the cafeteria, still stubbornly ignoring each other, but I know Rachel will kill me if I tell Eric what they're fighting about. Assuming Paige doesn't kill me first. "I don't know. Private stuff, I guess."

"Oh." He looks after them. "I hope they work it out."

"Yeah." My phone buzzes in my pocket. Text notification.

"Are you practicing here today?"

"I think so. Probably for a couple hours; there's no musical rehearsal. Want to hang out?"

He winces. "I promised Nina I'd help make a costume for her school play."

"Oh, that's cool." My phone buzzes again. "What's her costume?"

"A sparkly rainbow unicorn octopus."

"What?" Is Rachel texting me? Or Paige? Maybe Paige was crafting texts, all that time she was staring at her phone.

Eric jumps out of the way of some rowdy guys from the basketball team and shrugs. "Apparently everybody got to make up their own character for the school play, so she made up a rainbow unicorn octopus. I have my work cut out for me." He jabs a thumb over his shoulder. "I gotta run to the art room, actually, to see if I can steal a few supplies. See you later?"

He kisses my cheek and dashes down the hall.

Okay, who is texting me? I pull out my phone, fully expecting either Rachel or Paige. Neither of them usually hold out on me for long, so it has to be one or the other.

But it's not. It's Shane.

Can we talk?

Like maybe after school?

I stop, so fast that some poor pimply-faced freshman plows right into me and bounces off.

What does Shane want to talk to *me* about?

It has to be about the call, right?

Maybe he's mad I called him.

Maybe he's *glad* I called.

Maybe . . .

Stomach flip.

Rachel would be Judgy-Staring me so hard right now. But she's not here. And she has too many of her own problems to pay attention to mine anyway, so . . .

> I'm going to practice in the auditorium.
> You can meet me there.

Hesitate.

It's fine. Shane just wants to talk. It's fine.

Send.

And run for the bathroom.

Shane still hasn't replied by the time I walk into American History, and he's not in the classroom yet, either. Neither is Eric. So I sit down in my usual spot on one side of the room—same spot I've been sitting ever since that first day of the new semester, when I was trying to get Shane to notice me.

Shane walks in along with the bell, and Eric dashes in just behind him. I wait for some sort of acknowledgment from Shane—a nod, a look, a smile. Nothing. He just walks to his seat like he didn't text me five minutes ago.

"Hi," Eric whispers, collapsing in the seat next to me.

(What the hell, Shane?) "Hi. Find what you needed in the art room?"

"I don't know what you're talking about." Eric grins. "I definitely didn't borrow any glitter."

Mrs. Reed dims the lights and starts yet another slideshow about the atrocities of World War I. I'm starting to think Mrs. Reed has a morbid streak.

In the middle of a tangent about mustard gas (apparently a thing), my phone buzzes. *Crap.* I fumble around and manage to catch it before it slides off my knee. Eric glances at me, but Mrs. Reed doesn't notice.

It's a text message from Shane.

> OK meet you in the auditorium.

I lean back in my chair and try to casually glance over at him. He's looking down. At his phone?

I look at my phone. Maybe he's going to text something else.

But he doesn't. When I look again, he's doodling in his notebook.

Eric leans over, pencil in hand, and writes in my notes: What's up?

I pick up my pencil. Just thinking about Rachel and Paige. Totally. Me too.

My stomach twists around the lie.

Rachel and Paige are still mad at each other after last period, which is awkward, because Rachel is Paige's ride. "God forbid we do anything independently," Paige mutters as she blows past me and out the doors.

"You okay?" I ask Rachel.

She's hanging back with me, looking out to the parking lot like the last thing she wants to do is follow Paige. Which means she's definitely not okay.

"I'm fine." She lets her breath out with a huff. "Whatever."

And she marches after Paige.

"Oof," Eric says. He's standing next to me with his backpack, which looks more stuffed than it did this morning. Must be those "borrowed" art supplies.

"Yeah. Tell me about it." I glance back over my shoulder toward the auditorium. There are still people milling around, filling up my view. I can't see if Shane is waiting for me or not.

"Well . . ." Eric sighs. "Wish me luck with the unicorn octopus."

"Yeah. Good luck." Maybe Shane's already *in* the auditorium.

"You sure you're okay?"

Eric is frowning at me. (Quick. Paste on a smile.) "Yeah, sorry. I'm just thinking about piano. I better go practice, I guess." I jerk my thumb over my shoulder. "Have fun with Nina."

He's still frowning, but he squeezes my hand. "I'll text you later?"

"Yeah. Sounds good."

He shoulders his backpack, turns away, and then he's out the door, and I can make a beeline for the auditorium. No sign of Shane outside, so I heave open the door and walk quickly down the aisle, looking around at the dark seats. No sign of Shane here, either. The auditorium is just as quiet and empty as it always is.

I climb slowly up on the stage. Sit down on the piano bench. Where is he?

Maybe he changed his mind.

Maybe he flaked.

Maybe that's not such a bad thing. I mean, what the hell am I doing? Why did I actually come here? *I* should have flaked. We don't need to talk about that call. We should both just forget it ever happened.

I dig my fingers into my hair. If I'm here, I might as well practice. That's what I told Eric I was going to do. If I do it, then I won't have just told Eric a total lie . . .

I drop my bag on the floor, and that's when the auditorium door opens. A quick band of bright light from outside. A creak that echoes in the hall. I jump up like I sat on a porcupine.

It's Shane. I can't see his face yet, in the shadows beyond the stage, but I would recognize that silhouette anywhere. Big, broad, but still moving like he's not sure there's space for him. Shoulders hunched. Hands in his pockets.

"Hey," he says.

And all that guilty-comfortable-*you-know-me* of the phone call last night comes rushing right back. Hand on my shoulder at

Valentine's Night, smiling at me in the cafeteria, and every single time I looked at that text message . . .

I somehow find my voice. "Hey."

Shane stops at the front row of seats. But he doesn't sit—he stands. Hands still in his pockets, looking around. Like he's trying to avoid looking at me.

I can't take the silence. "You said you wanted to talk."

"Yeah." His shoulders hunch even higher. "I just, um . . . I did some thinking, after you called me."

Oh, no. "Look, I'm sorry I called. I wasn't thinking and—"

"No, it's fine. I mean, it's fine you called. I didn't . . . I don't mind." Shane pauses. Frowns. Juts out his jaw.

I recognize that look. Shane has a way of talking before his brain totally figures out what he's saying, and when it catches up, he stops and looks confused. It's the face he made when he tried to say *I love you* for the first time. He got there, eventually. After about ten minutes.

It's the face he made when we broke up, too. That vague and desperate frown. Hoping I can figure out what he's trying to say, so he doesn't have to say it.

"Why did you call me?" he asks.

There it is—the question I've been dreading.

I sit back down on the corner of the piano bench and stare at my feet. "You know about Cameron, and the competition, and what all this means to me. I guess I just wanted something familiar. Someone who knew me *before*."

"I don't know you now," he says. It sounds desperate.

And it stings. "Yes, you do. I'm the *same person*."

"No, you're not!" It bursts out of him, loud and echoing in the space. He ducks his head, looking embarrassed. "You keep saying that, Miles, and I know what you think you mean. But you're not the same. You play piano and you wear glasses and you probably have the same sense of humor or whatever, but you have a different name and you use different pronouns and you're just . . . you're living in the world differently. That changes you to me. I see you differently. You're *different* to me."

The sting turns to an ache.

But he's got me there. I wouldn't have believed him before now. I didn't believe him when we broke up. But getting my suit, performing in the prelim round . . . That wasn't Melissa. That was *Miles*. And there is a difference, somewhere.

Where?

I don't know.

Does getting a suit really change a person? Does a tie make you someone new? Do glasses?

They shouldn't. And they should. They don't. And they do.

"I get it." It's barely a whisper, but I say it. "I get what you mean."

"I totally get what *you* mean," he says. "Or I do now. For what it's worth." He runs a hand through his hair. "I get that in a way you've always been this person. Or, I mean, you feel like you've always been a guy on the inside? I don't know, I'm saying this wrong—"

"I don't even know." My shoulders feel so heavy when I shrug. "Sometimes I feel like I have no idea who I am and I never did."

Shane smiles a little. "That's everybody, though."

"I guess."

He stares at the floor. So do I.

"I'm sorry I'm different," I say.

"Don't be." His shoulders hunch up again. "I just . . . wanted to apologize. I was a jerk when we broke up. I freaked out because everything was changing—you were changing—and it felt really fast. It all weirded me out. I don't mean you're *weird*, I just mean I felt weird about it. It's not every day your girlfriend, you know, changes gender."

I can't speak. The lump in my throat is too big. But I manage a wobbly smile.

"I'm sorry." He looks up and his eyes meet mine. "That's what I wanted to say. You're not the same as you were before—as the person I felt like I knew. But when I saw you play in that competition round, I got it. Watching you play piano . . . Well, you're not the same as the person I thought I knew, but you're more *you*. I'm sorry if I ever made you feel like—I dunno—you couldn't be you."

I stare at him. He gets it. I've been waiting months for him to see me—really see me—and now he finally gets it. This bit of me, anyway. "Thanks." (I feel like a fool as soon as I say it.) "It's okay." (That isn't any better.)

"I miss you," he says.

My stomach flips. *No, no, no.* I don't want this feeling. This tug. But I say, "I miss you, too."

He takes his hands out of his pockets. Doesn't seem to know what to do with them. "Now what?"

My mouth is dry. "What do you mean?"

"What do we do?"

I can't swallow. "About what?"

He looks down at his hands. Puts them back in his pockets. "Can we be friends?"

Everything in me sinks. Sinks and twists into guilt, because *why* was I just shoving Eric—wonderful, funny, really-truly-*gets-all-of-me* Eric—out of my head to tell Shane I miss him?

And what was I expecting Shane to say?

"Yeah," I say. "Of course we can."

He lets his breath out. A gentle sigh. "Okay."

I suddenly want out of this conversation. I can't figure out what *friends* means. I can't figure out what anything means. And I don't want to. Not right now. "I should practice."

"Oh." He looks confused again.

"Sorry."

"No, I get it." Does he? But he's retreating. One step, then another. "Thanks for talking." He turns away, shoulders hunched, and wanders back up the aisle.

I turn to the piano.

The door creaks closed behind him.

I start playing scales, wondering how I'm supposed to practice now. How I'm supposed to focus, when everything inside me feels like a mixed-up tornado.

What was that, Shane?

What do you want?

And the million-dollar question: What do *I* want, and why the hell can't I just be happy with Eric?

CHAPTER EIGHTEEN

Rachel and Paige have constructed some kind of grudging truce by Monday morning. They don't glare at each other. They sit next to each other in homeroom. They even kiss in the hallway between classes. They don't really look like they enjoy it, but I guess they're trying.

Eric, on the other hand, looks like death.

"*Gesundheit!*" Rachel says, when Eric sneezes, very loudly, into the sleeve of his hoodie at lunch.

"Sorry." He pulls out a handkerchief and blows his nose. "Nina's got a cold and I think I caught it."

Paige scoots her chair away from him. "You think? You sound like you have the plague."

Eric looks offended. "The plague is a very different kind of illness. It has lumps."

"Gross."

"Miles." Rachel elbows me.

"What?"

"You're zoning out."

"No, I'm not." I *was* watching Shane, goofing off with DeShawn at the football table. DeShawn *and* that cheerleader Rhoda from Valentine's Night, because they're definitely a thing now. And I'm watching them just like I was watching Shane in homeroom, and in the hallway between classes, because supposedly we're *friends* now, even though he hasn't looked at me once today.

What the fuck is wrong with him?

Rachel is giving me a Judgy Look. "Your boyfriend is dying and you're zoning out."

I glower at her and gingerly rub Eric's arm, to show I am definitely *not* zoning out, and to try to stamp out the wave of guilt because I totally was.

"I'm not *dying*." Eric shivers and hunkers down into his hoodie. He's wearing his glasses today, and behind them, his eyes are red. "It's supposed to be spring. Why is your state so damn cold?"

"Because it's Wisconsin," says Paige, staring out into the cafeteria. "If it's not winter, then it's the humid armpit of hell. Those are the seasons."

Rachel sighs. "I have allergy stuff in my locker. Want some?"

Eric sniffles. "Thanks, Rachel, but it's definitely not allergies—"

"*Duh*, Eric. Allergy stuff has the same ingredients as cold stuff. I use it for both all the time." She pushes her chair back and stands up. "And if it'll stop you sneezing all over the entire school . . ."

Eric knows when there's no point arguing with Rachel (honestly, most of the time), so he stands up, too, stuffing his uneaten sandwich back in its paper bag.

As soon as they've left, Paige pushes her chair back. "I'm going to say hi to Josie."

"Who?"

"Josie Leyman." She picks up her tray. "We have a chemistry project together."

I twist around in my chair, watching her weave through the tables. Josie Leyman sits with Sophie (still dating Cameron), Daniel Young (on the debate team), Julian Wozniak (takes AP everything), and Hanna Herschel (probably going to Harvard). So I expect Paige to be awkward—hover outside the circle, maybe pull out this chemistry project and wave it to get Josie's attention. But she plunks down at their table like it's No Big Deal. Starts talking and laughing with Josie. Nobody gives her a second look.

What is happening? Since when is Paige friends with people who are friends with Sophie? What about all the Valentine's Night judginess? Sophie is *dating Cameron Hart.*

I turn away. Push dregs of pasta around on my plate. Go back to staring at the football table. Rhoda and Shane are laughing as DeShawn crams French fries into his mouth.

Ugh.

I get up and bus my tray. I'm going to find Eric, because feeling guilty is better than watching everybody else have a great time without me.

Whatever Rachel gave Eric, it seems to be helping. He doesn't sneeze once as we spend half an hour pouring different colored liquids into a vial to make "banana smell" in chemistry. Of course, he also can't tell if our vial smells like banana. Neither can I. The only thing I can smell is DeShawn and Marcus's vial in front of us, which is definitely not banana. Smells more like three-day-old fish guts.

Mr. Gracie is just launching into an explanation of the chemicals in coffee (Eric perks up at that), when the classroom door opens. It's Ms. Harding, the college counselor, red reading glasses dangling around her neck. She beckons Mr. Gracie over. They whisper together by the door.

Mr. Gracie turns around, squinting at us like he's never seen us before. "Eric Mendez?"

Eric blinks. Glances at me. Tentatively raises his hand.

Ms. Harding waves at him. "Can I see you, Eric?"

Eric gives me another look. An anxious one. And then he picks up his bag and sidles through the desks to the door. Ms. Harding pulls him out into the hall.

The door thunks closed. Mr. Gracie goes back to talking about coffee.

I slip my phone out under the desk and text Eric.

> What's going on?

But when the bell rings, he hasn't come back, and he hasn't replied. I grab my stuff and dodge through the desks ahead of everyone else.

I find Eric at his locker, stuffing books into his backpack. "What happened? Everything okay?"

"Um. No." He's trying to wrestle our enormous chemistry textbook into his backpack. The textbook is winning. "Nina's sick. I'm going to meet her and my dad at the hospital."

"At the hospital? What's wrong with her?" It's out of my mouth before I realize how blunt it sounds.

But Eric doesn't seem to notice. "Looks like pneumonia." He gives up and shoves the chemistry textbook back into his locker.

Pneumonia? Pneumonia is bad, isn't it? "Are you leaving now?"

"No, after last period." He gives me a tired smile. "It's happened before, Miles. She's more likely to get infections and stuff, especially in her lungs, because of her Down syndrome. She's always been fine, it just . . . freaks me out." He tugs his backpack zipper. "And freaks her out. She doesn't like hospitals."

I don't want to think about Nina in a hospital. "Do you think you have pneumonia?" (Maybe it's not a cold. Maybe it's something worse. Maybe . . .)

"I doubt it. I've never gotten it before." He nudges me gently with his shoulder. "I gotta get to class."

"Okay, but I'll see you before you leave school?"

"Yeah." He turns away.

"Should we meet somewhere?" I call after him. "Or I could text you?"

But he's already into the crowded hallway, looking anxiously at his phone, and he doesn't seem to hear me.

"Miles!"

Oh, for the love of . . . It's Shane, coming toward me, waving like he hasn't been ignoring me all day. Catching me off guard, which is all he seems to do these days.

"Hi, *friend.*" I turn and start heading toward the gym. I have just enough time to hit the bathroom before class, and with no PE this period, the men's room by the gym shouldn't be crowded.

"Hey. Wait!" Shane's annoyingly long legs carry him after me. "Look, I'm sorry. I know you're mad, but I wasn't sure where to start."

"With what?"

"With you," he says, like it's obvious.

"You have to figure out where to start with me?"

"With being friends—Look, Miles, can we just talk for a sec?"

"We talked yesterday, Shane. You said you wanted to be friends. I get it." Except I don't. All I feel is hurt, and that just pisses me off.

He groans. "I know I said that, but—"

"I have to go to the bathroom and get to class. Unless you want to come with me?"

He stops then.

Somehow this just makes me more annoyed. "Great. Whatever, Shane." I jog for the bathroom, to get away from him, and because otherwise I'm going to be late for class.

I usually really like Mr. Kashani, but today, English crawls by. Eric is in French, and Mr. Kashani's one shortcoming is that he's a real jerk about phones in class. He makes everyone sit in a circle to "promote discussion," and (let's be real) so he can catch anybody who dares to text. And if he catches you, you lose your phone for the day. The *whole* day.

I can't stop fidgeting. Chewing my nails. Thinking about Eric. Thinking about Nina. Thinking about Shane. Watching the clock over Mr. Kashani's head.

The bell rings.

Out comes the phone. No texts from Eric, so I text him as fast as I can, asking where he is and where I should meet him. Maybe I could offer to go to the hospital with him. Would his family think that's weird?

I'm still staring at my phone, hoping for a response, when I get out into the hallway.

Someone grabs my arm. "Aaaghh!"

"Miles! It's me!" Shane. Again. Lurking in a doorway this time and looking stressed.

"God, Shane, you can't just jump out at people."

"Can we please talk?"

"Now isn't really a good time—"

"*Please.*"

That brings me up short. I look up and meet his eyes. He's more than stressed. He looks confused. Anxious. Lost.

I know this look, too. I saw it before the last homecoming game against Hale High, our football team's archnemesis. I saw it when his grandma died last year.

It's important is what this look says.

I know I should ignore it. I know I should blow past him and go look for Eric. But if it's just a few minutes . . . "Okay. Fine. Let's talk."

"Not here."

"Shane—"

"Miles—somewhere else."

"Okay." (Think. *Think.*) "Let's go to the auditorium."

I grab his sleeve—that familiar, thick letter jacket sleeve—and pull him with me, pushing against the tide of people heading for the exit. Still scanning the crowd for Eric.

But I don't see him. And my phone hasn't buzzed in my pocket. Maybe he's late coming out of French. Or maybe he's texting his family and he hasn't had a chance to get back to me.

We reach the auditorium and I heave the door open. Propel Shane inside. The door creaks closed behind us.

Here we are again. Déjà vu.

I walk halfway down the aisle, and Shane follows me. When I turn to face him, we're close enough to the stage that the lights illuminate his face. "So." (Impatiently.) "What's so important?"

He steps forward, grasps my shoulders, leans down, and kisses me.

My brain hits the brakes so fast I forget to breathe.

Everything else vanishes.

Eric.

Nina.

Piano.

For a second, I'm just there with Shane. Falling back into a kiss that's so familiar, it's like the last several months never happened.

For a second, I might even be kissing him back. It's *Shane*.

And then, oh god, *it's Shane*. My brain switches back on with a gasp like I'm coming up for air after drowning and (*no no no*) I pull away, twisting out of his grasp. Heart hammering. Gulping for air like I really was drowning. What did I do? *Why did I do that?*

"I had to try," Shane says.

I stare at him.

Maybe I should say, *You had to try?*

Maybe I should say, *Are you kidding me?*

Maybe I should yell at him that I have Eric, and god *what have I just done to Eric . . .*

But Shane's shoulders have slumped and his whole face looks like gravity is dragging it down. He looks pathetic. And sad.

I let my breath out, rubbing my eyes under my glasses, and all I can manage is, "What are we doing?"

Shane retreats. Sinks down on the armrest of the nearest aisle seat. "I thought maybe you were right. I thought if I just tried harder, I'd feel like I used to, and we could go back to being . . ."

But he can't say it. He just hunches his shoulders until his whole chest caves, like he wants to disappear inside himself like a turtle.

"I meant it," he says. "When I said I miss you. I miss what we had. But I'm missing Melissa. I thought if I kissed you, maybe . . . but I realized I just wanted to kiss Melissa. Or—I'm sorry." He looks up. Anxious. Uncomfortable. "I didn't mean to say your old name, I just—"

"No. I get it." I get that he didn't really know who I was, underneath that *girl shell,* but when we were together, he told me I was awesome. And he meant it. And that's not nothing, I suppose.

"I'm really sorry, Miles," he says.

I shake my head. "No. It's . . . I wanted you to try, because I wanted to—I don't know—*change* you, so you'd realize what you were missing, and find me attractive again, or . . ." I pull off my glasses. They're fogging up. That chaotic tornado of feelings bursting free. "But that doesn't make any sense. I can't just stalk you like one day you'll wake up queer." My eyes keep filling up, but who am I even crying about at this point? "I just . . . I still liked you, so I thought you should like me anyway, and if I could just make you see that I'm really a guy but so what—"

"I know you're a guy." He looks desperate again. Frustrated, even. "I get it now. Really. It's totally cool—"

"I know, Shane, but you don't want to date me."

He's silent, then. We stare at each other. I know what he's going to say. He looks so sorry.

"No," he says. "I don't."

And it doesn't sting as much as I thought it would. Because I realize—finally realize—what I've been ignoring for a long time now: I don't want to date Shane, either. Somewhere along the way— maybe after Eric kissed me, maybe after he gave me his tie, or maybe some random day at school—I stopped loving Shane. All I've got now is some sort of empty fantasy that I held on to, because . . .

Well, because I just wanted one thing not to change.

I wipe my eyes on my sleeve. I need to find Eric.

"I'm sorry I want a girlfriend," Shane says.

I snort. "Yeah, woe is you, straight boy."

He looks pained. "I'm just trying to—"

"I know what you mean." I put my glasses back on. My eyes are clearing. "Seriously, though, if you like boobs, just be honest about it. We'll both be better off."

"Do you think you want to . . . I mean, are you thinking of . . ." He clears his throat.

"Ditching my boobs?"

"Transitioning."

It comes out stiff, but it comes out. I suddenly wonder how much late-night Googling Shane has been doing. Maybe more than I've been giving him credit for.

I think, for a minute, about pointing out that *transitioning* doesn't just mean what he thinks it means—hormones, surgery, all the stuff that's somehow supposed to make you a *real* trans person. Like you can't just *be,* without checking those boxes.

But now isn't the right time.

"Yeah," I say. "Eventually. I think so."

He takes a breath. Hesitates. "You looked good in your suit. At the prelims."

He sounds like he means it.

"Thanks."

"Now what?" he asks.

Now I need to go. I pick my bag up from the floor. "Well, we can try to be friends—if you want to."

"What does that even mean?"

"Hey, you're the one who asked to be friends."

"I know." He sighs. Runs a hand through his hair. "It's just . . . We weren't friends before I asked you out. So how do we even . . . ?"

"I don't know. I guess it'll take time—you can't just expect everything to immediately be rainbows and unicorns."

"I know. You're right."

My phone buzzes in my pocket. *Eric.* He's finally gotten back to me. What time is it? "Shane, I gotta go."

He blinks at me. "What?"

I fumble my phone out of my pocket. "I have to go meet Eric—"

"Is Eric your boyfriend?"

I look up at him. "Yeah." Wasn't that obvious?

"And he likes you for . . . or, I mean, he likes you as . . ."

I watch Shane, fumbling for words, and realize, then, that this is the difference. For Shane, doing his best, there is still *for* and *as*.

For who you are now.

As a guy.

But for Eric, there is no *liking for* or *liking as,* and there never has been.

There is just *liking.*

I don't have time to explain all of this to Shane right now. And I don't have time to answer his question. Because the text isn't from Eric. It's from Rachel.

> Hey, did Eric find u? He said Nina's sick.
> He was looking for u before he leaves.

Shit.

"Miles?" Shane says.

"Sorry. I have to go." I turn and run up the aisle, through the auditorium doors. The hallways are almost empty now. I jog past a knot of theater people on their way to the auditorium for rehearsal. Past Rusty Ziegler pulling his stash out of his locker to go smoke under the bleachers in peace.

Eric isn't at his locker. Or in the art room. Or at the bike rack.

Did he even bike? He said he was going to meet his dad at the hospital. Did he drive? I can't even remember.

My phone buzzes. I pull it out. Maybe it's Rachel, telling me where Eric is.

But it's not Rachel.
It's Eric.
And the text says:

You kissed him.

CHAPTER NINETEEN

When we were in middle school, Rachel, Paige, and I discovered the wonders of Google Translate. We all had Spanish together, and one day, Rachel came to school announcing that you could put Spanish words into the computer and make it say them. It wasn't really a helpful study tool, since we discovered pretty quickly that you could make the computer say English words, too.

Which meant, obviously, that Paige typed in *shit fuck boobs,* and we spent an entire afternoon laughing our heads off at the computer stiffly but cheerfully saying, "Shit, fuck, boobs" over and over.

It was so dorky and so middle school, but that's what pops into my head now. Because *shit* and *fuck* aren't enough to cover this situation, so why not throw *boobs* in?

I have to text Eric back. I have to make my hands stop shaking so I can text him back.

> What are you talking about?

Send. Regret immediately. *Why did I say that?* I don't know what he saw. Did he even see anything? Did someone else see something and tell him?

So I text:

> Did you leave already? Is Nina OK?

But I regret that, too.

> Nothing happened. Can u call me?

I don't know if that's right either, and he doesn't call me in the next five seconds, so I call him.

Voicemail.

How could Eric have seen me with Shane? How could *anyone* have seen me with Shane? We were alone in the auditorium. I would have heard the door open.

Except that the first time I met Eric in the auditorium, I totally blundered right past him, and didn't notice him at all until I'd already bombarded him with a bunch of Tchaikovsky. Because apparently when I'm wrapped up in my own ridiculous thoughts, I can just fail to notice another human who's right there.

And I was *kissing* Shane. I wasn't paying attention to anything else in the world.

What am I going to do?

"Miles?"

I turn around, stuffing my phone in my pocket. It's Shane, backpack slung over his shoulder, one of the high school doors slowly closing behind him. "You okay?" he asks.

No. I'm cold and I'm sweating. My heart is hammering so forcefully it's going to burst out of my chest. My stomach is tied in knots. No, I'm not okay.

But what do I tell Shane? "I, uh . . . I need to get home."

Which makes no sense. Going home isn't going to fix anything. Eric isn't going to be at my house. He's not going to suddenly pick up his phone just because I'm at my house. For all he knows, I could still be in the auditorium making out with Shane.

No.

Things will be better if I go home. I *have* to go home because I sure can't go back into that auditorium where I was kissing Shane . . .

Shane pulls his car keys out of his pocket. "I can give you a ride." He points vaguely to the parking lot, where his old white pickup is sitting, irritatingly perfect bumper dent glinting in the afternoon sun.

Great. Seems about right for the alternate dimension I've been dropped into. A ride from the ex-boyfriend I just accidentally kissed, so I can get home and try to call (again) the current boyfriend I just epically hurt.

But I don't know what else to do. "Sure. Thanks."

The truck smells like pine trees, just like it always has. Yellow foam protrudes from the seats like fungus. The gearshift grinds when Shane moves it. The fuzzy stuffed football dangling from the rearview mirror swings gently.

It's all so familiar. But there's no warm rush this time—I just feel sick.

I pull out my phone and text Rachel:

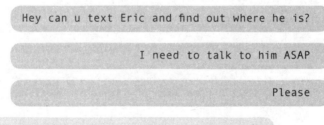

Hey can u text Eric and find out where he is?

I need to talk to him ASAP

Please

what's wrong?

I try to reply, but everything I type is wrong. Backspace, backspace, backspace. Delete everything without sending.

Turn my phone over, facedown, on my knee.

Outside, budding trees flash by. The crocuses are out—patches of purple and orange and white—and now the trees are waking up, too. Took long enough, but spring finally showed up.

My phone buzzes. I turn it over quickly. It's Rachel.

Miles?

Buzz.

What happened?

Buzz.

Is Eric ok?

Shane glances at my knee.

"Sorry," I say. "Just Rachel."

I turn the phone back over.

As soon as we turn onto my street, I grab the door lever, ready to bolt, but Shane pulls all the way into my driveway. Puts the truck in park. Turns off the engine. Like he thinks we're going to have a conversation now.

I don't want a conversation. I open the door. Slide out of my seat and down to the ground. *Get out of here.*

"Miles. Wait."

I turn around.

Shane's forehead is creased. "Did something happen?"

Yes. You ruined my life. Again. That's not fair, and I know it, but I think it anyway.

"It's fine, Shane. I just fucked something up and I have to go."

"Are we still friends?"

"Yeah." (Of all the times to ask.) "We're still friends. See you later." I slam the door and walk to my house as slowly as I can stand to.

The truck starts behind me. I can hear the grind of the gearshift from here. The engine rattles as he backs down the driveway. But I don't turn around.

I pull out my phone and call Eric.

Please pick up, please pick up.

He picks up. "Miles, I can't talk right now." His voice is low. Flat.

"Eric, just really quick—"

"Can you please leave me alone?"

My stomach knots all over again. "No! I mean, yes, I can, but just—I just need to explain for a second—"

"I'm at the hospital, Miles!" His voice breaks. I've never heard him like this before. "Nina is sick and I'm trying to be here with her and my family and not think about anything else—"

"Is she okay?"

"You're really asking me that right now? I just told you everything that happened with my ex. And then you kissed *Shane.*"

He sounds so hurt that I can't think of anything to say. There *isn't* anything to say, except, "How do you know?"

Which isn't the right thing. I know that as soon as I say it.

"I guess I should be grateful you aren't denying it." Now he sounds bitter. His voice is so cold it could freeze my ear off. "Honesty is worth something, right?"

"Eric, it was an *accident.* Shane was trying to—"

"Miles, I can't talk about this right now. Please leave me alone, okay? My sister is sick and I seem to have terrible taste in people that I fall in love with—"

My breath catches. "Fall in love with?"

Bitter again. "Well, I don't know what you thought we were doing . . ."

My head is spinning, because *falling in love with.* "Shane was trying to figure things out. We were figuring out that we *didn't* want to be together. That's what that kiss was. That's what he needed—"

"What *he* needed?" Eric sounds incredulous.

"Did you hear me? We figured out we *didn't* want to be together. Both of us."

Silence. I hold my breath.

But all Eric says, his voice flat again, is, "I have to go."

No. *No, no, no.* "Eric—"

"Miles"—his voice shakes—"I'm sorry, but I really can't do this right now. I can't do this again."

And he hangs up.

I go into my room.

I shut my door.

And I sit down on my bed, hands on the rumpled mounds of blankets on either side of me. I didn't make my bed today.

Why why why why why.

Why did I let Shane kiss me?

Why did I kiss him back?

Why did I stalk him and stare at him and spend all that time planning conversations we'd never have?

Why did I make that pointless, shallow-as-shit New Year's resolution in the first place? And why did it take all of this for me to let it go? Who do I think I am?

I rub my sweaty palms on my knees. Wish my saggy old mattress would swallow me up.

Who do I think I am?

I thought I knew the answer to that. Or at least, I thought I was getting closer. *I'm Miles. I'm trans. I'm a pianist.* It's what Stefania has been harping on for months: *Who are you? What are you doing?*

But this isn't girl hips that won't fit into boy pants. This isn't girl boobs that won't fit into boy shirts. This isn't about feeling like I'm put together with leftover pieces that didn't fit anywhere else.

I don't know who I am because I never realized I was that person who could kiss his ex and hurt someone he cared about.

Because even if I feel like I look all wrong half the time, Eric never seemed to think so. I still don't know what he saw when he looked at me, but he liked me. Which means, in a weird way, I was right, after all. Love can transcend short hair and clothes and pronouns and see who you really are.

And take your word for it.

And just love *you*.

My phone buzzes on the bed next to me. Rachel.

But I can't. Not right now.

I pick up my phone and text Mom to tell her I'm home and she doesn't need to pick me up. And then I do something that I haven't done since—I don't know, I got my phone?

I turn it off. Set it on my nightstand, shoving it between an empty tissue box and my alarm clock. There. Now I can't text Eric or call him. I can't do any more damage.

I lie down on my bed. Stare up at my popcorn ceiling.

It's so obvious and shallow and cliché, but it's true: Now that I've royally screwed everything up, I realize just how much I like Eric.

No, not like.

Love.

Not just in a stomach-flip way. Not just in a will-you-be-my-Valentine's-Night-date way.

In the watching-*Cinderella*-on-the-couch way. In the I-don't-know-how-I'll-go-back-to-practicing-alone-in-the-auditorium way. In the I-don't-care-if-you-touch-my-binder way.

In a safe, comfortable way I didn't even know I could love until now. It goes way beyond anything I ever felt, or thought I felt, with Shane. It's a different kind of familiar. The kind that's not so much about what you *had* as about what you know will always be there. It's low-key and profound, all at the same time.

My eyes fill up and tears run toward my ears. I can't breathe. There's a big block of iron sitting on my lungs.

Fuck Eric—he's being judgy and unfair and jumping to conclusions—and also *I really love him.*

Someone is knocking on my door.

My eyes are sticky. It takes me several blinks to really get them open. I'm curled up on my bed, and it's dark—the sun has gone down. Dusk is settling in outside my window.

I sit up and rub my eyes. "Yeah?"

The door creaks open. I fumble for my glasses.

Mom is standing in the doorway, backlit by the ceiling light in the hallway. "Your phone is off."

"Yeah. Sorry." (What time is it?) "I just needed to turn it off for a while."

"How'd you get home?"

I squint at my alarm clock. Six thirty. "Shane gave me a ride from school."

Mom is still wearing her pinstriped business suit—the new one she took to Stefania's tailor last week to get the pants hemmed. She came home talking about what a warm-hearted, funny woman Yula is. I wonder if we met the same Yula.

"Miles, are you okay?" Mom asks.

(No. But you wouldn't understand.)

"Do you want to talk?" she asks.

(How am I supposed to talk, when you'll just say this never would have happened if I could just be *straight* and date girls?)

But it pours out of me before I can stop myself. "I really fucked up, Mom, and I blew it with Eric and I don't know if he'll ever forgive me."

For a moment, she's frozen. Hand on the doorknob. Eyebrows raised. Like she turned to stone. And then the moment is gone. "Oh, honey." She closes the door behind her and sits down next to me in the dark, arms reaching out, wrapping around me . . .

I sob. Tears, snot, puffy eyes. It's ridiculous, and raw, and ugly, and I can't help it. I never want her to let go.

I don't know how many minutes pass. But eventually, I run out of steam. Eventually, I can breathe again. I can see again. All I'm left with is a pounding headache.

Mom says, "What happened?"

And I tell her. Everything. My New Year's resolutions. Shane ignoring me. Eric in the auditorium. Valentine's Night, and calling Shane, and talking to Shane. Nina's pneumonia. The bad-decision kiss and the texts and the *leave me alone.*

She rubs my back, gently, until I run out of things to say. And then, quietly, she says, "You really like Eric."

It's not a question, but I say, "Yeah."

"You turned your phone off so you wouldn't call him."

"Or text him. Yeah." I brace myself. *Here it comes.*

"Miles," she says, "I think we're more similar than you realize."

I'm sorry, what? "I hate to tell you, Mom, but I don't think the lake is that big of a draw."

She smiles. "Har-har. I meant that I think we both try to change people. You wanted to change Shane, so the two of you could go back to dating. And I . . . I wanted to change you."

In the dim room, shadows settle into the lines on her face. The last bit of light outside finds the gray threads in her hair. I didn't remember she had so many gray threads. When did she get them?

"You might have noticed that I felt . . . *uncomfortable* with the idea of you dating boys." (You don't say.) "The truth is . . ." The shadows move across her face as she frowns. "The truth is that I just didn't want your life to be harder. You're trans, and I know it's not the same as it was even five or ten years ago. There's so much online, and so many people and organizations out there . . . But, Miles, when you came out, you were suddenly so much more comfortable, like you'd found something you'd been looking for, and that was so great. It made me so happy to see you like that. But I still worry. And I thought if you were *straight*—transgender people can be straight, I read that—then you would have a slightly easier life. Being trans is already so much. People might say things or do things. Men can be— They can feel threatened. They can be threatening."

She sighs. She looks helpless. I've never seen Mom look helpless.

"I thought maybe you would experiment with your sexuality, too, since you'd just come out. And maybe if you liked girls, then down the road, it would be easier for you."

Oh. "Because I could be a straight man."

She looks sorry. As sorry as Shane. "I just didn't want you to make up your mind too quickly. You can be stubborn."

"I wasn't being stubborn, Mom. I just like boys."

"I know." She nods. "I get that now. I'm trying to say that I tried to change you, or hoped I could change you, and that was about me, not you. It was about my fear for you— not about who you are."

Well, that's not how it felt.

But I know what she means.

"I love you, Miles. I just want you to be safe."

"I know." I take a deep breath. "But I can't not be me, just because it might make life easier. It won't be easier. Not for me."

She nods again. "Yeah. I know."

It's getting darker. I can barely see the gray in her hair now.

"What am I supposed to do?" I feel like a little kid, asking it. But I guess that's the thing about parents—maybe you never grow out of hoping they can fix it for you.

She leans over and kisses my head. "I don't know," she says. "Maybe don't try to change people so much. That's what I'm trying to do." She pushes herself off the bed. "I brought home Chinese food. Dad's not home yet, so we could eat out of containers and watch *Home Habitats* judgment-free, if you want."

"*Reno or Demo*," I say. "And you can't say anything about marble countertops."

She sighs dramatically. "Fine. I'm going to change. See you downstairs."

"Okay. I'll be down in a minute."

She smiles and closes the door behind her.

CHAPTER TWENTY

Day One Without Eric is pretty literal: he doesn't come to school. Rachel and Paige and I sit and stare at his empty seat in homeroom.

"He hasn't responded to my texts," Rachel whispers.

"I saw him leave in kind of a hurry after school yesterday," Paige whispers.

And they look at me. But I don't say anything.

Until lunch. Then I tell them.

"*Dude,*" says Paige. She's giving me a strange look, like she wants to ask something and keeps thinking better of it.

Rachel is settling into Judgy Face, which means I better say something now before she gets going. "It was . . . a bad call, okay? A mistake. Shane's not into me anymore and I'm not into him. It felt like we had to kiss, to make sure, and now we're done."

"You have a *boyfriend*," Rachel says.

"I know!"

"You can't just lead him on if you want something to happen with Shane—"

"I'm *not* and I *don't*." I let my breath out, and everything inside me sinks down to my knees. "And it doesn't matter anyway, because I'm not sure I have a boyfriend anymore."

"Did Eric say he wanted to break up?"

"He said he wanted me to leave him alone."

Rachel looks thoughtful—so thoughtful I half expect her to

start stroking her chin. "That's not great news, but it's not the end of the world."

(Oh, no.) "Rache—"

"You should get him flowers—"

(I definitely should not.) "Flowers aren't going to fix this."

Rachel looks frustrated. "Have you explained? Have you told him? I mean, like, *really* told him how you feel? Really told him what happened with Shane was a mistake? I just feel like you should have the chance to explain."

(Yeah, so do I, but look where that's gotten me so far.) "I don't know, Rache." I can't argue this with her right now. "Maybe."

Rachel sighs. Like she's given up. "Whatever, Miles. You do you. For the record, I'm also mad you kissed Shane."

I rub my eyes. "I know."

"I could try to text Eric," Rachel says. "Or Paige could."

Paige stands up suddenly. "I have to go. Josie and I are still finishing up that project."

Rachel blinks at her. "We're *talking* here. And I thought you handed it in yesterday."

"No."

They stare awkwardly at each other, and then Rachel shrugs. "Fine. Whatever."

Paige turns and leaves without a word.

I look at Rachel. "Are you guys okay?"

"I don't know," she says.

Paige gives me a ride home after school, but she seems distracted the whole drive, chewing her lip and tapping her fingers on the wheel while WUPT plays in the background. And I'm distracted, too. Staring at my phone, which I had to turn on again, obviously. What if Eric called? Sure, it's unlikely, but not impossible.

But he hasn't called. Or texted. I open Instagram. He hasn't posted anything new, but he's still following me. That's worth something, right?

Unless Nina is so sick that he hasn't had time to unfollow me.

Maybe that's why he didn't come to school. Maybe Nina's so sick that he hasn't left the hospital.

I stuff my phone back in my pocket as Paige pulls into my driveway. "See you tomorrow."

"Yeah." But she's already putting the car in reverse, glancing over her shoulder.

And now I'm alone in my driveway, listening to a car rumble away, and it's like yesterday all over again. All I want to do is call Eric. Just to ask where he is. Just to make sure everything is okay.

And yeah, I want to explain. Maybe Rachel's right. Maybe if I could just explain, *really* explain . . .

Except he's not going to pick up his phone. I know he's not. He told me to leave him alone.

A damp, chilly breeze blows my hair into my eyes.

Fuck it.

I open the garage. My old bicycle is still in a back corner. I haven't ridden it in years. I yank it free of cobwebs and wheel it out. The whole thing is covered in layers of gray dust, but I don't care about that either. The tires are low, but they aren't flat, and that's what matters.

I sling my bag over my shoulder, throw a leg over the bike, and pedal out of my driveway.

The sun sinks lower in the sky, throwing long shadows behind me. Wind whistles in my ears and makes my eyes water. I should have grabbed a warmer jacket. I'm freezing now. My hands are turning white on the handlebars.

Down the quiet streets, turning away from the high school, pedaling over the freight train tracks. Down the hill and past the smaller houses and yards where the grass is only just turning green.

Eric's old Subaru is parked in his driveway. The porch light is on, casting a soft yellow glow over the front door of the house.

I hit the brakes. Tires skid. I drop the bike on the grass and dodge around it. Up to the porch. Ring the bell.

I hear it echo, inside the house. A muted, distant *ping-pong*.

And then silence. No voices. No footsteps. Maybe nobody's home. His family could have another car. His mom must have a car, right? Maybe they're all off in that car . . .

Click. A lock turns—I hear it—and the door opens. Just barely. Just enough for Eric to stick his head out.

My knees go weak. "Hi."

"Miles." Behind his glasses, his eyes are puffy. His hair is rumpled. "I asked you to leave me alone."

"I know. I know! But I just . . . you weren't in school today, and then Paige was driving me home, and I couldn't stop thinking about you and I got worried about Nina, so here I am. I know you're upset, and I get it, but it was a mistake. I really miss you. I need you, Eric. You're amazing and funny and I've never met anyone who understood all my practicing like you do. I honestly don't think I can do this competition without you."

He opens the door wider and slips out onto the porch, pulling the sleeves of his ratty blue sweatshirt over his hands. "All of that was about you," he says.

"What?"

"I asked you to give me space, and instead you show up here saying you need me in order to get through your competition. That doesn't have anything to do with me."

"I said I was worried about Nina—"

"Nina's fine. She has pneumonia but she's fine." He rubs his eyes, pushing his glasses up on his forehead.

"Is she home yet? Is she feeling better?"

"Miles—"

"When you weren't in school, I thought maybe something happened—"

"Something *did* happen. I needed space. That's why I wasn't in school." He drops his hands. His glasses land back on his nose, and now I realize why his eyes look so puffy. It's because he's been crying. And he's crying now.

"Miles." He blinks, but all that does is send tears down his face. "I told you what happened after my last breakup."

"Yeah. Your ex was a real jerk."

"And told everybody—"

"Eric, I know, but that doesn't have anything to do with us—"

"It has to do with *me*." His voice breaks. He takes a step backward, like he surprised himself, and runs into the door behind him. "Miles, I don't tell everybody what happened with my ex. You were the first person I told since we moved here. I told you because I trusted you. I thought you would understand."

It's like he punched me in the gut. "I *do* understand—"

"No, you don't. On the day I'm sick, and I have to leave because Nina's sick, you kiss Shane. That mattered more to you than I did."

"It didn't. It didn't matter more to me." (You're full of shit, Miles. It *did* matter. In that moment, it mattered a lot, or I would have blown Shane off. I would have said he could wait.)

"Well." Eric folds his arms. Hunches his shoulders like he's cold. "It made me feel like you were using me until someone better came along—or until you could get Shane back." He shakes his head. Takes a slow breath. "When we moved here, I was finally ready to start over and make new friends, but what Jocelyn did . . . I thought you'd get it, after that forum post about you. Jocelyn said this thing to make herself feel better, but then she kept saying it, because the more she said it, the bigger it got, and the more people paid attention to her, and . . . I guess she got something out of that. Maybe it wasn't even really about whether I was gay or straight or anything else. It was about me being creepy and perverted somehow. Like I might steal girls' clothes out of the locker room. That's how she said it, and she didn't spend any time thinking about the fact that I'm brown, and that just . . . that makes it even worse. She didn't spend any time thinking about how maybe people already assume I'm going to steal something, and now she's made me perverted on top of that. That's how people looked at me. For months."

Oh, god.

That's awful.

"I was excited to move because I thought I could just start over and finally nobody would know me, or know this thing that happened, but now . . ." He shrugs one shoulder. "I didn't mean to start liking you as much as I did, Miles. But then I did—and now I just feel like I shouldn't have trusted you either. I somehow keep picking the wrong people to trust."

Now my eyes are filling up. I look down because I don't want him to see that I'm about to cry. Don't want him to see how ashamed I feel.

And I notice that the bottoms of his jeans are rolled up, and he's wearing rainbow socks.

The socks seem familiar, but it takes me a minute to figure out why.

"You're wearing . . ." I point to them.

"Yeah." He wipes his eyes. "I felt like it."

So he kept his rainbow socks. The socks he used to wear, when he dressed a little different. After everything Jocelyn said—after she told him he was too gay, after she spread horrible, fake rumors about him—he kept the socks.

Which means he hasn't changed—not completely. He didn't give up the pieces of himself that Jocelyn didn't like. He held them even closer. So close that most people couldn't see them—didn't get to see them—but he kept them, the pieces of himself that he knew were right. He believed in them.

And that's the opposite of changing for someone else. And it's not changing someone else for you, either.

It's finding yourself in spite of everyone else.

"I really like them," I say. "Your socks."

He manages a small smile. But it looks like a courtesy. "Thanks."

I'm blinking furiously, trying to keep my eyes clear.

Don't cry.

It's slowly sinking in—not just what he said, but what he didn't say. That someone posting horrible shit about you online is awful, but it's not the same as people saying it to your face. It's not the same as everyone whispering wherever you go. It's not the same as someone you trusted taking a piece of you—a vulnerable piece—and twisting it into a weapon to hurt you with, until you feel so wrong in your own skin that you just keep hurting yourself.

I walk around school every day and people leave me alone. Rachel and Paige guard the bathroom for me. My ex-boyfriend calls me by the right name now. So do my teachers, most of the time. They're getting better.

It's a low bar—a really low bar—and it doesn't take away my fear.

But it does make me feel less alone.

"I made this New Year's resolution." *Don't cry.* "Before I met you. It was about piano, and the competition, and Shane. I should've abandoned the Shane part ages ago. But he was my first boyfriend, and I just hung on to that." My voice is getting shaky. "I'm not trying to justify what happened, I just . . . I had to explain. That's why I made the mistake. I'm kind of slow, I guess, at figuring things out."

He nods, but he doesn't say anything.

So I nod, too. And I realize—that's it. "Okay. I'll just . . . go."

He nods again. Still silent.

So I turn. Pick up my bike. Wheel it slowly down the driveway, hoping I'll hear his voice behind me. Hoping he'll give me a reason to turn back.

But when I reach the street, and finally turn to look, Eric has already shut the door.

CHAPTER TWENTY-ONE

Y ou did the right thing," Rachel says, when I tell her and Paige
    what happened the next morning. It's raining again, and the
hallway is a cacophony of squeaky shoes.

"Yeah." Paige stuffs her raincoat into her locker. "Sorry it didn't
fix anything."

We squeak into homeroom, and there's Eric. My heart leaps,
because he's back, and sinks just as quickly. He's sitting by himself,
at the back of the room, drawing in a notebook.

He sits by himself at lunch, too.

And I sit alone in the auditorium after school, wondering how
I'm supposed to channel joy when I just feel empty.

I'm on autopilot when I walk to Stefania's house for my next
lesson. It takes me several seconds to even realize I'm standing on
Stefania's porch, staring at her front door.

I knock, Stefania opens the door, and then I'm suddenly sitting
at her piano, playing through Tchaikovsky. Fingers moving while
my brain just thinks about Eric. Half-assed crescendos. Phrases
that sound robotic.

"Stop!" Stefania shouts.

I jump. She's glowering at me. I have a feeling she's been telling
me to stop for a while, and I only just heard her.

"Where is Miles today?" she barks. "Who's this on my piano
bench?"

"Sorry. I'm distracted."

"Yes, that much is obvious." She narrows her eyes. "*Why* are we distracted today?"

I don't want to talk about this. "No reason."

She raises an eyebrow. "Bullshit."

Now I'm annoyed. Mrs. Kim never asked about my personal life. The only time we talked about anything besides piano was the Coming Out. Even that was brief.

ME: So . . . I'm trans. I'm using the name Miles and he/him pronouns now.

HER: Does your mother know?

ME: Yeah.

HER: Okay, then. Miles needs to practice this Chopin more.

But I won't get out of answering Stefania. She'll just sit there in glaring silence until I cave. "I broke up with my boyfriend. Maybe. I don't know."

Stefania nods slowly. "Your boyfriend is . . . ?"

"Eric." My stomach twists. "You met him in the auditorium that one time."

"Ah. Reindeer-hat-man. I liked him." (Well, that's just great, Stefania. I feel so much better.) "So, what happened?"

I stare stubbornly at the page of music in front of me. "I made a mistake. Fucked something up." No way in hell I'm telling Stefania what I did. "Eric got mad at me."

"And then he broke up with you."

"No. It's unclear."

"You broke up with him."

"No!" Why is she pushing this? "I don't know if we broke up."

She nods again. "And this is what you're thinking about instead of Tchaikovsky."

Here comes the judgment. "I know, okay? Sorry."

But she just shrugs. "Everything out there"—she waves a hand at the window next to her—"impacts what goes on in here." She waves her hand at the piano. "Playing music is about what's in your head, not just your hands." Now she gives me a judgy look. "I thought you'd learned that by now."

I feel annoyed again. "Well, I'm not going to get anything done if I can't concentrate on Tchaikovsky."

She sips her coffee. "So how is the current state of Miles going to impact Tchaikovsky?"

"What? It's not. I'm just going to keep going."

"I see. Denial."

"It's not denial!" The annoyance shifts into anger. "I don't have time for denial. The competition is in, like, a month! The last thing I need on top of everything else is for Cameron to beat me again. Then it'll all have been for nothing."

"What will?"

"Everything!" My voice cracks in panic. "Breaking up with Shane, changing piano teachers, coming out, all the jackass forum posts, everything with Eric—"

"What forum posts?"

Shit. "Nothing." Try to shrug. "Just some jerks on the competition website's forum saying ignorant shit about me."

"What kind of ignorant shit?"

"I don't want to talk about it. It doesn't matter anyway. All that matters is the competition."

Stefania sets her mug down on the windowsill with a solid *clunk*. "Miles, when you started studying with me, I told you all I cared about was whether you were willing to work. Remember? And I told you to think about *why* you want to play the piano, and what this particular concerto means to you."

"Yeah, I know." Glower. "I remember."

She leans forward in her chair and says fiercely, "Competitions don't mean *jack shit*. You want to beat Cameron, and I'd love for you to beat Cameron, but at the end of the day, it's a single performance that a bunch of random people will have completely subjective opinions about. They'll turn those subjective opinions into some sort of score and then they'll pick a winner."

Anger flares back up. "Yeah, I know how this works—"

She holds up a finger. "Yes, they give you money. Yes, it looks good on a résumé, and yes, it has some meaning, to you, to everyone else. All these things are true. But if you win, it doesn't mean you're the best pianist. If you lose, it doesn't mean you're not a *brilliant* pianist. It's *just one performance*. Do you understand?"

"Okay, fine, I get it!" I'm shouting now. "Competitions are pointless and I'm not gonna win anyway, so I should stop caring."

"Why do you think you won't win?"

"Because the judges hate you!"

She stares at me. The room is silent, except for the faint ring of piano strings, echoing my voice.

It slipped right out of my mouth. Too long sitting in my brain, like a pot boiling on the stove until it finally boiled over.

"Excuse me?" Stefania says quietly.

Stop, stop, stop. "Cameron said the judges hate you. Is that why you're telling me competitions don't mean anything? Because I won't win because they don't like you?"

She leans away from me. Abruptly stands up. "That's enough for today. You need a break."

"What?"

Her blue eyes are icy. "I'll see you next week."

There's nothing for me to do except stand up, gather up my music, and leave. She clomps ahead of me. Opens the front door. Says nothing else. Closes the door behind me.

And then I'm alone on her front porch. Heart pounding. Palms sweating. The cool air burning my throat.

I want to scream. At her. At myself. At how pathetic and reckless that was. At how I don't care.

Because I *don't.*

I start walking home, fast. So fast that I almost trip over my own feet and faceplant in the sidewalk, twice. But at least it means that I'm far away from Stefania's house by the time I start to cry.

It's not like I had a lot of free time Before Eric, but now it feels like that's all I have, and all of it moves at a snail's pace. I text Rachel to distract myself, and she texts me back about a petition campaign she wants to start for more plant-based food options in the cafeteria. I sort of wonder where Paige is and why Rachel's not texting both of us, but at least it fills some time. I let Rachel fill up the silences at our lunch table, too, since all Paige seems to do these days is stare off into space or noodle around on her phone.

And all I seem to do is look for Eric—in homeroom, in the cafeteria, in the hallway. But whenever I see him, he's never looking at me.

I wait all of Week Two Without Eric for Stefania to call my parents and tell them she's dumping me as a student. But she doesn't, which means I have to show up at her house on Thursday afternoon like everything is normal. I'm figuring she either wants to dump me in person, or kick my ass.

Olga barks like she always does, but Stefania is silent when she opens the door. And silent as we walk back to the piano room. She sits down in her chair, picks up her coffee, and says, "B-flat major scale, please."

It's stiff. Formal. Like she doesn't know me at all. Or she's a robot.

That's how she is the whole lesson. Everything blunt and short and flat.

And it's so much worse. By the end of the lesson, I'm wishing she'd yell at me. Tell me to throw in the towel and give up on the competition. I wouldn't even blame her. I'm playing terribly.

I'm still thinking about it at lunch the next day when Rachel shoves a notebook across the table. "What do you think of *Plant-Based Is Planet-Based*?"

"What?"

"For the campaign." She points at the notebook. "We need a good slogan."

We seems like a bit of a stretch, especially since it's just me and Rachel at the table. Paige is off somewhere with Josie Leyman, working on their chemistry project.

I study the notebook page. "Well, it's better than *Meat Sex, Eat Plants*."

She hastily scribbles that one out. "It's Meat *Sux,* with an 'X.' You know, like tux."

"Why?"

"Because it looks cooler— Oh, never mind." She snatches the notebook back.

I glance at my phone. Partly to see the time, partly hoping (again) that maybe Eric texted. He hasn't. "Is Paige coming or what? She's gonna run out of time to eat."

Rachel lets out a frustrated grunt. "This chemistry project is taking over her life. I *told* Paige she should have taken AP Chemistry with me. Then *we* could be partners on projects, and she wouldn't have to put up with some track team bimbo."

"Oh, come on, Rache, *bimbo*'s a little harsh." I turn around and glance at Sophie's table. Debate Daniel, AP Julian, and Harvard Hanna are all there, but no Josie. "Is something still going on with you guys?"

"The *same* thing is still going on," Rachel mutters. "Now Paige doesn't even want to kiss me. What am I doing wrong?"

Across the cafeteria, Shane catches my eye and waves. I slide down in my seat. Pretend not to see him.

Rachel glares at me. "You're the one who asked! Don't try to hide now!" She throws down her pencil. "Where the *hell* is Paige?"

Paige misses lunch entirely. She catches up with us in the hall-way, looking frazzled. "Sorry. This project is taking way longer than I thought it would."

"No shit." Rachel gives Paige a look that could wither a cactus and hands her an apple she saved from lunch. "You're welcome."

Paige looks sheepish. "I still have more work to do after last period."

"Of course you do," Rachel says.

Which means that it's just me and Rachel, after last period, jumping puddles in the parking lot to get to her car. I'm planning to use the next hour to practice in the auditorium, surrounded by half-painted set pieces, before the musical takes over—but Rachel looked so lonely, slowly putting her books in her locker, that I said I'd walk out with her first.

"I really want to do this plant-based campaign," Rachel says, climbing into her car. "Do you think your mom would let me use her copier to make flyers?"

"Probably. I can ask her."

"We'll have a copying party this weekend! I'll bring snacks." She drives away waving a hand out the window.

I wander slowly back to the school, hands in my pockets, dodg-ing around the last few stragglers heading for the parking lot. I wish I hadn't told Mom that I was going to stay and practice. Now I'm stuck with it.

I glance at the bike rack, looking for Eric's bike, because I can't help it.

The rack is empty. But past the bike rack is a giant lilac bush, just beginning to flower, and half hidden, talking to someone who must be completely behind the bush, is Paige.

Maybe I can ask her to give me a ride home. I skip around the bike rack and stop, like I've run into a brick wall, because next to the lilac bush, Paige is leaning forward and closing her eyes—*and kissing Josie Leyman.*

Oh, *no.*

Paige can't be kissing Josie Leyman. Not blond-braid, track-team-sweatshirt, pink-running-shoes Josie Leyman. Not I-post-cute-cat-videos-and-sit-with-Sophie *Josie Leyman.*

But she is. Kissing her. Like slow-motion, end-of-the-movie kissing her.

Get out of here, Miles.

Too late. They lean away from each other, open their eyes, and Josie sees me. Her eyebrows go up, and Paige turns around . . .

Right. Time to run.

"Miles!"

No. Not getting involved. The auditorium suddenly doesn't sound so bad.

"Miles, wait!" My power-walking is no match for Paige, even in her big Doc Martens. She gets ahead of me and blocks the auditorium doors. "Miles, please. Can I talk to you?"

Well, I can't exactly go anywhere else now, can I? It's not like I can just turn around and run away again, although it's really tempting.

Paige just stares at me. Either she's waiting for me to argue, or she hasn't thought of what to say next.

I say the obvious. "Does Rachel know?"

Paige's face crumples. She folds in on herself like I gut-punched her. "No."

"What are you doing?"

"I don't know."

This is going nowhere. I reach past her for the auditorium door handle.

"No, wait." She grabs my sleeve. "Miles, I don't know what to do."

(*Why* did my two best friends have to start dating?) "That's not my problem."

"But I need you to tell me what to do!"

"Seriously? Maybe try not cheating on Rachel."

"I'm *not* cheating on—" She stops. Covers her eyes with her hands. "Miles, please. I'm so confused."

I've never seen Paige like this. She looks . . . fragile. So fragile that I can't be as mad as I want to be. I mean, we're basically in the same boat. "Okay, fine. Come on." I pull open the auditorium door and push her inside. "What happened?"

The door slowly closes behind us. Paige leans against it and slides down to the floor. "Nothing happened. That's what sucks."

I set down my bag. Sit down next to her.

"Everything with me and Rachel is great. Or should be great. She thinks it's great."

She definitely does not. But now doesn't seem like a great time to point that out. "You don't think it's great."

Paige looks like she might actually cry, which I've never seen her do. Not even when she got in a fistfight with Brandon Gibson in seventh grade because he called Rachel fat.

"I like Rachel," Paige says, voice low. "I really do. I mean, of *course* I do—she's been my friend for . . ." She doesn't seem up for the math. "When I came out, Rachel was so supportive."

(So was I.)

"Because my parents just . . . I mean, you know my mom. They didn't get it at first."

That's news to me. "They didn't?"

"No." Paige looks at me like this was obvious. "It's a phase, I should dress girlier to fix it, have I tried dating boys . . . you know. I mean, you came out to my mom."

"Yeah, but she didn't really say anything. She just sort of went with it."

Paige frowns. "Oh. Maybe it's different because you aren't *family*. She can't try to control your every move."

How did I not know any of this? Did Paige tell me and I forgot? Or did Paige just not tell me?

I'm not sure which is worse.

"Anyway, dating Rachel just made sense." Paige rubs her

forehead. "We were already friends. We both like girls. We both *are* girls."

"Okay." *This isn't about you, Miles.* "So if you like Rachel, why were you just making out with Josie Leyman?"

"Because *it doesn't make sense.*"

"You lost me."

"It doesn't make sense! It's not sensible or convenient. But when I kiss Josie—I don't know—I *feel.* Like the world stops spinning and time stands still." She looks at me, desperately. "I *know* it sounds cheesy. But I never felt like that with Rachel."

Oh. "So, you don't love Rachel. Or you're not *in* love with her."

Paige leans over her knees and bursts into tears, and whatever anger I had left evaporates. All I feel is terrible. For Paige. For Rachel. For the ways they kind of match up but don't fit together. For the way they have feelings that they never meant to use to hurt someone—and yet here we are.

Boy, do I know how *that* feels.

"Okay." *Think.* "What are we going to do about Rachel?"

Paige looks up, face red and tear-stained. "What?"

"You got me involved, Paige. Now I have to help you."

"Sorry," she mumbles.

"To be clear, *you're* the one that actually has to do something."

Paige digs her fingers into her short hair. "Maybe I don't. Maybe I shouldn't."

"Right, so you'll just keep sneaking around with Josie?"

"We weren't sneaking!" But she looks guilty immediately. "Okay, fine. We were. But we only made out a couple of times."

I'm starting to think the chemistry project has been finished for a while. "Paige, you're cheating on Rachel."

"Rachel says monogamy is a patriarchal power structure meant to—"

"I know, but Rachel also thinks she's in a monogamous relationship."

Paige looks thoughtful. "Maybe we could try an open relationship."

"Do you actually even want that?"

"No." She shakes her head. "You're right. That wouldn't be fair to Rachel. I just—I want to be her friend. I want to be your friend."

She could have thought of that before kissing Josie Leyman. Or before dating Rachel in the first place.

But that's not fair, and I know it. After everything *I've* done, I really know it.

"Paige, you'll still be my friend."

"But you were Rachel's friend first."

Oh, come *on*. "Look, I'll still be your friend, okay? But you have to tell Rachel. And you have to tell her your feelings, not just that you kissed Josie."

Paige sighs. "Yeah. I know." She wipes her eyes on her sleeve and looks at me sideways. "You're kind of wise, Miles."

What a laugh that is. "Paige."

"Yeah, yeah." She takes a deep breath. "I'll tell Rachel."

Rachel calls me just after eight, when I'm sitting in my room, trying to write an essay on memorials of World War I and streaming the classical radio station from Chicago on my laptop.

I know why she's calling before she even says anything, because Rachel is a texter, not a caller.

"Paige broke up with me."

Her voice is thick and low. She's been crying. I know because Rachel, unlike Paige, has cried dozens of times since I've known her.

I wait a second before saying anything, so I seem surprised. "Oh, Rache, I'm so sorry." That much, at least, is true. "What happened?"

"We were supposed to hang out tonight. Paige came over and said *we need to talk*." Rachel sniffs. "And then she said she's been hanging out with Josie Leyman, and I said *yeah, because of chemistry*, and she said no. So I asked what that meant, and finally she said she thinks we're better as friends and she wants to date Josie."

I try to sound confused. "What?"

"It gets better." Rachel sounds bitter now. "Because Paige is actually *already* dating Josie. She's been dating Josie behind my back."

"Crap." (I hope I sound genuine.)

"Yeah. Well. Go figure. That's Paige for you. I mean, god forbid she ever tells you what she's actually *thinking*. At least, not when it would be useful to know. Like, for example, when we're trying to *do it*. But no, it's just—*this isn't working for me*. Yeah, maybe because you're hooking up with some shallow *jock* girl on the side."

Well, I knew Rachel would be mad. "At least Paige told you," I say. "I mean, she should have done it sooner, but at least she did it now."

"Yeah. Fantastic." Rachel's voice drips with sarcasm. "I do have that. Thanks, Miles."

"I just meant . . . She felt bad and told you. She was trying to do the right thing, like I did with Eric."

I didn't know phone silences could be frosty, but this one practically freezes my ear. "How do you know she felt bad?" Rachel says. "Why are you taking her side?"

"I'm not taking her side." (Backpedal. Quick.) "I'm just saying she talked to you. She's trying to tell you how she feels. Isn't that supposed to be a good thing? You can't act like she never tells you anything when she just told you something *big* like this."

"I really would've thought you of all people would be on my side. You should get it. You kissed *Shane*."

The way she says it makes it sound like I kissed a dead rat. "Yeah, I know, and that's why I get where Paige is coming from. She told you because she cares about you, Rachel. You *just* told me I did the right thing with Eric. Why isn't this the right thing? Paige wants all of us to be friends."

"Who cares what Paige wants? How can I be friends with her now? She didn't even have the freaking *ovaries* to talk to me first— she had to go suck face with Josie Leyman. From the *track team*."

"So there's another queerdo in school. You should be thrilled."

"Oh my god, I can't believe *that's* what you're getting from this."

Now I'm upset. "What am I supposed to be getting, Rachel? Everybody does shitty stuff and makes mistakes they wish they could take back."

"Of *course* you side with her." Rachel sounds disgusted. "I mean, you guys have so much in common now, right?"

"What's that supposed to mean?"

"I'm your *best friend,* Miles. I've always been your best friend, but the second I actually need you, you go and defend Paige. But hey, now you guys can be cheaters together."

That's it. "Fuck you, Rachel. I'm trying to help and you're being totally hysterical."

"Oh, sure, play the man card and call women hysterical, Miles. Go be a member of the patriarchy."

Why is she getting so mean? "That's not what I'm doing. Paige *asked* me what to do because she cares about the three of us being friends!"

A pause. "She *asked* you?"

Uh-oh.

"She told you? Before she told me?" Rachel's voice trembles. "She asked you what to do and you told her to break up with me?"

Oh, *shit.* How do I fix this? "No. No, Rache, I told her to talk to you and tell you what happened. That's all."

"You just can't stand me in a relationship when you're not. You sulked every time the three of us hung out after Shane broke up with you. And now that you've messed things up with Eric, you want to tank my relationship, too."

What? "That's total bullshit."

"I don't care." She's crying now. "You and Paige were talking about me behind my back—"

"Come on, I was trying to help—"

"And you both just decided what was best for me without

asking how *I* feel. You're so self-centered! Just go around and kiss whoever you want, because who gives a crap about who it hurts?"

Lands like a slap to the face. "Rachel—"

"Defend Paige all you want, Miles. You can keep being friends because I'm done with *both* of you."

She hangs up.

Fuck.

I punch out an angry text to Paige: Thanks for the heads up.

Fling my phone across my bed. Stand up and yank off my sweater just so I can throw it across the room. *Fuck Rachel.*

I want to break something. Why isn't there anything in my room I can break?

Instead I fall over on my bed and scream into my pillow. Fuck Rachel. Fuck Paige. Fuck Eric.

And fuck me, for screwing it up with every single one of them.

My buzzing phone wakes me up in the middle of the night.

It's a text from Jenny Chang.

> That forum post about you is finally down.
> See you in three weeks babyyyyyyyy!!!!

CHAPTER TWENTY-TWO

There is no copying party with Rachel, obviously. She doesn't call or text me all weekend. It's probably the longest I've gone without talking to her in years. Then again, the last time we had a fight was in middle school, when I wanted to go on the Ferris wheel at the state fair and she wouldn't go with me because she was afraid of heights, so I told her she was a scaredy-cat. In retrospect, that wasn't even a real fight. We were friends again, like, fifteen minutes later.

On Monday (Week Three Without Eric), I wait outside school in our usual meeting place, but Rachel marches right past me. In homeroom, she sits on the other side of the room with Eric. By lunch, it's obvious I'm dead to her, so Paige hauls me off to sit with Josie Leyman, Sophie Hubbard, and the rest of their crew.

Now that they're no longer sneaking around, Paige and Josie have turned into the giggly couple that the old Paige would have rolled her eyes at. If they scoot their chairs any closer together, they'll be in each other's laps.

It's pretty clear nobody else at this table knew Josie was queer—or that she was making out with Paige. AP Julian eats his sandwich while frowning at Josie and Paige like they're a math problem that doesn't add up. Hanna Herschel glowers at me like Josie and Paige's current relationship status is my fault. And Debate Team Daniel looks between Josie and Paige and Julian in a way that makes me wonder if he sort of wants to make out with Julian.

Sophie decides to interrogate me. "How many hours a day do you practice?"

She's wearing a black turtleneck. That's new. So is her bright red lipstick. I don't even need three guesses to figure out whose influence is at work here. "I don't know. Three? Whatever seems like enough."

She looks triumphant. "Cameron practices at least five."

I highly doubt that, unless he also doesn't sleep. "My teacher says if you're practicing more than three hours a day, you're wasting your time, because you aren't practicing efficiently."

That shuts her up. She blinks at me. Looks like she just sniffed a turd.

"Paige told me about your piano playing," Josie says, giving me a big smile. "That's so cool."

I may not like anybody else at this table, but I can't really find fault with Josie. And I've been trying. But she's nice. When she smiles, she looks like she means it. She seems to really like Paige.

"Thanks." I glance over my shoulder.

Rachel and Eric are sitting together at our old table. Eric is drawing something in his notebook, occasionally sliding it across the table so Rachel can look at it.

What's he drawing?

"Cameron has been filling me in on the main contenders," Sophie says, apparently recovered. "Who do *you* think has a shot at winning?"

This is obviously a test. She wants me to say *I* have a shot, so she can shoot back with some withering response she probably got straight from Cameron.

Joke's on you, Sophie. I'm not falling for that. "Actually, I have to go." I stand up, picking up my tray. "See you later, Paige."

Paige opens her mouth, looking confused, but I'm not really interested in what she has to say. I just want to get out of here. I bus my tray and leave the cafeteria without looking at Eric and Rachel, or Shane, or anybody else. Practically run for the auditorium. Through the door. Down the aisle. Up onto the stage.

I collapse at the piano and dive into Tchaikovsky because I desperately need noise that isn't Paige and Josie giggling.

Escaping partway through lunch and hiding in the auditorium becomes my new normal. Sophie eventually runs out of annoying questions for me, but then she stops talking to me at all and talks to Hanna. Daniel and Julian mostly talk to each other about video games. And Paige and Josie giggle.

It's so bad that I even spend one awkward lunch period with Shane at the football table, dodging past Paige and pretending I don't see her waving at me. Shane seems happy enough to see me, but nobody else knows what to do, so nobody talks to me. Even Shane just talks to DeShawn. If it wasn't for Paige, craning her neck and shooting me hurt glances across the cafeteria, I might think I'd turned invisible.

So on Friday, I just skip the cafeteria altogether. Head straight to the auditorium.

Rachel is standing outside it, pinning a flyer to the bulletin board next to the auditorium doors. She carefully pretends not to see me.

I stop near her and look at the flyer.

Plant-Based Is Planet-Safe!
Rally and Petition-Signing

It's drawn in big black letters that look like they belong in a comic book, along with words that say things like *POW* and *BOOM*. Around the letters are hand-drawn plants and flowers wearing capes like superheroes. Small text near the bottom says, Design by Eric Mendez.

I guess that's what he was drawing and showing to Rachel.

"The flyer looks nice," I say.

Rachel doesn't look at me. Just keeps smoothing the paper against the bulletin board, like that's a totally normal thing to do. "Thanks."

"When's your petition signing?"

"Next Friday." She points to the flyer. "It says right there."

(Well, yeah, I can see that, but I was sort of hoping you'd talk to me.) "Oh. Cool."

She turns to face me. "Did you want something?"

"Um, is anybody helping you? With the petition stuff?"

"No, and I don't need help. One committed person can change the world by themselves." She looks ready to fight me about it. But instead, she just turns and walks away.

I'm so bored and lonely over the weekend that I actually log back into the competition forum, just to see if that post about me is really gone, like Jenny said.

It is.

But I don't search for myself. I'm never doing that again.

Instead, I scroll idly through the forum's main page. It's full of anxious posts now. What model is the piano in the hall? How's the action? Is the hall hot or cold? Do the judges let you play the whole piece or stop you partway through? How many copies of the sheet music do you have to provide for the judges?

(Oh, come on, pianoman5000, that answer is literally in the FAQ on the main website.)

Any other year, I'd be right there with them. Clicking through each question and answer. *What if someone else knows more than me?*

But this year, everything having to do with the competition feels oceans away. Who cares how cold the hall is when I'm stuck with Paige and Josie's cuteness all day? Who cares if the pedal sticks when Rachel's and Eric's silences seem deafening?

I know I should be focusing on piano. I don't have anything else to do. But every time I sit down to practice, I just think of Eric, sitting in the auditorium with his Chuck Taylors up on the seat in front of him. Or Rachel, tagging along to my suit fitting. Or all of us sitting at our lunch table, joking around.

I even miss Rachel constantly asking me if I have to pee between classes.

When I climb Stefania's porch steps on Thursday (Week Four Without Eric), I wonder if this is the week she tells me I'm a waste of her time and kicks me to the curb. It wasn't last week—last week was as awkward as the week before, but that was it. Maybe I should just do it for her. Tell her I quit.

Will Mrs. Kim take me back if I do?

When Stefania opens the door, she's wearing an enormous white sweater over black leggings, with her frizzy gray hair loose around her shoulders. No earrings. And no clogs, either. She looks smaller without them, just standing there in blue slippers.

For a few seconds, she stares silently at me. Blue eyes flat and expressionless. She might as well be made of marble.

Then, suddenly, she softens. Steps back, even smiles a little. "Come in, Miles."

I step inside. My heart is going a mile a minute. My practicing this week has been even worse than last week. She's going to tear me to shreds.

But Stefania stops in the kitchen instead of heading straight for the piano room. "I'm going to have coffee," she says. "Would you like some?"

"Um, what?" That sounded a lot like friendly small talk. "I mean, sure."

Stefania pops the lid on her coffee maker and puts in a filter. So she doesn't even have coffee ready? She never starts my lesson late. Except for that very first lesson, I've never seen her actually *make* coffee. She always seems to have a mug ready for herself when I walk in.

She spoons coffee into the filter and turns the coffee maker on.

"I'm going to show you something, Miles." She picks up a black photo album from the counter and brings it over to the dining table. It's a nice photo album—leather-bound, not plastic. She sets it on the table and opens it.

These are pictures. Of her. She looks just like she did in that video I found on YouTube. Young. Eyebrows like dark paintbrush strokes over her big blue eyes. Dark frizzy hair, twirled up on her head. Here she is in a red gown, at a piano, in front of an orchestra. Here she is in a blue gown, standing alone on a recital stage in front of another piano. Here's a yellowing newspaper article about her.

RUSSIAN PIANIST WOWS AT CARNEGIE

In the black-and-white picture, she's clasping hands with the conductor. *Stefania Petrova, 21, performs Rachmaninov with the New York Philharmonic.*

"Wow," I say, because I don't know what else to say.

The corner of her mouth lifts. "I hadn't even graduated from Juilliard yet," she says, tapping the newspaper article. She turns the page again. "Ah, yes. These are from Europe."

More pictures. Stefania with the London Symphony. With the Berlin Philharmonic. With orchestras in France, Spain, Russia . . .

"Why are you showing me this?" (I mean, if it's to make me feel completely insignificant, it's definitely working.)

"To show you that I was building a career," Stefania says.

"I know you were. I mean, I know you played with . . . I found a video on YouTube."

"Did you?" Her eyebrows go up. "That's interesting."

Has she seriously never Googled herself?

She closes the photo album. "The Tri-State Piano Competition used to be named after a big patron of the classical music world. Someone who had a lot of money, and gave some of it to start the competition. He had connections, too, and he liked helping young musicians start their careers."

The coffee maker beeps. Stefania leaves the photo album on the table and moves to the counter, taking down mugs and pouring coffee.

"This person heard me play at Juilliard. He introduced me around New York and helped me with the expenses of living in the city as a musician." She hands me a mug. "He helped start my career here in the States."

There's a *but* coming. I can feel it.

Stefania sips her coffee. "This person also turned out to have expectations of me that I was not interested in meeting. I made that obvious, and he didn't appreciate it. He seemed to believe he was owed certain things. Unfortunately, he had more money and more power than I did, and orchestras and conservatories and performing arts organizations need money. Which meant that people were more inclined to believe his version of things than mine." Another sip of coffee. "I graduated Juilliard and left New York. Met a medical student in Chicago, and we ended up here. And that's that."

I stare into my coffee mug, because I have no idea what to say. *That's that?* How can she say *that's that* about . . . well . . . that? I remember all the theories on the forum—*she got knocked up, she had an affair with her mentor*—and my stomach twists. I feel kind of dirty for reading them.

And I feel really bad for yelling at her—for throwing it in her face.

Olga comes padding into the kitchen, big tail slowly wagging. Stefania reaches down a hand. Olga sticks her nose into it.

"You asked if the competition judges hate me," Stefania says. "The answer is—I don't know. But plenty of people liked this person and appreciated the money he gave to the arts, and didn't take kindly to some upstart like me accusing him of . . ." Stefania considers for a moment, eyes narrowed. *"Unsavory things."* She smiles, a little demonically. "Of course, about ten years later three other ladies made the same accusations I did and it all became quite the scandal. The competition got renamed. This person got booted off orchestra boards. Etcetera."

I know I shouldn't ask. But I can't quite stop myself. "Who was it?"

Stefania gives me an appraising look. "If you really want to know, you can use Google," she says. "You don't need me to tell you."

"Why are you telling me anything?"

"Because you asked if the judges hate me, and I reacted poorly. I spent a very long time teaching myself not to care what other people think. But I suppose you can't ever stop caring completely." She scratches Olga behind the ears. The dog closes her eyes. "Plus, Pierre has hated me ever since Juilliard, so it's quite possible he's been filling those judges' heads with all sorts of nasty gossip about me for years."

That pulls me up short. "You went to Juilliard with Pierre Fontaine?"

She grins. "Did I not tell you that? I beat him in every single competition. I was his Cameron Hart. He hates my guts."

I snort into my coffee. "That's great." There's another question, hanging in the air between us. I have to ask it. "Did you give up piano because of that?"

Stefania raises an eyebrow. "Miles Jacobson, I did not *give up* piano. I thought I told you last week—winning competitions does not make you a brilliant pianist. And neither does touring the world playing with famous orchestras."

You still changed your whole career. Your whole direction in life.

But all I say is, "I shouldn't have brought it up. Cameron is full of shit. What he said . . . I shouldn't have let it get to me."

"Well." Stefania picks up the coffee pot and pours the last little trickle down the sink. "In this case, it's possible he's not entirely wrong. Still interested in studying with me?"

Easiest question I've ever had to answer. "Yeah."

She smiles. "All right, then. Let's go."

She starts for the piano room, but I hesitate. "I don't know what to do."

She turns back. "About what?"

"I'm not exactly full of joy right now. How am I supposed to play this piece?"

"Good grief, Miles. Nobody's full of joy all the time. Practice anyway, and the joy will come back around. Give it time." She points to the piano. "Now let's go!"

Through what I can only guess was a colossal effort, Mom has made it home by dinnertime, so we sit around the table together, eating the lasagna that Dad made. I can't totally remember the last time we did this. It's nice. Except for the part where Mom asks me how school was, and I give her surfacey answers because I just can't bear to relive the five thousand moments Eric and Rachel ignored me today. And also the part where Dad asks how my lesson was, and I give him surfacey answers because I don't want to tell him about Stefania. Not that he wouldn't care—I mean, it's Feminist Dad—but it would feel weird, to tell him, when I don't tell him anything important anymore.

Still, it's nice they asked. Dad especially has been asking me more questions lately. Yesterday he said, "How did you sleep?" when I came down for breakfast, instead of just his usual "Morning."

After dinner, I trudge upstairs. But I can't focus on homework. I open my laptop, ready to Google. It should be easy to figure out what Tri-State used to be called, and that'll tell me the name of the asshole patron Stefania told me about . . .

But I change my mind. Backspace, backspace. Delete the search I just typed. Maybe I'll find out someday, but I don't want to go looking for it. Not right now. It doesn't feel fair to Stefania.

I wish I could talk to Eric about my lesson. Or Rachel. Tell them what Stefania told me. See what they say.

But I can't. So I call Paige.

"Hey, what's up, Miles?"

"Hey, I just wanted to . . . Where are you?" The amount of noise on the other end of the line suggests Paige is inside a cement mixer.

"Track meet!" she shouts. "Josie's up next in the relay race. We're doing really well so far!"

We? Paige has never, ever had school spirit for anything. Not even the competitive composting league Rachel wanted to start last year.

"Oh. Well, it's not important. We can talk later."

"No, I'm here! Just a sec." The noise slowly fades and then suddenly drops. "Okay, I'm inside now. What'd you want to talk about?"

"Just something that happened at my lesson." *But I really don't want to talk to you about it now. Not while you're at Josie's track meet.* "You know what, it's nothing. How're you?"

"Great. Just hanging out with Hanna and Daniel."

Seriously? "Okay . . ."

"Miles, um . . . if it's not important, I better go. I don't want to miss Josie—"

"Can you just quit talking about Josie for one second and be my friend again?" It bursts out of me, in the split second before my brain can catch up. "Sorry, that came out wrong. I didn't mean that . . . Never mind. I gotta go."

And I hang up. Shove my phone aside and glare at my homework.

Why was Paige so desperate to keep me as a friend? She seems to have five new friends, and somehow I've ended up with none.

I pull on a sweatshirt and go downstairs. Mom and Dad are watching some cooking show in the living room.

Well, Dad is watching it. Mom is on her laptop.

"Can I borrow a car?" I ask.

They both look at me, and then at each other, confused.

"I want to practice at school," I say.

"We can move to another room if you want to practice here," Mom says.

"Won't the school be closed by now?" Dad says.

"There's a track meet, so it's open. Plus Janitor Bob is there Thursday nights, so if the auditorium is locked, he can let me in."

"Is Janitor Bob the hippie?" Mom asks.

"You can take my car," Dad says. "Keys are in my coat pocket."

"Thanks, Dad." I escape before they can say anything else. Pull on my shoes, grab Dad's keys, and head out the door. The nights are slowly getting warmer. For once, my breath doesn't cloud in front of my face. Maybe it's finally spring.

The headlights on Dad's old Subaru uncover the road in front of me bit by bit as I drive to school. I don't think I've ever been to the school this late, but it's not exactly hard to find in the dark. The whole ugly building is lit up. A giant glowing brick. The parking lot is almost full. I guess the track team is popular.

The lobby is empty, though. The track is out behind the building. I can hear faint, muffled cheering.

The auditorium door is unlocked. Sigh of relief. No searching for Janitor Bob.

I climb the stairs to the stage. Ditch my coat. Sit down at the piano, surrounded by silent, looming set pieces.

And I bang on the keys.

No chords. No opening of Tchaikovsky this time.

I just bang. Like I'm a little kid again, playing the thunderstorm game with Dad. I smash my hands on the lowest notes—resonant, dissonant noise. The piano vibrates. The bench underneath me shakes. I can feel the sound waves rolling through the floor. The echoes bounce back from the ceiling.

Now the high notes—tinkling like breaking glass. Sharp, percussive, and almost painful.

The dissonance is too much, so I switch to octaves and crash my way back down the piano. Hopping from note to random note, without caring what I play. My fingers just land where they land.

And when my hands get tired, I switch to chords. Strange chords. Weird chords. Chords that don't make any sense next to each other. F minor to B major to E-flat seven.

And then my right hand changes to a melody. Or some kind of vague melodic noodling. I don't know where it's going. I just play whatever notes come into my head, and put whatever chord I feel like underneath. The notes are my thoughts, blinking by like flipping TV channels, and the piano is my voice.

No Tchaikovsky. No Chopin. No Bach or Beethoven or Brahms.

Just me.

My notes. My feelings.

People love to say *music is a language,* but I think that's bull. You can't tell a story with notes the way you can with words. Music is more like impressions. Like the paintings where everything looks a little blurred, but you get the idea of flowers, or people, or water and trees. Except instead of flowers, it's just feelings. Anger. Sadness. Frustration. Joy.

I don't even know what I would have said to Paige, if she'd actually had a minute to listen. I don't know what to say about anything right now. But the notes tumbling from my fingers feel like some kind of truth.

The longer I play, the more the notes and the chords seem to lead somewhere. Here's a bit of melody that sounds nice. Here's a chord that isn't dissonant. And it's all still coming from me, and no one else. I can go any direction I want. I can tell any story I want . . . or the impressions of any story.

And without really knowing *why,* now I know where I'm going. The melody and the chords move down the piano. Lower and lower until suddenly—

Crash, crash, crash.

Into the beginning of Tchaikovsky.

I'm leaving behind the notes that were all mine, but it doesn't matter. There's a clarity here that I haven't felt before. I'm thinking only of my fingers hitting the keys, feeling only the piano vibrating through my arms into my shoulders.

And right when everything else falls away . . .

I know what to do about Paige.

I know what to do about Rachel.

And I know what I have to do for Eric.

CHAPTER TWENTY-THREE

I start at the beginning. With Rachel. Because she's the oldest friend I have.

On Friday morning (One Week to Competition), I roll out of bed early. Mom gives me a bleary look over her disgustingly green smoothie when I come downstairs.

"I'm not ready yet," she mumbles.

"I don't need a ride." I grab a granola bar from the pantry. "I'm biking today. Can I borrow a clipboard?"

"Sure." Mom blinks. "What?"

But I'm already running out the door, stuffing the clipboard into my bag. Luckily, Mom is obsessed with organization in the garage, so I actually find Dad's old bike tire pump in the first place I look for it.

With fuller tires, I take off down the street. It's cool and damp this morning, but the sun is already nuking the dew on the grass, sending steam rising into the air. The trees are leafy enough now to give me dappled shade on the road. If this keeps up, I might not even need my sweatshirt later.

Hive is still sleepy when I pull up. The only two customers are a couple of women in yoga pants. The barista yawns when she hands me the paper cup and my change.

It's a bit tricky to get back on my bike holding a cup of hot chocolate. I didn't think this part through. But I manage it and awkwardly ride off. It's slower going, one hand on the handlebars, trying not to spill the cocoa . . .

I'm going to be too late. Rachel's already left . . .

But she hasn't. I pull up in front of her house just as she opens her front door. She doesn't see me until she gets to her driveway.

She stops. We stare at each other.

"Hi," I say.

"Hi," she says.

"I brought you something." I wait, but she doesn't say anything, so I carefully slide off my bike, ditching it on the grass, and walk up her driveway. "Just some, um, hot chocolate." I hold out the cup.

She chews her lip. Takes the cup.

"Rache, I'm really sorry. I didn't mean to take Paige's side, and I didn't mean to hurt your feelings, but I can see why you're mad at me. So, I'm sorry. You're my best friend and I really miss you."

She looks down at the cocoa in her hand and mutters, "I miss you, too."

I pull the clipboard out of my bag. "I thought maybe you might need some help getting petition signatures today." Pump my arms up and down like a cheerleader minus the pom-poms. "Plant-based is planet-based?"

"It's 'plant-based is planet-*safe*.'"

"Right. Sorry."

She chews her lip some more. "I guess I could use the help. I mean, since you brought a clipboard already."

"Do you have extra petition copies?"

She rolls her eyes. "Obviously." She pulls a slim stack of papers out of her bag and hands me a page. I clip it onto my clipboard.

Rachel is looking doubtfully at my bike. "You actually rode that?"

I turn and look at it. "Yeah, what's wrong with it?"

"Well, for starters, you haven't ridden a bike in, like, five years."

"Yeah. Um, maybe I could hitch a ride with you? I'm realizing now that if I ride that from here, I'll be late."

"Super late." Rachel sighs. "This is why you need me, Miles. You can't plan for shit."

That sounded almost normal. I start to feel hopeful. "You'll give me a ride?"

"If you tell me I'm a better friend than Paige."

I freeze. "Rachel, I'm trying to be friends with both of you—"

"I know! Shut up." She turns to her car, flustered, like she's embarrassed she said it. Maybe she didn't really mean it and was trying to make a joke. "We can't fit the bike, though. I'll give you a ride back later and you can pick it up."

"Okay." I wheel the bike up her driveway and leave it on the porch. She's already started the car when I get in next to her.

"You really hurt my feelings," she says quietly.

I brace myself. "I know."

"Paige hurt my feelings."

"I know."

She puts the car into reverse. But we don't move. She brushes a stray curl out of her face, staring at her knees. "I kind of feel like maybe nobody will ever like me."

My building anxiety vanishes. "What? Really?"

She shrugs. "Paige said I'm *a lot*."

There's no denying that. "Rache, that doesn't mean nobody's gonna like you. I mean, if nothing else, you'll go to, like, Smith, or something, and every girl on campus will fall head over heels for you."

She gives me a tiny smile.

"Seriously. Rachel, they will all go vegetarian just for the chance to go on a date with you."

Her smile grows wider. "Shut up."

"Any protest you want to organize, you'll have a legion of ladies showing up."

"Oh my god, *stop*, Miles." But she's grinning as she backs down the driveway.

Even in the car, we're almost late. We don't have time to stop at our lockers. And Rachel's right, I am shit at planning. Because as soon as we walk into homeroom, we're faced with the new reality again:

there's one open seat next to Paige and Josie, and one next to Eric on the other side of the room.

Rachel glances at Josie, and for a second, I think she might start to cry. But she doesn't. She lifts her chin and says to me, "I'll see you in the cafeteria for petitioning." And then she heads over to Eric.

Which leaves me with that last chair next to Paige. I take a deep breath and sit down just as the bell rings. I'm figuring Paige is going to say *something* about me yelling at her on the phone last night.

But she doesn't. She just glances anxiously at me, and then past me to Rachel. I follow her gaze—and meet Eric's.

I smile.

He doesn't smile back, but he doesn't frown, either. He just looks back down at his notebook.

At the start of the lunch period, I meet Rachel in a corner of the cafeteria. She has her own clipboard and two pens. "We have fifteen minutes," she says, handing me a pen. "That should give us time to collect signatures and still eat if we're fast. Now, if anyone asks what we mean by plant-based—"

"Rache, I've known you forever, I know what you mean by plant-based."

She purses her lips. Turns pink. Crap, maybe I've pissed her off. Rachel loves telling people about stuff. I'm basically expecting her to become a professor someday.

But she just nods. "Well, that gives us more time for signatures." She turns and marches fearlessly into the cafeteria. "Sign for a sustainable lunch!"

I follow, waving my clipboard, hollering, "Plant-based is planet-safe!"

People in the lunch line turn to look. Cafeteria workers roll their eyes.

"Sign our petition for plant-based lunch options!" Rachel shouts.

"Demand eco-friendly food!" I yell.

At their table, Sophie and Hanna are staring at us. Josie is grinning. Paige looks stricken. Alone at his table, Eric looks up from his notebook.

Someone boos. Someone else whistles. Several more people laugh.

"Eat my farts, tree-hugger!" That must be Nathan Ryan, because he's been yelling that at Rachel since her middle school carpool campaign.

Josie pushes her chair back. Paige reaches for her sleeve and misses.

Oh, god, she's coming over here to make fun of me. *Or Rachel.* Quick—get in front of Rachel . . .

Josie stops and holds out her hand. "I'll sign. Do you have a pen?"

I stare at her. So does Rachel.

Josie just smiles.

"Yeah. Here." I hand her my pen and turn the clipboard around for her.

She prints her name and then scribbles her signature, turning the dot above the "i" into a heart. "Thanks, Miles!" And she turns and walks back to her table.

For a second, there's dead silence. You could hear a tater tot drop. Sophie, Hanna, Daniel, and Julian stare at Josie, who just goes back to her lunch. Paige looks between Josie and Rachel with wide eyes.

Rachel makes a valiant attempt to recover. "Plant-based is planet-safe! Sign for a sustainable lunch!"

"You need to get laid!" some guy yells from the football table. What's his name? Brad? Chad?

Shane shoots to his feet like someone lit a firecracker under his chair. "Shut up, man!"

And now Shane is coming toward us, with DeShawn and DeShawn's cheerleader girlfriend right behind him.

"Sorry about Tad," Shane says to Rachel, as he signs her petition.

She looks so shocked that for a second I think she might not have anything to say. "It's okay. Thanks for your support."

Shane just nods. DeShawn and his girlfriend sign my petition, and then they all troop back to the football table. The table cheers, except for Tad, who looks grumpy.

But now Daniel and Julian are getting up, and pulling Hanna Herschel with them. A few people are peeling off the lunch line to sign. More stand up from the tables closest to us.

Sophie stays rooted to her seat, shooting daggers out of her eyes.

I hold the pen out to one person, take it back, hold it out to the next . . . My world is just hands now, one after another.

And then there's a familiar hand. Silver ring on the middle finger. Carefully taking the pen and scrawling a familiar name.

I look up, into Eric's face.

He hands back the pen. "Do you have an extra petition?"

Somehow, my voice works. Somehow, it doesn't tremble. "I think Rachel does."

He ducks his head and walks over to Rachel. I hand the pen on to the next person, but I'm watching Eric, taking a petition from Rachel, fishing a colored pencil out of his pocket, holding the petition on top of his notebook.

Raising it all above his head and shouting, "Plant-based is planet-safe!"

The rest of the football table slowly gets to its feet. Even Tad, though he looks irritated. DeShawn's girlfriend seems to be negotiating with the other cheerleaders, pointing at us. But even without them, there's a line forming. Or a swarm.

There are people waiting for my pen, anyway.

"We want your involvement!" Rachel shouts. "Tell us what you want to see in your sustainable cafeteria!"

What? That wasn't part of the original plan. But Rachel's on fire now and there's no stopping her. I catch Eric's eye. He smiles.

I smile back.

We don't get all the cheerleaders, but we do get the entire football table. Josie brings over several other girls from the track team. Eric's presence seems to be attracting people in a lot of black, or with dyed hair, or a lot of earrings. Must be people who know him from art class.

And finally, here comes Paige, sidling through the crowd, looking as uncomfortable as I've ever seen her. She might be trying to get to me—I can't totally tell—but the crowd has other ideas, and she ends up face-to-face with Rachel.

They stare at each other. Paige holds out a hand for the pen.

For a second, I think Rachel isn't going to give it to her. She looks like she's thinking about it, twirling the pen in her fingers.

But it's just a moment, and then she hands the pen over. Paige signs. Hands the pen back.

And that's that. Paige turns and heads back to her table. To Josie. And Rachel's shouting again, waving her clipboard in the air.

By the time the bell rings, Rachel and I haven't eaten anything, but we have signatures filling our petition pages. Eric tears his peanut butter sandwich into thirds and we each try to eat one while counting signatures and walking down the hallway. We bounce off a lot of people.

"Sixty-four!" Rachel is ecstatic. "Can you believe it? Should we give them to the principal now?"

"We could try again on Monday," I say. Rachel's enthusiasm is contagious. "Let word travel a bit. Maybe we could get more signatures."

"Plus Monday is stroganoff day," Eric says. "Everybody hates the cafeteria on stroganoff day."

"Good idea." Rachel collects our petitions and sticks them in her bag. "See you guys later, then!" And she jogs away down the hall.

Leaving me and Eric. Eric, who's avoiding my eyes now, hands stuffed in his pockets.

I take a deep breath. "I'm sorry. I never actually said that to you, and I should have. It's the first thing I should have said. I'm really, really sorry for hurting you. I was being selfish, and you're right, I do sometimes get wrapped up in my own stuff. I'll try to be better at noticing that."

He looks up at me—dark eyes and long eyelashes, perfect behind his glasses.

The second bell rings.

My heart is beating so loudly that part of me believes Eric can hear it. "I get that it was hard to trust me, and when you did, I blew it. I don't know if you can forgive me, and I get it if you can't, but . . . I miss you. And I'm sorry."

He holds my gaze, while my heart hammers through the voices and footsteps around us, and then he looks away. "Okay," he says.

"Okay." And I turn and run for English.

Then there's Paige. My second-oldest friend.

I wait for her at her locker on Monday morning. We haven't talked since she signed Rachel's petition on Friday. She didn't even say goodbye when she left school with Josie.

She slows down when she sees me now, and approaches her locker like I might bite. Her hair is pulled back in a tiny, messy ponytail. I can actually see the studs in her ears—little silver stars. I've never seen her in a ponytail. Or without her barrettes. Her bangs hang into her eyes.

"Did you come to tell me you're just Rachel's friend now?" She sounds like she'd rather be elsewhere.

"What? No. Paige, that's ridiculous. I'm friends with both of you."

She stuffs her jacket into her locker.

"Look, I just wanted to give you these." I hold out two tickets. "The final round of the competition is on Saturday and it would mean a lot to me if you came. And . . . maybe you could bring Josie."

She looks at me in surprise. "Um . . . my mom can probably get us tickets."

"Well, I wanted to give you these to make sure you had some."

She hesitates. "Is Rachel going?"

"I haven't asked her yet, but I hope so." Time to change the subject. "Your hair looks nice." I might be lying. I can't tell yet. It's just so different.

"Josie said I should wear it up sometimes. I like it." She says the last part defensively, like I might disagree with her, which makes me wonder if she really likes it. And if Rachel ever told her to change her hair.

But all I say is, "Cool."

I hold out the tickets.

She takes them. "You're gonna kill it," she says.

And that, at least, sounds genuine.

Now there's just Eric.

On Friday, he smiled at me. And I smiled back.

On Saturday, I left him alone.

On Sunday, I liked a pencil sketch he posted on Instagram of Nina holding Mr. Pudge.

On Monday, we stand with our clipboards again and shout about sustainable lunch with Rachel in the cafeteria. And we run together to the principal's office to deliver our petitions full of signatures. The principal sighs as soon as she sees Rachel, but she seems impressed by the number of signatures and promises to consider our proposals.

Between classes on Monday afternoon, I run to Eric's locker and slip a note in through the vents on the door: *I'm sorry I didn't take your trauma seriously. I will work on listening more. And I like your rainbow socks.*

And then I leave him alone for the rest of the day, except for saying *hi* in American History. He says *hi* back.

On Tuesday, I get to school early and drop another note in his locker. This one says: *I'm sorry I made you feel like I was using you. I think you're awesome. I should have said that.*

I'm sitting with Rachel at lunch, listening to her ideas for an environmental club at school, when Eric sets his sandwich bag on the table and sits down.

"Hi," he says.

"Hi," I say.

He pulls out his sketchbook and starts to draw, and Rachel (somehow) manages to keep her mouth shut. She goes back to talking about the environmental club. And I let Eric be.

On Wednesday, I slip a third note into his locker: *I'm sorry it took me so long to apologize. Please tell Nina I'm sorry I was a jerk to you and I think she's awesome, too.*

Eric catches up with me and Rachel at the end of the day, as we're leaving school. "I could design posters for your environmental club," he says. "If you decide you want to do it."

"Really?" Rachel's whole face lights up. "That would be the *best*. I already have a spreadsheet with ideas. I'll email you. Thank you, Eric. To be continued!" And she runs for her car, pumping her fist in the air.

"She's going to email you as soon as she gets home," I say.

Eric grins. Actually grins. "I know."

God, I've missed that dimple. "The spreadsheet is going to be enormous."

"I know."

We sink into silence, and he turns and unlocks his bike from the rack. "I've been getting your notes," he says to the bike.

My heart jumps into my throat. "Do you want me to stop writing them?"

He pulls his bike from the rack. Considers. "No." And then he's on his bike. "See you tomorrow." He weaves down the sidewalk into the parking lot.

On Thursday, I leave the longest and scariest note. The one that shook my hand, writing it. It says: *I'm sorry I didn't tell you the whole truth about Shane. I made that New Year's resolution because I thought I still liked Shane, and if he could just see me as a guy and like me anyway, then that would somehow make me REAL. But I've been real all along. You've always seen that. I'm sorry it took kissing him for me to figure all that out. It's a weird way to realize you love somebody, but I'm weird. I love your socks, and your cartoons, and your glasses. And I promise to tell you all the truths from now on.*

He's not wearing his glasses on Thursday. But he is wearing rainbow socks. He doesn't say anything to me all day, but he smiles, once, when I sit down across from him, next to Rachel, at their lunch table. And then he goes on drawing.

On Friday, I leave one last note for Eric, a short one, along with two tickets: *I'm sorry I haven't returned your tie. I hope you don't mind if I keep it for one more day.*

Stefania drives me home after our last dress rehearsal in the auditorium. The sun is low in the sky and I'm starving when we pull up in front of my house.

"No practicing tonight," she says as I climb out of the car.

"I know."

"I mean it, Miles."

"Okay! I think if I practiced any more, my arms would fall off anyway."

She narrows her eyes at me, but apparently decides I'm not lying to her. "Good. Get some sleep." She gives me a quick smile. "You're ready." And she drives away.

I haul myself up the stairs to my bedroom. That dress rehearsal lasted two hours, and now my feet feel like they're made of cement. My head weighs a hundred pounds. I have to rely on gravity to change out of my suit.

I stash the suit in the closet, except for the shirt, which, after that epic dress rehearsal, is going in the wash as soon as I have enough energy to haul myself down to the basement.

Someone knocks at the door.

"Yeah?"

The door opens, and there's Dad, in his old UW-Madison sweatshirt and slippers. Holding a narrow cardboard box. Looking awkward. "Hey, Miles."

"Hi. Sorry. I thought it would be Mom."

"Oh. She's here, she's just putting a frozen pizza in the oven."

"Gourmet."

He grins at that. Clears his throat. "So—big day tomorrow. Feeling good about it?"

He wants a simple answer, but there isn't one. I can't lie to him, so I shrug. "I guess. Better than last year. I think."

"That's good. Um." He points vaguely at my bed, and then wanders over and sits down on it. "I got you something."

I guess I'm supposed to sit next to him. Right? When was the last time I sat next to Dad?

His sweatshirt sleeve brushes my arm as I sit down. He smells like graham crackers. I'd forgotten that smell. I've never been able to figure it out, but my dad always smells like graham crackers to me.

"I guess when I say I got you something . . ." He looks down at the cardboard box in his hands. "Well, I didn't actually *get* it for you. It's mine. Or it was mine. It used to be mine."

"Dad."

"Right." He hands me the box.

I take off the lid and there, carefully folded, is a tie. A shiny, skinny black tie, with a delicate floral design stitched on it in white thread.

"This is your jazz tie," I say, because I've seen it before, in the picture he has in his office of him with his old jazz band. It sits on top of that old upright piano that's buried under books. He must be in his twenties in the picture. Big glasses, dark curly hair that looks a lot like mine, white shirt, and this black tie.

"Well, I don't play a lot of jazz anymore," Dad says. "But I thought, hey, it's probably not too flashy for Tchaikovsky."

I carefully unfold the tie.

"It was always a little short on me," Dad says. "So it might fit you better."

I stand up. Go over to the mirror. Hold the tie up to my neck.

It's perfect. Narrow enough to look like it belongs on my smaller frame. Subtle enough that it will blend in with my suit, but still stand out, just a little. And it doesn't *seem* too long.

I turn to face Dad. "What do you think?"

He looks. For a long time. At the tie, at my face.

He gives me a thumbs-up. He can't seem to say anything, but I get it. This is hard for him, but he's trying. The thumbs-up is what he can do.

"Thanks, Dad." I lower the tie. "I really like it."

He clears his throat and runs a hand over his head—balding now, his graying hair buzzed close. "Well." He stands up. "Come down for dinner soon, okay?"

"Okay."

He manages the smallest smile, and then he leaves, closing the door quietly behind him.

I look back down at the tie in my hands. Turn it over.

Ties have these loops sewn on the back of the fat end, so you can tuck the skinny end in and it won't flap around. Eric showed me how to do it.

This tie has two loops on the back. One is white with tiny blue letters stitched on it that say, *For Arthur, xo Tanya.*

The second one is blue, with tiny white stitching that says, *For Miles, xo Dad.*

I'm down in the basement, shoving the laundry load containing my concert shirt into the dryer, when the doorbell rings.

Good grief, are Mom's clients showing up to the house now instead of calling? Mom's been turning off her phone after dinner. It's a big step for her.

The basement door creaks open. "Miles?" Mom shouts. "You've got a visitor!"

What?

I give up trying to detangle this massive knot of shirt sleeves and just fling the whole thing into the dryer. Hit the start button. Run up the stairs too fast and hit my head on the lintel of the basement door. Yet another project Mom never gets around to. She keeps saying she wants to make this doorway taller, since it was apparently designed for hobbits. Dad's constantly bumping his head—he's probably losing hundreds of brain cells a week.

Where did Mom go, anyway? She's disappeared. So has Dad.

But at the end of the hall, standing awkwardly just inside our front door, is Eric.

Eric in his glasses. Eric with his jeans rolled up above his ankles, revealing rainbow socks. Eric in his green Chuck Taylors, with that silver ring on his finger, and that silver hoop in his ear.

Eric, in my house.

I'm wearing a giant T-shirt with a puppy dog on it and sleeves that hang down to my elbows. My hair is a frizzy mess. My jeans have holes in both knees. I'm barefoot.

But it's too late to change any of that now, because Eric's turning around . . .

"Hi," he says.

I pad down the hallway. "Hi."

"I got all of your notes."

"I meant everything I said." I glance into the living room—wondering if Mom and Dad are in there, watching us—but it's empty. "Or, I mean . . . everything I wrote."

"I know." He takes a breath, hesitating. "Nina and I would really like to go to your concert."

Stomach flip. "Really? I mean, that's great."

"We don't have a ride, though. My mom's car is in the shop, and she and my dad need the Subaru for errands. We kind of split that car—Dad takes the bus in the winter, and now I'm biking so he's using it."

"Oh." Stomach flop.

Eric glances down at his shoes. "I was thinking... Or, I thought I'd ask..." Looks up again. "Could we hitch a ride with you? Or Rachel? I guess I could have asked Rachel." He frowns.

"Rachel's riding with us. Which means we'd only have one seat, but..." My brain is going a mile a minute. Think, Miles. *Think.* "Uh, I need to make a quick phone call. Can you wait here a minute?"

He looks confused, but he nods.

I race upstairs to my room, so fast I lose my balance and almost face-plant into my door. (Thank god Eric didn't see that.) Grab my phone. Dial.

It rings. Once. Twice. Three times.

"Hello?" It's a man's voice. Low and gentle.

Did I dial the wrong number? "I'm, um, I'm looking for Stefania? This is Miles. Jacobson."

"Oh." The voice brightens. "Hi, Miles. This is John, Stefania's husband."

He exists. I mean—of course he does, even if I've never seen him. And he sounds so ... mild-mannered.

"I'll get Stefania for you. Just a moment."

And then Stefania says, "If you're calling to ask if you can practice, the answer is still no. No practicing!"

(How is she married to someone so calm?) "I'm actually wondering if there's any chance you could give my friend Rachel a ride to the competition tomorrow? Another friend and his sister need a ride in our car, and we don't have room for them and Rachel."

A pause. "Would this be our friend Eric, the reindeer-hat-man?"

"Yeah."

Another pause. Maybe this was a mistake. I should offer to drive with Stefania myself. Or maybe I should just call Paige. I could ride with her . . .

"Rachel's the one who came to your suit fitting," Stefania says.

"Yeah."

"Good. I like her. Give me her address and tell her I'll pick her up at noon."

My knees buckle. *Whew.* "Thanks, Stefania, that's really nice of you—"

"Address, Miles."

"Yeah. Okay." I give Stefania Rachel's address, start to thank her profusely again, and get hung up on.

Now there's just Rachel.

> Is it OK if u ride with my piano teacher tmrw?

Rachel: Um ur kind of hot piano teacher? Hell yeah it's OK.

Me: Thx and please don't tell her u think she's hot.

I run back downstairs—too fast again, and I slip on the last stair. Catch the banister just in time. Try to look natural. "You can ride with us."

Eric smiles—that self-conscious smile I remember from the first time I met him. But somehow it looks different to me now, now that I know about Jocelyn, and Sam, and the hardest things that happened before he got here.

I hope (I really hope) that smile means he's trying to trust me again.

"Thanks," he says. "I really appreciate it."

I shrug. "It's no problem."

"I'm sorry I didn't tell you about everything with Jocelyn sooner." His smile fades. "I sprang that on you. It wasn't fair to expect you to just immediately get it—"

"No apology necessary. Ever."

He looks at me. Searching. But I really mean it, and he must see it, because he nods and looks away.

"I can give you your tie back." I point at the stairs behind me. "My dad gave me a tie and I can wear that tomorrow, so . . . Do you want to come upstairs and I'll get yours?"

He blinks. "Your dad gave you a tie? That's awesome."

How does he do it? How does he find the right thing to focus on, the bit that matters, in everything I say? "Yeah. You want to see it? It's really pretty, actually."

"Sure."

He follows me up the stairs and down the hallway, and just as I'm opening my door, I remember my bed isn't made and my room is a mess, but *too late now*. Eric's in my room and all I can do is kick an old unwashed binder under the bed and hope he doesn't notice.

He doesn't seem to. "Hey, I've never seen your room before."

"Yeah, I guess that's true." We were always in the auditorium, or at his house with Nina. "It's not always this much of a pit, I swear."

He looks at me sideways. "Sure, if you say so."

"What's that supposed to mean?"

"I've seen the inside of your locker, Miles."

"And I've seen the inside of your car." I pick up the black tie with white stitching and hold it out. "Here's the one from my dad."

He takes it carefully. "It's beautiful."

"Right? It's subtle but nice." I slip Eric's tie off the hanger, where it's draped around my suit jacket in the closet. "Here you go."

We trade ties. I drape the one from Dad over my suit jacket and Eric puts his in his pocket.

"I should go," he says.

I nod, even though I don't want him to. "Yeah. Sure, of course."

We go back downstairs. I open the front door for him. A cool, damp breeze rushes in, blowing my hair into my eyes. It smells like spring.

He pauses on the porch and turns back. "Thanks for the notes. And the tickets. And the ride."

"You're welcome."

"See you tomorrow?"

"We'll pick you up at noon."

He smiles. And then he jogs down the driveway, picks up his bike, and pedals away into the twilight.

CHAPTER TWENTY-FOUR

I wake up to birds chirping in the tree outside my window. It was so warm last night that I left the window open, and now there's a warm band of sunlight across my face.

For a few minutes, I lie in bed, pretending today is not the day it actually is. Pretending I can just stay in bed, listening to the bird cacophony, while the stripe of sunlight moves across my bedroom floor.

But today *is* the day, so I get up.

I shower. Style my hair. Put on my newest and cleanest binder and (yes) my underwear with the little stars on them. Clean my glasses. And then throw on jeans and a T-shirt because it's too early for a suit.

Mom has eggs and a banana ready to go when I come down-stairs.

"I have a showing in half an hour," she says, sliding a cup of orange juice across the table. "But it's over at eleven, so I'll be back in plenty of time to pick up Eric and—what's his sister's name?"

"Nina."

"Right. Should we bring some snacks in case she gets hungry? Why don't you ask? Or we could just throw something in a bag." Mom picks up her briefcase from the counter. "Love you, sweetheart. See you in a couple hours."

She kisses my forehead and races out the door.

I eat slowly. I feel like I'm dreaming, which I remember from last year. Competition day finally arrives, and I drift along, hyper-aware and sleepwalking at the same time. Time crawls and it flies.

I take the orange juice with me into the living room and fold up on the couch. Flip through TV channels until I find a home improvement show. Let the arguments about marble or quartz countertops wash over me.

TV always makes time go faster, and after two episodes, Dad emerges from his office, sees me on the couch, and says, "Aren't you going to get ready soon?"

"Yeah." I turn off the TV, peel myself off the couch, and head upstairs.

Fresh deodorant. Suit pants. White shirt. (Sideways check—flat.) Black socks. Dress shoes. (Rock back and forth—laces tight enough.) Wash my face. Check my hair.

It doesn't take me as long, this time, to tie my tie. I don't even have to resort to YouTube. The tie from Dad fits perfectly. The right length, the right width. The knot fits between the points of my collar like it was made to be there.

On with the suit jacket. One last look in the mirror . . .

Downstairs, the front door bangs open. "I'm here!" Mom shouts. "Sorry I'm late. Let me just change—"

"We have time," Dad says.

She clatters up the stairs. "No, we don't, we have to pick up Eric and Nina!"

I pick up Eric's drawing of the laughing waffle playing the piano, fold it carefully, and put it in my jacket pocket.

Mom emerges from her bedroom as I leave mine. She's wearing nice jeans and a blouse, and switched her heels for sandals. "Arthur, come on!" she yells.

"I'm coming." Dad follows her, wearing a checkered button-down shirt that he usually reserves for client meetings. He smiles when he sees me. "Tie looks good."

I smooth it, suddenly awkward. "Thanks."

"Come on, come on!" Mom's already halfway down the stairs.

We throw granola bars and bananas into a bag. Fill up a water bottle. Mom grabs her purse. Dad grabs his keys. And then it's out the door and into Dad's Subaru.

And now the nerves hit.

Today is the competition.

We're going to pick up Eric.

My phone buzzes.

Rachel: omg your piano teacher

I guess that means Stefania found her house.

Eric and Nina are sitting on their front steps when we pull up. Nina jumps up immediately, waving a stuffed animal in the air, and runs flat-out for the car. Eric dashes after her, managing to catch her hand and slow her down.

I get out of the car. "Hi."

Nina looks me up and down. "Look sharp," she says, giving me a thumbs-up.

"Thanks, Nina. So do you."

"I look pretty, not sharp." She holds up the skirt of her flowery dress to prove her point. And then she holds up her stuffed animal. "I brought Small Pudge. Is that okay?"

The stuffed animal is a rather tattered cat that does look a little like Mr. Pudge.

"Sure. Totally okay."

"Eric said I should ask."

"Thanks for asking."

"Okay." She pushes up her little pink glasses. "Let's go, Eric."

"Yeah. I'm coming." But he's looking at me. "I like your tie."

"I like yours, too." I point at the black tie—the tie that I borrowed—that he's wearing over a purple button-down shirt. He's still wearing black jeans, but between the shirt and his new, sky-blue Chuck Taylors, it's the most color I've ever seen him in.

"Let's go, Eric," Nina says again.

"Okay." He ducks past me and climbs into the car. "Get in the middle, Neens. You're the smallest."

"I am the smallest," she says proudly.

"That's right. Where's your seatbelt?" He looks up, smiling at my parents while fiddling with Nina's seatbelt. "Hi. Thanks a lot for giving us a ride."

"Do you want a snack?" Mom says. Because she may be a high-powered career woman, but she's also constantly anxious she's falling down on her mom duties if she isn't feeding everyone in sight.

I climb in on the other side, squashing in next to Nina's poofy skirt and Small Pudge. And off we go, Nina studying the granola bar collection. She finally chooses one and hands it to Eric to open for her.

"What do you say, Neens?"

"Thank you."

It's a forty-minute drive to Milwaukee, and I definitely spent some time last night worrying about how awkward it would be. What would I say to Eric? What would he say to me?

Turns out I didn't need to worry, because Nina keeps up the conversation all by herself, telling us about Mr. Pudge's adventures (some of which must be made up), about the goldfish that's still in her school classroom, even commenting how our car looks like their Subaru.

"Except ours is not clean because Eric trashes it," she says seriously.

Eric looks surprised. "No, I don't."

"I heard Mami say you trash it."

I raise my eyebrows at Eric. He just grins sheepishly and goes back to looking out the window.

It's almost one o'clock when we pull into the parking garage. (One hour to go.) Mom grasps Nina's hand as we cross the street, leaving Eric to fall into step next to me.

"How are you doing?" he asks.

I have butterflies in my stomach. And you're talking to me. "Okay. Getting nervous."

He smiles, and it's not so self-conscious this time. "You'll be great."

"I don't know."

"Okay. Well." We reach the steps of the concert hall. "Consider this: You chose your own name. You chose to live as the gender you really are. You're literally rewriting your narrative. Not to sound pretentious, but you're, like, a wild card. Compared to all that, a little Tchaikovsky should be a piece of cake, right?"

Is he joking?

But except for his vague smile, he looks serious.

He knows. What I've been trying to do for months—he gets it. Rewriting and rewriting myself, because he did the same thing, moving from Seattle and finding me, and deciding to trust me. He's *doing* the same thing, deciding to trust me again. He's not switching genders or names or pronouns, but he's still choosing who he wants to be.

Finding yourself, in spite of everyone else.

All I can say is, "Thanks."

And then we're through the giant glass doors and into the lobby of the concert hall. It makes the prelim venue look like a cheap rec center. This lobby has plush red carpeting, soaring white walls, and sunlight pouring in through skylights in the ceiling. The doors to the concert hall itself are enormous—twice as tall as I am, and made of rich dark wood.

The lobby is also *huge,* which is just as well, because it's already filling up with people. I see Andrew Morris sidling through the crowd, heading for a side door—probably on his way backstage. A younger girl who must be in the Junior Level follows him, fiddling anxiously with her sleeveless yellow dress.

Most of the people in the lobby are older. Anxious-looking parents, rolling programs in their hands. Anxious-looking grandparents, leaning forward any time anyone says something to them. And the usual group of curious retirees who have just come for the concert and are (yet again) the only people who look like they're enjoying themselves.

"Miles!"

It's Rachel, barreling toward us from across the lobby, with Stefania just behind. Rachel grabs me in a tight hug. "I was hoping I got kicked out of your car because of Eric," she whispers in my ear.

"Nothing happened," I whisper back.

She pulls away, narrowing her eyes at me. I can practically see the gears turning in her brain. "I'll work on him."

"Rachel," I say patiently, "please don't."

She just grins, turns away, and compliments Nina on her dress. Nina stares at Rachel with her mouth open, which is fair. Rachel is wearing her suit jacket from Valentine's Night over a black-and-white button-down shirt with a bright yellow tie. She looks like a really gay bee.

Stefania comes over and puts her arm around me. "Your friend Rachel is a firecracker."

Uh-oh. "She didn't rant about climate change the whole ride, did she?"

"It was feminism, and yes, she did. We had an excellent discussion about the lack of female representation in the conducting world."

Well, as long as they both enjoyed it.

"Hey, Miles!"

I turn around. There's Paige, just coming in, with Josie behind her.

Paige gives me a quick hug. "Mom and Shane are just parking the car."

"*Shane?*"

"Yeah." She lets me go.

"I didn't give Shane a ticket."

"My mom did. I told you, she can get tickets. He just texted me last night and said he wanted to come, so I got him a ticket. I thought you guys were friends." She turns away and goes back to Josie.

Great. Shane is going to be in the same concert hall as Eric. It's not like that's ever gone horribly wrong or anything. There aren't even assigned seats. He could end up in the same aisle as Eric, or *next to him.*

I grab Mom's sleeve.

She turns around. "What?"

"Shane is coming. He came with the Kims."

She smiles and nods. "That's nice of him."

I give her a Look. "Mom. *Eric* is here."

"Oh. *Oh.*" She looks quickly around and pats my arm. "Leave it to me. I'll run interference. Go sign in."

I pull Stefania away from talking to my dad about pianos, and we head for the sign-in table. The same old ladies from the prelim round are sitting behind it. It's probably even the same card table. Déjà vu.

Patrice gives me a wink, puts a check mark next to my name, another next to Stefania's, and hands me a program. No printed warm-up times today. The finals function more like a regular concert, which means an army of runners backstage telling everyone where to go when.

I've never been able to decide if that's better or worse.

I wander slowly toward the side door that leads backstage, opening my program. The Junior Level always goes first. Then intermission. Then Senior Level.

I scan through the order. Cassandra O'Brian, Andrew, Jenny . . . There I am. Second-to-last on the program.

Right before Cameron Hart.

Crap.

I hold the program out to Stefania, jamming my finger at it.

She just raises her eyebrows at me. "What?"

(*What?* Look!) "I'm second-to-last."

She's not looking. "Who cares, Miles?"

"Cameron is *last*. He's going to be the last thing the judges hear."

That gets her attention. She grabs my program. "How much you want to bet Pierre is responsible for this?" she mutters. "Probably bribed someone."

This is turning into a nightmare already, and the competition hasn't even started yet. "He was last on the program last year, too. And he *beat* me."

Stefania looks up. "Don't let this get to you. This is an entirely different year. I mean, look! You're not even the same person. You have a different name."

I scowl at her. "I *am* the same person."

She sighs. "Of course you are. That was a bad joke, sorry." Pats my shoulder. "Let's go backstage."

"Miles, wait!"

I turn around. Eric is weaving through the crowd toward me.

Oh, no. Did Shane show up? Is Eric coming to ask me what the hell I was thinking, inviting *Shane*?

But he just says, "I wanted to say good luck."

He's so close. Close enough I could count his eyelashes behind his glasses, if I really tried.

"Oh. Thanks." With him here in front of me, I feel calmer. I can breathe again. I reach inside my jacket pocket. "You know, I think I've got a pretty good good-luck charm already." I pull out the piece of paper and unfold it. "This really cool artist made it for me. I call it *Laughing Waffle in Concert*. He didn't sign it though."

Eric grins and fishes a pencil out of his pocket. "I'll sign it now." He gently takes the drawing from me, and, with it flat on one palm, scribbles his name on the edge.

He holds it out and as I take it, our hands touch.

"Kick ass, Miles," he says.

Through the side door, into a hallway that looks a lot like the hall-way everybody waited in during the prelim round. But this one is wider and taller, with floors of polished cement. Stefania's clogs echo off the walls and ceiling.

There's also nobody waiting in this hallway. It's empty, under a wash of harsh fluorescent light. We walk all the way to the end of it, to another door with a flyer that reads TO WARM-UP ROOMS. Stefania opens the door.

Here's the noise.

It's a big open room, carpeted in gray, filled with stiff-looking couches and chairs. On the couches and chairs are all the other contestants, and their accompanists, in their gowns and suits. Those who haven't managed to snag a seat are crowded around the water cooler that's sitting on a table in the corner.

"Miles!"

I barely have time to brace myself before I'm tackled by Jenny Chang and Trilby Malone, both in sleek black gowns.

"Girls Club Plus Miles reunited!" Jenny shouts.

I look around the room. Cassandra O'Brian is glaring at us from her spot on a couch. Andrew Morris is giving us some serious side-eye from the water cooler. "Where's Andrea?"

Trilby brushes a stray wisp of red hair from her eyes. She got her braces off since I last saw her. Her teeth are really straight. "Stomach bug. She was vomiting all day yesterday and had to pull out last-minute."

"That sucks."

"See, this is why I only eat plain white bread for twenty-four hours before any performance," Jenny says. "You can't get food poisoning from bread."

(I've known Jenny for long enough to know she's perfectly serious.)

Trilby rolls her eyes. "Jenny, it wasn't food poisoning. It was the flu."

The door behind me opens. I tense up, ready for Cameron, but it's a girl with long, straight black hair, wearing a lilac sleeveless gown and holding a copy of Brahms's Piano Concerto No. 2. She hesitates in the doorway, gives us a nervous smile, and then sidles past us. We watch her pick her way through the maze of competitors, ending up in a corner by herself.

"Who's that?" Trilby whispers.

"Lily Shimada," Jenny and I say in unison.

"Oh, the new girl. Jenny told me about her." Trilby lets her breath out. A nervous sigh. "She's playing Brahms Two. That's . . . She can compete with that."

"She'll crumble under the pressure," Jenny says. "She's never done this competition before."

Trilby looks at her sideways. "You didn't crumble under the pressure your first time."

"Of course not!" Jenny glowers. "What's your point?"

Stefania's hand lands on my shoulder. She firmly steers me away from Jenny and Trilby, over to the wall. "We get twenty minutes to warm up with an actual piano, so I think we'd better run through things a bit mentally, don't you?"

"I don't see a closet to hide in."

The door opens again. This time, it's Cameron. He breezes through, dressed entirely in black—black shirt, black suit, even a black silk tie. It makes his pale skin look like marble, and his blond hair stand out like gold. Behind him, Pierre is dressed in black slacks and a black turtleneck sweater.

Jenny and Trilby turn to look at me and pull off a very synchronized eye-roll.

Cameron sees me. He smiles.

I turn back to Stefania. "How about the hallway?"

"No." She's giving Pierre such a ferocious look I half expect him to burst into flame. "I have a better idea."

She pushes me toward the door on the other side of the room. The flyer on this one says WARM-UP ROOMS THIS WAY.

"We're not supposed to go to the warm-up room yet—" I say, but Stefania's already opening the door, shoving me through.

Another hallway, also empty. Two doors with signs on them—WARM-UP ROOM #1 and WARM-UP ROOM #2—but Stefania ignores them. She opens a heavy-duty door on the other side of the hallway and pushes me through.

Into darkness.

No, not darkness. It's not pitch black, it's just dim. Another janitor's closet?

The space is too big for that. Way too big. My eyes adjust and I realize I'm standing on a black floor and the ceiling above me soars away. There are big dark stage lights up there, and all sorts of rigging. Around me are black music stands (grouped together like groves of short trees), stacks of armless chairs, a big bass drum, a set of four timpani (tops covered by circles of cloth, coppery bottoms glinting).

"Are we backstage?" I whisper.

"Yes," Stefania says in a normal voice. "But we're quite far back. No need to whisper."

I don't want to be backstage. What if I hear applause? What if I hear someone else performing?

Of course, then again, I don't really want to hang out in a room with Cameron Hart throwing me smug glances every ten seconds, either.

Sigh. "Okay. Now what?"

"Now, we breathe. Ready?"

Just like in the prelim round, we breathe together, slowly, in and out. I close my eyes and let my muscles relax, one by one.

Listen only to my heartbeat, and the vast, waiting silence of the space around me.

We shake out our arms, hands, legs. Roll our shoulders. Lean forward and stretch. Lean back and stretch.

And then I close my eyes, let my breath out, and, just like before, start mentally playing through Tchaikovsky in my head. Every note. Every phrase.

Distantly, I hear applause. The junior competition is starting. Here's the opening of a Mozart piano concerto, far away.

Tune it out. Mozart blurs into muffled noise. I focus on Tchaikovsky. Chords. Phrases. Notes. Sing it all in my head . . .

When I finally reach the last chord and open my eyes, there's a different Mozart piano concerto in the distance, which I guess means I've tuned out at least one performance.

"Did you get all the way through?" says Stefania.

"Yeah."

"Good. Then let's go listen."

"Listen to what?"

I get the raised eyebrow. "Everyone else's performances. This competition is also a concert, and at concerts, one supports other musicians."

Uh, since when?

But it's too late to argue, because Stefania is dragging me off through the backstage area, dodging an upright piano, a celesta, more percussion instruments (chimes, marimba, xylophone), and an enormous set piece that looks like a cardboard castle.

The Mozart is getting louder. Stefania slows down, walking gently so her clogs don't clomp. We round a corner, and there are two stagehands in black clothes and black headsets staring at us.

And between them is a big stage door with a small glass window in it. Through the window, I can just see the corner of a piano—and a hand reaching down for the lowest keys . . .

A stagehand points to us. "You next?" he whispers.

"No," Stefania says, "we're just listening."

He looks confused, but Stefania looks calm and confident, so he shrugs and goes back to noodling on his phone.

We listen through the last bright notes of the Mozart. Final chord. Applause erupts, muffled by the thick door. The stagehands put away their phones and haul open the door. A girl who looks like she's twelve or thirteen comes through, visibly shaking, followed by a middle-aged woman with glasses, who must be her accompanist—and probably her teacher.

"Good job," Stefania whispers to her.

She looks up at Stefania, like a deer in the headlights. "Thanks?"

The woman in glasses pats the girl on the back and steers her away, probably headed for the hallway and the room full of everybody else.

Running feet. A boy appears, breathless, followed by a harried-looking man who's just as breathless. The stagehands heave open the door again. More applause. A moment of quiet. And then the opening of Mendelssohn's Piano Concerto No. 1 in G minor.

I stuff my hands in my pockets so I don't bite my nails. Stefania folds her arms, listening seriously, nodding her head along.

What is she doing?

The next young pianist shows up partway through the Mendelssohn. Her black hair is braided down her back and her dress looks big on her.

"Where's your accompanist?" says one of the stagehands.

She points. "He's out there."

Must be another student of the same teacher. I feel suddenly grateful that Stefania doesn't have a stable full of young pianists, all competing for the same prize.

Stefania steps closer to the girl. "Deep breath," she whispers. "In . . . out . . ."

What is she doing? This girl isn't my competition—we're still in the Junior Level. But what is Stefania doing coaching her?

Mrs. Kim always left me alone before performances and competitions. She was always my accompanist, but I never saw her before it was time to warm up on an actual piano. And then all we did was play through the piece. Last year, I sat in the lounge with Jenny and Trilby and Andrea, talking and biting my nails. Sat there until it was time to warm up—hating Cameron's cool confidence, hating the way Pierre stuck to him like a bodyguard.

The Mendelssohn finishes. Applause.

The stage door opens. The boy and his accompanist come through. Stefania whispers, "Good job."

The boy shoots her a relieved look as he leaves.

Stefania raises her eyebrows at me. *Fine, I get the message.*

"Good luck," I say to the girl.

She stares at me in surprise. "Thanks, Miles," she whispers, and then the stage door is open again and she's out, followed by the same man that accompanied the boy.

Wait. How did she know my name?

Applause. Another Mozart concerto begins.

Stefania sees my expression. "You looked up the other competitors online, didn't you? So did she."

"Yeah, but she's in the Junior Level. I'm not her competition."

Stefania shrugs. "You've been runner-up for three years. People know who you are."

That's a weird thought. Obviously, some people know who I am—Jenny, Andrew, Cameron. And other people beyond them. That nasty post on the online forum made that obvious. Plus, after a few years, you get used to seeing the same people over and over again.

But I had no idea anybody in the Junior Level would know me.

The girl finishes her Mozart. I watch her bow through the tiny window. The door opens and she comes backstage, shepherded by her accompanist.

I give her a thumbs-up.

Her face brightens. "Thanks." And she's gone.

I'm not ready when intermission arrives. Were there fewer Junior Level competitors this year, or did time just seem to go faster?

"Let's go," Stefania says.

We head back through the backstage area, out into the warm-up hallway. Cassandra O'Brian is just opening the door to one of the warm-up rooms.

On an impulse, I give her a thumbs-up.

She looks confused. For a second, she can't seem to figure out what to do with her face. She settles for glaring at me, and closes the door of her warm-up room with a bang.

Stefania and I go back to the room full of everyone else. It's weird to come back to it, after listening backstage. It looks just the same as it did this time last year. A different city, a different lounge, but Andrew Morris is still hanging around Cameron, hoping for a conversation while Cameron ignores him. Jenny is still talking nonstop while Trilby nods and looks dazed. Jason What's-His-Name from Indiana is on his phone. Nadiya Name-I-Also-Can't-Remember is playing air piano.

The only difference is Lily Shimada, clutching her Brahms music in her corner.

Stefania says she's going to the restroom, so I sit down on a couch with Jenny and Trilby. Jenny breaks off her monologue on the difficulty of finding adequate high heels to play in.

Trilby looks relieved. "Where have you been?"

"Listening to the junior group." Cameron is looking at me, but I ignore him. "They sounded good."

"You listened to them?" Jenny looks baffled. "Like, out in the audience?"

"No, backstage."

Jenny and Trilby blink at me. Next to the couch, Nadiya stops playing air piano, looking sideways at me like I've just declared Mozart the coolest composer of all time.

And then Trilby shrugs and stands up, smoothing the creases out of her gown. "Well, I have to go warm up."

"Good luck!" I give her a thumbs-up.

She stares at me. So does Jenny. And I realize I've never once told them *good luck*. Even though they've been my "competition friends" for a couple years now.

They've never said *good luck* to me, either.

Jenny recovers. "Um. Yeah. Good luck, Trilby."

"Thanks." Trilby wanders to the door, still looking confused.

Now it's just me and Jenny.

"Thanks for reporting those posts," I say, quietly, so no one else can hear me.

Her face turns serious. "Anytime, Miles." And she carries on talking about high heels.

Andrew leaves to warm up. Cassandra comes back in tears. Nobody asks her what's wrong. People just watch her from the corners of their eyes, like they're afraid whatever happened to her will rub off on them, as she grabs her coat and flees the room.

Where's Stefania? Am I supposed to go listen to more people? I'm not sure I can. Not when it's my group . . .

Nadiya leaves to warm up, and Trilby comes back.

"How'd it go?" I ask.

Trilby lets out a shaky breath. "I don't know. Okay, I think? I don't know." And she wanders away. Nobody wants to stay here after they finish. Why would they? They all head to the lobby.

Jenny sighs and stands up, smoothing her dress.

"Good luck," I say.

Again, she looks confused. But then she smiles. "Thanks, Miles."

And now it's just me, Cameron, and Lily. And Pierre Fontaine, who is currently rubbing Cameron's hands like some obsessive athletic coach. It's not even cold in here.

The door to the hallway opens. It's Stefania—finally. Pierre looks at her disdainfully. Stefania ignores him. She sits down next to me on the couch.

"Almost time," she says.

I nod. Tap my fingers on my knees.

Lily heads for the door to the warm-up rooms.

"Good luck," I say.

She pauses, hand on the knob, and turns to look at me. So does Cameron.

Lily smiles—just a little. "Thanks," she says. "You, too." And then she's gone.

I listen to myself breathing as the minutes pass. Listen to Stefania breathing. The creak of the floor under Pierre's pacing footsteps. Finally, I check my phone. "I guess we should go."

Stefania nods, and we both stand up. I reach for the door.

"Good luck, Miles," Cameron says.

I turn to look at him. He's in full smirk.

I take a breath, and keep my voice level. "Thanks. You, too."

CHAPTER TWENTY-FIVE

The warm-up room is small. Small, fluorescent-light-white, and sterile. The only things in it are two upright pianos and two piano benches, just like in the warm-up room in the prelims. It's a squeeze for Stefania and me to both sit down.

"What would you like to do?" Stefania asks.

I rub my hands on my pants to warm them up. "I don't know. Start at the beginning, I guess? Maybe a few times, just to practice starting."

She nods, and plays the opening fanfare.

The upright pianos are bright and tinkly, without any of the depth of the grands we'll play onstage, and this warm-up room doesn't have carpet on the walls. The sound bounces chaotically off every surface. Close and claustrophobic. My eardrums vibrate.

I manage to make it up to the first big orchestral tutti, and then I pull my hands from the keyboard.

Stefania stops, too. "Want to start again?"

"Yeah. I mean, no." I rub my forehead. Rub my eyes under my glasses.

Stefania is silent. Waiting.

"Sorry. I hate these warm-ups." I lower my hands. "They feel useless. It doesn't matter what I play like in here. I know I'll go out there and get nervous and make mistakes. And then Cameron will win. Again."

"What makes you think you'll make mistakes?" Stefania says quietly.

I stare at her. "Because it's a performance. A competition. That's what happens."

But she just calmly raises her eyebrows. "That's what happens?"

"Yeah! Things never go according to plan in performances. That's how they work. I'm going to go out there, after all this practice, and my fingers will still get away from me and I'll have to recover, and the whole time I'll be wondering if *that* was the mistake that handed Cameron the win—"

"Or this could be the best time you've ever played it," Stefania says.

I turn and look at her. Is she joking?

But her face looks totally serious.

"It's a performance," I say, like she'll get it if I just say it one more time.

She shrugs. "So? It could still be the best time you've ever played this piece. It's statistically possible."

"Uh, sure, and all the air in this room could randomly go under the pianos. That's statistically possible, too, just pretty unlikely."

Stefania rolls her eyes. "You assume, because it's a performance, with nerves and pressure and the knowledge that you can't simply start over, that things will go wrong. Your fingers will cramp. You'll hit a wrong note. You'll forget what comes next—"

Grimace. "Not helping, Stefania."

She sighs. "All of that is just assumptions, Miles. Yes, more likely, with nerves, that you'll mess up. But don't make it *even more likely* with your assumptions. This could be the best time you've ever played it. It's not all out of your control. You choose what you think is possible."

It hits like a ton of bricks.

I choose.

Just like I chose my name. Just like I chose to live as *me*. The *me* who is a boy and was a girl, who is a puzzle of masculine and feminine pieces, who is brand new and exactly the same.

You're kind of a wild card, Eric said.

The door opens and a runner sticks his head in. "Miles Jacobson? You're up next."

I can choose.

We stand up. Follow the runner down the hallway, through backstage, past the silent instruments, to the door I was standing at an hour ago.

The door opens. The applause grows suddenly louder as Lily Shimada comes through, followed by a tall Black man—her accompanist, and probably her teacher.

"Good luck, Miles," Lily says. She gives me a thumbs-up.

"Thanks," I say, and then she's gone.

The door is opening for me. *This is it.*

I walk out, Stefania clomping behind me, into the bright, warm light of the stage. Applause kicks up like a wave, drowning out our footsteps. We reach the two grand pianos in the center of the stage—one with the lid all the way up, the other with the lid on the short stick.

We stand together, each at our piano. Bow. *Dodge the flying tomatoes.* Straighten up. Sit down.

The applause dies away.

I lean down to adjust the piano bench. The knobs on either side are slippery under my fingers. Are my hands sweating? Or is it leftover sweat from everybody before me?

(Gross.)

I stick out my right foot. The toe of my dress shoe finds the sustain pedal. Wipe my hands on my pants. Touch the pocket of my jacket, where Eric's drawing is stowed. *Laughing Waffle in Concert.*

I look through the piano in front of me—past the long strings, shimmering under the raised lid—to Stefania, sitting at her piano across from me.

I nod.

Stefania gives me a tiny grin, and then she launches into the opening fanfare, throwing herself at it like she always does. Bright. Percussive. It's just a piano, but in my head I hear horns, cold and clear and tragic.

I lift my hands.

This could be the best time I ever play it.

Take a breath.

I am a human wild card. I choose my own path.

I am free.

I slam my entire joyful being into the first massive chord. The piano vibrates, strings turning to a blur, pedal rumbling under my foot.

I am the crashing chords of joy.

I am the reaching, searching melody.

I am the cascading arpeggios and the waves of scales and the pounding octaves.

I am queer.

I am trans.

I am full of joy.

Sweat trickles down my back as I switch gears into the nimble, spritely development section. Angelic, harp-like arpeggios. The phrases float away and Stefania takes over, the orchestra part ratcheting up the tension again. Doom forcing its way back into the story.

I let my arms hang by my sides. Stretch my fingers. Take another breath.

And dive back in.

On and on and on, to the big cadenza. *Take your time, take your time . . .*

I listen to the sound from my piano, floating up around me and fading away into the hall air. I let my hands do what they know how to do. I've played this hundreds of times. Thousands of times. I can do this.

Gathering steam. Gathering speed. Brighter. Louder. Faster.

Now Stefania joins me, and we both rush toward the end.

The last run of octaves.

Chord after chord after chord . . .

Into the final note, leaning my weight on the keys. Looking up, into Stefania's eyes. And *lift*.

Hands up. Breath out.

I did it.

I made it.

I'm smiling. I don't know when I started but I'm smiling, and Stefania is smiling.

Applause crashes in. I hear a whistle—Rachel. She always blows me a whistle at the finale.

I stand up with Stefania. Turn to the audience. Bow. *Dodge the flying tomatoes.*

When I straighten up, I look out into the audience, but I can't see anything or anyone. It's too bright onstage.

We turn. The stage door is opening. I walk through it, and Stefania follows.

I bump right into Cameron. Is it me, or does he look nervous?

I'm breathing like I just ran a marathon, but I say, "Good luck, Cameron."

He glances at me like he barely knows who I am. But there's no time for him to catch up, to come up with some smug response, because Pierre is pushing him through the door onto the stage. The applause rises again. Now the door is closing.

Stefania grabs my arm. "This, you don't need to hear."

Back we go, past the instruments and the stands and the chairs. Out into the hallway.

And then she lets out a squeal and pulls me into a hug so tight I can't breathe. "You did it! Miles, you did it. That was *wonderful.* You kicked ass, and I am so proud of you."

What is . . . what's wrong with my eyes? Everything's turned blurry.

I hear myself say, "I think it was okay."

"It *was* okay. It was great. You did a great job."

My eyes are blurry because I'm crying. Tears roll big and fat down my face. Sniffling into Stefania's shoulder.

She said I did a great job. She said she's proud of me. She wouldn't say it if she didn't mean it. I've known her long enough to know that.

For a long time, we just stand there. I cry. She hugs me.

And then, finally, she gently pulls away. "Cameron will be coming back before we know it."

"Yeah." Mighty sniff. "Definitely don't want him to see this."

"Where's your handkerchief?"

I blink at her. "My what?" (Brain catches up.) "I don't have one."

"Miles, all men have handkerchiefs in their suit pockets. Get one for next time."

We go back to the room with the couches and chairs. It's totally empty. The only signs of the competition are the empty water cooler and the paper cups strewn across the table and the floor.

Stefania pulls a pack of tissues out of her purse and hands me one. I blow my nose.

It's over.

Wipe my eyes.

It's over.

"I guess we should go out to the lobby?" I crumple the tissue and stuff it in my pocket because I don't see a trash can in here. "There's the reception. The results . . ."

"Miles." Stefania gives me a serious stare. "Whatever happens with the results, you played an extremely respectable Tchaikovsky. It belonged to you. You showed everybody who you are and what that music means to you. What piano means to you. You should be proud of that, whatever the judges say."

"Yeah. Okay." (Easy to say now.)

Stefania picks up her purse and we leave the room, walking back up the hallway to the lobby.

I get through the door and Rachel immediately tackles me with such force that I stagger sideways.

"You were amazing! Miles, that Tchaikovsky was *so good*!"

"Is Cameron done?" I look around, but the only people in the lobby are the other competitors. "Is it over?"

"No." She lets go of me. "He's still playing, but who needs to hear that? I ducked out as soon as you finished."

I love Rachel so much my heart hurts. She might complain about how the only classical music that's ever played was written by dead white guys (accurate), but she also shows up to all my concerts, and she always has, and I'm really glad she didn't miss this one.

The other competitors are looking at us. Most of them look annoyed. I don't see Trilby or Jenny, but Lily Shimada waves at me. I wave back.

Applause echoes distantly from behind the doors to the concert hall. *That's it.* Cameron must have finished.

The Tri-State Competition is over.

The doors open. People slowly wander out into the lobby, blinking in the light.

"I will give you all the gossip later," Rachel mutters in my ear. "Because let me tell you, Cassandra O'Brian crashed and *burned*."

I barely hear her. I'm watching the door for . . .

"Miles!" Mom bursts out, power walking past a startled group of retirees and blasting toward me, arms outstretched. Rachel jumps out of the way just in time, and Mom wraps me in a hug almost as tight as Rachel's. "That was amazing, sweetheart."

"Well done." Dad is just behind her. Squeezes my shoulder. "Really good Tchaikovsky."

"Hi, Miles!" Here's Nina, waving Small Pudge in the air. "Good job!"

"Thanks, Nina."

"I was not bored of the piano," she says seriously.

I grin. "I'm glad about that."

"Kicked *ass*." Now Paige is hugging me. "Cameron looked scared as shit."

"It was really good!" Josie reaches out and squeezes my arm.

"Miles! Excuse me, I have to see my former student!" It's Mrs. Kim, in an incredibly floral dress, sidling past Paige. "That is why you're studying with Stefania." She pats my cheek. "So good. *So good.*"

"Thanks, Mrs. Kim."

Shane looms behind her. "Hey, Miles."

Crap. I totally forgot he was here. Where's Eric? But I don't see him. Nina's right here—how far away could Eric be?

"Hi, Shane. Thanks for coming." I don't move to hug him, and he doesn't move to hug me. But he smiles, and nods at me. Retreats, tucks his hands in his pockets, and wanders away. Giving me space.

Where is Eric?

But now Mom has my arm and I'm being dragged away, through the lobby, out a pair of glass side doors, into the sunshine. There's a wide patio out here, under the shade of tall leafy trees. And on the patio are buffet tables full of brownies, cookies, small cut veggies . . .

Nina heads straight for the cookies and Mom lets go of me to run after her. Dad has stopped just outside the doors, talking to Mrs. Kim and Stefania. Paige and Josie wander toward the punch bowl, and Rachel says she'll get me something to drink and goes after them.

Where the hell is Eric?

What if he left? Maybe he saw Shane. Maybe Shane said something to him. Maybe he just decided he didn't want to be here after all and he's gone to wait by the car.

Rachel shoves a paper cup of soda into my hand. "Drink something." And then she's gone again, heading for the food table.

The paper cup is turning blurry. *Crap.* I'm going to cry again . . .

"Hey, Miles!"

I turn around, and it's Eric. Rumpled, breathing quickly, tie knot loose, and holding a single rose.

He's here.

"I thought you left." My voice comes out choked.

He looks embarrassed. "I did, but just because I realized I didn't have any flowers to give you. Your performance was . . . It was amazing. Better than the last time I heard it. It was just . . . There was nothing else while you were playing, and I realized I should have brought you flowers, and I didn't. So I ran out as soon as you finished. It just took me a little longer to find a flower than I thought it would."

He holds out the rose.

I take it, pinching it tightly between my fingers. I'm not going to drop this one. "Thanks. I thought you left because of Shane. Or me."

"Well, technically I did leave because of you." He rubs the back of his neck. Looks self-conscious. "But. Um. I thought it was nice that Shane came to hear you play?"

How is he this wonderful?

I smile, tentative. "Yeah."

He takes a deep breath. "Would you go out with me again?"

Stomach flip. Heart going a hundred miles an hour. "Really?"

"Really. And, maybe . . . a real date. Not a pretend date that turns into a real date."

"Yeah." I'm smiling. It's already hurting my face. "Sure. I mean, yes."

He's smiling, too. Dimple and all.

I can't hug him, holding a soda cup and a rose. I look around, but there's nowhere to set either of those things.

Time to take a risk.

"Eric Mendez, may I kiss you?"

He takes the soda cup from me. "Yes, please."

I lean up, free hand around his back, and kiss him.

I'm sure there are people watching. I'm sure there will be some asinine forum post about it later. But right now, I really don't give a fuck. I am here, kissing Eric, and I feel all the joy I felt onstage. I am just as much *me* as I was when I played Tchaikovsky.

That's enough.

Despite Mom's best efforts, Nina still manages to eat at least four cookies, and when Eric finally tells her she can't have any more, she wraps a few up in napkins and puts them in her pockets, to take back to their parents. I introduce Eric and Rachel and Paige to Jenny and Trilby, who seem pretty relaxed now. They must be feeling pretty good about their performances—but I don't ask them. This is the break, the time we all try to think about everything *but* our performances. At least for an hour.

Cameron doesn't look relaxed, though. He hovers on the edge of the reception, glancing around like he's expecting a ninja attack.

"Good afternoon, everyone."

The amplified voice makes me jump. Everybody turns to the older woman with dyed blond hair who has climbed up on a small raised dais with a microphone. She's wearing flowing blue pants with a flowing blue tunic that is definitely a set and was definitely bought at a new age store that also sells incense.

"As many of you know, I'm Janet Sofby, the executive director of the Tri-State Piano Competition."

Light applause. Everybody here knows who Janet is. She's been announcing the results for years, so the judges don't have to make eye contact with the people they critiqued.

Wait a minute.

The results.

She's about to announce the results.

"Thank you to each and every one of you for coming out today to support the Tri-State Piano Competition and all of these amazingly talented young artists. Let's give them all a round of applause!"

Applause. Whistles. Yeah, yeah, let's get on with it.

"The standard just gets higher and higher every year, and we are so inspired, hearing all of these young people play. What an exciting future for classical music and piano performance in particular!"

Oh my god, Janet, hurry up.

"Now the part you've all been waiting for." She smiles benevolently, like she has no idea there are at least thirty pianists ready to tackle her and yank the results out of her hands. "First, for the Junior Level . . . In third place, we have Matthew Zhang. Congrats, Matthew!"

More applause. A stunned kid in glasses wanders forward, climbs up on the dais, and shakes Janet's hand. A photographer darts forward and snaps a quick picture—probably going up on the website later. Janet hands the kid a certificate and he leaves the stage.

"In second place . . . Christopher Merritt. Congratulations, Christopher!"

The whole scene repeats, except that Christopher has a lot more acne than Matthew.

"And in first place, the grand prize winner for our Junior Level . . . Amanda Chin!"

It's the girl who knew my name when I told her *good luck*. I join in the applause by whacking my hand against my leg because I'm still holding Eric's rose. Amanda looks thrilled—she accepts her trophy with an enormous smile.

"Now for the Senior Level." Janet adjusts her notecards. "This was a truly exceptional year. The judges had a very difficult time choosing the winners."

Nobody cares, Janet. Just tell us. Just put me out of my misery.

The rose trembles in my hands.

"In third place . . ." Janet beams at the crowd. "Trilby Malone!"

Trilby, who is standing next to Jenny, looks completely shocked. She's never placed before—Jenny was third last year—but she hikes up her dress and hurries forward. Jenny applauds, but her smile looks tight and anxious.

"In second place . . ."

Trilby has her trophy and is walking back into the crowd. Jenny is biting her lip. Andrew Morris and Cassandra O'Brian are practically on their toes, ready to leap for the stage.

"Miles Jacobson!"

I'm frozen.

I can't breathe. I can't move. I swear my heart has stopped.

And then it drops down to my feet.

Cameron beat me.

I'm second.

I *almost* made it. Almost.

Again.

Somehow, I make my feet move. Make myself walk up to Janet. Shake her hand. Force a smile. Picture. Trophy.

In the crowd, Cameron is smiling. That smug, infuriating smile. He knows what's coming.

I step off the dais. Back into the crowd. Eric grasps my hand. Rachel and Paige are looking at me anxiously. I catch sight of Shane, over Paige's head, looking annoyed.

Where's Stefania? I want to know what she thinks.

I want to get out of here before Cameron wins.

But it's too late.

"And finally, in first place, the winner of the Senior Level of the Tri-State Piano Competition and a trip to National . . . Congratulations, Lily Shimada!"

Silence.

Then someone claps loudly. Turn around—it's Stefania, standing behind me. (Where did she come from?) And now everyone else joins in. Lily walks up to Janet, looking shocked. Her smile for the picture looks dazed.

I don't blame her. She did the thing nobody thought was possible. She beat Cameron Hart.

And Cameron . . .

I turn and look at him. The smile is gone from his face. He looks catatonic. Next to him, Pierre looks furious.

Cameron didn't place. He didn't win anything. So I . . . I sort of beat him.

I catch Jenny mouthing at me, *Oh my god.*

Trilby's mouth is open. Andrew Morris looks baffled. Cassandra O'Brian is crying again.

Up on the dais, Lily turns to leave, but Janet catches her elbow. "As you all know," Janet says, "the winner of the Tri-State Competition's Senior Level automatically gets an audition slot at the National Young Artists' Piano Arts Competition in New York City this summer. But this year, the judges felt that there were *two* outstanding performances that deserved spots at the National Competition, so for the first time, we will be sending two pianists to New York City."

Stefania reaches out and grips my wrist. She's next to me. When did that happen?

Janet's smile is practically blinding. "Miles Jacobson, would you please come back up here? You're going to New York!"

Stefania squeezes my wrist, *hard,* and then Rachel is screaming next to me. Enthusiastic applause from all around me. Eric gently nudges me forward. Mom and Dad are clapping and looking completely confused.

I'm moving toward the dais. Janet grasps my hand and pulls me up. I'm suddenly between her and Lily and the photographer is snapping away.

"You sounded great," Lily says next to me.

Camera flash.

"Thanks. I—didn't hear you play. I was warming up."

"That's okay." The photographer has retreated. Lily is pulling away, with a smile that's nice and intimidating, all at once. "You'll hear me in New York."

And now we're back off the dais and into the crowd. Stefania grabs me first, hugging me tightly. And then Mrs. Kim hugs me, and then Mom hugs me. I lose sight of Lily. Rachel is yelling about how exciting New York is. Paige is explaining to Josie how the competition works. Nina is eating a cookie from her pocket stash.

I slip past Eric, who helpfully blocks Rachel by starting up a conversation about New York, and tap Jenny on the shoulder. She turns around, her face red and her eyes teary.

"Miles!" She smiles quickly and reaches out, squeezing my arm. A sincere squeeze. "Congratulations!"

"Thanks, Jenny." But I feel so bad for her. "I . . . sorry . . ."

She waves a hand. "It's okay. I didn't play as well as I hoped to."

"You're an amazing pianist." I hope she believes me; it's true.

She blinks quickly. "Thanks. But hey, you and the new girl beat Cameron! Did you see the look on his face?"

"Oh my god, Pierre is making a *scene*." It's Trilby, at my shoulder. She points to the dais, where Pierre is having a quiet but heated conversation with Janet, who seems very calm in the face of his waving arms.

I look around for Cameron. He's standing alone by the punch bowl, still looking catatonic. Even Andrew Morris has abandoned him and is talking to Lily.

"Excuse me." I leave Jenny and Trilby and go over to Cameron. "Hey."

He jerks. His eyes focus on me. His face settles into a glower. "Oh, hi, Jacobson. Come to gloat?"

Get over yourself. "Not really."

"Yeah, well, Stefania *bribed* the judges." He practically spits it at me. "Pierre's telling Janet."

Oh, come *on*. "She bribed them to give me second place?"

He clearly doesn't believe it either, but he hangs on madly. "Stefania lies and cheats her way to success and now she's teaching you to do the same."

Well, fuck you very much. "You are such a shit, Cameron."

"It should be *me* going to New York and you know it." His mouth twists into a sneer. "I played *Rachmaninov*."

I just shrug. "I guess the judges weren't into subtlety."

He turns red. "I'm not gonna give you a compliment, if that's what you're looking for."

"It's really not, Cameron. I was going to say good job and hope you're okay, but honestly, at this point, I don't know what I was thinking." I turn away. I'm done wasting time with him.

"They just want diversity!" Cameron yells after me. "That's the only reason you guys beat me. You're just tokens!"

Maybe that would have hurt once, but now it's just the opening I've been waiting for—I give him the finger over my shoulder.

Janet seems to have shut Pierre down. She's now talking to the photographer, leaving Pierre fuming by himself. He shouts for Cameron and the two of them storm away, back into the lobby.

I watch them through the glass doors. Pierre is clearly shouting as they cross the vibrant red carpet and sweep through the main door to the outside, down the steps to the sidewalk and out of sight.

Stefania is next to me again, sipping impassively at her soda. But I see a twinkle in her eyes.

People are starting to leave now that the excitement is really over. Jenny and Trilby hug me goodbye. Andrew even manages to say congratulations, although it sounds like every syllable is being yanked out of him.

I get a last hug from Paige. "Rocked it," she says in my ear. And then she takes Josie's hand and heads for the door, followed by Mrs. Kim, who waves at me, and Shane, who gives me a thumbs-up.

"I suppose I'd better go, too." Stefania gives me an intense look. "Now we start working toward the National Competition. You need to fix that pinky finger before New York. Let's go, Rachel."

She clomps away.

"Talk to you tomorrow?" Rachel gives me a quick hug.

"Yeah. Thanks for coming, Rache."

She smiles. "Always."

Man, it's so good to have her back. "Hope the drive back is okay."

Her smile turns to an excited grin. "We were *just* getting to second-wave feminism. It's going to be *great*." And she runs after Stefania.

And then it's just Mom and Dad and Eric and Nina.

"Ready to go?" Dad asks.

"Yes," Nina says.

"He was asking Miles, Neens," Eric says quietly.

"Oh. I'm sorry."

I smile. "That's okay, Nina. I'm ready to go, too."

Dad leads the way, back through the lobby. I turn back once to look at the banner over the now empty card table. And then I walk out the front doors.

Eric takes my hand. "You're going to New York."

"Yeah." *Holy shit.* "Yeah, I am."

"My boyfriend is going to New York."

I pause. "I'm your boyfriend?"

He glances at me. "Is that okay? Sorry. I didn't mean to assume—"

But I'm smiling. I can't seem to stop smiling. "I'll be your boyfriend if you'll be mine."

He grins. Dimple. "Deal."

CHAPTER TWENTY-SIX

The Sunday before the last week of school is warm enough for a T-shirt and sunny enough for sunglasses. Which means I'll have to figure out what to do about sunglasses this summer, now that I'm wearing my glasses all the time.

Maybe I'll just squint and look rugged.

But it's not an immediate concern, here in the dim auditorium. The musical is over, and the set pieces are gone, and my only immediate concern is this passage of the second movement of Tchaikovsky, which keeps tripping me up.

"Take a break!" Eric shouts from the second row of the audience, where he's sitting with his new blue Chuck Taylors up on the seat in front of him.

I pull my hands from the keys. "I can't take a break! One movement was fine for Tri-State, but National expects you to play the whole concerto."

"And that's months away." Eric's shoes come down. "Take a break and come visit me."

I lean back and stretch my hands. "Fine." *Ouch*. My knees are stiff when I stand up. "What are you drawing?"

"First page of the graphic novel." Eric holds up his notebook as I sidle into his row. He's divided the page into squares, and inside the squares are rough sketches of what I'm guessing will eventually be people. Right now most of them look like stick figures, some with empty speech bubbles over their heads. "I'm still working on the layout but I think it's going okay."

I study the page, imagining those stick figures filling out into characters, and the empty speech bubbles filling with words. "It's really cool that you're finally starting it."

He raises an eyebrow. "Finally? I've been working on it for ages."

"You know what I mean. You're starting *this* part. Putting it all on paper."

"Yeah." He sets the notebook aside and sighs. "But I could use a break, too."

I lean my head on his shoulder. "What kind of break?"

"Pizza break?"

I roll my eyes. "You're obsessed with the pizza here now."

"I'm obsessed *that there's pizza,*" he says, like this is both very obvious and extremely important. "And we can get to it without freezing our asses off now."

I find his hand and twine my fingers with his. "Give me fifteen minutes? I just want to get through this one phrase and then we can get pizza."

I kiss him, quickly, and stand up. As I walk back up to the stage, I look at him, bending over his notebook again. At his earring, glinting under the dim lights. At his glasses, which he's been wearing every day since the competition. At the look of deep concentration on his face.

I sit back down at the piano. And just for a minute, I close my eyes and breathe in the auditorium. The vastness and the stillness and the silence, except for the *scratch-scratch* of Eric's pencil.

I am Miles Jacobson.

I am trans. I am queer.

I am a human wild card.

Not *almost.*

I just am.

I lift my hands, open my eyes, and begin to play.

AUTHOR'S NOTE

Hello, friends!

When I started drafting this story in 2019, I wanted it to be a lot of things: a coming-of-age narrative, a rom-com, a love letter to classical music, a reminder that trans and queer teens exist outside of big cities on the coasts—but most of all, I wanted it to be joyful.

Trans and queer folks deal with plenty of Not Joy in real life: the recent slew of anti-trans legislation, an ever-growing pile of banned books, online trolls, op-eds that question whether our identity is just a trendy fad (*insert facepalm here*).

So, I wanted to write a story with a happily-ever-after. I wanted to write a story about all the *other stuff* that's part of being trans and queer. The fun stuff, like finding your first suit, or looking in the mirror and seeing yourself. And the stuff that's just about being a human in the world: falling in love, accidentally hurting your friends' feelings, awkwardly bumping into your ex at the pizza parlor you can clearly never set foot in again.

Miles has a lot of things on his mind in this book, and some of them are about identity, because when it's literally who you are, you can't *not* think about it. But being trans is also only a piece of who Miles is. This is not a story in which Miles has to prove himself to anybody—except, maybe, himself.

Miles's journey is about finding himself, in spite of everyone else. About fully, shamelessly, and triumphantly forging and inhabiting his own moments of joy. I wrote this story because I believe, firmly, that joy can be an act of resistance in challenging times. And trans and queer folks, especially now, deserve all the joy.

Thank you for checking out this book of my trans heart, and I hope, very much, that you enjoyed it.

Edward Underhill

ACKNOWLEDGMENTS

To Nicole Maggi: You were one of the first people to believe in this book, and I wouldn't be where I am today without your incredible mentorship.

Patricia Nelson, agent extraordinaire, thank you for championing this story, for always having my back, and for calling Eric a "marshmallow human" on our very first phone call.

Thank you to Sylvan Creekmore, the OG editor, for being this book's biggest fan and its most honest critic. Somehow you understood from the beginning exactly what I wanted this story to be, and you patiently and thoughtfully guided me there.

To Sarah Grill, for fearlessly steering the ship for the last half of this journey; thank you for your enthusiasm, your empathy, and your incredible work bringing *Always the Almost* to publication day.

Thank you to my copy editor, Angus Johnston, for saving me from embarrassing grammar mistakes, and to my authenticity reader, Jon Reyes, for your keen eye. So much gratitude to my amazing publicist, Sarah Bonamino; Rivka Holler, Brant Janeway, Mary Moates, and everyone on my incredible marketing team for a million things I know I never even saw; and Christina Lopez for assistance with line edits. To production pros Lena Shekhter, Melanie Sanders, Nicola Ferguson, and Eric Meyer; all the folks on the sales teams; and Sara Goodman, Eileen Rothschild, and the entire team at Wednesday Books, I'm endlessly grateful for your support.

Kerri Resnick, your cover concept literally made me squeal. Myriam Strasbourg, I had no idea what I hoped my cover illustration would look like; turns out your art was my wildest dream.

To the authors who offered advance praise for this book—Dahlia Adler, Jaye Robin Brown, Mason Deaver, Jason June, Adib Khorram, Bill Konigsberg, Emery Lee, Miel Moreland, and Phil Stamper—your support for my story completely bowled me over, and your kind words were truly an embarrassment of riches.

Thank you to the best critique partners a guy could ask for: Deanna Day, for early notes on an early draft; and Jennie Bates, for the most important tarot read of my life. Thank you to Rebecca Rabinowitz for wise and thoughtful conversations about language. And thanks to the 2023 debut group, many of whom went above and beyond to keep us all sane and organized, and put their hearts and souls into lifting all our books.

A very special thank-you to Erik Rose for the cutest laughing waffle drawing(s). I am so happy your art ended up as the case stamp. Special thanks also to Robyn Gerry-Rose, for assisting in a tiny, socially distanced celebration of good news, when the world wasn't allowing for a whole lot of that.

Thank you to all the friends who kept me going through writing and revising this book during a global pandemic, especially Clara Brasseur, Jen Ferguson, Claire Forrest, Caroline Huntoon, Bryn McDonald, and Sarah Rosenthal.

Thank you to the amazing music teachers I've had over the course of my life. To my parents, thank you for recognizing that the only way to keep me off Dad's computer was to give me my own (aged) laptop and allow me to stay up too late writing stories. To my grandma, who preordered this book but didn't live to see it released—thanks for insisting you wanted to read this story, even though I have no idea what you would have made of it.

Laura, thank you for believing in my stories before they make sense, listening to me babble about people who don't exist, and reminding me to celebrate. You make the best cake.

Finally, thank you to all my readers, from the bottom of my heart. You are the reason this story is here, and your support means everything to me.